THE YELLOW BALLOT

a diversion

Edwin Ahearn

The Yellow Ballot

Dusatia (Duszacja)

Republic in east-central Europe, bordered by Germany, Poland and the Czech and Slovak Republics.
Area: 75,385 sq km (29,100 sq mi)
Population: 6,350,000 (1995)
Capital: Korava (Kvorvava).
Language: Dusatian

Historical: Briefly an independent kingdom in the 16th Century, Dusatia became a province of the Polish kingdom, but in 1712 was annexed to the German Empire.   Reconstituted as an independent republic by the Treaty of Versailles (1919), it again became a "protectorate" of the German Reich in 1938, and with a native National Socialist government retained some shadow of autonomy until 1942, when German military rule was imposed, first on the capital and then throughout the country. Liberated by the Red Army in 1944-45, Dusatia shortly thereafter became the People's Republic of Dusatia, *i.e.*, a communist dictatorship, and member of the Warsaw Pact, with Soviet medium-range ballistic missiles and divisions of the Red Army on its soil.
In 1961, a new premier, Niemek, was installed. A youthful hero of the resistance during the Nazi period, who narrowly escaped execution by the Gestapo, he now instituted a policy of liberalisation, dissolving the notorious VDKR, a

Soviet-style secret police, and making conciliatory gestures to the West. When, in 1962, Niemek spoke openly of a desire to dismantle missile sites, what Moscow characterised as his "CIA-inspired deviation," like the Budapest uprising six years before, and Czechoslovakia's Dubcek reforms six years in the future, was brutally crushed by swift military action, East German, Polish and Red Army tank divisions invading from three sides. The deposed Niemek was made manager of a provincial fertiliser-factory, and the liberalising elements ruthlessly purged from all positions of responsibility; the secret police reappeared in a more efficient incarnation as the SNJR, which the gallows humour of the time aptly pronounced as the German word *Schnur*, a noose. Undisturbed by the events of 1968 in neighbouring Czechoslovakia, the satellite government retained its unloved grip up to the economic crisis of the late eighties on the eve of the Soviet break-up. In 1990, Dusatia overturned the "Muscovites," and Niemek, now past 70 and in retirement, was recalled to fill the figurehead role of President, while real power was held by Anton Gorat, who had emerged as leader of the Action for a Democratic Dusatia. After "acceding" to the premiership in the immediate post-communist chaos, Gorat strengthened his position a year later in the first democratic general election in Dusatia's history, and has since guided the painful transition to private ownership and a market economy, holding together a working coalition drawn from a patchwork-quilt of political parties.

I

Now my first and last sortie into Central European power politics is over, what I'd like to tell is a tale of high adventure, with épées in it, and epaulettes, and the world well lost for a gallant quip, a fairy tale for not-quite grownups, more heartwarming, more uplifting, less grainy than the reality. Instead, I'm obliged to write a kind of book which, as fiction, I don't care to read, where the shabby heroes are only marginally preferable to the grey and seedy villains, and triumphs are equivocal, relative disaster averted, mediocrity saved, as our best shot at virtue. Yet it may be (offered with no real hope) that if I recount what happened, as soberly and precisely as I can, that bright, romantic other realm will be glimpsed through the cracks, and a faint scent of its impossible pageantry sweeten the murky winter air of the Dusatia that is, east of the Oder and south of the Odra.

It begins, however, in Bosnia, in Sarajevo, that city where an assassin's pistol killed so much more than an Archduke, and sent swashbuckling Europe down into the abyss, to suffocate in the Pripet Marshes and the mud of Flanders. At the moment, December 18, not much is happening here; Belgrade is quiet, Zagreb blanketed in snow; little is heard from Prague or Bratislava, Warsaw, Minsk and Kiev have only routine cares; all my Slavonic beat is quiet — I say Slavonic, but I have been twice to Bucharest, where I could cope with their Monty Python Latin, once to Budapest, where I had to use an interpreter, who had wonderful legs and a costly thirst for Veuve Clicquot — quiet enough that it seems safe to go home for Christmas.

"Where is home?" Mireille asks. She's French, *de vingt ans*, a famine relief worker, and we've been to a chamber-concert together. Now we're back at my hotel room drinking riesling, and I'm reasonably sure she'll spend the night. Not serenely certain — what man ever is, with the hoped-for first time — and an undertow of anxiety is muddling the luxurious anticipation of helping disengage the hundreds of little claws that keep her slenderly swathed in some diabolically affectionate greeny-blue material with a slight sheen.

"Sevenoaks." We're speaking French, and I say the name twice, translating it for her, *Sept-chênes*, a spongier place than the

Anglo-Saxon sturdiness of the original. "Or near there, on the Weald. It has apple-trees, Restoration panelling, and, not to brag, the best privately-owned Shakespeare library in the home counties." A place of homecoming for three of us, always has been, and it comes to me that if this evening results in a sustainable juxtaposition, I can invite Mireille, who must be due some leave, to spend Christmas with us, *à l'anglaise.* My mother will genuinely like Mireille, while visually measuring her as a possible bearer of grandchildren, and my father fail to exclude envy from his jocular approval. It was a latish marriage for him; he's completely faithful, I'm sure, and entirely satisfied with his choice, even complacent, but Mother, with all her intellectual and social gifts, her slightly preoccupied charm, could never have been one thing Dad never had and part of all men yearn for, a being Mireille effortlessly (though I don't mean merely) is, an adventure, a universal trophy, what Americans call a babe.

"Shakespeare? Your father's hobby?"

"My mother's profession." No longer teaching, she is still at work on *Shakespeare: Continental Productions and Publications before 1750,* an unexpectedly voluminous book, labour of many years. When I come home, I'll interrupt them both at writing, she in the library at a console, he in his more modest study, by far the likelier to greet me by reading aloud a choice passage just penned, memoirs in longhand on ruled pads, or sometimes irascible or explanatory letters to the *Times* or *Guardian,* to be typed, actually typed, my father dislikes printouts, by a woman who comes every other day.

Chiming with my thoughts, the small computer on the rickety desk beeps twice, and the screen — the lid of its attaché-case format — tells me I have mail. From the agency in Vienna, relaying a terse query from Albertson in London, *What about the constitutional crisis in Dusatia? ITN had coverage today.*

"What constitutional crisis?" I challenge, my professionalism impugned. I ended a five-day stop in Korava, covering the election, a week ago. Something to the same effect I type as a reply, but then, judiciously, decide to do some checking before dispatching it.

"I have to make some phone-calls."

"If you would prefer — " reaching to the low coffee-table,

where her little blue envelope of a handbag reposes.

"God, no, please stay. But I may be a quarter-hour or so."

"I am not bored."

"I might have to go back to Korava — " apologetically, as if my thought of taking her to Sevenoaks has been a spoken invitation.

"It's the price you pay for your brilliance."

"I'm not especially brilliant — " at the same time registering *she'll sleep with me*: she believes flattery improves performance.

"You must be. An Englishman fluent in Czech, Polish, Dusatian."

"I'm as much Dusatian, English only by patrilinear standards."

"And birth."

"By birth, I must be American. I was born in Walter Reed Hospital, in Washington, my mother having gone into labour on her way to a White House reception."

"Americans are strange people. Did you like America?"

"No one ever asked me. Before I was six months old, my father was moved to Paris. When I was four I spoke as much French as English, and was more at home in Dusatian." My father's idea; in the Washington posting he'd been dismayed by how easy it was to meet Americans named Bauer or Rossi who spoke not a word, respectively, of German or Italian, and had urged my mother to use her own language with me, rather than her very correct, occasionally archaic English.

"*Formidable.*"

Pavel Orbicz; too late for the studios; ask the hotel switchboard to ring his home number. The usual interlude in these parts when attempting an international call, even to a capital city not 400 miles away; strange warblings, phantom ringing signals, a phantom conversation in (I think) Ukrainian; a very distant operator speaking Serbian followed by a very near and moist one asking in Viennese German what number is wanted, clicks, more warbles, at last an authentic ring, and Pavel picks up.

"Hi, buddy — " I used his language, but he, knowing my

voice, goes instantly into his free-wheeling American. "I was just saying to Katja, betcha we gonna hear from Mark."

"Have you got a constitutional crisis?"

"Do we have a constitutional crisis: Does the pope eat kielbasa?"

"What happened? I thought Gorat had enough support to form a new government."

"Just about, yeah, if he can make it stick. You know the Loyals protested the election?"

"Something about the ballots being the wrong colour?" It had seemed to me a typical clutching at straws by a graceless loser.

"Yah. So, Vock got the court to, to what, stop the results from counting till they make a ruling?"

"Issue an injunction?"

"You got it. So the University students did a protest march, and then the appeals court nixed the injunction and said, go ahead, so the Loyals had their thugs out in the streets; *Gaspodi*, this better be a safe line, and then the top court — "

"High court."

"Okay, good, the high court upheld the original gizmo, and set one side the election results pending the judges' decision. So this p.m. we got no government, but we got the thugs and the students both in the streets, and some heads get biffed, Angèle had her half-dozen out there, too, they want to abolish the high court, taxes, et cetera. Tear-gas in the end, and then there was freezing rain, everybody went home, to be continued, okay?"

"Jesus." The uneasy suspicion I should have stayed on till the election was altogether over now becoming a guilty certainty, though I'm a little soothed by Pavel's breeziness, more so by having found him home; a crisis of the first magnitude would have put him on twenty-four hour watch at the station.

"So, we gonna see you? You can stay with us, Katja is saying hi right now."

"I'll be in Korava tomorrow." Somehow. "You'll be at the studios?"

"If it still there, somebody might try to blow us up, we got flatfeet with machine-guns all round the building, you better have a badge to show. You wanna stay our place?"

"If the agency books me, I may have to stay at the

Schweitzerhof again. I'll let you know, but thanks. Best to Katja."

"Sure thing, buddy."

Ringing off, I delete my rude original message, and send off an acknowledgement, with a request for plane routes into Korava in early morning. Mireille, frowning, is reading my indispensable paperback *Pickwick*. Trying to read; her English is hardly up to it.

"Qu'est-ce *self-acting*?" She has not begun at the beginning. I circle to see the place indicated by her small tight thumb; soft hair tickles my cheek, and our CO_2 mingles shamelessly.

"Self-acting ink, *une encre qui écrit par elle-même, de l'encre automatique.*"

Frown. "*Comme d'une planchette?*"

"*Ah, non. —* " recalling the scene, "*Parce-que M. Pique-ouique l'a jetée —* " her eyes are soft, and I abridge my exegesis with a kiss.

Though filled with wonders, the time is short till I'm apologizing again; I ignore the computer when it chirps another newlaid piece of mail, and buy myself ten more minutes before the phone begins to sound.

London, Albertson. Eleven p.m. there. He can't possibly tell I'm naked; my composure is unimpaired. One of the three American network giants, ANS, for whom I've done pieces before, wants from two to five minutes on their evening news tomorrow; they'll have a camera crew in Korava. They pay very well.

"Exclusive?" I venture. When using freelancers, all the American networks like to festoon the footage with logos — microphones, cameras, the reporter's blazer — to convey the impression that they maintain a full-time staff everywhere from Ulan Bator to Tierra del Fuego, but this time Albertson has told them I'm already contracted for international distribution. Indeed, there is a sudden heavy, if transient, demand for stories from Korava, and Albertson tells me I'd better get some writing done, fast; at present, apart from RTPD (Dusatian TV) reports, everyone is translating stuff from the French agency, who have a man there; his taped piece, overdubbed, was what ITN used earlier.

I smile; everyone, then, is probably being misinformed; I know the man. He's Belgian, actually, Albert Dufoireau, young, slight, but because of his vanity, not acumen, referred to in the community as Hercule Poirot.

Shortly, a weary-voiced but still competent Susan Brent comes on-line to tell me I'm on a seven-thirty flight from Sarajevo to Kiev, whence, at noon, I'll take a shuttle back to Korava, where I'm booked at the Schweitzerhof. I then soothe Albertson by assuring him I already have authentic background material, which I'll work up on the flight, and have in his hands early afternoon. He has been inclined to sarcasm over my sleeping through this crisis in what has become my own potato-patch, but now I have him if not purring, conditionally mollified. The wakeful eyes of Mireille are very bright in sidelong illumination, and there is small chance of my getting sleep, not before — I scan the day ahead — late tomorrow night.

Last night I was at the brink of asking Mireille to come with me, but she, reading me, said she had to be back in the field, feeding babies and the old. The French bureaucrats are annoyed that *the Anglo-Saxons* are hogging the credit for relief efforts; everywhere one looks, one sees the Stars and Stripes, one sees the Union Jack, but the bloody banner of France, where is he raised, hah? Mireille in turn is exasperated at her government for thinking in such terms, but (shrug), her field-jacket with the tricolor shoulder-flash is by now making its way south and west, to villages left unfunctional by civil war. I hoped her morning smile, seraphically blurred, would be slow to fade.

Pavel's talk of freezing rain has made me nervous about the steep, always precarious-feeling descent into Korava's airport, but at two in the afternoon the landscape is merely moist and dreary as we drop through low cloud and align with the main runway.

The gloom is by contrast with my first arrival here, the golden summer of 1992, as propitious a start for my career as could be contrived. After Oxford, I'd had eight months in London, rooms in High Holborn, many days reading at the British Museum, and written a callow, opinionated book on the "*Dvůr Králové*" Ms (which also entailed my first visit to Prague); published, it happily sold no more than 517 copies, some of which must surely by now have been left on buses or out in the rain, vanished into dusty secondhand bins; if I survive long enough I may outlive the book entirely, and be able to deny it ever existed.

Equally mortifying to recall is my first passionate love-affair, which, after many yearning nights, I swore would also be the last, abandoning (I hoped) not sexuality but sexual captivity. Emerging, scathed but at last clear-headed, from both false starts, I discovered that disintegration of the Soviet empire eastward of Berlin was an opportunity for one who could communicate in several Slavonic languages and write coherent English; when in Prague I had already written and sold a report on a literary conference there, and Albertson, urging me only to concentrate on subjects of interest to human beings, took me on as a correspondent at large for that vast, awakening, troubled territory, former vassals and former constituent republics of the USSR, at first excluding what had been Yugoslavia, at the time already amply covered. My happy breakthrough assignment, after only a month, was to report on my mother's homecoming.

In acceding to my father's desire that I be brought up speaking her cradle language, my mother (I was told much later) had not failed to point out that for Dusatian there's no payoff on the order of being able to read Goethe or Dante in the original. She was the more eloquent and certainly the more imaginative of my parents, and for me as I grew it was a mounting disappointment gradually to recognise that in terms of wider usefulness — except as a stepping stone to other languages — Dusatian was near the bottom of the list, a minor twig on the West Slavonic branch, with no significant literature, bar a couple of folk-tale collections made in the nationalistic 1840s. All Duszacji writers, if they desired wider recognition, abandoned their mother tongue; even Bedric Grdacz the one Dusatian writer of any note (1871-1958) declared independence from Germany with stories and a novel in Polish, and his scholarly work on French and English literature was written in German (as "Friedrich Graz"), not published in his cradle tongue until near the end of his immense life.

German cultural domination accounts also for early experience of Shakespeare; plays were given in German at the Imperial Theatre between 1840 and 1855, where *Hamlet* and *Twelfth Night* were repertory pieces. Even when Dusatian renditions began appearing, they were translations from the German of Schlegel and Tieck, holding the stage unchallenged until after the First World War and independence, when versions derived directly from the English texts were staged. In 1931, Korava University made plans for a complete Dusatian edition, under the general editorship of Grdacz, beginning with the histories, and the first, the two parts of *Henry IV*, were both published and performed in 1936 at the renamed National Theatre. Though these were more accurate and in most cases nearer in spirit to Shakespeare's poetry, audiences did not at first take to them, missing the familiar, plushy comfort derived from Schlegel and Tieck (a shock which most Germans had yet to experience) and resenting the fathering of "low street talk" on their Alabaster Bard. The "University Vandals" were out of favour during the Nazi period, but after the second war and "liberation" by the Red Army, the newer texts became standard at the once-more renamed People's National Theatre.

Now the university, with a surprised but poker-faced Grdacz enshrined as a "prophet of the proletariat," resumed the task of translating the plays, reaching the final group by about 1954. My mother, whose English had benefitted from contact with British Intelligence officers at the end of the war —

"*British* Intelligence officers?" I wondered, when my father first recounted the tale to me in full. I was about nine, and my ancient English history consisted of King Harold with an arrow in his eye, and some old singers called the Beatles.

"Oh, yes, we were still quite important then; there were British agents all over those parts, till the Red Army arrived. Mr. Churchill never reconciled himself to the postwar Soviet dominance formally conceded at Yalta, and hoped to leave some spores of British influence. He was a child of Empire, and couldn't possibly foresee that when the war was over, Britain would be no more than an offshore European island."

My mother's elder brother was in the Resistance — her brother, always, not my uncle; I never knew him. He was killed in 1945, reportedly by the Gestapo, but more probably, my father asserted, by Communists in his own cell of the Resistance, who, with the Red Army rolling near, were less concerned with Germans than with independent-minded Dusatians who might oppose Stalinism with the same ardour as they had Nazism. But before that, her family had concealed a British agent, a very blue-eyed explosives expert, who could (and did) recite page after memorised page of Milton and Herbert; he taught the fourteen-year-old girl Marvell's *Nymph Complaining* (still a favourite), explaining what it all meant, and after leaving that sanctuary was eventually captured and presumably executed by the Germans.

After the war, university, and an advanced degree (1953), my mother became a favoured disciple of the venerable Grdacz, and joined his team of translators, much the youngest of a trio assigned the remaining late plays (*Hamlet*, *Macbeth* and *Lear* having been done in the first wave). She was teaching, too, and regularly denounced by one or another of her orthodox students for bourgeois readings of Shakespeare, regularly admonished, and — after promising to adopt "realist" interpretations — repeatedly rescued by the intervention of National Monument Grdacz. After his death, however, soon barred from teaching, her work as a translator was subjected to such scrutiny, such idiotic emendations proposed to bring Shakespeare in line with the people's revolution, that she gave that up, as well, and fell back on her reserve vocation, as a piano teacher.

The events of 1961-2, the attempted break with Moscow under the leadership of Niemek and the brutal consequences, were particularly poignant for my mother, whose family had known both Niemek and the girl who became his wife as Resistance fighters in the Nazi period.

"He was a young man still," my mother mused. "And hoped a quiet revolution might succeed; Khruschyov was seen as, in part, a Westerniser; had he not visited America? Many of us thought Niemek might `pull it off.'" The inverted commas are always audible when my mother, speaking English, descends to colloquialism.

Among the less momentous of the Niemek reforms, she was reinstated at the University, both as teacher and with the translation team, which in her absence had produced only a shabby

Timon, spun so as to ascribe his woes to the endemic faults of capitalism. There followed, she always said, her happiest months in Dusatia, till one morning Korava woke to machine-gun fire, and Soviet tanks in the streets. In the subsequent purge she lost her post, and her credentials, and at this point my father comes into the tale.

Shortly after Niemek's overthrow, the British embassy in Korava and the Dusatian in London had shut down; charges of spying in London, of "counter-revolutionary interventionism" here (giving medical treatment to students wounded by Red Army bullets), several preliminary rounds of tit-for-tat expulsions. As always, after an icy silence, pique gave way to practicality, and my father came to Korava as an interim chargé d'affaires. He was not, strictly, a diplomat, but a specialist in what you might suppose to be sometimes mutually hostile interests, Economic and Cultural Affairs (Later, in Paris, this uneasy pairing obliged him, disgustedly, to arrange an embassy party for some "prancing ninnies," here tactfully encoded as Mike O'Lamprey and the Mossless Ones. Dad is fond of Purcell.), but he'd been well-liked in Moscow where he was posted, and was the only one at his grade immediately available.

He coped, and stayed on for a time when reestablishment of full ambassadorial relations came, about the same time as my mother's loss of credentials. Being fluent in English, she obtained work at the British embassy, with the help of my father, whom she'd already met; as part of the thawing process he'd wheeled in an elderly Knight Commander of the British Theatre to read some Shakespeare at the university. One cultural event led to another, and eventually Dad was able to marry Mother, and take her with him to his next posting, in Washington.

When I recounted this history to Pavel, he said, "No sweat, just like that? Such marriages, it could be an ass-pain getting a visa, I could tell you some stories."

"Dad had pull." The first version I was given, as a child, was that he hinted, quite untruthfully, that the Royal Ballet might be moved to omit Korava from their forthcoming tour of Eastern Europe, which would indeed have been a potent weapon, European high culture being symbolically as indispensable to those regimes as American junk music to its dissidents. When I was old enough, however, my mother confided that in fact Dad's leverage came from his having obtained for the Dusatian Foreign Minister some rather rare Anglo-Indian books, often bruited in Bombay, banned in Birmingham, burned in Boston, dealing with a wild array of erotic whimsies (copiously illustrated); less than the threat, the mere floating possibility of exposure had sprung my mother's visa with exemplary celerity.

She has not yet outlived her wonder that the British Council would pay her, a Dusatian, to talk about Shakespeare to Americans, more than once at the hallowed Folger Library, and later on to the French, though still in English, in several charming and tasteful venues. All the time, she continued to work at the Dusatian translations, building on her own bits in the official project.

When I reached school age, she and I were more often in England, Dad having acquired the Sevenoaks place, and it was there she completed the last of her translations, *Anthony and Cleopatra*, in 1973. This, with its three companions, she sent to an old friend at Korava University, who thanked her, praised the texts, but admitted there was small chance of either publication or performance in Dusatia. Slavonic versions of Shakespeare being in little demand west of the Elbe, she recognised this meant a production anywhere was as improbable as, for example, destruction of the Berlin Wall, the re-establishment of Lithuania or the Ukraine as sovereign states, or a democratic election in Moscow.

Which, after silent decades, became exactly true. With the fall of the "Muscovite" regime and the election of Gorat, the newly confirmed Dusatian president, Niemek, himself back from long provincial exile, invited a small group of distinguished political emigrés to return to Korava, a festive reunion, a healing of old wounds, and part of the celebrations was a production of my mother's *Anthony and Cleopatra* at the National Theatre, "People's" no longer. And that, if you'll excuse the extent of this explanation, was the occasion of my first visit, for the very pleasing task of filing a story on my mother's homecoming, and the acclaim that greeted her after the play. Which I followed up with *A Translator Comes Home*, a signed Sunday piece in the *Observer*, reprinted in the *New York Times*, among lesser places.

It occurs to me here — now, that is, as I hump my minimal, functional, still leaden bags through token Dusatian formalities, and look for a taxi — that the presidential box at the theatre on the night of the *Anthony and Cleopatra* contained as much potential for drama as there was on stage, with most of the principals of my story there as guests. Besides the Niemeks and my parents, the just-elected premier, Gorat, flanked by National Hero Major-General Stepan Vock, in dress uniform and about a hundredweight of medals, most bestowed by the Soviet Union he had ended by unexpectedly humiliating. Standing behind was the enigmatic, elegant, educated Juan-Micel Herder, probably unaware he was watching, amongst so much else, his wife-to-be, down below in the role of Charmian. How, exactly, he qualified as a prominent Dusatian repatriot, like most exact information about him, is unclear, but he was to become a powerful broker of mutation in the evolving market economy. He remains influential, imperturbable, cultured, and enigmatic, even politically. His natural affinities would seem to be with the Right, but at parties in his baroque villa on the outskirts of Korava, whose previous tenants have included archdukes, the president of the old republic, the Gestapo, a dance-school, and the Soviet military staff, and where under current management celebrity of some kind seems the main criterion for entrée, I've met socialist, Social Democrat and Catholic Renewal MP's, and the fiery young anarchist known only as Angèle, as well as National Loyalist adherents including General Vock. But, still with the presidential box that festive night: at the far flank was the remarkably colourless jurist, Wirath, clothed in his seamless integrity, accompanied as everywhere by his adored, orchid daughter, Christa, then 15 and just coming to the threshold of her celebrity. Wirath is now admired, incorruptible Chief Justice of the High Court that will rule on the validity of the election, and perhaps make it impossible for Gorat to go on as premier. Conceivably, gathering every imaginable ally, Vock will be in a position to form the next government.

I, though invited to sit with my parents, chose to remain a working journalist, down below with the nameless. But then as since, my mother's ancient association with the Niemeks, and my fluency in the language, opened up Dusatia for me; those things, and of course Pavel.

II

My cabdriver is a Slovak, one of some thousands who migrated here during the brief prosperous years, and now, in a time of widespread unemployment, had become an issue in the election campaign; the National Loyalists, almost the extreme Right (there are a handful of even more rabid neo-fascists) hinting but never quite advocating forced repatriation, and using the "Foreign Workers" issue to seduce blue-collar votes away from the Left.

"How is Korava today?"

"Quiet." He has been at first cautious, but hearing his own language he gives me another rear-view look, and decides I'm all right. "Plenty of cops on the streets. You know about Vock?"

"More than I want to." I'm flicking out a dry-fly, and get a bite.

"I used to think he was a good man. Now — why is he picking on poor Slovaks? They were glad enough to see us when *that* was doing eighteen-hour days — " jerking his head in the direction of the giant Cicada Works, on the skyline leftwards.

"You worked there?"

"Good money, then, plenty of overtime, but Slovaks were the first they let go when it went bad. I've got a wife and kids."

Gorat's first term as premier, his early efforts at transformation from a centralised to a market economy, were given an unrepeatable boost by the Cicada phenomenon, in origin, curiously, a Soviet legacy. Long ago, back in the forties and early fifties, Dusatia manufactured the Podarny, a decent motor-cycle, and the Soviets gradually converted that factory to produce a light all-terrain military vehicle, which became standard in the Warsaw Pact countries. Production peaked in the latter seventies, but fell off sharply thereafter, and with the disintegration of the military alliance, Dusatia would have been left with a large, derelict motor works, but for the design flair of a young engineer, who was able to show how existing machinery could be adapted to produce the Cicada, a perky, durable little sports vehicle with some features even the Japanese hadn't thought of. Turned out in a paint-box array of brilliant colours, it sold well in Poland and what was then still Czechoslovakia, and became a sudden rage in the eastern regions of reunified Germany, among students and young would-be executives, for whom Mercedes, BMW and Porsche were out of financial range, Volkswagen too dull (of their home-grown environmental menace, let us not speak). These later export successes were made possible by new capital, recruited by Jiri Podarny grandson of the old motor-bike king, and largely assembled by that Juan-Micel Herder I've already pictured in the presidential box at the National Theatre. His money was somewhat mysteriously acquired in exile; he was rumoured to have worked for the American CIA, but that alone would hardly explain his apparently bottomless fortune.

Cicadas began turning up in the UK in 1994, and at the same time were becoming the fashion in certain patches of the USA; Boston, Madison in Wisconsin, Berkely in southern California come to mind, all notable for their universities. The summit was reached when the Cicada Works dispatched five hundred cars destined for Yokohama.

At that time, there was a delivery backlog amounting to some 60,000 units, and a new assembly plant was planned for the depressed eastern province of Dusatia. Rather than the bursting of a bubble, reversal, when it came, though swift, was a cumulative series of deflations. It began with recall of a large number of cars with a dangerously defective fuel line, unfortunately not before some models from that run had been sent for review to the most widely-read consumer magazine devoted to cars. Fiscal retrenchment in Germany coincided with staling of the Cicada fad among the young, and a snappy new "leisure vehicle" emerged from Korea, priced well below its Dusatian rival; a massive layoff at the Cicada Works was, if not the beginning, the nightmare confirmation of that economic decline which led to Gorat's current political troubles.

"Maybe I'll go home," my driver says, as we come to the semi-circle driveway of the Schweitzerhof, a new building unsuccessfully trying to echo the Victorian Gothic of its smaller, palmier predecessor. "Except, for my kids, this is home. For me, too, if they don't put Vock in charge. Maybe I'll join in the candlelight march tonight; there ought to be some Slovaks out there."

General Vock was Gorat's ally, until they quarreled about immigration policy, and he resigned his army commission, announced himself a convert to National Loyalist "philosophy," got himself elected, and almost instantly became leader of their parliamentary party. In uniform (which is how he campaigned) or business-suited, he is always dapper, and only a certain thickness of both waist and features gets in the way of the dashing image he pursues. As an orator he sticks doggedly to Loyalist themes, keeps it simple, uttering their formulas with what seems a deep conviction — although it is all a pallid and less strident echo from the intemperate rhetoric of the party's founder, Míloczy. He, with his near-peasant accents and crude, angry ironies, has not been tested in a general election; though he has a noisy national following, he remains an autocratic provincial premier in the north, awaiting his moment. Since he has frequently excoriated the inadequacies of the parliamentary system, holding that wide executive powers vested in a single leader better serve the needs of an emergent country, it is fairly clear what he thinks that moment would entail; an impasse sufficiently grave (as, for instance, an election paralyzed by dispute) to justify constitutional changes making parliament a mere adjunct of a ruling rather than ceremonial president, with Míloczy as man of the hour.
As for policies — but here I can't do better than to insert one of my "backgrounds," taped while the election campaign was still raging:

"The hopes of the Loyalists lie in the personal popularity of Míloczy, and of his leading advocate, former-General Vock, best known for his outmanoeuvring of a half-demoralised Red Army at the time when this country, like so much of eastern Europe, was breaking free of the Warsaw pact and of Soviet political hegemony. The General, while maintaining strong ties with the army, is now leader of the parliamentary Loyalists, in whose rhetoric certain stated principles are a source of uneasiness for many. *Regional co-prosperity*, signifying an interdependence among relatively weak states created in the break-up of the Soviet

Union and the breakdown of the Warsaw Pact, is not in itself an unattractive idea, but such words take a decidedly sinister turn when associated with other phrases like *a re-examination of artificially-imposed frontiers* and *our ethnic loyalty, which transcends national boundaries.* To many observers, these slogans, like the National Loyalist banner in the sacred red, white and black colours, wake echoes from an older, more dangerous era, a past best buried, and the implacable hostility of Míloczy to any flirtation with NATO, his open contempt for the United Nations, together with Vock's obsession with modernizing the army, do nothing to soothe the anxieties of adjacent states. The integrated Europe of today, with its interlocking economies and increasingly open borders has no place for a country trying to goose-step out of economic troubles under the banners of national pride and military aggrandisement, and a neo-fascist Dusatia would find itself increasingly isolated and ostracised. In this confused and confusing election, however, plagued by splinter-parties and characterised by scare and rumour, the Loyalists seem certain to gain strength in the new parliament, though few believe they'll come anywhere near a majority."

After that I received a phone-call from Vock's secretary, and having persuaded her I would have no difficulty communicating with her boss (who spoke only Dusatian and military Russian), was thanked by him for the profile but genially upbraided for the term "neo-fascist." As a result I did a lengthy interview with him, most of which was never shown, although NPR in the USA played much of it on sound radio, and several newspapers carried my print story, largely a transcript (we spoke Dusatian, and I redubbed it later, Pavel supplying a voice for Vock's translated answers). What struck me was the shallowness of the ideas, even their non-existence except as neo-Pavlovian dinner-bells, since every attempt to get at the thought beneath the slogan was met by another slogan. Agreed, a successful military commander doesn't need to be a giant intellect.

We stand for national integrity.
Yes, General Vock, but what exactly does that imply? I imagine every political party would claim to stand for national

integrity.

They pay lip-service to the idea. Only the National Loyalists have a four-point programme to ensure national integrity.

Four points?

You can find it in the manifesto. You really should have read our manifesto. A commitment to what is uniquely, historically Dusatian, a renewal of national purpose, eradication of all remnants of the Soviet colonial era, unification of the Dusatian race.

To take just one of those points, General —

They cannot be considered in isolation; the four points are interdependent.

Yes, but, "unification of the Dusatian race." According to figures put out by your own information office, though they have been widely disputed, as many as a million and a half ethnic Dusatians are now living within Poland, the Slovak Republic and in the Olava region of the Czech Republic —

(with an impish grin) *And more also in the United States, especially in Western Virginia. But we do not expect those Dusatians to renounce their American citizenship.*

But the question is, will it be your policy to assert sovereignty over these alleged ethnic Dusatians living in neighbouring states?

We are the party of all Dusatians. National integrity is our goal.

National integrity, if necessary at the expense of your neighbours?

No one need talk of this being at anyone's expense. The Loyalist party has positive aims, national renewal, a turn away from the discredited, divisive policies of the Gorat bloc.

(Stonewalled, I abandoned that line) If the Loyalists were to attain a working majority in the next parliament, what would be your first legislative proposal?

That might depend on the circumstances at the time. We need not get bogged down in timetables and agendas; our goals are clearly stated.

Yes, General, but where are the means of attaining those goals? How will the Loyalists go about "renewing national purpose?"

As a great American president has said, we must learn to ask what we can do for our country.

(We did several more turns on this same treadmill without advancing an inch, and I switched to another of the "points.") Can you tell me, General, what your party's ethnic policies mean in terms of immigration and the immigrant workers already in Dusatia?

This a question that must be clarified, but it is clear that the present high unemployment among our own people make it imperative to adjust our policies, in a context of national renewal.

Adjust your policies with a view to what?

To affirm our commitment to what is uniquely and historically Dusatian.

Perhaps, if he hadn't been a national hero (though now somewhat shopworn), I might have gnawed away at this, but the unheard clink of the medals and the imagined racket of victorious tanks, *our* tanks, filing into the capital under a blizzard of spring flowers, made me what no effective interviewer can afford to be; shy. Like the hapless Soviet commander, like the bewildered negotiator from the Kremlin, I caved in, and with small sincerity wished him well.

Scarcely installed at the Schweitzerhof I hear from my camera crew, and meet them downstairs in the bar. Though indeed supplied with plentiful ANS logos, for whom I've filmed with them before, the pair is as freelance as I am, brothers-in-law who've driven their van overnight from Prague, where they also make commercials and industrial films. Within three minutes the major partner, Svoboda, is renewing his insistent proposal that we join forces on a permanent basis, and produce a multilingual news magazine show, which (he asserts) can enjoy world sales to dwarf "*Bévach*" (something popular, I gather, from the USA), and make all our fortunes. As before, I turn this aside, and we work out a list of shots needed today; I'll meet them again at about the time the candlelight marchers arrive at the presidential palace. Back in my room, I send off the stuff written on the plane, and decide I'll walk over to RTPD. A few discouraged snowflakes are vanishing on contact with the dully gleaming pavement; on an overcast afternoon mere hours from the solstice, at much the same latitude as London (or, if you like, Saskatoon), there isn't much in the grey stone of the old capital to lift the spirits; my lack of sleep and an unwise scotch with the camera crew are making me mournful rather than tired.

In the cobbled expanse of Grdacz Square, which, when I was first here, was identified by painted signs hastily put up to conceal the hated former name, *Karel-Marx Placza*, there is little traffic, some litter from last night's clashes — tear-gas canisters, a broken placard which had had something to say about the high court — many police. A few are ordinary city police in their dark blue uniforms, but there is a more formidable, warier, better-armed contingent of the "brown police," the *dzhăndarmi*, functionally something between coppers and a provincial militia (here, district militia, Korava being administratively extra-provincial); a quartet of their armoured cars are parked in front of the National Theatre. They can at need deploy helicopters, water-cannon, sharpshooters.

Nearing the studios, I at last come upon some civil unrest, a knot of about twenty National Loyalist supporters carrying signs extolling Vock, wearing the red, white and black rosettes. The police are in some disagreement with their evident leader, square-framed, of moderate height, perhaps forty, with a thick moustache; he is of that dark-haired tribe with skins the translucent no-colour of a peeled cucumber, whose chins and jowls can never seem clean-shaven, a bluish bruise of beard always lurking. At first sight, no more than an aging street tough, and I can't understand why the commander of the *dzhăndarmi*, tall, very fair, holstered, belted, walky-talkied and dispatch-cased in shiny brown leather, is treating him with such apparent deference, all-but apologising for his orders banning any demonstrators on the same side of the street as the studio entrance. Press pass displayed in one hand, nib-sized microphone to my pocket recorder in the other, I make for the debate, proclaiming meaninglessly, "World News!" In a window two floors up, an RTPD camera is already craning down, and someone behind it, perhaps Pavel, must be cursing my interlope. As the darker, broader of the two men turns towards me, I see that while he may be a thug, he's not a stupid one; the deep eyes are disconcertingly intelligent. I've seen him before somewhere, but before I can ask anything a diagonal rifle is pressing me back, the officer shouting over the shoulder of his minion to the effect that interviews at this time are inappropriate.

He'll always walk with something of a limp, but when I first met Pavel he was still barely mobile. A newsreader and interviewer for RTPD who had become assistant supervisor of News and Public Affairs, he had been shot in the thigh when a student group tried to annex the studios at the demise of the "Muscovite" government. During the dinosaur's dangerous death-throes, he had precariously maintained a deadpan compliance with official dictates, while doing all he dared, both on the air and backstage, to discredit "that senile gang" (his own term); typically (as I was to discover) he was amused rather than embittered by the irony, that he should now be assailed as a pillar of the *ancien régime*.

During the Festival of Reunion, having had separate TV talks with my mother and my father ("an old and valued British friend of Dusatian liberties"), he asked me to do a kind of mutual interview with him; I was at first reluctant, feeling rather like the utilitarian but unloved vehicle proverbially bringing up the rear of the Lord Mayor's Show, but he had been so helpful in making facilities available for a visiting journalist, so generous in sharing usable anecdotes, that I couldn't refuse, and we ended up making chaos of late-evening programming by nattering on (live) for more than eighty minutes (Pavel was and is strongly opposed to forcing all topics, whatever their inherent interest, to fit a predetermined fifteen, thirty or sixty-minute frame). Passing over my mother's genetic contribution, notwithstanding a generous helping of Kelt from my father's grandparents (two Irish, one English-Scottish, one Scottish), I strike most Dusatians as an archetypal Anglo-Saxon, and it was a marvel, therefore, that I not only understood and spoke but made idiomatic jokes in their seldom-acquired language; at the same time I was discovering that I could be comfortable in front of winking cameras; I turned the tables by interviewing Pavel on tape in my staid, his fluent if sometimes lurid English. This one we trimmed down to a commercially viable twenty-four minutes, and its sale to ITV was the start of my second career, to run in parallel with print journalism. As, and more valuably, of a genuine friendship.

Surrounded, he points a pistol finger, thumb cocked, to acknowledge my arrival, gives instructions complete with framing gestures to a junior producer, signs what must be a requisition for a hovering girl, leans through an open office doorway to tell somebody named Firenc he'll see him at four, accepts a video-cassette from a second and faintly flirtatious gophermaid, and reaches to grab my elbow.
"You gotta be kidding, pointing a mike at Rietz. Come on."
He hauls me off to his keep, tells a secretary on the outer ramparts, "No calls," and ushers me into the inner office, one side all windows looking out on the street, where the Loyalist demonstrators have grumpily withdrawn to the farther pavement. Littered desk, swivel chair for scanning a row of active but silent monitors; one evidently plugged in to prehistory is showing an episode of *The Avengers*.

"I tell you, my friend, don't try anything cute with Rietz, this guy is bad news."
A serious warning, and right up to this moment of writing, I'm still not sure Pavel knows his version of English is a tongue never spoken by any live human; modernised somewhat by Radio Free Europe DJ's, it's largely the dialect of classic Hollywood gangster movies, of which he owns a large collection, mainly on 8mm reels, though with a few newer tape transfers (he passionately loathes "colorization"). Pavel's own face, with its firm, straight eyebrows, large liquid eyes and broad strip of mouth with jutting lower lip, was made for the chiaroscuro of black and white films, and at times of excitement or drama (which occupy quite a lot of his life), he leans to a twitching, wincing, teeth-baring style hybridised from Cagney, Bogart, Edward G. Robinson — familiar names in his pantheon, though he can cite many lesser

gods mainly mysterious to me; Sydney Greenstreet (the fat one), Peter Lorre (the little one), Richard Conte, Richard Arlen, Richard Powell, Elisha Cooke...

"Rietz?"

"Rietz," Pavel emphasised. "Erhardt Rietz. No, no, he's as Dusatian as I am, but, you know."

I do; in 1919, when independence first came, of families with German names, whether by intermarriage or Germanisation, a stubborn or snobbish few declined the stampede to give them native Dusatian forms, and some to this day continue to call their sons Hermann and Hans, their daughters Bertha or Gretchen.

Before telling more, Pavel makes certain the intercom box on his desk is switched off, then makes surer still by unplugging it. These precautions, like his concern last night about the security of our phone-line, are not a relapse into the paranoia — or more justly, rational terror — of the era when *Schnur* might lurk in any shadow; as Director of News and Public Affairs for state radio and television, Pavel must maintain publicly an appearance of virginal impartiality among the forces contending for Dusatia's soul.

"Oh, yeah, Rietz is a hoodlum; he organises hoods for the Loyals — that's what he does now, but you wouldn't believe his *curriculum vitae*. He started out with *Schnur* when he was about twenty, and they must have liked his work, he got up to major, only nowadays he didn't know about any torture or people vanishing, he was just a communications expert."

"Wouldn't that entail a certain amount of wiretapping and surveillance?"

"Tell me about it; if we wanted to call some minister a shit we used to ride our bikes out into the boondocks to make sure we weren't eavesdropped. So, whatever, the guy was good at what he did; about '86 he was mystically changed into regular army, same rank, to become communications officer for Javelin, you know Javelin?"

"Vock's old division." An élite armoured unit conceded to be among the best the Warsaw Pact ever had.

"Vock was very big on communications — his own, and any he could overhear. He must have pulled strings to get Rietz, and it was Rietz who intercepted the Soviet orders — you know the story?"

I do, mostly. It was in the final days of the "Muscovite" regime, and when the Action for a Democratic Dusatia began filling the streets of Korava with silent candlelight marchers, Vock's division was in the east, actually engaged in a joint-exercise with Red Army assault infantry. His staff intercepted and decoded orders from Moscow telling the Soviet units to close down the training, and be prepared to "restore order" in Korava, using whatever force was necessary. Instead, next morning at three a.m., a Soviet battalion woke up to find Vock had his tanks surrounding their field headquarters. Without firing a shot he took twelve hundred infantrymen with their vehicles, keeping his erstwhile colleague their commanding brigadier under good-natured but determined arrest. That, with Vock's subsequent nearly bloodless capture of Strbjena, the main Soviet base in Dusatia, is now virtual folklore.

"You know where Javelin is now?"

"Strbjena?" After negotiating the Red Army pull-out, Vock had treated the base like his personal prize.

"The artillery, maybe. The tanks have been *redeployed* just outside Viczony." The place of Pavel's birth; he enjoys explaining that his surname, Orbicz, has nothing to do with circling satellites, but records an ancient, once baronial association with the Viczonja region. More to the point, his point, is that the old city is hardly fifty kilometres eastward of the capital.

"Vock, he could have tanks ringing the Assembly, the presidential palace, ringing the studios here, at two hours' notice."

"*Vock* could? He resigned from the army, didn't he?"

"Oh, sure. Javelin is now commanded by Firkus, who was Vock's staff chief; he is like Vock's shadow. Vock still gets to all their dinners; just before the election he reviewed them in uniform. The company commanders I don't know about, but down to major all the officers think Vock comes somewhere between Guderian and God; if he said go march on Moscow, they'd go."

I discover I am very English, after all, staggered by this warlord vision of Vock, by the very idea of normal authority brushed aside by a division's transcendent loyalty to, technically, an individual civilian. But it was true that back in '89, Vock had in effect independently declared war on the Soviet Union, and there is no doubt about Pavel's anxiety.

I say, "That would be a coup."

"That's what we're talking. Not right away, but that's where Rietz and his torpedos come in. I got a mole into Rietz's organisation. Kid where I take my car, you know, a grease gorilla — "

"Grease monkey, I believe that is, but I think the term is obsolete."

"Whatever, he works on my car, I'm the TV big wheel, he says to me, `Mr Orbicz, sir, I got a yen to be investigative reporter.' I say, fine, go volunteer for Rietz's roughnecks, when I come in for gas, wise me up what's going down. He's a good kid, body-builder, pumps iron; he hears some Loyalist crap about foreigners taking bread out of our mouths, he says `Is that true, Mr Orbicz?' I say, no, it's not foreigners, it's the aliens, little green guys from UFO's, he looks at me real hard to see if I'm kidding."

"Rietz?"

"Yeah, well, he's doing some illegal stuff, but it would be hard to get him arrested, never mind convicted. My guy knows there's a whole lot of weapons somewhere, but Rietz runs a sports club with a range, strictly legit, his militia all train with the same three assault rifles, also legit. But where he's dangerous right now is, he's trying to make a riot. Last night his people got some of the students throwing stones, the *dzhăndarmi* got there with tear-gas, then it was raining and got too fucking cold for them. See, he starts a riot the cops can't handle, Niemek's gonna have to call in troops, and that's Javelin. Tonight we may not be so lucky. He gives his hoods lessons in how to get people to blow their tops."

"Can I use any of this?"

"You mean, naming names? Sure, if you don't care about getting your head bashed in. You see how the cops are with Rietz. All over the world, same thing; you march for world peace or against hunger, cops say, real sweet, but you're still blocking traffic, we're gonna have to bust some asses. But you wave the flag and say you're saving the country from the egghead loony queers, right away three-quarters of the flatfeet would like to join you. Listen, buddy — " his hand is on my forearm — "Don't badmouth Rietz on the air. We kinda used to having you around."

Pavel, as should emerge as this tale progresses, has never been easily intimidated, and in my mind I cancel what I might have said on-air, substituting *certain elements*, vague entities who *are thought to believe they may profit from civil unrest.*

Pavel, looking like the world's worst poker-player holding aces over queens, asks me innocently about my piece for the American network. As he must have guessed, I plan to do a street scene, with the waxy-fingered marchers as background for my exposition.

"Where you gonna be?"

"I thought, by the railings in front of the presidential palace."

A nod. "Could be worse. Me, I'm setting up cameras on the northeast corner of Grdacz Square, you know, by the steps down to the river. I just got a hunch there might be better pictures there."

"More action, you mean."

"Could be."

I thank him, and he resumes his summary; with a riot the police can't contain, Javelin rolls into Korava, "and they're in place; the high court comes down with a ruling nixing maybe thirty, forty election results, practically all of them Gorat supporters — "

"Is that likely?"

"There's five judges, but only one means anything. Wirath will decide it."

"That's good, isn't it?" — knowing his seriousness, his earned reputation for incorruptibility.

"Cuts both ways. Sure, nobody's going to get to him, he'll make up his mind by the book. You can't buy him and you can't scare him, but same token, if you, if even Niemek was to go to him and say, you gotta let the election stand, it'll tear the country apart if not, he'd say, law is law, the chips have to fall wherever."

Probably true, and this is where Pavel brings me up to date and fills in gaps in my knowledge of the constitutional dispute, but it might be better if I set down the whole story, including bits I already knew, had already dispatched by E-mail to a voracious Albertson.

Though conspiratologists on both sides of the question have asserted otherwise, I'm satisfied that it began with a simple mistake: one of the printers contracting to produce the standard ballot form for the election had to scrap an entire run at the last minute, after discovering a misspelling; rushing through a replacement run, without time to order fresh supplies, he had used paper on hand, which happened to be pale cream rather than the standard white.   In obtaining their injunction to suspend declaration of the official results, after the Centrist coalition's narrow victory, on grounds that the substituted ballots violated the constitution, the Loyalists, as ever after, called the colour yellow.

"Yellow!" Pavel rants, thrusting an example at me. "Is this yellow?" The answer is no; almost anyone without a whiter page nearby for comparison would call it white.

Since, by the meagrest margin of butter-fat, however, it is not, Vock's forces were correct in the letter of the constitution, which stipulates white as the proper colour; a curious provision, but one which has an origin in loathed history. Through all the many years when an "election" meant the ritual of casting votes for the people's choice, predetermined in a meeting of about ninety people of the sole party, the ballots naming each lone local candidate were printed on pink paper. Later, and through the eighties, the so-called Parliamentary Agenda was also on pink paper, this being nothing but a list of measures again decided in advance by the politburo, which the assembly was required to approve. "In the time of the famous Brezhnev Doctrine," Pavel tells me, "We used to call the pink agenda Mrs Brezhnev's bloomers — not in public." (When he hears, for the first time, of the pun this contains in English, his delight is enormous.)

But it was this memory, together with insistence on the word *yellow* that permitted the Loyalist leadership to reject the charge they were trying to upset a valid election on a nitpicking technicality: yellow was the chosen colour of the Centrist alliance. Not of any political party — Gorat's Social Democrats use blue — but in an election with at least fourteen different parties fielding candidates (plus an added sprinkling of independents), those pledged to support the Gorat coalition saw a need for ready recognition, and yellow was used freely in posters, buttons and leaflets, while "Vote Yellow for Unity and Progress" was a familiar slogan. So that the National Loyalists, joined by the other losing parties, could assert, some of the dimmer ones even believe, that the distribution of the "yellow" ballots was a deliberate attempt (who can tell how successful?) to influence voting.

What Vock and his allies wanted from the court was a declaration invalidating all those elections where the "yellow" ballot played a significant part. Since the last-moment printer's run had been distributed mainly in immediate vicinity of the capital, hardly a Loyalist stronghold, Gorat's Social Democrats and the other Centre parties would be disproportionately affected; the best guess was that from 35 to 40 deputies would face new elections, only half a dozen of them belonging to the Right. Even so, in the interim parliament, the Social Democrats would still far outnumber the Loyalists, but Vock, depending on a complex of alliance, trading and perhaps intimidation, would be within range of a working majority, and could demand Niemek name him as premier.

"Is there a premier now?" I ask.

"Well, Gorat still has the office — you know, the office, *byró*, the place where his desk is, but they're leaning on Niemek to name a, what, janitor?"

"Caretaker."

"Yah. The betting is it's gonna be Dalerant — " the bland, vain, unctuous Catholic Renewal leader.

"Why him?"

"He's a healer. That's what he thinks, but if he gets it it's because his one real strength is his weakness; one thing everybody, Vock, Gorat, everybody agrees on is he'll be real easy to junk. But you see? Vock is made premier, he already has his tanks in place, protecting us, how hard's it gonna be to find an excuse for a semi-legal coup? He takes over TV and the newspapers, suspends the constitution, and then it's bye-bye Niemek, and Miloczy for Fuehrer. Or maybe we have a civil war. Either way."

As he says, eether way. Not insensible to the gravity of Pavel's fears, at the same time I'm trying to work out how much of this I can safely and comprehensibly squeeze into about forty-five seconds of television time; the bane of the unread word and the dominating picture is that too often we must show events without the history for their full understanding; neither in Peoria nor Budleigh Salterton has Dusatian politics been the object of constant and informed scrutiny. What can make them even care?

"Sure," Pavel snarls (has he read my thoughts?), upper lip peeling back, more Bogart than ever. "Big deal for us, but we're nothing but pipsqueak nickel-and-dime operation. So Miloczy comes muscling in behind Vock's tanks — so what on world stage? Hell, there must be a couple dozen *cities* with more people than all Duszacja. He gets bright idea to invade Slovakia, great; if Slovakia can't kick our asses here to Wednesday, you and the French got your armies down in Bosnia, ready to roll, and Uncle Sam makes with the cruise missiles — it's no dice for Miloczy; today Korava, tomorrow, Korava. But, listen, Mark my friend — " suddenly in his native language. "I don't want to see my country go Nazi because a printer was in a hurry."

I offer, "But surely, if it came down to saving the country from Miloczy's dream-world, the Left, even Neo-Communists, would support Gorat."

"I wouldn't count on it. Gorat trod on a lot of toes these past couple of years. Some of those bozos might think a bad dose of fascism is the best way back for them, creating the pre-revolutionary condition, they used to call it. Or civil war."

"How soon will the court have a decision?"

"Who knows? Five, six days, a week at most, we think. Meantime, let's hope the *dzhăndarmi* can keep Rietz from starting his riots."

All at once I remember where I've seen Rietz before, four or five years ago, when I went to one of Herder's baroque parties.

Pavel is interested; this deals with what we might call Rietz's Lost Years, between communications officer for General Vock, and organiser of thugs for political Vock. "Herder? I heard more than one time he's been bankrolling Vock's operation; hell, somebody told me he bankrolled Miloczy from the start, but you know. Herder, he like collects big people, Niemek, too. You sure it was Rietz? He was a guest there?"

"No." I can be definite; all the male guests were in dinner-jackets, and Rietz, blue-jowled, was in what might be a sort of uniform or livery, a tight, many-buttoned jacket without lapels. "I had the idea he worked for Herder — a chauffeur, perhaps."

"Uh uh. Nobody hires Rietz for a chauffeur, he drives like a frigging madman. *Gaspodi*, this could be a conflict, maybe the Loyals find a way to get to the incorruptible Judge Wirath. You know his daughter, Christa."

"Of course." Since sitting in the presidential box at what was her father's as much as my mother's homecoming, Christa Rasch (as she is now known) has become Dusatia's one internationally-recognised figure, and a member of that smiling, gesturing, shimmering multi-national stock company that appears in an eternal repertory of gala premières, restaurant openings, celebrity parties and benefits for various trendy diseases and social causes. *Figure* is an apt word, since she's done it mostly by modelling, and her lovely, large-eyed, heavy-lipped, faintly loony face had appeared on the cover of *Elle* and *Vogue* even before she added to fame by making two weirdish cult films (one winning a special citation at Cannes) with a young, intense, ostentatiously bisexual *auteur*, a French Canadian who lives in Switzerland and works mainly in North Africa. Like me, Christa was born abroad, but in her case both parents were Dusatian; I now learn, somewhat surprisingly, that she is back in Korava.

"Home for Christmas?"

Pavel nods, and gives a wicked smile. "But she's also supposed to be engaged to Jiri Podarny, and he's here trying to make another economic miracle." Podarny, who used to be, according to the popular newspapers, an entrepreneurial genius, has been downgraded by recession to a status more nearly matching his very slight intellectual gifts, and apparently no true Christa-watcher believes she'll ever marry him.

"Podarny has flirted with the Loyals, but that cuts no ice. But if what you say about Rietz working for Herder is true, then maybe it's true Herder is one hundred percent behind Miloczy and Vock, and Christa is with the Herders all the time. You know I don't give two cents, but there was rumour Herder was boinking her; could be, but now she's like *this* with Mara Herder, you don't see one without the other. This I don't like."

This, to me, is incomprehensible; Mara isn't my idea of anyone's bosom friend. Having abandoned a less than brilliant stage career when she married, she was hostess for my second appearance at a Herder party. Over-groomed, I'll allow her a certain blonded beauty, but her studied elegance left me chilled. True, in her new role as chatelaine, she might have disliked me for recalling her in the servile part of Charmian.

Not much to the point, as Pavel is. "Like I say, our good judge cannot be bought or pushed around, but if Pop Wirath has a soft spot, it's his daughter; she says she wants the moon, he goes looking for a longer ladder."

"You can't believe he'd let her friendships influence a constitutional ruling."

Pavel parodistically gives me up for lost. "Come on, you used to be so smart. Sure, I don't think Christa goes to her father and says `You gotta throw out the yellow ballots account of my friend Mara Herder.' We're talking subtle, which Herder knows how to be. I don't like it."

He begins a fresh tirade on the apparent covert alliance the wild-card Rietz is evidence for, but here his secretary, a long-nosed woman, very motherly at about twenty-eight, taps reticently at the door, and in obsequies of apology reminds Pavel of the production meeting for the evening news and tonight's remote.

"Yah. Listen — " me. "What time you gonna get through tonight?"

I shrug. "Depends. If there's anything to shoot, my crew will keep shooting, and I'll be with them."

"Like if Korava goes up in flames, thanks a million, sure. Assuming that doesn't happen, I ought to wrap about ten; Katja's gonna have supper, soup and a bottle of Bulgarian merlot, not bad. She tells me, don't come home unless I bring you, okay?"

I make a doubtful noise; ten here is four in the afternoon in New York, and if there's usable live footage —

"Bring your computer, leave my number with the Schweitzerhof. Listen, maybe nothing's gonna happen, maybe something gets started, there's enough *dzhándarmi* there to snuff it out — that's gonna make good pictures, huh? Strangest thing, about an hour after I get this funny feeling the trouble might start in Grdacz Square, guy at the Interior Ministry, friend of mine, gets the same identical funny feeling. Like your mom would say, 'swounds, but this is pissing strange."

"Passing strange."

"Same difference."

I don't ask how long he's been saving up that one.

III

I've omitted to mention that earlier, when being installed at the Schweitzerhof, I'd run into the Belgian, Dufoireau, an encounter quite easy to forget. Puffing up his normally nearly concave chest, he asked with cumbersome modesty if I hadn't seen his ITN piece.

"On the kroon devaluation?" innocently — something about an alleged Estonian currency crisis he did at least six months ago, and buggered up so badly he'd almost lost his job.

We're no longer in exclusive possession; the siren-voice of crisis has been heard, and the afternoon Lufthansa flight from Berlin, which meanders here out of its way to Warsaw, before going on to Riga and St Petersburg, has disgorged a consignment of journalists, almost all old acquaintances; for German-language consumers, handsome Horst Scheiden (print) and rather forbidding Gunther Üwe (television), Amy Highcote, the diminutive, chain-smoking Reuters correspondent with her absurd mop of desiccated straw hair and eternal dark glasses, yes, even in the brownish murk of late midwinter afternoon at $51^0 40'N$, Ludmilla Matsirova, Russian TV, ripe, glossily dangerous, regrettably strictly lesbian, though she enjoys erotic badinage with males, Trev Hassett, a breezy, hard-drinking Australian about forty, with whom I am in occasional competition for both printed and broadcast space; he formerly worked in South Asia, and from there brought back the useful conviction that any story, no matter how exotic its detail, is ultimately reducible to the simple terms of small-town gossip. A proposition he cynically holds to be self-confirming, since the audience he calls the "teleclones" can't follow anything more complicated. Also a couple of faces new to me, Hong Kong Chinese and Polish. This flock is in possession of the hotel foyer, surrounding a pyramid of luggage and portable equipment. Recognised, I keep the greetings short, but inform them about the candlelight march, and do not refuse anyone a quick briefing on where matters stand in Dusatia; some other day I may want authentic local information in any of their particular back yards.

There are two late items from RTPD radio: President Niemek "with the concurrence of all parties" has asked Dalerant to become interim premier, and he will address the nation (no doubt with his accustomed smarminess) tomorrow. Also tomorrow, the Chief Justice, Wirath, is holding a news conference at noon. Not, it is emphasised, to announce a decision in the "Yellow Ballot" question, but to "clarify the issues and put forward his timetable." This I more or less overhear while the concièrge is handing me a short list of phone messages, with the face of one who hadn't planned to be my personal receptionist (buy her flowers soon), and farther down the barricade of high desk an assistant manager is shortly trying in a mélange of tortured tongues to relay the news to my confrères. "Come on, Kearns, you speak the bloody language," Trev Hassett snarls, and my two quick translations (the other Polish), together with the assistant-manager's superfluous German (both Horst and Gunther speak excellent English) trigger diaspora, everyone scurrying to phone and E-mail. Such items are not the stuff of Clark Kent scoops and world exclusives.

But Rietz and Herder, Herder and Vock, Mara Herder and Christa, are mine and Pavel's, and without a word said I know that he and I are wrestling with the same divergent and perhaps incompatible questions. Both of us are newspeople, looking at what might in some tortuous fashion be a story, and a story is something you find a way to tell, doing your best, like any biologist or sociologist, to minimise observer effect. Once published, the revelation may and often does alter the course of events; to report authoritatively that some prominent statesman has his hand in the till is likely to modify behaviour, for both him and those his office affects. But that's not the same as manipulating events as-yet unreported, and I know that Pavel is passionately interested in forestalling what he suspects; he passionately wants Wirath to reject the Loyalist claims and let the election stand as announced. So do I, and again like him, would like to see Vock and the baleful threat of Miloczy altogether discredited. But beyond even that, for which we hardly have the ammunition, we want them *stopped*, now, even if it's accomplished behind the scenes, in such a way that there's no story left to report: I would rather be Dusatia's Unknown Benefactor (though how I can is worse than unclear) than win prizes for reporting how the National Loyalist coup came to succeed. Albertson would be disgusted with me.

Another strand to complicate the weave — and here I can't tell how far Pavel and I are in accord — is the absence of any hero. Certainly it isn't Gorat, a man and statesman I've come to dislike greatly. He's 54 now, large and heavy but not obese, began as a teacher and educational administrator, and then, past forty, in one of those metamorphoses far rarer in western Europe than here, became a performer, with an odd mixture of folk songs, traditional and American, and rambling topical monologues filled with lumbering irony. On the basis of the murky amateur tape I've seen of a performance in a "people's club," all cigarette smoke, beer, and unruly audience participation, any booking agent would have advised Gorat to keep his daytime job, but he was able to make a living at it for several years; he's generally remembered now as a courageous public critic of the régime, but in fact his lampoons of generic political bumbling, mixed with far harsher treatment of such targets as American hypocrisy, geriatric Nazis in West Germany and English football fans, for a long time enjoyed official approval, as shown by occasional television appearances, and his participation in the "World Festival of Socialist Folk Art" in East Berlin, where he sang an interminable, scurrilous German version of "This Old Man," dedicated to President Reagan (to translate, for example: *This Old Man, Standing firm, Filled with Mrs Thatcher's sperm* — the German is much cruder).

It is true that latterly Gorat became an acknowledged leader among those drawing attention, at first discreetly, to the advancing senile paralysis of Warsaw Pact governments and the progressive impotence of Moscow; he edited and largely composed an "underground" newspaper whose undergroundness eventually became a joke; it was said the police would confiscate a copy being read on the street because they were the only ones in Korava who didn't know where to buy it (actually, though it had a tiny cover price, it was mostly distributed free). For this period, I know, Gorat has or had the admiration of Pavel, then 25 or so, for whom he was an exemplar, though they knew each other only slightly.

The Action for a Democratic Dusatia was engendered at the University, and like all such movements, no matter how worthy their shared aims, was soon wasting much of its energy on wrangling over the next step, attempted internal coups, the formation of more activist or more gradualist splinter-groups. Here, Gorat for the first time developed or demonstrated an innate political aptitude, and swiftly emerged as a unifying leader, organising, if not originating, the impressive silent candlelight marches that in growing strength expressed the popular desire for change. When, with the police declining to suppress dissent and the army, or part of it, openly ignoring its directives, the "Muscovite" government at last conceded defeat, Gorat became de facto premier, and as soon as it had been agreed the new constitution would be, with minor adjustments, that of 1919, again showed acumen by instantly recalling the old hero, Niemek, from the provinces to be figurehead president, a post in which he has been reconfirmed ever since without opposition.

So far, so praiseworthy. If disappointment with Gorat came less precipitously than with Vock, it was not much lesser in the end, as it became plain in his manoeuvrings that the good he strove for was that of Gorat at least as much as his country. He's far better off now, and if he still chooses to appear in public in the same unpressed, baggy, old-fashioned chalk-stripe black suits, it doesn't quite efface the image of telephoto paparazzo pictures of Gorat on summer holiday, deckchaired in svelte white linen and a panama at his mountain retreat in the Czech Republic — and the change of attire is a fair equivalent for the contrast between the comfortable, motherly Mme. Gorat (Deresza) who campaigns with him, and the lithe bikini-babe draped by his knees across the border. That's salacious gossip, but his acquisition of the choice property, and its location, are of more than passing interest, since it was a Czech company that bought a controlling interest in the western Dusatian coal-mines when they were de-nationalised; indeed, Gorat's personal control of the privatisation process, of the list of those who would be permitted to bid, appears to be the key to his fortunes. Curiously, he seems to have made little if anything out of the Cicada phenomenon, since title to the factory ("requisitioned" by the Soviets) reverted by law to the Podarny family, and Herder declined government loans or guarantees when swiftly raising the cash to launch the enterprise.

Yet more disillusioning than his questionable financial probity has been the unprincipled trimming, trading, backfilling and temporizing by which Gorat has kept himself in power. On issue after issue — amnesty for bureaucrats who served the "Muscovites," disposition of former Church property, redemption of the "people's bonds" with their impossible 9% interest rate (a late, desperate expedient by which the old government had tried to re-invent capitalism to save communism), institution of a minimum wage, safety regulations for mining and industry, he has appeared on all sides of the question, given and then backed away from assurances, invented ectoplasmic language to embrace incompatibles, and in most cases somehow achieved uneasy compromises, often with the promise of future "re-examination," which leave no one satisfied, and seldom look much like a lasting settlement.

Written down, this indictment seems less awful than it does in my heart; nothing I've said, clearly, would prevent a better-tailored, less swarthy Gorat from being a successful and even revered political figure by the Thames or the Potomac; or unchanged, including the awful suits, on the banks of the Seine. Like irascible parents, we of the ancient corruptions should not make infant democracies the whipping-boys for our own shortcomings; Gorat has not gone back (anyway, not much) on his commitment to a free economy, and has piloted a precarious course between the Right, with its nationalist idiocies, and the Left with its nostalgia over the days when a loaf of subsidised bread was unimaginably cheap (not figuring in the cost in personal liberty). But here, as when I'm in Whitehall, I can't help longing for a leader who leads, for principle, for vision that isn't just another marketable *thing*.

At Grdacz Square as early as six-thirty, sober marchers are already assembling, and I hope those with their candles burning have brought spares. Standing in twos and threes, some larger clumps, they'll be here to swell the main march, which, coming down the long slope from parliament, will enter the square on the south side, and swing right in front of the National Theatre to take east-running Avenue of the Republic, past the presidential palace, ending at the broad space not far beyond in front of the building, blended of Parthenon and Petit Trianon, where the high court sits. Thus completing a solemn tour of the three branches, legislative, executive and judicial, by a route made traditional in the last months of the "Muscovite" period.

There are many police. At the presidential palace, solid lines of *dzhăndarmi* inside the railings to discourage any forcing of the gates, another strong detachment on the steps to the high court, but though there are brown uniforms here in the square, by contrast with midday — does Pavel's friend at the Ministry doubt the resolution of the browns in dealing with Rietz? — the largest presence is of "blue police," the municipal force. Sinister in masked helmets and with perspex riot shields on hand, about sixty are marshalled in the northeasternmost corner, by the balustrade next to where broad stone steps descend to the riverbank. Between their parked vans and the corner of the Avenue RTPD has put up a plank platform on skeletal steel supports, with four cameras, all but one still hooded. Kept by the police from being any nearer the steps, my crew has its van practically in front of the National Theatre. As I greet them, I note a weathered and out-of-date playbill, recalling the belated arrival of *Evita* in Korava ("Performed in Polish," the poster warns) sometime last year.

Certainly the effect of a candlelight procession is meretricious, a tug at the heart that can be and has been used to lend an unearned sentiment to some worse than unworthy causes, and yet the rippling waves of tiny flame, eddying down from parliament, are a stirring sight. Down below, talking to Svoboda's portable camera, I have recorded my short intro, and we have both clambered to the roof of the van, he to film, I to deliver sober prose explaining this event, but my voice snags and breaks as the slow-pacing leaders flow into the broad square, earnest, sad and hopeful faces of old and young men and women, small children, softly laved with golden light, the waiting reinforcements swelling the stream; all this is something more than the great television I know and murmur aside that it will be. True, we are very near exact midwinter, when the lighting of candles, log fires, vicarious coloured lights, answers a more atavistic need than political desires. It's growing colder, though with practically no wind, and

snow is gently but persistently falling, beginning to whiten
cornices and car roofs.   There are many flags, the horizontal
tricolour, green, narrow gold, blue, of Dusatia, but only a
sprinkling of signs, most asking simply for *Unity!*, though I see
and point out to Svoboda one insisting *The Election Must Stand!*
— I speak a translation for the tape. This will probably have to be
remixed later, although Novak, younger of the team, the
technocrat, is in the back of the van, riding the controls, and has an
uncanny knack for his job; he makes cuts on the fly, saving much
editing time later, and can rewind, cue, and cross-fade in existent
footage while monitoring and mixing live sound and pictures.

As the great river of Koravans continues to fill the square
I keep turning over my left shoulder to keep an eye on the
predicted trouble-spot, and am surprised to see, out on the cobbles
of the square, a small gathering, eight or so, without candles, two
of them holding the poles that suspend a cloth painted with the one
word, *Freedom* (which tickles my cameraman). All are young,
with a sort of unisex appearance, and their evident leader is, of
course, Angèle, less immediately recognisable now the trademark
mane of tousled near-black hair, since her second spell in prison,
has yielded to a more ruly, more practical close helmet, brushed
back. No one has ever seen her with a hat, and even at this
distance I can see the glisten of ice-crystals in her hair. Though 26
now, with a career in mainstream journalism apparently behind
her, she could still easily pass for eighteen, not much more than
the average age of her tiny, devoted following.

Well behind them and to their left, at the head of the steps,
I can see the front ranks of another and larger group, how large
impossible to determine since many more could be packed on the
steps below. The helmeted police have already extended in a
double line, half watching the candle-bearers, half practically
nose-to-nose with this flanking contingent.   Just as I point
Svoboda in that direction, a sudden surge pushes back the police,
and the would-be disrupters are able to establish a stair-head,
spreading in front of the balustrade, some armed with cudgels,
though diffident about actually swinging them at the police. More
shove up from below; they look very like Rietz's toughs outside
the studio earlier, but there are no red, white and black rosettes,

and I see that some are carrying signs proclaiming allegiance to Dalerant.

To *Dalerant*! It is preposterous: while he sometimes makes questionable political use of the archbishop of Korava (who would do anything, it's said, to bring himself nearer a red hat), and more than once has come close to asserting that the sole hope of escaping eternal damnation is a vote for Catholic Renewal, he is simply not a man who stirs strong passions; his supporters are lukewarm, his detractors casually dismissive. Besides, he's just been made, however temporarily, premier; why riot for him now?

The crazy necessary logic of what must be Rietz's choice comes clear in my mind, as, solidly contained to their front, the bruisers, of whom there are at least thirty, achieve a near breakout to their right, in my general direction. Threatened, Angèle's little band, the banner foundering, retreats, while Svoboda, calling out something about better pictures, goes humping down the steel ladder on the side of the van, and I, with misgivings, quickly follow.

Though it becomes nasty, the struggle is brief; a numerous reserve of police trotting across, truncheons coming into play, to capture the foremost of their adversaries; recognizing failure, others are already disappearing back down the steps. At the same time I see that Angèle, followers dispersed, is backed up almost against the van, and that a sergeant of police with a couple of subordinates is about to seize her. Getting Svoboda's attention, I intervene.

"What do you think you're doing?" I bawl.

"Police business. Get away!" The sergeant, with a looping arm tries at a range of twenty feet to wipe out the camera's prying gaze.

"Why are you arresting this woman?" — proffering the mike for his answer.

"Police business. Disorderly conduct; we have a riot here." The rapidly subsiding struggle scarcely substantiates his claim.

"She did nothing. I have it all on tape."

"I have orders." But his hands are no longer at her shoulder and wrist.

"When the tape is played in court, you'll be charged with

abuse of police powers — " a magical term since the well-publicised case of a police captain who'd gone about the black market in a vigilante spirit, and caused arrest of a completely legal seller of eggs, destroying most of her stock in the process; the captain was last heard of as a waiter in a working-class restaurant.

"Let him arrest me," Angèle says, even-voiced, all the defiance in her eyes.

He is wavering. I gesture to Svoboda to cut the camera, and in a more friendly spirit say, "You think whoever gave you your *orders* will come forward when you're on trial? He'll be the first to call you a rogue copper once it's on the front page of the newspapers."

The likely truth of this sinks in; I'm going to win; he huffs a little, and saves face by admonishing Angèle to stay well away from trouble if she wants to avoid trouble for herself. Wordless, her glowering contempt is articulate enough.

The officer looks at me, and I assure him this part of the tape will be destroyed. To his men, he points out some imaginary place of potential danger, and so achieves a reasonably dignified exit. Angéle meets my eyes, and nods curtly; understood, to thank me would be a violation of her creed.

Angèle: small, dark, very slim, wound tight, "philosophical anarchist" journalist; prominent in student uprising of 1991; it was her wildly fired gun, when attempting to "liberate" the TV station, which had wounded and might have crippled Pavel.

She escaped the more serious charges connected with the affair, and was sentenced only to a year (of which she served less than eight months) for "illegal discharge of a firearm," Pavel having bluntly told the prosecutor that if she was charged with attempted murder, or even felonious assault, he would decline to identify her as his assailant. As a fiery undergraduate she had, he told me in justification, contributed to Gorat's underground newspaper, her singling out of the "Muscovite marionettes" allowing them to overlook or condone her implicit condemnation of all government. "We were on the same *side*," he said, this at a time when walking was still agony for him.

Notwithstanding her record, Angèle went straight from prison to the most respected national newspaper, and become a frequent talking head on television (with Pavel's sanction, though not his presence), not in the least harmed by her tense, youthful good looks, "a shaggy adolescent volcano," as one muddled commentator put it; eventually blown apart by her own eruptions, in particular the notorious prediction that "a few judicious assassinations may be necessary if our freedoms are to be saved — " the last-straw indiscretion in her brief, turbulent career as a political journalist; she still contributes passionate jeremiads to a grubby little newspaper, and is still displayed by the smart set, though both radio and TV are careful to filter her views through the intermediary of an interviewer, building in the disclaimer. Most men, despite her extravagances, find her (often to their shame) enormously attractive physically.

When I was last here, just before the election, Gorat for the fourth time having given a perfectly reasonable excuse for last-moment cancellation of our interview, I found myself with a camera-crew already paid for, and no one to shoot. At last scrabbling up my courage I phoned Angèle, and she sullenly agreed to appear, insisting on Republic Park for venue, which I assumed in some mysterious way symbolised her libertarianism; we sat on a bench in a light, cold rain; glossy pigeons, several gawkers, occasional noises off. She had arrived on time, flanked by a couple of even-more-youthful disciples, and I hadn't realised how tiny she is, not shorter than several women I know (Amy Highcote of Reuters, for one), Angèle was pencil-slender inside a capacious, well-worn fleece jacket; the French jeans, bagged at the knees, were faded and frayed, but her philosophy, I noted, didn't bar use of either lipstick or some artful eye-shadow and the blouse under the voluminous jacket was a rippling silklike fabric. Would she support anyone in the election?
"You must understand, this election, whatever its outcome, is irrelevant to the real needs of the Dusatian people. All over Europe, everywhere in the world, you have these farcical charades, where people are asked to choose between forms of slavery, and told that is freedom."
(I overcame fright) "You will concede, at least, that there

is a greater degree of freedom now than when ballots had the name of just one candidate, approved by Moscow?"

"Instead of three or four, none of which will upset Washington? I'm sorry, you want me to say there's more freedom in the exercise-yard than in the cell, when the real point is, it is still prison."

(Tempted to ask about her own spell in chokey; resisted) "What, practically, is your remedy? You do agree that we must have some form of government?"

"For what? To make laws limiting my right to choose my own life? Let us say there are suddenly no more laws against robbery, murder, and so forth — does that mean you will become a wild animal? Those who make laws are saying that without fear of punishment, people will be worse than wild animals. That is not my belief."

(This was going to become a rotten interview if I really debated the point) "Surely it isn't simply a question of wilful crime? You're demanding the right to choose, but choices will inevitably come into conflict; with no ill-will, people may differ, for example, on the best use for a piece of land — "

"The land belongs to all the people."

"In the absence of all law, isn't it likely to belong very soon to the strongest and most ruthless?"

"So you have been taught to believe. This is the virus of our history. What I anticipate is a new future, where competition and conflict are seen as we now see cannibalism and human sacrifice — of which, to be sure, these things are simply different forms — as bad memories of a savage past."

"You seem to be anticipating a new species."

"No, sir, a new resolve, a new determination to shed the constrictive clothing of the past — for an awakening."

"May we take it you expect none of these developments as a result of the national election now imminent?"

(Angèle has no palate for irony) *"As a direct result? Not possible. But every election must be seen as another stage in the progressive disillusionment — which is to say, the gradual awakening — of a free people."*

(cut soon to "Thank you.")

She probably never appreciated my tact in not asking about her "few assassinations" remark, which I felt was adequately recalled by calling her "controversial" in my intro; if I had brought it up, incautious as she is, she would no doubt have reaffirmed its validity, thus that of her surveillance by the police; hunched and gloomy in a filthy mac, a blatant plainclothesman was among our bystanders.

As far as I know, this tape, admittedly quite odd, a Central European philosophical anarchist saying virtually nothing about the election I was supposed to be profiling, was used except for tiny snippets only once, overdubbed in Ukrainian, in a magazine programme out of Kiev called *PanSlavia*, and even they complained about the abstract content. As for me, I ended less scared, somewhat more exasperated, and with a reluctant near-liking, though I was and continued for some reason largely immune to the erotic element others found so imperative. Oh, it was plain, whatever weighty reading she'd done since, her intellectual development had run out of gas when she was about fifteen, and the combination of badly digested ideas and ferocious intolerance made her a dangerous beast, yet I understood now Pavel's forbearance; she is everybody's bright, half-mad, foul-tempered daughter or little sister — an assessment that would put me high on Angèle's hit-list, if she knew.

That since seven a.m. yesterday I haven't slept is becoming the dominant fact in my life, but in the production studio rented from RTPD, the edit goes swiftly, with only a moment of irritation when we can't find a short bit of film; by ten past ten we can send New York nine minutes to play with: their evening broadcast is half an hour, which means that when you take out commercials, promos and various time-consuming bits of graphic over-production, they have about twenty-one-and-a-half minutes to deal with the entire world, and would allot nine whole minutes only to some domestic catastrophe or scandal, but it's just past four in the afternoon there, giving them hours to choose which bits they like. Pavel, who was on live from Grdacz Square, and can reshow great chunks of it on his evening news hour, has an easier time, and comes in to lounge watching me while I'm still making up a cue sheet for our satellite transmission.

"Okay, you ready to go?"

Still with a vague sensation of guilt or foreboding, I accept the inevitability of supper.

"Whaddya know — " as we belt ourselves into his BMW. "A violent pro-Dalerant demonstration. Gee, whiz."

Obviously he believes it no more than I do. Vock wants a riot, but couldn't let Loyalist supporters disrupt an obviously peaceful demonstration; since most in the candlelight march would at worst accept the return of Gorat, Rietz couldn't have his bullies masquerade as Gorat supporters; Dalerant was a choice of desperation. "How are you reporting it?"

"Dalerant expected to deny any connection, hard to see what his faction could hope to gain by unrest — " this in Dusatian. "You?"

"Twenty-five seconds of the clash, no mention of Dalerant, *certain elements*; it comes immediately after I talk about what Vock hopes for."

A grin. "You would have been a natural for the Ridiculists."

This links to my earlier reflections. About a decade ago, at the same time as Gorat was taking charge of the Action for a Democratic Dusatia, Pavel had a loosely-organised group quietly seeing to it that banned publications and accurate accounts of censored news stories were distributed, going on to various forms of mild disruption and dirty tricks — "ridiculism," Pavel calls it, on the analogy of *terrorism*.

By this time it was becoming obvious that the prevailing system had no resources for reversing economic decline, and a choice target for the Ridiculists had been Oszanow, the Dusatian Minister for Economic Development. An unpleasantly obese man, Oszanow was widely believed to have accumulated a personal fortune, and rumoured to have an insatiable appetite for very young girls, thirteen to fifteen his preferred range. In 1989, being driven to a provincial capital for a public meeting where he would soothe disgruntled agricultural workers with his well-worn "teething troubles" speech, insisting collectivism was bound to bring universal prosperity, given another forty years running-in time, Oszanov was delayed by an unexpected detour, small but official-looking arrow signs which took him up into the foothills, and then lost interest. Meanwhile, at the moment when his speech was supposed to begin, the doors to the packed, seething provincial People's Hall opened, and a complacent, adipose pig waddled down the central aisle.

"The one thing really killed those guys," Pavel recalls. "Being laughed at. The poor bastards couldn't even do a proper investigation for fear of giving it more publicity. We had a ball at the station; started to do a piece about the minister, showed about fifteen seconds of the pig, then pulled it like it was a foul-up. Eight seconds dead air, then Katja comes on with her wide eyes — she wasn't even eighteen then, looked innocent as the angels — and she does an apology; `That was, of course, *not* Mr. Minister Oszanov — ' it was beautiful.

"That night," he adds sentimentally, "was the first time we screwed." Pretty, slender Katja, whose otherworldly air of innocence, not incompatible with a witty UHF flirtatiousness, caught my attention when I was first at the studios, before I knew her name; I might well have tried my luck with her, but soon saw that Pavel regarded her as his. She had begun in girlhood as a dancer, at fifteen won a year's scholarship to Kirov, but with a mother dying of cancer had come home, tried out as a reader of news for children, and been an instant success, attracting fan-mail from pimpled youth and wistful age, and everything in between, none of which did anything to alter her extraordinary, calm practicality — though here I'm jumping ahead to later meetings with her, now Pavel's wife, and mother of two boys, as which, to my eye, she has lost none of her enigmatic (though straightforward) air of fragile indestructibility. All right, that's word-play, but resort to it is admission of my inability to capture the elusive charm of one who never thought for a moment about being charming.

She greets us phone in hand with the one word, "Station," and while Pavel makes a face and takes the phone, lets me kiss her cheek, and asks what are my plans for Christmas.

"Of course run it," Pavel says. "Steal a minute from weather, everyone can see it's snowing." His evening news is on right now.

After tonight's preservation of the peace, I've been wondering if I can't get back to Sevenoaks after all, and return for Wirath's decision, which, if he has to announce a timetable, can now hardly come before Christmas. But Katja wants me to join them for an "Anglo-Dusatian" feast; she's roasting a goose, and has found and purchased what she calls a "Krauss ent Blachvil" pudding.

"Okay, run over," Pavel says. "It's only gymnastics, on tape, following. Yes, use the file picture, the one where it looks as if he's spitting." He disconnects and rolls his eyes. "If I'm not there when we declare war on New Zealand, they'll phone me to see if we should carry the story. Up in Kerpacza, Miloczy just announced he's holding one of his rallies tomorrow night, and will have a statement about the Yellow Ballot."

"Marvellous." Experience makes us sourly aware of what that means; panning for gold. Miloczy boasts of speaking from only the sketchiest notes, which, urged on by the enthusiasm of his spellbound listeners, he can spin out almost indefinitely. Somewhere, seldom at the beginning, sometimes at the end, often passingly in mid-spate of crude but evidently effective rhetoric, will come what for all but the faithful may be the real point of the speech, but still we must go on listening, remaining alert through tedious repetitions and meaningless mouthings, to be sure nothing of note has been missed. I don't take the bet when Pavel offers me five crowns for every minute under an hour, if I'll give one for every minute over.

The soup, a peasant dish made with marrow-bones, leeks and lentils, is soothing, the wine remarkably breedy for four nicker or so. Swapping our evening's adventures we remain in Dusatian for the comfort of Katja, whose progress in English has been muddled rather than helped by Pavel's archaic variant; she speaks a rich, rolling ballet-school Russian, and in her clipped, somewhat Saxonised German can become a new personality, precise and didactic.

I don't refer to the encounter with Angèle, who obscurely annoys Katja. Uncountable hours without sleep are beginning to haul me down; desultorily we review the political scene, and decide Pavel's nightmare of tanks in the streets and a Loyalist coup must recede after tonight's events, unless the one unknowable, Miloczy, can stir up fresh trouble.

"He's impatient," Katja holds. "That's why he never stood for parliament; he has no patience for haggling, compromise, manoeuvres. But this Yellow Ballot mess is his best chance ever."

"Maybe his last chance, if times get better," Pavel says. "But this is all trickery. The Loyalists' best legitimate shot was '93, when Vock was still our hero. After he broke with Gorat and came out for Miloczy — at one time the Loyalists looked like winning eighty to ninety seats; with that kind of base, they would have won this election; Vock would be premier right now. But there was another Loyalist candidate over in Obdana — "

"Jan Tidjak," Katja supplies.

"Tidjak; for no reason he decides to go after the President, calls him the old man in Gorat's pocket, the 1962 rebellion was nothing more than another kind of communism, and Niemek had spent his whole life kissing up foreign dictators. *Niemek*!"

Yes. Admittedly, my portrait of Niemek comes largely from my mother, who reveres him, but this was a man of the Resistance who was about five minutes away from execution by the Gestapo when the Soviets arrived in '45.

"Right. Then Stalin brings him to Moscow for the victory parade, makes him Hero of the Soviet Union, and Niemek turns round and tells Uncle Joe the politburo style is not compatible with Dusatian traditions — he's a kid, not even twenty-five, can you see it, that terrible old man? So Niemek is not in the plans for the new Dusatia, but some people believe that was what saved Niemek from being shot, or vanished away to Siberia, after the suppression in '62 — "

"Khruschyov had heard the story," Katja explains, "and Khruschyov loved anything that made Stalin look foolish, so they say."

As happens rather easily in a country trying to find some continuity with a largely rejected past, we have strayed into legend, and I have to bring Pavel back to the more immediate point.

"The National Loyalist support melted away, everybody

was offended; Vock disassociated himself from Tidjak's remarks, and after a talk with Miloczy Tidjak steps down as a candidate for reasons of bad health. But the damage was done, and Gorat knew how to exploit it; the Loyalists ended up with twenty-four seats instead of ninety; but for the economy going bad they'd be history by now."

Pavel here begins to remind me of the complex mathematics of alliance needed to give the Loyalists a fragile working majority, but my yawning can no longer be controlled.

I'm offered a bed, but while it's true that where there's a modem I am still on line, my communications may conflict with Pavel's, and I shan't feel easy here about rising at four to catch up with some writing. By now, Amy Highcote has found an interpreter, two hundred Virginia Slims and a large bottle of vodka, and as usual is covering the story from her hotel room, watching local television; Albertson will have picked up the late news from Reuters. He has an annoying habit of acquiring instant expertise, and though yesterday he didn't know Miloczy from Stravinsky, and will have forgotten all about him in a month, he's sure to call and instruct me on the potential importance of the speech tomorrow night.

I decide to summon a taxi, but Pavel, with a glum look at the accumulating snow, doubts we'll rouse one, and says he'll drive me.

Where I am to be for Christmas may be decided tomorrow, depending on what first Wirath, then Miloczy, have for us; so I tell Katja, who repeats her invitation, upping the ante with a friend of hers as guest, "very beautiful, very brilliant, single, wants so much to meet you," and a promised showing of "Al'stair Seem," one of the few dameless and doughless films in Pavel's library. This appetite for a self-conscious, stereotypic "Englishness" is something I'm familiar with from my mother, but while in her case it's easy to trace back to an adolescent crush on a rather glamourous, poetry-spouting intelligence officer, as renewed in her rescue by my father (who, frankly, strives hard to be a cliché), with Katja I can't guess the origin. But if not much to do with the habitual me, it is still very sweet.

Pavel's mood is unwontedly subdued on the drive.

"We got some footage of you with Angèle." In his voice there is an unfamiliar note I'm unable — or perhaps reluctant — to identify. Though not affecting his laconic driving, sliwowicza after Bulgarian merlot may be a factor.

I explain the incident.

"So, da-da-da-*dah* it's Kearns to the rescue." There's a tension never felt before with Pavel, and I come a step nearer the unthinkable.

"It bothered me. Christ knows what she thought she was accomplishing there, but she wasn't starting a riot. He had orders!"

"That's Gorat. Not straight from him, but that's where it comes from. He's gunning for her, ever since she said we were a country of sheep, led to disaster by a cunning old goat."

I silently salute Angèle for a neat double reference, but still can't see the use of her. "She's wasting her time with all that anarchy nonsense."

We had slipped into Dusatian, but Pavel, rousing, snarls back into his gangster English: "Whadda you want, she's nuts. She sure is something, though, ain't she? Bugsy like a starved panther, how would you like those claws in your back, huh? Never once thought about it, did you?"

This, a sarcasm, at last lets me acknowledge perception; jealousy. Pavel envies that I was the one to save Angèle from arrest, but beyond that —

"What would you give for a long weekend and a wide bed with Angèle in it? *Gaspodi*, I'd like to fuck her till she is meek as marshmallow and twice as sweet."

"That might take more than a weekend — " and more than a little help from his friends, I almost say, but recognise in his overripe tone a state not for mockery, far outside mere changing-room vainglory.

Actually, I'm appalled. "You can't possibly be in love with Angèle. She tried to kill you."

"If a dame pulls her gun on a guy, he is not allowed to hold the torch for her? This is not the rules of cricket, my dear old chap!"

"But you're in love with Katja. You would have to be

loony — "

 "No, no, I *love* Katja, my boys, being married to Katja.
You are *in* love with Katja, my friend."

 We have arrived at the Schweitzerhcf, the driveway being
patiently cleaned by an elderly man with what looks like a coal-
shovel. Pavel is laughing at my dumbstruckedness.

IV

Absurd as it is, I've anticipated Albertson's most urgent exhortation, and kept our own camera crew for the Wirath event, though essentially identical footage will be made available by RTPD, on whom we'll depend thereafter — for clips of the Miloczy address, for instance, though I judge the world appetite for Dusatian news has already peaked, and will subside until we have a decision from the high court.

The *Gadzete*, Korava's chief morning newspaper, who had sent a man to police headquarters and attempted without success to question some of the demonstrators (charged and released), asked *Who Were These Hooligans?* just below the fold; a large photo of the peaceful march was contrasted with a small one of the attempted disruption, and their disbelief it had any connection with Dalerant was not disguised. The tabloid-sized *Novjétny*, less read but editorially pro-Loyalist, had Vock's statement deploring the incident, and calling for calm, but darkly hinting it could at need be imposed, but their front page led off with Miloczy's coming speech. He will, they promise, reveal additional scandalous irregularities, quite apart from the Yellow Ballot, in the recent election.

Pavel rings to ask how I slept, and, still generous (though with information I can't print), to tell me he has spoken this morning with his mother in Viczonjy, and she says the tanks of Javelin Division had their engines running yesterday evening, the racket easily audible at a distance of three miles.

For the morning the press corps is swelled if not exactly joined by an entourage, seven in number, enclosing a genuine American network newsman, who has been "on assignment," filming a series about organised crime in eastern Europe, and has come overland from Warsaw, his arrival delayed by mismatches between available roads and the fleet-carrier dimensions of their vehicle, which looks equipped for communication with, at need, Alpha Centauri. The ensemble has a brisk, terse competence about them, and their star, with his forthright, manly smile, when introduced (by Trev Hassett, who knows him), has a forthright, manly handshake, and says, "Hi, I'm Whitburn Farley," (or some such invertible name) with the tone of one repeating what is universally known. When I mention my work for a rival network, he increases the squareness of his jaw, and recites a litany of the Jims, Audreys, Scotts and Barts he knows or has worked with "over there;" my inability to match him christian name for name blights any chance of a lasting relationship. He'd arrived in a rumpled though expensive suit, but when later he emerges ready for action is exquisitely costumed in flak-jacket and drab fatigues, with one of those caps whose fleecy crown is a pair of earpieces folded up to overlap on top. Thus clad he strides forth, turns up at the Wirath news conference, and is afterwards found to have powered his way to interviews with Niemek, Dalerant, and even the elusive Gorat, but finding no sniper fire or Molotov cocktails erupting in the streets, has flown away after fourteen hours, leaving the roadies to repack the giant land-cruiser and depart westward. I am later reliably told Farburn's salary, not counting various stock-options and benefits, is $1.8 million. Per annum, I mean, not for eternity.

The Wirath news-conference, I say, but it is no such thing; we gather at the court building in a small auditorium, and Wirath, looking less than his 68 years, slight, neat and grey in a grey suit, stands at the lectern and reads a statement, already distributed in four languages. We learn that, taking into account the Christmas holidays, and considering that Wirath is to hear statements from those who brought the complaint and those opposing it, as well as evidence from the printer and from election officials in districts where the questioned ballot was used, a decision can be expected on or near the 28th of December, that is, a week from tomorrow. Having announced there would be no discussion today as to the substance or the merits of the case, he steps back, and looks bored and impatient, while a lesser official, never identified, answers, or rather turns aside, a series of questions, those from foreigners mostly in English, all almost entirely on the substance or the merits of the case. So as to appear on the tape Svoboda is making, I ask whether there are to be any interim reports before the 28th (probably not).

Finally, Farley Whitburn, having again introduced himself with all the cumbersome modesty of a two-ton Lincoln (car), wants to know if the judge can "assure the American and worldwide public that there is no perceived threat to regional security such as might at some future time call for deployment of U.S. or, could be, multi-national military personnel," the sort of question that might be put by a recently-arrived, verbose Martian who's been too busy getting depressurised for a proper briefing. Mutely appealed-to by the minion, Wirath gives Whitley a stare whose temperature would register only on the Kelvin scale, and utters the single English word, "Yes." Amid the inevitable laughter, Trev Hassett next to me mutters, "Gawd, that's a relief, eh?"

For me, the rejoinder is a reminder: don't be numbed by the colourlessness of Wirath; here is a redoubtable intellect, and a man who has earned his spurs resisting intimidation.

A boy pianist of near-prodigy standards, his attention had shifted to law, where he could memorise statute and case as the young Mozart did once-heard scores. Though he took his degree at 19, he never practised, and as a LlD at only 24, became professor of international and constitutional law at Korava University in 1956, which (I quote my father) must have been much like teaching Roman Catholic theology in Riyadh. Honoured during the nine-month Niemek period, he became, briefly, Dusatian representative at the United Nations, and, notwithstanding his lack of personal charm, was greatly admired, especially by the French and the Scandinavians (he already had a modest international reputation, having published *Magna Carta and the Bill of Rights* in the Harvard Law Review, and *Voltaire, Rousseau, Beaumarchais: thèmes littéraires du Code Napoléon* in a French journal). Though quickly removed from the U.N. post after the suppression, he was allowed to go back to teaching, and survived indiscretions of a seemingly impossible naïveté, such as publicly stating, when some dissidents were put on trial for "anti-Socialist tendencies imperilling the state" that such a crime was a constitutional absurdity. He had evidently become that occasional plague of totalitarian rule, the untouchable good man: other such cases have been, even for Nazi Germany or Pol Pot's Cambodia, Verwoerd's South Africa; that they have argues for the existence of a moral force which can sometimes, though not inevitably, survive to rebuke the cynical. Practically, Wirath could have been barred from teaching as readily as my mother was; the Soviet Union had made Shostakovitch publicly abase himself, and had penal camps stocked with those whose sole crime, mental hospitals filled with patients whose only madness, was political deviation; the emigration policy of the D.D.R. was "shoot to kill;" any international repercussions from Wirath's silencing would have been no more than a nine-day nuisance for such governments. After a dozen years, his sacrosanct immunity came very near running out.

In the mid-seventies, having managed to smuggle out and have published in London a compendious indictment of constitutional violations by the post-Niemek government (for which my mother, she won't mind my now revealing, was unnamed translator of the English version), all the more devastating for its unheated, scholarly, even technical tone, Wirath, in one of those bureaucratic bits of muddle or inattention to which such régimes are especially prone, was nevertheless permitted to attend an international law conference in the Hague. Perhaps they thought it would proclaim to the world their liberal and forgiving spirit.

On his arrival, Wirath was furtively approached by a French-Polish double agent, who had penetrated *Schnur.* and showed the jurist convincing evidence that when he returned he would be arrested on a fabricated charge of espionage. Imperviousness exhausted, Wirath asked for asylum, though not before a hasty marriage to his clerk, a much-younger widow, who, had she gone home, might have become the target of a thwarted vindictiveness by no means alien to *Schnur.*

All available evidence suggests Wirath intended the marriage to be nothing more than a legal convention ("He's, what, forty-five," Pavel said, "And never had a hard on for anything but a nice piece of case law."), but a seduction must have occurred, since Christa was born next year. Not long after, domiciled in Switzerland, the wife slipped away with a Norwegian ski-instructor who had slalomed into her life, and it's possible Wirath didn't notice she was gone until about 1985, equally preoccupied with his treasured daughter and his *magnum opus*, a well-intentioned but eventually unreadable book on *Legal Foundations for the Idea of the Individual in Western Thought*, published initially in French, respected and shelved in several additional languages. At home the memory of his somewhat quaint courage was kept alive as part of the golden legend of Niemek's Revolution; his return to become Chief Justice at the fall of the Muscovites was popular and inevitable. Unlike Trev Hassett, who rolls his eyes upwards to express his feelings, I do not dismiss Wirath as a kind of Dusatian Polonius.

I make an attempt to see Vock (no one can say where he is) and, still with my crew, succeed in a brief meeting with Premier Dalerant, who tells me winningly he is particularly interested in close ties with the United Kingdom, with which Dusatia enjoys a special historic relationship of mutual respect. He has, I'm sure, for Burnley Whitfar, already hymned the immemorial Dusatian friendship with Washington, and will shortly be making the same assertion for Berlin, Warsaw, and perhaps, though implausibly, Canberra and the Orient at large. Even Dalerant's unction, surely, couldn't postulate an ancient, special cordiality with Moscow, and would be forced to settle for *a new era of cooperation*. As with his earlier, agreeably brief and subdued radio and television address, he is positioning himself beyond the certain eight days of his tenure, for conceivable deadlock and the search for compromise.

The two Czechs, after editing, wish me well and point their van towards Prague. There is a feeling of watchful calm in the snowclad capital, and but for those idling tanks in Viczonjy, and Miloczy's contribution still to come I would, like them, be anticipating Christmas at home, not without regret for Katja's feast, and meeting with her brilliant, beautiful, single friend. I put in a call to the French relief centre in Sarajevo, and fail to make contact with Mireille.

Examining my feelings for Katja, as I have been on and off since last night, I'm not sure there's all that much to examine, certainly no occasion for sentimental reappraisals; I am in love with her (if I am) only as I've been in love with dozens of women (well, more than two or three); I like her, admire her style, and find her attractive. Very attractive; the trouble with a sudden, half-joking insight like Pavel's is that it brings into conscious consideration what has (if it has) been only a small snag beneath the surface, and, since life is no more than the sum of what we perceive, largely creates what it seems merely to identify. Inescapably, next time I see Katja I'll be monitoring my own seismic activity, preventlessly watching Katja, trying to read her feelings for me. In a rational sense, I don't ask her to have any, am sure both she and Pavel chose well, but the conceit that drives the mating self treacherously wants her to cherish a fantasy or two about me, can re-explain in those terms what already has appeared; the pressing Christmas invitation, the "English" touches. I've noted in the past that the purely lustful circuits know no impossibility, take into consideration no friendship, no difficulty of time or space or circumstance (why am I writing inside-out clauses?), which is why, when we let them run the whole show, we get ourselves into such grisly messes; it requires only the smallest dash of reason in the mix to see that I can never, shan't ever sleep with Katja.

The test of post-revelation re-exposure isn't long delayed. Back at the hotel, bearing December roses from Turkey for the concièrge, I return another Pavel call; he asks where I plan to view the Miloczy rally, and suggests I do so from his home, where I'm invited for dinner.

At our first real meeting, Katja was a new bride, and asked me to teach her to make "English tea" (the beverage only, not the afternoon orgy of starches) — typically, she had already provided herself with an earthenware pot and a large tin of Jackson's Darjeeling. Most of my crowd in the High Holborn period used electric kettles and teabags, but at her behest I resurrected the orthodox ritual; an unexpectedly intense experience (and the tea actually was better), Katja very concentrated, asking the reason for everything, apt to bestow light confirming touches of her fingertips to my arm or cheek; I had no difficulty understanding why Pavel adored her. Typically, too, six years later, she still retains the entire process; most newcomers almost at once decide that one or more of the steps is pure superstition, and may be omitted or altered without harm. Not Katja; she carries pot to kettle, scalds, brings the water to a real boil, uses a cozy (we made do with a folded sweater before), puts milk in the cups first, all with a teasing challenge in her eye and the set of her chin, as if to say ironically, *Have I learned well, Master*? I wonder why I've always pretended her sensuality is somehow remote, veiled, unconscious, even accused myself of imposing my own reading on a natural human warmth; she is in fact very assured and at home with her sexual component, which, far from immuring, she brings, only slightly veiled, out into the light so as to laugh at its lugubrious self-importance. We are being monitored by the four-year-old, Vasz (for Vaclav), with his mother's large, eloquent eyes, and some exaggerated grimaces caught from his father, who quite soon comes into the kitchen to scoop him up and lug him back to bed. If there's anything new in the quick glance he has for his wife and me, it's neither serious nor accusing.

The back room where we wait for Miloczy to come on is quietly furnished in firm, plain upholstery, rather garishly decorated with framed posters from Pavel's beloved era, when Alan Ladd or John Garfield, trench-coated and armed, pressed their backs against brick in spook lighting, Ida Lupino and Lizbeth Scott and unnamed generic blondes leant or sprawled with cascading hair and precarious decolletage, quaint upright cars with yellow headlights rocked and skidded or spewed forth tommy-gun fire; to be here is like entering a burial vault at Carnac, domain of ancient gods whose sovereignty has passed from the earth, but whose likenesses, only here, still have the power to conjure nostalgia for what we've never known.

We're not exactly watching, muted to silence, the climactic medal round of a home-grown quiz show, offensive to Pavel's responsible nature, in which contestants in their own animal costumes answer zombie questions and perform embarrassing forfeits; the most I can do for the idiomatically untranslatable title is *What Beast Does Best?* — tonight, the answer appears to be a lady giraffe with purple spots.

A knock at the side door. Pavel goes, and out of sight

down a few steps I hear him say, "Christ, you shouldn't come here. Come in, then," and he reappears followed by a bulky youth with a bland, almost a foetal face, inadequately clad for the clear, frigid evening in a blue work-shirt, open to display a grimy underthing, and baggy brown trousers over what look like agonizingly uncomfortable cowboy boots.

"Where'd you leave your car?"

"Right outside," thumb. "But it's not my car." He shows a coy shame. "I took a Volvo we're working on."

"Okay — " Pavel relaxes slightly, though he still shows signs of puzzled annoyance with the youth, whose last words have confirmed what I've instantly assumed, that here is Pavel's mole in the Rietz outfit, the would-be investigative reporter. Now I see him, Pavel's "grease gorilla" seems less an error of idiom than a sly Nabokovian stroke of descriptive illumination; the boy, surely not twenty, short-legged, is all torso and arm; the sleeves of his shirt are stuffed to bursting with taut muscle. He goes by the name of Arni — I put it that way, suspecting the name was borrowed from a more celebrated *Mitteleuropa* brawn-builder, latterly mega-star of mega-buck mega-movies, packed with mega-destruction and micro-interest.

One of my flights to Sofia happened to be on the eve of some world grease-up of freakish muscles there; the plane was half-filled with about six English and American contenders, and for three hours I was wearied by their tiny-minded narcissism, their mincing talk of *Abs* and *Pecs*. I have heard of your steroids, too, well enough; God hath given you one metabolism and you make yourself another. You strut, you amble, and you lisp; you nickname Gray's muscles — Go to, I'll no more on't, it hath made me queasy.

But Arni, as in Pavel's description, seems inoffensive; the more to wonder, with Pavel, at why he would risk blowing his cover (pre-cooked lingo, ready-to-use) with this uninvited visit.

It is, he says he thinks, too important to wait. He'd hoped to see Pavel at work today —

"I was in early — "

— because last night, after the stillborn disruption of the march (Arni in attendance, though he never reached the head of the steps), he had gone home with Rietz — or to one of his homes, a flat fairly central in Korava. Rietz is excited by Arni's physique — the boy is shy with this, but only to avoid seeming vain — and has invited, perhaps pestered him before. So he did, and they did, or at least (if I'm following correctly) Rietz did and Arni let him. I understand there to be a girlfriend in the offing, but for Arni there is no conflict — no connection — between that and his acquiescence with Rietz's designs; not for a moment, I'm convinced, would he think of himself as anything but a heterosexual, to whom this unexampled thing has happened. And, as it happened, if he needed justification, that was lavishly present; he has come of age as an investigative reporter.

There are various post-coital behaviours, instant sleep, elation, garrulousness, depression, renewal. Rietz is a boaster — not about his prowess as a partner; he evidently can't resist impressing his conquest with the importance, daring, cleverness of his daytime activities. From the other side, in the *Schnur* years, Rietz decidedly would have classified a Rietz as a security risk, but there is practically no limit to human capacity for excepting oneself from a sound general rule.

What he crowed was that the failure of the evening's provocations didn't really matter, because Wirath was going to decide the Yellow Ballot issue in favour of the Loyalists. Rietz knows, because they have captured the judge's daughter, Christa, and are holding her as a hostage.

Before we can do much more than look stupefied, the Miloczy rally in Kerpaczy is under way with a waving of many flags, Dusatian and the vertically-banded red, white and black of the Loyalists. Pavel swears, picks up a phone, presses a single number, and is talking to RTPD. Looking at me for concurrence, he tells Firenc that he's unable to watch the Miloczy address, and that Firenc is to ring him to report any points of substance as soon as it's finished. After a listen, Pavel says to me, "Firenc can make a copy of the tape and drop it off here on his way home, okay?"

I nod, Pavel tells Firenc, okay, and the remainder of our discussion with Arni has the flickering background of a gesticulating mime Miloczy, intercut with shots of a rapt, silently rowdy or wildly applauding audience.

Katja, as stunned as any, starts to offer Arni tea, changes it to Pepsi, changes that to diet Pepsi. He humbly accepts, and she fetches it, serving it on a tray American style, open bottle and a glass filled with crushed ice. Arni turns the glass round, then swigs from the bottle.

"It is preposterous," Katja says. "You can't kidnap a Christa Rasch."

"Christa *Rasch*?" Arni chokes on his cola. He has been troubled over the abduction of Judge Wirath's daughter; but now, clear for the first time who she is, is devastated, personally incensed. Two or three years ago, he must have been one of the many, not all adolescent boys, deeply stirred by Christa's celebrated "penitential" scene (costumed, if that's the word, in sandals and a long white lace mantilla) in her second film. That Rietz, boasting, hadn't exulted over which Christa had been abducted means only that he assumed everyone, even Arni, knew who Wirath's daughter was.

Arni recounts the details as far as he knows them: Wirath was to be told, and assured his daughter would be unharmed if he decide the constitutional issue correctly; meanwhile any attempt to inform anyone of the abduction would have "very unfortunate consequences." Rietz found it priceless that Christa as yet didn't know she was a prisoner; she had gone for relaxation and some skiing to a mountain retreat of supposed friend, driven there by his wife, Christa's avowed best friend, and been told that recent snows had interrupted telephone service. Force would be used only as it became necessary.

"Herder," Pavel says. "Bastard. He has a place, sometimes it's a private lodge, sometimes it's an hotel, up in Kerpacza, north of Kerpaczy." Miloczy's province.

"Yes, Herder, that was the name." Really, if Arni is going to be a journalist, he's going to have to get his nose out of manifolds and muscle-mags, and find out who's famous in Dusatia. But if Christa had gone to the lodge, it was with Mara Herder alone; I was seen and nodded to by Herder not far from parliament earlier today.

I ask when Wirath was to be informed, and Arni thinks late last night, whether by telephone or a visitor he can't say, bringing in the rather eerie possibility that when giving his briefing and listening to idiotic questions earlier today, the judge was concealing frantic anxiety over his daughter. The depth of emotion can't be doubted.

"Say — " Pavel is grimly humorous, and I realise he's gone into English deliberately to exclude Arni. "I guess this is where we find out just how incorruptible Wirath is."

"He may just go on as if nothing has happened."

"Anything but Christa, that's what he'd do. Ever since the kid was born, she was his *life*. Maybe fudging a decision is the only thing he wouldn't do for Christa, but I don't know." Pavel shakes his head like the wearied Bogart. "It's too close to call."

"There's always a chance Wirath will quietly take it to the police, if he hasn't already."

"Christ's overcoat, he mustn't do that, he wouldn't, he's smart. That would mean the Grey Police, you know, like the Feds, and Wirath has got to know Rietz has his people all over that operation. These palookas don't kid around, they're playing to keep. I bet Rietz has got his phones tapped, and a tail on him wherever he goes."

Quickly bored by all this incomprehensible foreign jabber, Arni wants to know if he hadn't been right to bring the story. Pavel pats a massy shoulder and tells him he's done well; clearly he'd like to dismiss the boy, but has concerns about his safety.

"Don't go to any more meetings of the bully squad, you're finished with this story, you got more than we ever expected. If anybody comes by to ask, just tell them Ljuba doesn't like you being out at night so much. Rietz won't dare challenge that; he's going to be thinking of something else Ljuba might not like. Something I don't think he wants the world to know."

"Ljuba doesn't have to know everything — " Arni's face makes its best attempt at cunning.

"Have you finished your drink?"

"I thought — there might be some way I can help. For Christa Rasch, you know."

"Okay, stay a while," abruptly decisive. "Sit quiet. We have some thinking to do."

Thinking, I think; in an orderly country we'd be discreetly tipping off authority, and congratulating ourselves on a terrific exclusive. What about Pavel's friend at the Interior Ministry?

"Miloczy," Arni says, eyes on the screen where the small figure is still gesticulating. "He's crazy."

Pavel says in self-directed scorn, "Yeah, we thought Herder might try to influence Wirath through his daughter. Some influence. He throws those frigging bashes of his, you can meet anybody from Angèle to Dalerant, and all the time he's a bug in a rug with Miloczy's operation. I'm gonna blow those guys sky-high, put out the story on the air."

"Wait," I caution.

"They wouldn't dare harm Christa, once I sang. Okay, they can still use her for a hostage, but they're washed up as a party — who's gonna vote for the guys who snatched Christa Rasch?"

"There is no proof — " Katja is quiet and concise. "Christa doesn't even *know* she's being prisoned."

"If you accuse them," I concur. "They'll just produce her, all smiles, say Wirath must be having paranoid fantasies. Christa herself will say, `Kidnapped? I was just on holiday with my friend.'"

"It would stop them, anyway."

"This time. If the Loyals are going to be on the scene, this country needs people like you — working. An accusation without evidence might even help them; Miloczy will say it shows the lengths his enemies will go to — "

"Yah," with a gesture at the TV. "He plays on distrust of *the media* like a violin, up there in Kerpacza. I bad-mouth the Loyalists, my position, all their griping about *bias* comes true — I would be gone in a minute."

"You'd be lucky to stay out of jail. I assume you have laws about criminal libel."

"You bet. That was Angèle's second rap, six months for saying Dalerant was the pope's old whore, but they sprung her out after eight weeks, she was too disruptive."

Katja: "She has said often, the worst prison must be freer than the regular Dusatian life, because prisoner is not a slave to money. But she didn't stay there when they tell her she can leave." Seeing Pavel's eyes when he mentioned the name, I no longer find Katja's dislike of Angèle so unaccountable.

"How about if you break the story, my friend?"

It is a seductive notion, front-page stuff from Mexico City to Tokyo, *SUPER-MODEL AND ACTRESS CHRISTA RASCH HELD HOSTAGE*, my by-line. "If we can get someone higher-up with the Loyalists than Arni to talk. Otherwise, same thing, except I'll be expelled from the country, and not invited back." Not even my mother's considerable credit balance would save me; the political pressure on Niemek would be too much.

Silence. I think we're all experiencing alienation, trying to grapple with what we can't quite see as real.

Pavel stops shaking his head. "Okay, we can't go public, so, what?"

Katja is also eyeing me, even Arni, tiring of the captionless, Chaplinesque performance by Miloczy, has turned in my direction.

What is expected of me? Admittedly, as little as Pavel reminds me of bluff, kindly old Colonel Zapt, I am the visiting Englishman with a blood-connection to Dusatia, ready to do my bit. But any uncanny resemblance between me and Christa is purely circumstantial, our foreign birth to distinguished exiles. Hardly enough to let me masquerade as her, so convincingly as to deceive even her father, till after the coronation, I should say the High Court decision, has been safely accomplished (patience; in a little while I'm going to ask you to believe that the village nearest Herder's mountain lodge is named Zrndja).

"What about your friend at the Ministry?" — a question to which I am never to get a direct answer, though Pavel is plain enough.

Unnecessarily, with a glance to quiescent Arni, his voice lowers. "Have you thought about, this could be a set-up? The kid is on the up-and-up, sure, but Rietz is no dumbbell, and this is just the kind of sucker play *Schnur* used to pull; maybe he checked out the kid, maybe he figures out how come the cops know exactly where to be last night. Like you say, they can have a feel day — better if they can get to the Ministry of the Interior."

"Field day," involuntarily. I am, and think we all are, perversely attracted to the idea that something so hard to believe as Christa's abduction could indeed be pure fiction.

Clear-minded Katja says, "What is needed to be known is, if Wirath was threatened."

"We can't phone and ask him, I know Rietz has got him bugged, it's all over, or else it's real bad news for Christa."

"I could go and see him." Wirath had said today that he would give no interviews while the Yellow Ballot was still under consideration, but I could surely invent a reason for him to admit me.

"So you ask him if he's been told his daughter is kidnapped, he says, are you nuts? — well, you know — " Pavel recognises the turn of phrase as distinctly un-Wirathian. "So what does that tell us? Either he's decided to play ball with these punks, or he can't make up his mind what to do but is holding it close to the vest — or he thinks you must be nuts. I tell you, he believes Christa is in danger, this isn't gonna be the same Wirath."

Perhaps not, and even the everyday Wirath is hardly a worldling in practical matters, yet I can't help wanting to believe that if there is a kidnapping, the judge will have found a way secretly to set in motion the proper, stealthy counter-measures, some Dusatian approximation to S.A.S. at this moment closing in on the mountain-lodge in the north. Followed by a wave of arrests, and the National Loyalists buried in an avalanche of big headlines.

My headlines. There comes, as rarely, a stirring of the genuine journalistic lust; we sit here — well, Arni sits, the rest of us haven't thought to — and try to think of what others can do to forestall what my first duty is to regard as a story.

I say, "There is a way to find out whether Christa is being held at that place. We could go there. I could — " recognizing Pavel can hardly take the time away.

"No — " Katja's hand is on my forearm.

"What's your story, if you show up there?"

"I've been wanting to do an interview with Christa — " even as pure fiction, it's hard to say without making a face; I don't do celebrity gawps. "I came up to Kerpaczy to interview Miloczy, and heard a rumour Christa was at Herder's lodge."

Trying to find a less confrontational way to confirm the kidnapping, Katja wonders whether I might telephone Herder, citing the same rumour, but recognises that if Herder (as is probable) denies any knowledge of Christa's present whereabouts, we have learnt nothing. Also, Pavel adds, gently enough, have increased the danger to Christa, if they really do have her.

"Look, sugar, these guys are desperate. They think we're

moving in, they're gonna move her someplace we can't find her —
or where, if we do, we can't do a thing about it. Herder's lodge
can't be more than sixty, seventy kilometres from Strbjena — " the
fortress military base inherited from the Soviets, evidently still a
personal fief of Vock and Javelin Division.

Since we have no means of moving authority without the
same risk to Christa, he concedes, we must either do nothing, or
act for ourselves. "Okay, you show up at the lodge, Christa's there,
whadda you gonna do next?"

"If Mara Herder wants to keep up the pretence of a
friendly holiday, I don't see how she can object if I ask Christa to
drive into Kerpaczy with me, to tape an interview at RTPD-
North."

Pavel regards me with unhumorous irony. We both know
that this would in fact be a crux, and possibly a dangerous one. It
may be conceit on my part that I'm relying on my standing to keep
me from harm; if these people are willing to kidnap an
internationally-known figure, daughter to the Chief Justice, why
should a journalist of far lesser eminence make them suddenly
shy? But there is a difference, as I tell Pavel; I intend to make it
clear on arrival that many people, RTPD, the London agency,
miscellaneous and if necessary invented others, know exactly
where I am.

"You better take Arni with you."

"What for? I'm going to turn up at this lodge on an
innocent visit; how do I explain Arni?" Rietz could, readily, in
more than one sense, and the thought buttresses my objection.
"There may be someone there who knows Arni from Rietz's
militia." Only too likely; Christa so far may be a captive
unawares, but the captors must have some strong-arm potential
lurking.

"All to the good. Arni's gonna be your driver, he does that
sometimes, anyone from the militia recognises him, they'll just
think Rietz found a way to keep tabs on you."

Arni has been attentive since overhearing his name
spoken; just as Pavel turns to him and I note that Miloczy must be
finished, the screen now showing the RTPD logo, the telephone
warbles. We all betray the tension of the past hour by jumping;

Katja picks up, listens, and proffers the phone to Pavel. "Firenc."

The conversation is brief, and Pavel makes a couple of pencil notes.

"Firenc will be here with the tape, about twenty minutes. Miloczy says he has evidence that, as well as the Yellow Ballot, there was widespread intimidation to prevent Loyalist supporters from voting. Frigging liar; the only place there was any strong-arm stuff it involved his goons. He also says Dalerant has a secret deal with Gorat, and they've both got Niemek snowed, and that there's a conspiracy with `Slovak interests' to kibosh any effective new immigration laws. That's all Firenc got out of it, he says the rest is the same old shit."

I scowl. I'll have to file a story, provide some clips of the speech; Albertson will be most provoked if all the other services have it and not us, though I can't believe the world is much interested, and Miloczy's rantings seem remote and abstract with the abduction of Christa to consider.

Nevertheless, "Perhaps I really should get an interview with the Fuehrer, while I'm up north. I'd love to demand his evidence for these accusations."

"Good luck — " and Pavel begins briefing a reverently attentive Arni. He is to provide a car, and Pavel will fix everything with his boss. He must do exactly what Mr Kearns tells him to, and if, when we reach the ski-lodge where the goddess is immured, he is recognised by anyone from Rietz's militia, he is to shake his head slightly — Pavel demonstrates — so as to convey *don't say anything, I'm working undercover*. Whether the bland features of Arni can achieve such subtle communication has yet to be tested.

Having expressed itself in thinly-camouflaged concern for my safety, Pavel's obvious wish he could go with me now finds another outlet. He gives me a slightly formal, man-to-man look, and speaks Dusatian. "This trip, you're working for RTPD, too, okay? We'll give you support, if you want a camera-crew, you can go to RTPD-North in Kerpaczy. But you break the story live on RTPD, same thing lead interview with Christa."

"Simultaneously," I say, thinking of all the markets that might want it.

"Okay, but it's our tape east of Berlin — not Moscow, the old Warsaw Pact countries, I mean, you can have the rest of the world, okay?"

Katja makes a reproving sound, but I find cryptic comfort in attention to business, and Pavel and I shake on it.

Arni, aglow with the importance of his new responsibilities, brings up a small remaining problem by asking the exact whereabouts of Herder's lodge. That it is north and west of Kerpaczy, somewhere above 1200 metres, and not far distant from the Polish border, is hardly adequate. Katja has just suggested there might be something in the data-bank when Firenc arrives with the cassette of the Miloczy speech.

He is about my age, but very boyish, friendly, a little dandified. I have seen him often doing the news, but he now also writes and directs. His education was in astronomy and meteorology, and he first came to RTPD to do weather and "celestial events," eclipses, comets, meteorite showers, solar flares, man-made intrusions. While Dusatia has so far had small success attracting foreign revenue with its ski resorts in the mountains of the north, Firenc's duties between mid-October and April included a twice-weekly "skiing forecast," imitated, I believe, from Austrian, Swiss or American TV, telling the public (as a short-skirted blonde successor still does) how much snow, of what consistency, would be found at each of the most popular spots.

This experience is what Pavel has in mind when he innocently asks Firenc if he knows just where Herder's lodge is. Firenc does; he has stayed there as Herder's guest. They have, he says, in the clear mountain air, a fairly nice little 17.5 cm telescope, but it's a good idea to phone ahead, because half the time Herder uses the place as a private guest-house and it's closed as a hotel. At best, its capacity would be no more than ten or twelve couples.

If curious about Arni, Pavel has him too well trained to ask questions, and he gives my driver-to-be exact instructions beyond Kerpaczy, taking what is actually the Berlin road, but short of Mlhave Pass and the Polish frontier, turning off on the lesser road to Zrndja.

"Where?" I interrupt.

"Zrndja. It's a village. From there, anybody can put you on the private road up to Eagle's Nest — they keep it open with a plough."

After Firenc's departure, Arni also leaves; he'll pick me up at the Schweitzerhof in the morning. We sit with fiery sliwowicza, knowing we'll have to view the Miloczy tape. Efficient Firenc has provided a cue sheet indexing what he sees as the major points, and in my current mood I'm inclined to trust his judgement rather than watch the entire ham performance.

Pavel waits till Katja is out of the room before going to a little wall-safe, from which he brings out a supple leather case, zip-closed, holding a pistol, a Walther 7.65 automatic, with room also for three spare clips of ammunition.

"You know how to work this?"

I do, but am unenthusiastic in the extreme.

"Listen, buddy, you wanna crack the whip at lions, you better have a gun ready." It must be a line from some old film.

"I'm only going because if I don't, somebody else will get the story. If it turns nasty — "

"Christa Rasch, to hell with her, Miloczy can take over, no skin off your nose, I got that right?"

"Well." I am struggling to rephrase the same thoughts rather less discreditably. "I don't have a permit to carry a gun."

"Put it in the glove box, if you're stopped it's not your car, it's not Arni's car, you don't know nothin' about no gun. Out in the sticks, a press pass wows the cops; I'll give you an RTPD card."

Still with distaste, I take the leather case with its baleful cargo, and thus accomplished, will go on this quest perilous, my Sancho Panza beside me — my Sam Weller, rather; not adoring Christa, I'm less like Don Quixote issuing forth to deliver Dulcinea from durance vile than Mr Pickwick setting out on some lunatic midnight adventure to thwart the machinations of Jingle — it's unpleasant to recall that in that episode, there is indeed what Pavel calls a set-up, designed for Pickwick's humiliation, the false tale of an elopement planted on a — but in his case, uncharacteristically — gullible Sam Weller.

V

December 22. Before Arni arrives, I ring Kent, waking my mother, to say I probably can't be home for Christmas. There's no snow, she reports, but it's very cold — and I see the glamouring mantle of hard rime on the stiffened grass, the low sun dull brick-red, scarcely casting a shadow, the wondrous, pregnant hush of an English midwinter morning. I wonder if the carollers have been round, but it would give away too much to ask. I suppose because of Dad's long years abroad, we make quite a fuss of carollers, and the experienced have learnt to make us their last stop, so as to enjoy the pies (pork, mince) and potent wassail, free from concern about effect on performance.

Apparently one of the channels (Mother never keeps track) has shown the long version of my coverage of the candlelight march; she congratulates but then gently upbraids me for pronouncing names almost in the accents of Prjanu — a boisterous suburb of Korava, on the wrong side of the river. I can't explain to her that no one in Dusatia wants to talk posh nowadays; at the university and in Pavel's domain, they all strive for the sound of the honest, unpretentious artisan.

"You will be here for the New Year?" Her voice, transmitted naked through a thousand miles of space, bouncing openly off a satellite, nevertheless becomes confidential — "Your father is getting his K at last, in the New Year's List. We're having a little gathering on the first, you know, Brie and bubbles, in his honour, some of the F.O. people, and Charles-Marie is coming over." The usual old buffers, I conclude, boring, though in the nicest way. Then, once again a connection with Katja, Mother throws in an added inducement: "The Forbeses are sure to bring Stephanie; she'll be looking forward to seeing you." Stephanie Forbes, slender, stylish and (quite likely) enjoyable, not to be connected with plump Steff, a know-all brat, or her successor, horsy Stevie, strident in corduroy; what happens to these creatures in a couple of years of Cambridge (Christ's as chrysalis)?

Sir Matthew Kearns, and, as my mother implies, about time. I promise the soon-to-be Lady Elena I'll do all I can to be there, not adding, Pavel-fashion, so long as I ain't rubbed out by Rietz's hoods.

Inspired by Katja's forlorn idea, but with a different objective, I then ring Herder at home, where he also has his offices, a sleek state-of-the-art pearl of communications and data in that mellowed baroque shell. Passed fairly rapidly through ascending underlings, I reach him, and as soon as he knows my voice he switches by choice into his faultless English, cultured mid-Atlantic, as befits one who spent academic time at both Oxford and Stanford (McGill and the Sorbonne are also in his dossier).

"Kearns, I intended to give you a call. Will you have time to come and see us while you're here? I hope our little crisis-in-a-teacup isn't running you too ragged." Soapy bugger.

Deferring the half-invitation, I ask about a plastics factory on which I've read he's doing a feasibility study. I ought to explain here that as a wholly above-board adjunct to my journalistic wanderings, making clear there can be no conflict or overlap of interest, I'm paid a retainer by a London group, to keep an eye open for promising investment opportunities, with a bonus for successful closure. Herder, unsurprised, unleashes impromptu a barrage of statistics, projected production, eventual capacity, other more arcane numbers; only the estimated work-force, six to eight hundred, makes any impression on my retentive faculty. Reading grunts of imperfect comprehension, Herder offers to fax me a prospectus, adding, "I actually think we've found the capital here at home. But there's going to be a major expansion at Cicada — an entire new factory, if it can be financed. Podarny is thinking specialised heavy vehicles; your people might want to explore that."

I thank him (though it reeks of disaster), then, ever-so-casually, come to my objective. I've been wanting to interview Christa Rasch (my face must learn not to contort with that lie, if I'm to repeat it at the ski-lodge), and had heard she was staying *chez* Herder —

"She was. Such a lovely girl. She's gone again now."

"She's turning out to be quite elusive."

"Oh, deliberately so, I think. She gets weary, I guess, of

the eternal goldfish-bowl. Not — " having accomplished that masterpiece of slime, he is swift to remove potential offence — "Not that she wouldn't be delighted, I'm sure, to visit with someone of your stature." *Visit*, American, *colloq., folksy*: = converse.

"I'm sorry I missed her."

"You're leaving?"

"I'll be back here for the High Court ruling."

A little humming assent. "Nothing quite like Christmas in merry old England, is there? Your mother is well? Give them both my very best."

I thank him, and we disconnect in a squall of good wishes.

It now seems to me most unlikely that Christa's captivity is a fiction. If Rietz made it up, it means he had rumbled Arni, and expected the tale to go straight to Pavel. I, of course, was not meant to be a primary plantee, but my friendship with Pavel and our frequent collaboration are generally known; Herder would have to think it not less than probable I am in on the secret. Herder is adroit, but the most cautious conspirator born could not decline the opportunity I gave him to lure me towards disastrous public accusations — a little fluster, some superfluous vagueness about Christa's whereabouts: curiously, if he'd given me more tangible reason to believe the kidnapping story, I would be less inclined to; as is, I'm all-but certain it must be genuine.

Also, perhaps, I have laid down a little archaeology for my appearance at the ski lodge. Presuming Mara Herder doesn't pretend no one's home, or shoot me and my driver on sight, or add us to the bag of captives, she'll be obliged to start out pleasant, and hope to hold together the story of a little holiday with her dear Christa; it's almost certain she'll telephone Herder for the next move. For whom my tale of being in the north and hearing word Christa is there will dovetail quite reasonably with our conversation; my present hope is that he'll decide I suspect nothing and reluctantly sanction my whisking Christa away to be interviewed; only when she isn't returned will it become apparent they've lost her. It appears I'm Quixote after all; I've evolved a plan whose success leaves me without a single headline; Wirath will be unable to substantiate the attempt to intimidate him, and Christa — perhaps the hardest part of this whole, what's the word,

this scenario, will be convincing her she may not go back to the
interrupted holiday with her good friend Mara.

The car is a fairly new Toyota, and, I'm relieved to see by
its orange plates, intended for rental, not borrowed from some
unaware patron of the service garage. Arni's driving is practised
and unremarkable, and soon I'm learning all there is to be told
about Ljuba. I had faintly imagined one of those distressingly
Americanised, slovenly adolescents to be seen in the environs of
downtown Korava's one McDonald's, or the new roller-blade rink,
perhaps with a gold ring in an unexpectedly pierced part or two of
her body, and am rebuked to discover Ljuba is a nascent zoologist
with university plans, as well as a middle-distance runner, who
expects to be in the next Olympics, where, according to admiring
Arni, she's certain to win a medal for Dusatia, silver at minimum,
in the 1500m. I get more information than I require about their
intimate life when he laments the sexual fasts they endure when in
intensive training, periods which seldom coincide (Arni exhibits
himself regularly, and has been as far afield as Warsaw to do so).
Who can't sadly foresee the end of this tale, when blossoming
Ljuba tells bewildered Arni she'll always want him for a *friend*?
A kindly lie; a friend will be exactly what she can no longer
imagine him as.

The Kerpaczy road has a brand-new number, D-1,
celebrating the three substantial stretches of motorway completed
while the Cicada boom was on, their link-up languishing now for
lack of funds. Yet the more traditional portions are still good road,
and the whole has been thoroughly scraped clear of snow;
climbing gradually under a hazed sun we make good time, and
eventlessness makes it possible for me to resume the intensive
instructing of Arni for the part he is to play, principally to maintain
a close-mouthed discretion, but, like Hamlet's revenant dad,
intimating that he could, but that he is forbid, make some hairs
stand on end. We stop for a robust lunch (tumescent puce
sausages and sauerkraut) not far short of the provincial capital,
Dusatia's second city.

It is purely imaginary that the sun dims and the chill deepens as we cross the border into Miloczy's province. The *dzhăndarmi* here have stiffened caps, trousers that vanish into shiny black calf-boots, and an aplomb verging on arrogance, but there are strict constitutional limits to the powers of a provincial premier. It's true that in Miloczy's first year, when there was a wave of arson, vandalism and gang assault, which the police did little to prevent and less to investigate, many families of foreign extraction, Slovak, Czech or Polish (ethnic Germans had been mostly left alone) either found other parts of Dusatia to settle in, or returned to what Miloczy calls "their own lands," although many had been Dusatian nationals for generations. Niemek's threat to send in army units to protect minorities brought about improvement, and also quietened Warsaw, which had been rumbling undefined threats of intervention, but a sceptical Pavel believed Miloczy had stopped short of driving out all his ethnic scapegoats because their uneasy presence was a useful target at election time.

But Miloczy, it must be conceded, has kept unemployment for his province at half the national figure, and part of his method is visible as we breast the ridge on the southern outskirts of Kerpaczy, and see on the opposing slope the grandiose new civic and administrative centre, still under construction, a new legislative chamber, new government offices, a soaring hall for public meetings as well as concerts, a capacious neo-classical Museum of Dusatian Art and Craft. How all this is paid for, depending whose economist you believe, is either fiscal wizardry or chicanery, an unconscionable mortgaging of the future; in view of the monumental nature of his building, I hesitate to call it a pyramid scheme, but it does involve so-called super-bonds, which invest only in the differential between market price and pro rata maturation of the original bonds. With Miloczy's fierce nationalism, it's odd that his own province is owned largely by a few German and Swiss banks. Bolasz, however, his fiery little economic shaman, is adamant that full employment and a growing tax base will reverse the tide of deficit, and have them all out of the pop-shop in a dazzling decade; since his balancing of the books also takes in dark hints at the confiscation of Church property (which his chief regularly denies), Bolasz may one day be known as the creator of Paganomics.

Part of the embracing xenophobia, a very small BERLIN now has second billing on the destination signs, under a large MLHAVE, a hamlet and high pass on the frontier with Poland, a small corner of which must be scampered across to reach Germany; at its birth in 1919 and until Stalin, at the end of the world war, moved Poland westward on the map, most of Dusatia's northern border was with Germany, now touched only for a few kilometres in the farthest northwest.

The road is still good, our climb still intermittent and gradual; for much of the way we shadow, at times cross and recross, the railway line, and this too puts out a branch where we at last leave the main road leftward, Fridova, a quiet little town with a bulbous-spired church, the shops and dwellings fronting on the main square steep-roofed, three-storeyed, startled-looking, not much changed since Austerlitz. The branch railway, which we soon lose as our winding way begins in earnest to tackle its climb, probably serves ski slopes farther westward; I catch one glimpse of a short red-and-white diesel train crawling west before we part company.

Especially on tight turns, there are patches of rutted snow now, not yet enough to call into question Arni's decision not to put on tyre chains. After a sustained, curving climb, we drop into the dell where is hidden the village of Zrndja, and I don't explain to Arni my short bark of a laugh on seeing the name on a painted metal roadside sign.

Together with a few television antennas, that identifying sign may be the most ambitious development in the past fifty years for Zrndja, a shabby, huddled place the most devoted antiquarian would hardly find charming; Arni, with youthful, urban contempt, mutters, "These places are backward as snake's arse."

Here, we go astray, choosing of possible lesser continuations one introduced by the silhouette representation of a sexless downhill skier. With less than two kilometres of winding way among dark, close-set pines and spruces, we come out on an opening and a small sub-village, entirely alien to the mediaevalism of Zrndja proper; on the roof of the small railway station a bold board proclaims the place as Dvygarmiscz, one of the newest and most popular of winter sport venues, its name shamelessly borrowed from Bavaria. The station itself is an elderly brick and slate building, steep-roofed, with snow-freaked ivy and a weathercock, but adjoined by an extensive car park, few private cars, four hirable conveyances too discreet to call themselves taxis. The station approach is a new-built miniature precinct, including an "American Drugstore," a wine-bar, a Brothers Grimm chalet shared by a ski-shop and one displaying pricey woollens; all this we take in on a quick sweeping turn, and soon leave behind.

Back in gloomy Zrndja, we do what we should have; I ask at the jumbled general store for directions, and soon we are nosing up what we had taken for a dead end, swinging back across the face of a formidable steep, and then back again to mount by a narrow but well-kept road.

Mountains have been proximate since leaving the main road at Fridova, but till now the roads have stayed square in the lap of hilly terrain; with a sharp turn we are abruptly on a mountain, toiling up a steep way between rock face and inadequately-guarded edge, looking out over snow and a deep declivity, the clothes-hanger pylons of a ski-lift mounting on the other side. At about half the corners there are widenings which would permit meeting cars to pass; we encounter none.

After this precarious Alpine section, we're once again among trees, having mounted to the domed summit of a blunt bluff, crowned with half-a-dozen large houses or small hotels, perhaps alternating as either. Our destination, *Eagle's Nest*, is the last square-pillared entrance on the road, though a matching exit, its posts similarly crowned with perched stone raptors, is a few yards beyond. The drive is a tilted loop to be traversed anti-clockwise, and at its summit reaches the four broad steps up to the front double-door of the lodge; halfway back down on the farther side there is appended a clearing, parking space for perhaps a dozen cars, currently one-quarter filled. The dark-blue Herder sports car, a Mercedes, is one of the three.

Tremendously placed, at the very brink of a wide valley with a backdrop of sharply defined mountains, the house itself is nondescript, unsuccessfully blending the kind of featureless lines popularly known as "modern" thirty or forty years ago with some tacked-on touches of the traditional, louvred wooden shutters painted green, a cuckoo-clock balcony over the entrance. The front doors are tinted glass and bronze.

Mara Herder says, "Of course," and smiles. She isn't actually confirming I am who I say, but assuring me I'm unforgotten, standing aside to permit ingress, maintaining the smile somewhat mechanically in place for hulking Arni.

"I'm surprised you found us." There is no real cordiality here, but that shouldn't be over-interpreted; Mara at any time has the firefly's secret of illumination without warmth. She is very youthfully dressed, white tailored shirt open over tee-shirt, and jeans that aren't really but are produced to look rolled up to mid-calf, an under-and-over strip of blue brocade in her cheek-length very blonde hair; her age is no more than three or four years beyond mine, but her careful composure has always carried her outside any such consideration; now, for the first time, I get a glimpse of the girl that was. And wouldn't have liked her; one of those self-assured, self-righteous, head-wagging little gorgons, remember? with permanently pursed lips, never wrong, never in doubt, who lead exemplary lives, blameless and blameful, dedicated to the perfection of rebuke.

I say that her husband had once invited me to ski here, perfectly true so far as it goes, though it was mere social noise; in reality, a venue for our sport was only vaguely mentioned.

"Have you brought skis?" Mara re-digests my garb, not what anyone would wear on his way to winter sports.

"I had no idea I was coming here." This launches my barely sustainable story of coming to Kerpaczy in an attempt to see Miloczy, stopping at RTPD-North, where one of the news people had told me Christa Rasch was said to have been spotted as passenger in a car, a blue Mercedes, going north on the Mlhave road — "and I remembered you had this place. As I mentioned to Juan-Micel when I spoke to him on the phone, I've been trying for an interview with Christa. So I rang Pavel Orbicz, and he found someone who could give me directions — Firenc Kjebik, I believe he was a guest here once — and came up on the off-chance she might be here."

There's purpose in this litany, a roster of those who, in the event of my disappearance, would know where to start looking, and this time, I manage to get out the nonsense about my eagerness to interrogate Christa without any facial rictus. That may merely be context, the initial absurdity lost in posing as the kind of carrion-hound who, for the sake of a story, a piece of mere gorblimey, would do what I say I'm doing, break in uninvited on a secluded holiday.

My salvation is that Mara is even more uneasy. The quick sideways slew of her eyes tells me the incredible is true; Christa is here, and Mara would very much like to deny it, but is afraid she'll appear at any second.

I also note there are some extras in this scene. Beyond this vestibule, a big, dark stair with carved banisters descends, creating a sort of strait, and the open water a few steps beyond is a wide, well-windowed lounge, which, like the lodge itself, maintains an ambiguity between private retreat and exclusive hotel; even this partial view lets me see that the furnishings, upholstered chairs and low tables, are gathered in several sub-groupings where couples or foursomes could clump for tea, strictly continental breakfast (too far to stoop for eggs), conversation, cross-flirtation. And a pair is there, seated quite near the entrance-archway, rather far from the windows, which offer, almost compel, the vista of mountain snowscape worth at least 25% on the bill. With most of the light behind them, one can't be dogmatic, but at an imperfect glance they appear even less like devotees of downhill than Arni and I. Though the nearest one, who is sideways-on and watching us, is sporty in a bulky sweater, red sawtooth stripes on white, his bulky frame and rounded shoulders are those of an aging boxer, and his companion, younger and more linear, just turning this way, has immediately that ratty, furtive urban air which transcends race, and forms a kinship between the Gorbals housebreaker and the backstreet Bangkok pimp, the black-marketeer in Moscow and the black car-stripper in Washington. The two, in short, look just like some of Rietz's.

Perception instantly confirmed. Mara has struggled with, "I don't know where Christa is — now," the last word most reluctantly wrung out, when the younger man stands, unclings trousers from his thighs, and emerges in our direction. With a better view of my companion, his approach becomes more purposeful, and eyebrows go up in clear recognition, when Arni, showing an imitative gift the unkind might call another simian trait, duplicates Pavel's discreet, don't-hail-me head-shake, a performance I can be seen to fail to see. The man, probably twenty-five, wearing his one suit (or noting the fit, possibly the one suit of a friend or relative, shorter in the leg and broader across the chest), stops short, peering, and with slow-motion comprehension, turns instead to Mara.

"New guests, Mrs Herder?" Here in full ripeness the clogged Prjanu accent whose encroachment my mother earlier detected in me. I see by the foot of the stairs his companion is now slouched, younger than his poor posture and balding head, not forty, big-knuckled, bulgy-necked, very solid.

I have watched Mara introduce a premier to the conductor of a very famous orchestra, a billionaire industrialist to a papal nuncio; *chez* Herder everyone has been some way notable, and though her origins are far from aristocratic, Mara always maintains a cool elegance, perhaps to be achieved only by former actresses who marry into that role (examples abound). Here, however, the graciousness perceptibly grinds gears, as she apprises me of Mr Lisuk, who is staying with us for a few days, with his friend Mr Jenadju, equally without capsule biography, who, from the stairs, raises a thick, blunt hand and moves it from side to side. As for me, I announce Arni's name, and he ducks his head shyly. "My driver," I add, and the identification is an obvious relief to Mara, who dislikes the undefined.

"Here for the skiing?" — to Lisuk, with a straight face; my question couldn't be more ludicrous if I said polo.

"Just taking it easy for a while," but before I can elicit fresh improbabilities Lisuk backs away, and moves to rejoin Jenadju by the stairs.

"Perhaps at least I can offer you coffee, tea?" Mara improvises, and before Arni can consider responding, puts him quite literally in what she sees as his place by suggesting he move the car into the less obstructive space provided lower down the slope, "and I'm sure they will have coffee for you in the kitchen."

In the kitchen, an established filing-cabinet, or a sort of broom cupboard where animated utensils may be stowed out of sight till they're needed again.

I'm not happy about this division, but it's either too early for panic or too late; the terms of my entry here have set in motion a sequence that can't be aborted. Mara's hand is hovering over the plunger to a small desk-bell, and just as I am about to accede to coffee, Arni to do what he's told, Christa appears, coming downstairs, lithe and provocative in what I'm certain is a prop ski-suit, designed, not to fend the icy airstream of a downhill run, but to cling and flatter. It is bright orange with some odd splashes and zags of contrasted blue, white and scarlet, and traces even the sweet hollows of her perfect flanks — of, at least, the one perfect flank visible on her descent. Delete *flatter*, above; though some might so delude themselves, this is an outfit to be worn only by one whose body can dispense with deft enhancements and shrewd deceits, a body like Christa Rasch's. Reprehensible that the world makes such a to-do over accidental harmonies of skin and muscle and skeletal geometry, all-too often to the neglect of more hard-won achievements, but in those superficial terms the world has made no mistake in placing Christa among the elect. Arni does not actually drop to his knees with a gesture of humble reverence, but his bland face has that look of the devout peasant vouchsafed a vision.

Served by a short, plump woman I'd guess to be Polish, Christa and I confer over coffee and biscuits in the lounge. At first, Lisuk and Jenadju, drinking beer, are our nearby neighbours, but they can scarcely follow when I suggest to Christa we move over to the windows, too far for eavesdropping.

We begin with Mara still hovering, preserving her smile, though my guess is that she's almost frantic to make a phone-call, while anxious to monitor our talk. Probably she can call on reinforcements for Lisuk and Jenadju, but while Mara is clearly in local command, she isn't going to make any irretrievable move without consultation. The needs of secrecy must be why Herder has no reliable lieutenant on the spot — Mara has intelligence, and I don't doubt her resolution, but her job as Herder's wife can have done little to develop a faculty for independent action.

I have been worrying over a plausible hook on which to hang my improbable desire for an interview, but Christa's self-absorption soothes away anxiety; she is so universally courted that my request seems unremarkable; though unable to recall my name unprompted she knew me again by sight, and that I am a journalist, therefore a courtier ordained. All her surprise goes to my arriving here without a camera crew.

This is a weakness in my credentials, not one I've overlooked; the most inept and neophyte of head-hunters would want this mountain hideaway background for his 'Christa Rasch At Leisure' piece, but all my plan centred on getting her away from here, and if I had turned up prepared to film, it's conceivable Mara would have preserved the illusion of an innocent holiday, and I would have been obliged to force the issue, or else tamely make my film, and leave defeated. I reply that I was unsure of finding her here, but (improvising) if I now can make a phone-call —

"The lines are down," Mara, quickly, with a helpless shrug. "We are used to that here, the snow — "

She must strain to follow the English that is Christa's choice with me; their usual language is German. It is sad that Christa is halting and ungrammatical in Dusatian, though that shouldn't surprise me; she was brought up and schooled largely in Switzerland, and her Dusatian mother vanished before she was three; her Dusatian father wrote and spoke in a medley of tongues, principally French and German.

With proper humility, I suggest that Christa, perhaps, would drive with me into Kerpaczy, where I have the use of a studio at RTPD. The world, I imply, is waiting to hear from the celebrated daughter of the man whose decision —

Her nose wrinkles, but Mara, taking no chances, interposes. "You cannot mean this for now, today?" To Christa, in German: "It would be four or five hours driving at least, both ways, and then the interview. There is more snow forecast."

"This is such a drag," Christa concurs. "Does this have to be right now? When I come back to Korava, you can have all the time you want. I'm supposed to be on vacation."

Oh, no, no, no; we can't have an answer to send me away, without private talk with Christa. I suggest we might be able to fix something mutually convenient for tomorrow, and before another word, Mara, fearful I'll leave, go where there are phones, and return in greater strength, makes her move to hold me incommunicado, by saying they can put me up for the night;

several rooms are available.

"You're very gracious; I never meant to impose myself."

She is very relieved, and given the excuse of seeing beds are made up for me and my driver, hastens away to make her report. After a moment, very casually, Lisuk gets up and leaves the lounge.

If, when he hears the news, Herder decides the kidnapping can no longer be kept a secret from its victim, and, very probably, that I too will have to be detained, I guess he'll either come here himself, or dispatch someone he trusts, most likely Rietz — it's possible that for this operation I have the hierarchy upside-down, and Rietz, the experienced, is in tactical command (but Herder may have done some spookery for the C.I.A.). In any event, they'll try to maintain the precarious pretence of a hideaway holiday, probably till morning, when they can have reinforcements deployed. Before then, I have to inform Christa, more, to convince Christa, of the truth.

Smiling lazily. "I can't believe you came all this way just to talk to me."

She can believe it; this is fishing for hype. Leaning forward, I say quietly, "I was told that you had been kidnapped, and were to be held hostage to influence your father's decision in the Yellow Ballot affair."

"*What*?"

"Hush." Her exclamation has attracted Jenadju's lumberingly covert attention. Rapidly so as not to allow her a chance to interrupt and delay me by calling me mad, I lay out the case — not yet why she must, but why I might believe the story. The evidence, recited, is slight, omitting Arni as mole, and almost at once I'm guessing at what might give Christa pause, the absence of any other authentic members of the normal Herder circle — doesn't she find Lisuk and Jenadju odd as guests? More like, for example, guards? At this moment, signalled to by Lisuk from the archway, Jenadju gets up and follows him from the lounge. New instructions?

Christa laughs. "I'm used to them, they're around all the time, or the other two."

Exactly, my face conveys (shifts of guests, in alternating pairs; commonplace). "You haven't been skiing?" They'd never take the chance of her finding a telephone or even an acquaintance at the foot of a ski-lift.

"Tomorrow, if Mara's okay. Her darned back has been acting up."

"Suppose you wanted to go into Zrndja, or over to Dvygarmiscz, to give your father a ring?"

Now she gives me a quizzical look, head prettily tilted. "I was going to, today, tell him not to worry, yesterday really, but..."

"Mara couldn't find her car-keys?"

"Her car. She forgot, Mrs Bacewicz, the housekeeper, you know. She had to go into Kerpaczy for supplies — "

In a £28,000 sports car? I fail to ask.

" — then, today — " a gesture of lassitude. "Then you showed up."

But she is troubled, the great dark eyes. Something I could never have achieved, if she hadn't at some level of consciousness already registered strangeness — if the bosom friendship with Mara did not have, and on both sides, an inherent artificiality. I say, "Mara is phoning Juan-Micel right now, to decide what to do about me. The phones here aren't out, they're just unplugged." They were made to be moved from place to place, with a plug to be inserted in any of the boxes liberally distributed along the wainscotting; one is on a little table by the archway, and a quick glance on the way in has confirmed my guess.

"That's crazy — you're not playing with a full deck." She is up in a ripple of orange, aiming at the phone to prove me wrong. I grab her arm, and endure a killing look.

"If you want to check it for yourself, isn't there a more secluded phone?"

"What's the difference? On the balcony, yes."

"Quickly, then."

Rather surprisingly, my urgent conviction works with her. While her face retains contempt, the certainty she'll prove me wrong, she wastes no time. If she was wearing anything remotely flounceable, she would flounce impatiently, as she goes through the archway and up the stairs.

Her balcony should, I think, be called a gallery, at the head of and at right angles to the stairs, bridging the alcove with double-doors apparently leading to the kitchen, a short passage, open with a balustrade on the right; below and opposite is the door, marked *Private*, through which I believe Mara has vanished. Above, at the end, where another turn finds four more carpeted stairs, up to what must be the sleeping-quarters, a lacquer table has a bronze eagle lamp, and a telephone.

Going to it, she scoops up the lead in her palm, and raises it, letting out a small "*Oh!*" when the end with the little plug appears. Without delay, she crouches to see where it may be inserted.

"What are you doing, Miss Rasch?" — a coarse voice, but quiet. I turn and see Lisuk, the younger of the resident thugs, has come silently to the head of the stairs.

"It's unplugged," Christa says, displaying the plug, then turns to resume her search.

Brushing by me, Lisuk reaches to grasp her wrist, saying absurdly, "That's no good, the lines are down."

Both my hands go into pockets; the left touches my little recorder, but the right comes out holding Pavel's automatic, with which I dig at Lisuk's elbow.

"Let go," I instruct him. "Not a sound." Christa makes a small, high one, not to be described.

Reactions to being confronted with a pistol — and for most of us, this would remain true no matter how often it happened — are initially emotional rather than analytical; before he can inhale and register that the weapon hasn't been cocked, I do so; it would require inordinate faith in phenomenal eyesight to flout its threat because the safety is still on (as it is).

"Jesus bloody Christ," Christa says, as she straightens.

Below, I see nothing stirring, but am anxious to get out of sight. "Is your bedroom up here? Shut up," I advise Lisuk, as he contemplates speech.

"Yes, right here," blankly, and we go up the four carpeted steps to a corridor of eight doors, four on each side. Second left is Christa's, and she throws it open, letting me wave sullen Lisuk inside.

Seeing a key in place, I tell Christa to lock the door. She does so mechanically, and then, more alert than she looks, crosses to vanish briefly, locking the farther door of the bathroom she has been sharing, she explains, with Mara. Hers is a large room, double bed with its accompanying furnishings, and a space by the windows, raised by two room-wide steps, with breakfast table and chairs, as well as two highbacked easy chairs for contemplating the alpscape, now in failing light. Christa, I note, is no fanatic for neatness; various discarded or yet-to-be-worn items of attire are draped over the backs and arms of chairs or bundled on the floor.

Lisuk speaks, and this is crucial for Christa's perceptions; a more intelligent, less servile conspirator might have the wit to chuckle and soothe, cast me as the melodramatic victim of paranoia. But he snarls, "What the hell do you think you're doing?"

I'd like to hear an answer to that question. A line has irretrievably been crossed, but it was his actions that did it, and so far mine have been pure reflex; this scene was in none of my plans.

With a moment to think, Christa is visibly lapsing into doubt, the desire for there to be a mistake somewhere, so that she won't have to believe in Mara's treachery. I murmur inadequately, "This must be a terrible shock for you. Herder wants to see the National Loyalists in power. There's nothing he won't do."

She is, I think, not entirely clear about which ones the Loyalists are, but does say, "He has all kinds of politicians coming to see him. He doesn't think it makes much difference who runs the government."

"That's for public consumption. In reality, he has Rietz on his payroll, and Rietz hires thugs like this for the Loyalists. You do work for Rietz, don't you — " to Lisuk, who doesn't reply.

I tell him to put his hands on his head, and Christa, at my suggestion, moves behind him to go through his jacket pockets, giving her little whimpering cry as she fishes out a revolver, a cheaply-made snubbed thirty-eight, fully loaded. Car keys, house keys, a disposable lighter.

"Sit down," I tell Lisuk, while Christa, as if she does it every day, unlatches the cylinder of the revolver, tips out six bullets which she puts in my pocket, and throws the emptied gun onto the bed.

"What now?" avidly.

"I think we had better leave."

"We'll have to do something with *him*. Knock him cold? You got a silencer for your gun?"

Well, obviously we can't take Lisuk with us, but I'm more than a little shocked by Christa's callous pragmatism. In her defence, the world she lives in when all is going well is somewhat aside from reality, and she's showing signs now of low-level hysteria, the reasonless elation that sometimes follows shock.

"We'll tie him up. And gag him," I supplement. "You have something we can use?"

Top drawer, some cloth belts, and a silk square which Christa starts to misfold, and after a pettish exhalation, methodically folds again. Any protest I would have predicted from Lisuk at this point might have been an offer to change sides, or minimally a statement of his complete indifference, so that we could leave him unsecured here and he wouldn't raise an alarm. Instead, we have captured a true believer; he tells me it makes no difference what I do to him, because Miloczy is Dusatia's destiny.

"God help Dusatia, then." We stand him up again, and turn him round, and I tell him to put his hands together behind his back; his indifference to his own fate doesn't reach as far as defying me to shoot him.

Christa, by no means gently, ties his wrists with one of the belts. That done, I feel safe in letting her hold the gun, which she does, casually, while I gag him quite expensively, the square folded into a strip still displaying a name prized by the label-conscious. Seating him again with a push, I lash his ankles, and reassure him he'll be found before long.

"Are we leaving right now?"

Thinking aloud, I observe that Mara quite soon will be looking for her, if she isn't already.

Christa gives the lazy, faintly demented smile the world knows. "With you gone missing, too, and my bedroom door locked? She isn't about to break it down."

"She'll be looking for him, too." I'm worried about getting out with no more gun-play, worried also about Arni.

"We can go down the back stairs, through the kitchen —" Christa unwittingly gives hope of solving the second question.

She stuffs some unabandonable things in a curiously puffy fat cylinder of a bag, and then, deciding she's not clothed for flight, with the practical unselfconsciousness of a fashion model accustomed to backstage quick-changes, zips away and strips off her orange skin, and is briefly within centimetres of a stunning nakedness.   Swiftly she puts on practical stuff, flannel shirt, trousers of a fine corduroy, wool socks, softer boots, a loud, bright blue, American-style windcheater jacket, with the Coca-Cola logo on the back; bought second-hand at some maison de grot, it probably cost her five times its price when new. This done, her spirits seem suddenly to have ebbed. She looks across at me, sad-eyed and in impossible doubt, trying to invent a way I could have conjured it all up, Mara's treachery, the deliberately disconnected phone.

Her eyes go to the empty gun still lying on the bed. I pick it up and slip it in my trouser-pocket; no sense in leaving it, but after her regret that I couldn't shoot Lisuk without making a noise, the idea of an armed Christa does not appeal to me; I can dump it beside the road somewhere.

But of course that revolver, its original bearer, are elements Christa can't possibly ascribe to my legerdemain. She tugs on really an ugly hat, a sort of baggy cap that pulls down over her ears and shadows her face (a prop for when she wants to go unrecognised?), picks up the fat bag by its canvas handle, and moves to unlock the door.

Still with the gun in my right hand, I hold up the left to stay her. I listen at the door, and can hear nothing. Glance back; Lisuk is watchful, and I wonder what volume of inarticulate noise he'll be able to achieve through nose and gag. Never mind. In the corridor, Christa locks the door and pockets the key, and just then from below Mara's voice calls, "Christa?"

We scuttle along the corridor and down a wide, steep back stair. In a sort of vestibule to the kitchen, a place lined with plates dishes, tureens, silver serving vessels and every kind of drinking glass, I very nearly run into Arni. He leaps back from the pistol with a noise and a face more appropriate to a venomous snake, but seeing it's me, marvelling it's Christa, quickly recovers.

"I was going to try and find you. They think you think I'm working for you, but they think I'm spying on you, but the skinny one — "

"Lisuk?" I note, meanwhile, that Arni's torrentially agglomerated Dusatian may be too much for Christa to follow.

"Yes, he came and blocked us in." After Arni had moved our car, that was, into the parking bay, Lisuk had positioned his in its narrow entranceway, so that no one could leave.

"A Cicada?"

"That's right, a white one." Arni, who works on Volvos, Lexi, Pavel's BMW, has an unpatriotic sneer for Dusatia's pride. I, contrariwise, grin; thinking to hobble possible pursuit, I have kept the keys taken from Lisuk, two keys, ignition and boot, which are hung on a loop of bead-chain, its fob a fat-bodied plastic insect, as with all Cicada keys.

We pass into the large kitchen, and come to the back door. Arni has said that after Lisuk went back in, "the bald one," Jenadju, was hanging about the front steps; since our foes still regard Arni as an ally, I send him out to see if he still is. An encounter with Mara alone doesn't worry me; what can she do if Christa simply says she's leaving now? With that thought in mind I uncock the Walther, and return it to my pocket.

The way we have just come, Mrs Bacewicz enters the kitchen. Her little cry on seeing us is just like Christa when shocked, but Mrs Bacewicz gestures behind herself, and begins to say Mme. Herder is looking for Christa.

I put a finger to my lips, and murmur to the cook-housekeeper in Polish. Her face shows surprise, then tilts sideways pleasantly; if we were in range she'd embrace us, embrace Christa at least.

From outside, Arni whispers, "Okay."

In one thing Mara Herder, perhaps inadvertently, told the truth; it has begun to snow, though not heavily. There is a dank, threatening chill in the air.

Under the eaves, we make our way to the corner of the lodge, and Christa is petulantly curious. "What did you say to her?"

"I told her we're eloping."

"Shit."

VI

Dark pines freighted and lobed with snow make it possible for us, darting from tree to tree, to cross to the parking bay with small chance of being observed from the house. I motion for the others to join me, crouched beside the white Cicada, and ask Arni, the professional, if he can disable the two remaining cars, the Mercedes and a nondescript black coupé of unknown eastern European make. With a pang I deduce it may well be the sentimental Mrs Bacewicz's.

Arni nods, and maintaining his crouch waddles to the black car, works up the front lid, and with a swoop extracts the distributor leads, which he throws, bolo style, far out among the trees and the snow. The bonnet of the Mercedes is not so easily solved, and the car is kept locked; Arni turns to me to shrug, then from a pocket produces a Swiss Army knife, and with methodical ferocity attacks the two near-side tyres in turn. "Serves her right, bleeding bitch," Christa approves, as the costly car subsides to rest on its rims.

As Arni comes back, panting, I tell him to follow us in the Toyota, then think of an improvement; his double-agent persona is worth preserving. "Are you sure they think you're one of them?"

A complacent grin and nod. Very well. In the house, anxiety about the treble absence must be mounting. There may be, as Christa said, hesitation over breaking into the locked bedroom to learn the truth, but the sound of a car starting must attract attention. Rather than following me in obvious convoy, Arni is to return under the eaves by the corner of the house, and as soon as I'm moving, come running to start up the Toyota in pursuit. Singlehanded pursuit (if he ever has to explain, he can say he meant only to shadow, not to intercept); I emphasise that he must be under way before anyone can come from the house to join him in his chase. He understands, and goes crouching away through the trees.

When, still staying low, I open the Cicada's door and motion to Christa to get in, she stares, and flaps a hand back at me.

Yes; this is of course the passenger side, and it is I who must get in first and hummock over behind the wheel. Long enough away from England I can make the complementary mistake, and gallantly open the door for my passenger on the driver's side.

In place, Christa's bag thrown in the cramped slot (in unproved theory, additional seating) behind, I turn the key, and am shocked by the roar; the automatic chokes of many Cicadas respond over-enthusiastically to cold weather. Not waiting for the idle to steady down, I put us in gear with a jerk, and as we emerge between the guardian eagles catch just a glimpse of Arni bounding through the trees.

Christa, elation returned, laughs, but for me the sensation of successful escape instantly dies. When Pavel spoke about Christa being spirited away to the Strbjena military base, it seemed to assume Vock as party to the plot. I was dubious; while Vock might be told a way had been found to exert pressure on the High Court, it would surely be policy to insulate him from the actual crime, and to keep the secret in the smallest possible circle. On the other hand, we are deep within the province that is practically a Loyalist armed camp, and Herder must be important enough to Miloczy that he would have us stopped by the provincial police under his direct control; in the period of his premiership here there have been a long series of imprisonments without trial and more than one disappearance from police custody inconclusively investigated by Korava.

Considering the road, the dusk, the unfamiliar car, I am driving too fast, taking the tight curves with a squeal of tyres. As we come to the last and steepest of the straights in this mountain section, which ends with a sharp swing left above a precipitous drop, I get a strong whiff of petrol.

Beside me, Christa sniffs, and says, "*Essence* — " choosing French perhaps because from a pocket she has dug out a battered packet of Gauloises. In the hand nearest me is the disposable lighter taken from Lisuk.

I grab her wrist, at the same time bringing the car to a jolting stop.

"Get out."

She stares, and I repeat the demand less peremptorily. It

has come to me that in the disastrous mass recall of Cicadas two years ago, the defective fuel line was especially dangerous "if the car was driven downhill at high speed."

The hand-brake is on, but I don't turn off the engine; the starter will be a far greater risk when I resume, as I must. I'm going to have to roll down to the turn, where there's space for Arni to get the Toyota past, and I'm not facing that brink without gears as well as brakes to stop me.

Having almost forgiven my unprovoked assault, Christa is at road-edge, on packed snow; it strikes her as unpardonable that we could have been killed. I too might have found an expiring millisecond to resent dying for a cigarette, hers.

Arni in the Toyota, little lights on, comes in sight; luckily we have traversed enough of the straight that he has ample time to stop, leaning out to ask what's wrong.

A new idea comes; I had intended to leave the Cicada somewhere, but as Christa says, we could have been killed, and if we had there would be no police alert for us, no road-blocks, a clear posthumous run back to Korava. I get out, explain the fuel-leak to Arni, and ask if he carries emergency petrol, as most Dusatian drivers who venture far from the main cities usually do. He begins to argue that I can't have lost that much fuel, and that the Cicada is too dangerous, but when I explain my purpose he is rapturously eager; this is an exploit worthy of that other Arny, the movie one.

Having extracted Christa's bag, we slop petrol from a yellow twenty-litre jerrican all over front and back seats; the reek is overwhelming. I roll down the passenger-side window, slightly dampen one end of a crumpled handkerchief by wiping it over the front seat, and while Arni is replacing the jerrican in his boot, walk about twenty yards down, to a place, a rocky bulge, where I can be completely off the road without too much danger of taking a header.

Christa, chilled, is by now installed in the back seat of the Toyota. Chin resting on the stuffed bag hugged upright in her lap, she watches, as Arni, its door open on the driver's side, on my signal puts the other car in drive, leans in to release the handbrake, and as the car begins to roll, risks walking beside a few paces, steadying and aiming the wheel.

With Lisuk's disposable lighter I set fire to the dry side of my bundled handkerchief, an exercise made trickier by the whipping breeze. The Cicada, holding wonderfully straight, comes up to where I stand, moving at no more than a brisk walking-pace. When it is almost by me, I toss the burning handkerchief through the open window, and at once duck away beside my rock.

There is no instant whoomf, only, when I raise my head, the flare of disappointingly ordinary blue and yellow flame, which draws attention to how far darkness has advanced. Still gathering pace, the car, flame flickering, rolls on, and then comes a brilliant eruption and a muffled bang; I feel the warm shock-wave on my face. Burning now on the outside in several places, the car still rolls, and I wonder if it has enough momentum to carry it over the low snowy bank edging the road at the turn. As it reaches there, comes a second, far greater and much louder explosion, the petrol tank, and this time I turn away from the heat, as the Cicada dives over the brink, and vanishes in a spout of smoke and flame.

Arni is pounding the wheel of the Toyota with both fists and asking the world if it saw that. Christa, too, if less noisily, is also excited, and as I get in says with unpredictable wryness, "Cut. Print it."

The answer to Arni's triumphant question is, I'm afraid, only too well, and I suggest we get away before the curious or the authoritative begin to arrive. He concludes his rite of exultation, but still doesn't move, staring moodily to the front.

"I was thinking, it would be much better if I was here to tell them what happened."

He means, what we would like them to think has happened, and he's right; before concluding we're dead, our hunters are going to want to know what's become of Arni in the other car, for police purposes as describable as the discarded Cicada.

Shaking his head, Arni goes in gear.

"Do you think you could do it?"

"What's the problem? I was following you, you went down the hill like crazy people, there was an explosion, you went over the edge — "

"You saw the explosion and the car go over. Don't be too sure about us — " this in case Christa's survival becomes known while Arni is still in possible danger. A trained police or insurance investigator would know the car went over the edge at no great speed, and determined forensics establish, no matter how complete the destruction, that it had no occupant, but if ever, none of that analysis will occur tonight. "Can you do it?"

"You won't have no car."

"We'll take a train from Dvygarmiscz." There are bound to be evening trains for Korava.

He'll drop us off in Zrndja, and return; if anyone that matters sees him coming from that direction below the site of the crash, he can say he was going too fast to stop, and had to find a place to turn round. But considering what we have done to their mobility, it's likely no one from the lodge has yet arrived on the scene, and Arni's intent is to go there, make his report, and as soon as possible slip away.

Well, but it's almost certain they'll want to borrow him to provide transportation for someone — as I think it through the danger for Arni increases, and I tell him a couple of hours is enough time, and after that he must manage to get away, even if it means making obvious he is no ally of theirs.

"I can take care of myself." Arni tries for a peripheral view of Christa, to judge how she's affected by his modest heroism.

We pull up in a dark spot, not hard to find in Zrndja, and in explaining, half-apologizing to Christa that because Arni can't be longer away we'll walk from here, less than a mile, manage to offend her a little with the implication she's unapt for exercise. I retrieve the leather case for the pistol, put both in my small valise, and find the other weapon, the revolver, digging at my thigh. Still with misgivings, I hand it to Arni, scrabble up the ammunition from my jacket pocket, and tell him to keep it out of sight, and use it only in the last extremity. Phlegmatically, he reloads.

There's one more loose end. "Back at the lodge, when we got away. Why didn't I disable the Toyota?"

Arni is baffled, Christa says, "What?"

I tell her in English, and as if being patient with a slow child, she instantly explains: "You were only going to move the

Cicada out of the way, and take this car, but when you saw Arni coming, we just took off."

Arni says, "What?" and I translate for him, adding that I had from the first a spare set of keys for the Toyota.

"No you haven't."

"Yes I have." The penny eventually drops, but I coddle myself this tendency to literal-mindedness might be a help in his deceiving the enemy. In any case, I can't now cancel his mission, which has become an offering, his knightly tribute to Christa Rasch; Sancho and the Don have changed roles. The sweet remains oblivious to his devotion; when we get out of the car and I wish him well, repeat he must get away on his own as soon as he can, Christa gives him neither kiss, nor favour to wear on sleeve or helm.

As the tail-lights dwindle, I wonder whether I've got this right. My reasoning has been explained to Christa, and she accedes, though her belief is that her celebrity would daunt any police who stopped us. Perhaps, but I hope she won't test her theory by proclaiming herself as soon as we're back among people; police who intervene to offer protection can metamorphose into new captors. I pick up her bag, which isn't heavy; she informs me there's a snap-on shoulder strap tucked in an outside pocket, and determinedly takes my valise.

The small road for Dvygarmicsz could hardly be darker; once, twice cars sweeping past give us a moment of illumination, and we can't miss the way.

"What if there's no train?"

"There must be. But we can hire a car at the station, spend the night in one of the hotels, and get a train in the morning."

"I can call my father, let him know I'm okay."

"I wish you wouldn't, not till we're safe. Pavel is quite sure Rietz has his phone bugged." We'll come back to life for the kidnappers, and the hunt will be on again.

"He's going to think I'm dead, when the news gets out."

"The news won't get out." Here I'm absolutely sure; there are going to be no *CHRISTA RASCH DIES IN FIERY CRASH* headlines, because Herder and the Loyals would then have no leverage on a grieving Wirath. Most likely the crash itself can be hushed up, but if not any information about its supposed occupants can come only from the Eagle's Nest. Belatedly, it occurs to me that even as a loyal Rietzling, Arni, when he describes the event, should show some emotion over the loss of Christa. Perhaps he'll think of that.

Some moments of silent march. "What was going to happen?" Christa is thoughtful and something like plaintive. "They told papa I wouldn't get hurt if he did what they wanted with this election thing. So he does, they let me go, what's to stop him saying, no, that's not what I meant, I only said that because they had me? He would make sure I was safe, first."

A nasty point, and one I've discussed with Pavel. We agreed Herder's or Rietz's people meant to hold on to Christa till they had control — of the police and army, at least, hence, according to Pavel, the media; then (urtext) Wirath could flap his gums all he wanted, it wouldn't faze them. Well, but as in the long-ago days with the Muscovites, before Christa was born, a protesting Wirath could become an international embarrassment for a National Loyalist régime, and my private belief (now I ponder it, perhaps Pavel's too) is that they mean to kill him. It would harmonise with the history of such movements, and in fact strengthen the Loyalist case for law and order, if they were to engineer an assassination by some deranged *Leftist* catspaw, outraged at the Yellow Ballot decision. Christa they would see as no long-term threat, her kidnapping story dismissed as something between a psychotic reaction to her father's death, and a pathetic publicity stunt.

All this I condense and euphemise for her consumption into, "They think, once they're in power, they can keep your father quiet."

"They don't know papa." (So I'm spelling it, stress on the first syllable, but English readers should take startled note that for most Americans it would be indistinguishable in pronunciation from the less antique and more petmaking *poppa.*)

Looking back, now, on that anxious walk through a pitch-dark tunnel of pines, as a working journalist I ought to be ashamed (but I'm not) that my chief preoccupation is not what sort of story I can make of this. Though less tenuous than it was, there are still difficulties with substantiation when, on the other side, there is Herder's benificent public image: Arni's initial evidence; we can imagine what can be made of how that was obtained. My own testimony; that of the scandalmonger who stands to profit most from these charges. What we must have for a sustainable case, either in the responsible press or a court of law, is for Wirath to confirm he has been threatened (and I can imagine his declining, for reasons of state), and the victim still in her current mood of belief — and I wouldn't predict what she'd say, given ten minutes alone with the persuasive Herders. And before any of that, we have to be sure the plot has failed, and that is my dominant obsession.

A settlement begun by missionaries from the Mastercard sect, the railway outpost comes as a shock, with its characterless, shadowless, dangerless cosmopolitanism: how, here, can there be thoughts of violent crime and corrupt politics — thoughts of anything, except the hallowed rite, tendering and acceptance of the plastic wafer, mystical union with the cashless? At the station, we discover there's a connection for Korava in about twenty minutes; I use secular currency to acquire tickets, and am sold four, two additional for Fridova-Kerpaczy-Korava, finding that this branch line has a flat rate, my tickets equally good westward to the end of the line at Obdana, just across the Oba from Germany, and little if any more distant than Fridova.

There are scattered people about, many of them ski couples, bold sweaters, bright nylon anoraks, young, robust men, attractive women. Having put on tinted glasses and pulled down her dreadful cap, any attention Christa gets is as a slender, supple example of the latter; there are no sudden flares of recognition. We stroll out and visit the "American Drug Store," which a thoroughly insular Brit would call about equal proportions of Boots, Marks and W.H. Smith; I buy bars of chocolate and some petits beurres, and glance at the headlines on newspapers, German and Polish as well as Dusatian. Dalerant's soporific advent and the Wirath news conference have combined to drive politics from the front page; a relief for me. I informed London that I was going up-country after a story, but any unexpected development would have

Albertson in a flap.

Again passing phone-boxes at the station entrance, I'm tempted to ring Pavel, not only to let him know where things stand, but possibly to get us some help; a phalanx of police, not controlled by Miloczy, waiting for us at Fridova to escort us through Kerpaczy, would enormously improve my morale. I'm stopped by Pavel's immense respect for the eavesdropping capabilities of Rietz — that, and the hour; while there is no longer a reason for Pavel not to bring in his friend at the Ministry, if he's unable to reach him, my call to Pavel may have done no more than inform our adversaries. Reasonably, we should be all right; Eagle's Nest thinks we're probably dead; no one is hunting us. Yet I'm tensely anxious to be moving. From a counter reeking logically of onions and inexplicably of rosewater, I purchase and consume another large, fellatious, steamed sausage, Christa a doughy pretzel, chanting current cant about complex carbohydrates.

There are sections of double track east and west of the station, but trains going in either direction stop at the single platform on the same line; when at last it appears the train for Fridova adds to my impatience by pulling within a few yards of the platform, and halting just short of the points. A nasal horn sounds, and from the other direction, a train crawls in, displaying OBDANA as its destination.

Most waiting are returning to Kerpaczy or Korava, and this train has few takers moving to the edge of the platform. Almost empty, its three carriages, doors at each end, disgorge even fewer. Two, dark-suited, are of about the same order of improbability for a ski resort as Lisuk and Jenadju at the Eagle's Nest. One, broad, moustached, hatless, has a strip of sticking-plaster on his forehead. It is Rietz.

Christa and I are well back near the station-building, but Rietz on his way out will pass within five yards. Inconspicuously as possible, I edge myself round to give him my back, at the same time trying to obscure his view of Christa, who is puzzled.

Preoccupied, crossing behind, he comes back into my view, is virtually past us, nearly at the gate. He glances, sees, recognises Christa. Rietz lunges to grab the shoulder of his companion a step or two ahead, telling him, wait.

The westbound train is moving. Tugging at Christa's arm, I bolt for it, wrench open the last of six doors, scramble up, and turn to pull her after me by a wrist; with a cat's quick, sure feet she comes aboard trying still to tell me this is the wrong way.

Inside the door is a pivoted iron bar that serves as a latch, and I ram it into the locked position, as Rietz overtakes, reaching for the outside handle. Too late; he'll run out of platform before he can try for the other door; through the back window I see both men come to a frustrated halt, and as I turn away get a contemptuous stare from another passenger, as if on some mean-spirited whim I have prevented a fellow-latecomer from catching the train.

"This is the wrong way," Christa persists.

I explain, but can't explain to myself why Rietz is here; it is far too soon, presuming he was in Korava, for him to have arrived as a result of a call from Mara Herder when I came to the lodge. Best conjecture is that Herder was troubled by my phone-call this morning, and Rietz came up to make sure the kidnap team was fully alert. Why he would come by train is beyond all guessing.

Christa complains that we're getting farther away from where we want to go, but to get off at the next stop and take a later train eastward is a very bad idea; whatever forces Rietz can raise, perhaps including provincial police, will be on the watch for us.

"We can go all the way to Obdana, and slip across the bridge to Pauernkirche. Once we're in Germany, we'll be all right." This has a curious sound, and it occurs to me that I have read numberless books, seen countless films, with hunted people seeking safety by slipping across the German border, and in not one of them was the slipping to be done *into* Germany. *Autres temps, autres meurtres.*

Momentarily comforted in comforting, my anxiety flutters over to Arni, and the peril to him in Rietz's arrival. It's three-quarters of an hour since Arni left us in Zrndja; by now he is probably at the lodge, certainly has told his story of witnessing our flaming demise. Meanwhile, Rietz will have been expected there (I'm assuming they kept somewhere secluded a working telephone with a muted ring, or possibly just a flashing beacon to announce incoming calls), and expect to be met by car at the station. He'll ring the Eagle's Nest, and whether he or Mara is first with momentous news, he'll soon tell her he has just seen us, not even singed, racing for a train in Dvygarmiscz. More than when doing it, I wish I hadn't given Arni the revolver, which if anything can only increase his danger; there are, I'm certain, other firearms at the Eagle's Nest, and a born killer on his way there; without tangible reason, I find it easiest to be afraid of Mara Herder, with her icy dispassion.

It's about Mara, about both Herders that Christa begins to talk, picking at the scab of incomprehensible betrayal. Most sourness centres on what now must be called Mara's affectation of unfailing solicitude; in a pat bit of parlour psychology I begin to connect the friendship with Christa's early loss of her mother.

All of this constantly counterpointed by the mathematics of worry, a tense algebra of too many unknowns; what Rietz can do to have us intercepted before we reach safety. We sit with a table-slab between us in a carriage not a quarter filled, our sombre-faced reflections keeping mindless pace. It feels like a graveyard time between midnight and one, but is still short of eight p.m. The train, in no hurry, winds through a sparsely-peopled dark, makes one stop and then a second, at minor stations, disgorging a few skiers and what must be waitresses, hotel porters, cashiers, picking up others; most of the passengers appear now to be Germans. Long ago this line used to meander into Germany, but with main lines both south and east, the railway bridge at Obdana, destroyed in 1945, was never important enough to replace.

With a jolt, we stop again, nowhere. We are on a rightward curve, and have halted in a double-tracked section short of the next station, no doubt to wait for an eastbound train. The station ahead is no more than a strip of hooded platform with dull yellow lighting, and the steep-roofed building behind is like a small farmhouse; no shops or dwellings are visible. In the forecourt, illuminated by a single stark sodium lamp on a high pole, I can make out at least three cars. One might well be the black coupé I assigned to Mrs Bacewicz, from which Arni jerked the distributor cables. The other two are provincial police, *dzhăndarmi*, and with that to go on I can now discern on the platform the glisten of jackboots and the peaks of caps, and know with the certainty of nightmare that Rietz is there among them.

The Fridova-bound train nosing into the station, I give Christa the news; it is likely that when our train comes to the platform there will be a policeman assigned to each of its six doors, and while still inclined to believe she can escape arrest simply by unveiling and proclaiming her identity, she does not dispute with me when I tell her what we're going to do. After the briefest of stops the other train is moving again, lurching abruptly over the points, passing us. As if alighting, Christa and I pick up our small baggage and move to the door. There is no one in the nearest seats, and a narrow upright partition hides us from the rest of the carriage; no one notices us going to the door on the wrong side for the platform. I pull up the massive iron latch.

As soon as the eastbound train is past, ours creeps forward; I open the door and step down onto snow over shifting ballast; Christa, having tumbled out her bag, leaps somewhat over-dramatically, and has to be caught as she stumbles. I reach to push the door to, but can't completely close it without risking more noise than is prudent.

The train masking us from the station platform, we follow till it waggles across the points and makes its stop. It would be easy to cross the second track and go down the far embankment, but I want the north side if Obdana, as I believe, is north and west of here. When all attention on the platform must be to the front, we go quickly across, down a shallow embankment knee-deep in snow. A three-foot fence, five taut strands of barbless heavy-gauge wire strung between frequent stanchions, is easily crossed, and beyond is a track, well-rutted, which follows the railway, the lights of the station, especially the high, glaring sodium lamp, quite close. That is leftward, and we don't go there; at least one lounging man was left to guard the vehicles, but left front, through a brake of weedy trees, there is a road, and after all there are dwellings, a small huddle of dark houses and possibly shops.

We hear shouts coming from the station, but haven't been seen; it was too much to hope our hunters would all board the train and be borne away, and the unlatched door on the wrong side is going to give them a clue. Not losing time, Christa and I slip through the hamlet where only small chinks of light show through curtained windows, and see that just beyond there is a parting of ways. The road, well-kept, curves away rightward to unknown destinations, but puts out a minor spur, and a signboard at its opening says *OBDANA 18*. Eighteen thousands of metres, say eleven miles. Here like a narrow lane or wide alley between ancient brick wall and wooden fence, the way won't remain so; its sign bears the little stylised silhouette of a stunted conifer, used in Dusatia to identify a footpath, a nature walk, or, in these parts more commonly, a mountain trail.

I look in Christa's face, and she grimaces. "Unless we can pinch a car."

"Or ring a bell, and yell 'Here we are!'"

Another volley of shouts from the station; I haven't heard the train move off; some habitually punctual German passengers must be getting testy.

"If we hadn't gone the wrong way, we could be almost in Korava by now,"

True, and if she hadn't trusted Mara Herder, I could be in Kent. I decline to be annoyed; though rendered timeless by fame and certified desirability, Christa is really only twenty-three, and kept younger by coddling.

There isn't any choice; a search may already be fanning out from the station. I find and attach the shoulder-strap to her bag, shrug it up, and stride out.

Something may strike you about that exchange, my reading of Christa's face. The night has grown lighter; like the drawing of an immense, heavy curtain, the overcast is moving off to the south, discovering a brilliant three-quarter moon, still waxing, enough for trees to cast faint shadows on the snow. Where not outdazzled by the moon, a fantastic excess of stars prickle the sky.

Though a sense of being visible makes me uneasy, it is as well we can see our way. Almost at once we're climbing, steep and straight, and when we reach the brow after a dogged half-mile, the surface, which may well be asphalt under a slight mantle of fresh, little-trodden snow, gives out, and the continuation, less abruptly uphill, is an uneven track where two can barely go abreast. We are, quite inexplicably, mounting across the curve of a vast treed hillside, and the path appears to be the boundary between forest and what when spring comes must be high pasture. Ahead, the final peaks of the range crowd like a daunting barrier, though I know and tell myself most lie northerly of our route. There is a steady, frigid breeze in our faces, sometimes working up to an agonizing gust, but except for cheeks and ears, I'm not cold, and for once Christa has no complaints; I let her make the pace, and her condition is better than I would have supposed, slender legs striding steadily. Because she has gloves, I let her carry my valise, thrusting my hands alternately into my pockets from time to time.

The gradient relents, and we're stumbling among trees, little snow underfoot, but it's darker, and the path is rocky and uneven. This is dreadful, annoying as well as arduous, with sudden gouges and barrier tree-roots detected only by lurching or stumbling into them, and the way itself not easy to be sure of; a long time and much physical and emotional energy are consumed, and doing my best to contain (in the military or firefighting sense) the endlessness of our halting often angry progress, I calculate that at this pace we can't be in Obdana before three a.m., still an absurd sum, because that means we shan't get there at all; neither of us can keep this up for five more hours.

Like an abrupt cut in a movie, we emerge into a district of the moon, treeless, rocky, wind-scoured, utterly disheartening. On our right, a steep rock-slope rises to what must be a knife-edged summit, and the trail, climbing again, is like a little shelf notched in the mountainside.

Christa stops, turns, and as I just avoid slamming into her, says, "Are we going to die up here?" She is, I see, more fatigued than I'd thought, consequently more affected by the cold, holding her shoulders hunched.

"Not unless they shoot us — " I'm thinking unreally of a helicopter pouncing out of the silvered sky.

"How can they know we're here?"

I shake my head; they can't. Even if Rietz and his auxiliaries found out, questioning passengers, that we were on the train till shortly before they boarded it, they couldn't guess the direction we'd taken; anyone who knew the country would say this route would be attempted on a midwinter's night only by mad people.

Fine snow comes squalling, but it can't be fresh; the sky is cloudless, or streaked only by immensely high wraiths of tenuous cloud. At the summit, three hundred feet above, a fiercer wind is tearing away visible plumes of old snow. Any counting of blessings is premature, but on the north side, without this sheltering bulk, we could scarcely have survived the wind, while even a moderate new snowfall would have been enough to make this trail a killer.

"Soon," Christa pronounces as fact, "I'm going to have to sit down and cry." She is struggling now against chattering teeth.

"It's a mountain pass," I point to where, still a long way off, the notch between heights is plain against the sky. "There has to be a shelter at the top, it's the law." One my mother often refers to with proper Dusatian pride. The summer she began working for the British embassy, she and my father did some epic walks, and there is, starring one of the wayside shelters, a scandalous family story I am never going to be old enough to hear except in roguish allusion.

"How far?" She makes this a challenge, any wrong answer punishable by her refusal to move.

Why would I know, idiot? "Fifteen, twenty minutes, if we step out."

And she does, heartened by what she knows to be sheer cobblers. Though exposed and at times precarious, the way is fairly good going, our climb gradual, the footing mainly solid rock scoured bare of snow. In half the time of my feckless estimate, we have made palpable progress, the pass ahead now three-dimensional, the higher side receding into background.

Glancing up to the right as we skirt a lessening of the slope, a wide, shallow bowl, I see indistinctly movement, a flickering, then quite clearly an advancing crest with the roll of an ocean breaker. With a warning shout I push at Christa's back, and seeing we can't outrun the avalanche, virtually leap on her back to pull her down below the parapet.

She fights me, felinely, twisting to bat at me with her hands, having scraped away a glove against her hip. Mainly by dead weight and the grip of my knees I partially subdue and partially cover her, folding my arms behind my head, as the peculiar tearing and multiple rattle arrives.

It is brief, a minor avalanche, and we are at its edge. Unidentified missiles patter on my back, a larger chunk of rock or ice thumps me in the kidneys with the vicious authority of a veteran boxer. When at last I start up, Christa now lying perfectly quiescent, something has painfully bruised my elbow, but what feels like the worst of my injuries is high on the right side of my face, a set of near-parallel scrapes, from which a little blood comes away on my numb, testing fingers. For the first time I'm consciously aware that Christa is left-handed.

Where I stand, a flat slab of rock weighing perhaps three or four hundred pounds has come to rest jutting out above the path, just about over where my head and shoulders were. But not thirty paces back, the trail has vanished in a littered slope of snow and debris.

Christa is gathering herself, looking about with wide, wondering eyes. "I thought — "

I know what you thought, silly bitch, and am less offended than exasperated by monumental illogic: in the centrally-heated comfort of her room at Eagle's Nest, door locked and a wide bed nearby, a gun in my hand, she has safely stripped in front of me; could this same man, half-frozen, two-thirds exhausted, wobbling on an arctic mountainside, be seized with a sudden frenzy of uncontrollable lust? I pick up my valise, which has almost gone sledding down the slope. "Get on," brusquely. At least any fears I had of trackers following us through the night have vanished; not for days will the way we have come be open again.

The shelter is there, wooden above, massive stone below, tucked against the rocks just below the head of the pass, and I'm too done to go on a dozen paces for a glimpse of the prospect ahead. A slab of door, checked by a massive coil-spring, opens grudgingly, and bangs shut behind us. With small and no doubt filthy windows partly covered in snow, it is very dark inside, and I'm sure it must be very cold, but refuge from the wind feels momentarily like a sudden wave of warmth.

With the aid of Lisuk's lighter, I find an iron stove, bundles of firewood and kindling stacked nearby. Wide wooden shelves against two walls are for sleeping, and there is also, and rather drolly, a partitioned space with a proper porcelain loo, connected to absolutely nothing but a noisome pit beneath, though an ancient pail beside suggests a degree of maintenance. On the wall behind is a faded list of things we mustn't use the lav for, none especially relevant to current concerns; the preoccupations of authority are endlessly strange.

Christa is, I believe, sitting on her bag next to the stove. With numbed fingers like alien sticks I manage to open my valise, laboriously tear off and awkwardly crumple several sheets from a ruled pad. It's not until flames are catching at kindling criss-crossed in the stove that it comes to me that we're going to survive. I add some larger bits of resiny wood, and by flickering flamelight see Christa is passively weeping where she sits.

Not quite cured of annoyance with her, I can't withhold a consoling hug across her shoulders. "We'll be all right."

She looks at me, eyes like holes in night. "Will we?"

"Lap of luxury, if only we had sleeping-bags."

"You carried one here. I'm sitting on it."

It's true; she empties it, stuffing the contents into the first thing unpacked, a drawstring laundry-sack; opened out the bag cunningly metamorphoses into a sleeping-bag folded in quarters. It seems very thin, quilting hardly perceptible, but Christa assures me the insulation is a miracle of space-age technology, the bag a new triumph of Swiss design intended for an Everest expedition.

While she spreads it on one of the shelves, I do more exploring. In a crude cabinet against the back wall there is an assortment of treasures, left here, one presumes, by a succession of guests; some stumps of candle, a couple of battered aluminium pans, a cracked whitish beaker and chipped enamel cup, a flat packet of institutional toilet-paper in spartan dun squares, even a small cardboard box containing a few aging Polish tea-bags. I'm conscious that more than three feet away from the stove, it is still very cold in here, but before I can succumb to lassitude take both saucepans, collect the pail from the loo, and carry all three outside to pack them with snow. The moon will shortly set, and the stars are numerous beyond conceiving.

Inside, I place all the containers on or near the stove. I add more fat split logs, but decide against damping down some fuel and keeping the fire in till morning. By first light there may be a full-scale search for us, and a slight plume of smoke could be enough to end it.

The stove-door closed down, though I have lighted a candle-end, it is very dark again, and from the darkest corner Christa asks me if it's after twelve.

"Quarter to one."

"Christmas Eve eve. Are you coming to bed?"

"You should use the sleeping-bag." What exactly I plan for myself is unclear.

"That's crazy. It's cold; we'll keep each other warm." I hear the snaps as she unfastens her windcheater.

She's perfectly correct, and it's not possible to ask her please not to claw me if our contact becomes too intimate.

"If it bothers you, I'll keep my pants on." She has, then, evidently completed her undressing, and is now sliding into the bag. Pinching out the ineffectual candle I blindly grope in that direction.

Christa's English, as I've tried to represent it, is not so much mid-Atlantic as Concorde, darting back and forth, taking its usage where it finds it (there may be some antipodean elements, too); the lingua franca, I suppose, of international co-productions and fashion shows, overlapping into the adjacent grotty world of rock music concerts; when she uses a word like *smart*, it is usually but not invariably to be understood in the American sense. Whether her retained *pants* are Yank or Brit is a critical question, the difference between sleek but substantial corduroys, and (as recalled from the earlier striptease), no more than about a half-ounce (14g) of pale *couleur de rose.*

Shivering as much with fatigue as cold I divest myself of outer clothing and sensations as it were turned inward on *chaste*, work into the bag next to her. British. Instantly she turns, wrapping herself against me, and I say "Ow," as her fingertips unerringly find the scrapes on my cheek.

But this is a chosen context for contrition; she murmurs abjectly, and meanwhile her left leg slides up outside my right thigh. Apology recruits a ceremonious and then a tender kiss, and shortly we go on to more.

Whether or not we actually make love, like most such puzzles, like the golden oldie about the unheard tree falling in the forest, is not the metaphysical riddle it pretends to be, but merely a demand we define our terms; what do we mean, *sound*, what do we mean, *boink*? Enough that there are exaltations, languors, bliss of the highest order, and that when we drift asleep in a universe of savage cold, our own microclimate is, if anything, too warm.

      My first waking act is to extract enough arm from the sleeping bag to touch the back of a warmed hand to the tip of my nose, which is indeed icy like nothing alive; emerging to pull on cold, damp clothes will be a brief but traumatic ordeal. Apart from that terror still to be met, and a hunger that is going to get worse, I feel good, as if I have been especially clever, though with miles to go before any chance of a bath, neither of us is going to be an olfactory treat by mid-morning.

      It doesn't matter — and the focus of my wellbeing shifts from me to her, from complacency to *tendresse*, and a wonder at the ingenuity or esoteric experience she brings to the restrictive theatre of a sleeping-bag. When she is hoveringly awake, I murmur some of this, tell her she should do a book — I'll ghost it for her, if she wants; *Things To Do in a Sleeping-Bag with Christa Rasch* surely has potential as an international megabook. While recognizing (I think) that this is grateful whimsy, she doesn't neglect to note that she has a manager, through whom all projects must be cleared.

      Before my hands go numb again, I scribble some notes, and Christa, who has retreated back into the sleeping-bag, half emerges again to say plaintively, "I thought you were going to light the stove."

      And I do so, raking out ash, salvaging half-burnt wood; it's too much work to explain about the smoke, and I crave a hot drink, even stale Polish tea laundered in far-from-boiling water. Christa, shuddering, tiptoes over to rummage for fresh underwear and socks, dresses swiftly, tastes greyish tea and makes a face. She accepts a biscuit, but chocolate, no. It seems I should have known she can't eat chocolate — she strokes a cheek to illustrate the reason, and finding it wind-roughened, rummages again for a tiny polythene bottle of costly balm, which she caresses on with a gentle middle-finger.

      "It's like being a racehorse, isn't it."

      "A racehorse?"

      I don't explain. I wasn't, in any case, at risk of being in love. Christa's personality can be grating: with her astonishing beauty, it could be demoniacal and still she'd have courtiers by the busload. But some men, many men, young men in particular are actually attracted to her sort of self-absorption, discovering a challenge, at the extreme, a *raison d'être*; my experience concedes that it's perilously easy to accept such a woman at her own evaluation, and live on nuggets of pride to be grubbled from identifying and anticipating her needs, whims, winning a flicker, it doesn't have to be of gratitude, mere acknowledgement — much the same abject triumph as when finding a food momentarily relished by an especially finicky cat. While not denying a servile thread in my own character, nor censuring the life which inevitably comes to exploit it, I won what I think may be permanent personal immunity at twenty-three, in my enthrallment when first let loose in London, of which the details are too painful and much too tedious to recall. The only point that's germane is that Germaine (that was her name) shared many of the traits I detect in Christa, above all the amazing, the insolent, the naively charming, the miraculously self-fulfilling assumption that admirers exist to rearrange the world to her likings, all men, by definition (their own as much as hers), being admirers.

      Petruchios are born, not made, nor do the Christas have any need to be kately quarrelsome or crosspatch or even overtly assertive; for the naturally chivalrous man the only survival is through a sort of ironic distancing, investing nothing of his emotions in reflexive service.

      We're not in much hurry to resume; I fed the fire generously to heat water for our near-tea, and it would be a shame to let its warmth be wasted on an empty shelter. What's left of our trek can't be so bad; it will be all downhill, and making generous allowance for misery, I'm certain we covered more than half the distance last night. What our reception will be in Obdana is another question. We sit by the stove, I on the emptied pail upturned, she on her reassembled bag, and she returns to the treachery of the Herders.

"Why would they hate me?"

"They don't. I'm sure they genuinely like you — " a retrospective caress goes with this, but Christa is intent on her puzzle.

"They would kill me. They want my father to think that."

"No need to take it personally; it's all for Miloczy's cause."

"Who is Magda Gödele? In history? Mara admires her; she says she was a truly dedicated woman."

"Magda *Goebbels*?" I didn't know she had any admirers; my skin starts to crawl.

"You got it. Who is Magda Goebbels then?"

"She poisoned her own children, all of them. There were six, and she had given them all names beginning with an *H*."

"What did she kill them for?"

"Because all their names began with *H*."

Christa, annoyed with me, turns away, but through this exchange I hear for the first time the eerie echo of old darkness to be found in the triumvirate of Herder, the overeducated, with his chill former-actress wife, Vock the former military hero and present parliamentarian, and, inspiring them both, the gutter orator and loony dreamer, Miloczy. Is it possible to speak of political ecology, where similar organisms come to fill the niches created by parallel conditions? But by this arrangement, Herder should be the theoretician, the philosopher, the reasoned fanatic. He hasn't emerged publicly in that role, and Christa still rejects it.

"Vock comes to see him, sure, but he's buddy-buddy with Angèle, too — you know Angèle?" She rolls up her eyes to express her distaste, whether of Angèle's opinions or her visual style I can't guess, but have no trouble imagining the two women dislike each other.

"He even gave her a gun, for her birthday, a little one."

"But real."

"I guess. It was a joke — "

"Angèle can't have a gun, she'll go to jail; she was convicted before. She's the one who shot Pavel."

"Pavel Orbicz? — " her head had given an interested little half-turn when first I mentioned him. "He's great, I think he's cool, he knows all about old movies and stuff. It was just a joke, because of what she said about assassinations."

The humour escapes me; this Herder present links much too neatly with my thoughts about the necessary killing of Christa's father; not a leftist, but an anarchist assassin, the principle is the same. She has access to those circles; half-mad at the best of times would hardly need much prompting from Herder to punish what she would perceive as betrayal, the ideal scapegoat, a potential Marinus van der Lubbe, a Jack Ruby. I don't want to put Angèle behind bars again, but when I get back to Korava mean to have that gun taken away from her, under threat of arrest. If I get back to Korava.

When we're assembled for departure, I contribute a large bar of chocolate to the treasure-trove in the cabinet. I mean to add Lisuk's lighter, but Christa snatches it up; she has already reproached me for failing to buy cigarettes in Dvygarmiscz. Evidently she goes through life like the Queen, carrying no money. The near-fatal Gauloises were discarded as too stale.

VII

Obdana, hemmed between high bluffs and river, straggles along the margin of the Oba, which the Germans call the Ohn; less abrupt banks on the northwest side allow Pauernkirche to be a smugger, more focused little town girded by the visible remains of 14th Century fortifications.   But while Pauernkirche outdoes Obdana in the possession of a shopping precinct, two supermarkets, a factory where they make clothes-pegs (the squeeze kind, with metal spring) and another for paintbrush handles, a hospital, a strip club, the Dusatian town, in the one place where it widens into more than a skein of dwellings, has about half of a perfectly preserved mediaeval square, dominated by its church, splendid with carved wood from weathered door to burnished choir.

This is opposite the end of the plain footbridge, low to the water, connecting the two towns (the highway arches across half a kilometre downriver, next to the forlorn brick pillars of the vanished railway-bridge).   In response to the daily stream of Dusatians, largely housewives crossing with empty and returning with loaded shopping-bags, there has always been a trickle of German antiquity-hunters coming the other way, but a couple of years ago the cobbled square was used as locale for the climactic final scene in an enormously popular costume-drama series on German television, and now, several times each day, a tour coach from Bavaria or the distant Rheinpfalz, having done Neuschwanstein, and nipped over to Salzburg (for the sake of technicolor Trapps, not hallowed Mozarts), stands at the German end of the bridge, while its passengers troop across to visit and snap the church portico where winsome Trudi with the forget-me-not eyes at last made her definitive choice between Ritter von Schnobb, swashbuckling aristocrat, and Hans Eselgesang (I may not have these names quite right), sincere but hard-up minstrel (no prizes are to be won for guessing [a] what Trudi's choice was, or [b], in hardheaded real life, whether the actress playing Trudi subsequently married an indigent poet, or a remote, still wealthy member of the Hohenzollern clan with a bent nose and a villa near Positano. Incongruently, both the fictional and actual matches are equally judged "romantic."). Border formalities are normally perfunctory, but if there is still to be an effort to stop Christa and me, it is there, surely, that its attention will be concentrated.

By contrast with last night's undesired saga, this morning has been practically a saunter, both way and weather easier, or made so by clear sunlight, our final descent into Obdana by a stair of more than one hundred steps cut into digestible portions, swinging back and forth on the craggy slope. As when we tackled the high pass by moonlight, we have no real choice but to go forward; it has occurred to me that the open door on the train last night might have persuaded Rietz we'd managed to transfer ourselves to the eastbound train as it passed, which makes our present whereabouts less inevitable; a watch that has to spread its resources to keep us from leaving the province at any point (which, indeed, may believe it has already failed) is not as daunting as a reception committee waiting for us to come down from the heights. We arrive in a little back-alley a row of cottages away from the river, so far as can be told unobserved.

Another distinction for Obdana is as the quarterly meeting place of the Foresters (as I can best translate the name, literally "woodgoers"). Nothing to do with either old-time hunters or newfangled environmentalists, it is a kind of masonic order (though never at odds with the clergy) for smallholders, recently taking in some ethnic nonsense borrowed from Miloczy, but with the sole observable function of assembling in February, May, August and November, singing traditional songs, and getting drunk. For this reason the town has, most of the year, an excess of rentable beds. A dismal restaurant where we stop, still well short of the town centre, also claims to be an hotel, and after coffee whose granular settling reminds me of calomine lotion, and some sort of bun fresh from the next-door bakery and surprisingly good, I suggest we take a room so that we can each have a much-needed bath.

Approached, the proprietress gives us the fish-eye survey of a woman who doesn't have to be told why a couple wants a room at ten in the morning (though honestly, it can't be all that common, can it?). As Christa, despite everything and contrary to her own despairing assessment, still looks absolutely beautiful, the woman must wonder why she'd waste her time slumming with me, on whom lack of maintenance and especially of a shave are damningly apparent, to say nothing of the lacerations high on my face. But she takes my money and hands over a key, telling us it's up the back stairs, first landing. And the bath? Shower cubicle in the room, immersion up another flight, towels. Two, not large, clean but somewhat threadbare; I rustle notes in my wallet, and we are issued two more, with a face that plainly believes an excess of towels must play some murky role in unspeakable erotic practices.

The room has wallpaper stained with damp, a matchwood chest of drawers with a patched and cloudy mirror behind, and a sagging iron bed.

With a glance to this last, Christa, debating who is to bath first, introduces as a consideration, "Are you gonna want to do it?"

Astonishingly, it is a genuine request for information, without any hint of coy challenge, a clue to the casual candour of the set she belongs to, its tolerant if lukewarm norms; outside such a circle, what man would or could afford to say no? even leaving out that one of the world's certified desirables is doing the asking? "Not before I shave," rubbing a chin capable of far outravaging chocolate.

We end by each having a bath and then both having a shower, lewdly cheerful, though the water at the end is hardly more than *chambré*. As for the interlude on the rhythmically querulous bed (it keeps saying "I *ask* you," in exactly the tone of a wronged cockney shopgirl), well, it can't and needn't always be magic; *satisfactory* sounds like a laconic comment from a school report, and if you didn't know who wrote it you wouldn't know whether you were being commended or ironically damned with faint praise, but here I mean no more and blessedly no less than I say. There is a sensation of closure, too, as if the confrontational act formalises and completes what the sleeping bag began; and for me at the very still end, a rush of glad awe for her physical perfection.

With barrier mountains northward, open to the south, the gorge of the Oba here is noted for its moderate climate, and the day is still bright; Christa at my urging puts on something less defensive, a short, slender tube of soft honey-coloured material capable of emerging unwrinkled from its ordeal in the bag; she wears tights but retains socks and the boots. The time may at last be near when her recommended tactic of exploiting celebrity comes into its own.

Dressing, working at her hair in front of the post-impressionist mirror, she grouses that among many things abandoned in our flight from the Eagle's Nest is an irreplaceable Just Saint-Just original, actually signed by *le maître*. Abstractedly, I tell her there is every possibility it may in time be recovered, although in just what circumstances is somewhere near the heart of my preoccupation.

Within the next hour, we'll either be captives, or practically safe, and it makes me uneasy that if and once we reach safety, the news of Christa's kidnapping can become, for the lifespan of a gnat, the world's biggest growth industry, headlines, interviews, the book, the movie (but who'll play Christa?). Not the species of story I've ever sought, and I hope it's clear my goal has never been either wealth or notoriety beyond the quiet recognition of my peers, but if I let this one get away I'll earn contempt instead, and the just fury of Albertson. A story to cut across class barriers, ready-to-wear for the tabloids, yet amenable to the tasteful tailoring of the serious press, *Observer*, *Guardian*, *New York Times*, who can compose their soberer headlines to emphasise the political aspect, the text soon subsiding into the perils of "Ms Rasch," can, as so often, come back for a second and third bite of the apple, disputing the conclusions, deploring the methods of their more monosyllabic brethren; what would Cicero be without Catiline, Jeeves without Bertie?

To be the ringmaster who starts this circus, I have to have Christa, but my nerves say, *not yet*. Albertson would authorise me to offer probably a pretty hefty sum to bind her to us, and when Christa says it would have to be done through her manager — perhaps her manager *and* her agent — want me to make that approach too; her manager is in Paris or Zurich or Los Angeles, as far as I can make out. What I want is not to be rushed, time to talk to Pavel, to — the august thought surprises me — Niemek.

Where does that come from? The president and I have exchanged polite words, largely about my mother, on two or three occasions, but now I want a real talk with him about, well, the future of Dusatia. About Vock and the Javelin Division, whatever armed forces Miloczy can command, the potential of Rietz's street toughs. It resolves for me; maybe, as Pavel said, they had been counting on a pretext, the shadow of legality, but I am afraid that for the Loyalists, revelation of the kidnapping plot, with criminal charges looming, arrest minimally of the Herders, followed very probably by an adverse decision from Wirath, will make them desperate enough to attempt seizing power by force. In what Albertson would call an act of outright treason to my profession, I want official sanction before proceeding on a course which may lead to civil war.

I'm not unsympathetic to the Albertson position; in the right mood I'd defend the principle that a journalist must tell the truth, and, as Pavel says, chips must fall wherever. Whether I'd have the same scruples if all this were happening in Belarus or Slovakia is hard to say.

Making sure Christa is safe melts into the question of keeping her quiet. I venture, "If we get out, I don't think you should go back to Korava till after your father announces the High Court decision. It's a pity about Christmas — "

"That's no big deal. Even before Mara came up with Christmas at the lodge, I wasn't planning to spend it with papa. I was going to Marrakech with Guy and some kids." Guy, the film-maker. It shouldn't shock me to find how onesided Wirath's feelings for his daughter are; doesn't all unconditional devotion come to be taken for granted?

"Does Mara know that?"

"Oh, yes. She was very against how Guy — how I am with Guy."

I don't ask. The repellent idea of a dual-purpose Christa, bed and bait, may be just my nasty-mindedness. "Is there anywhere else — "

"Where are you going?"

"I have to go back to Korava. But I don't matter nearly so much."

"You don't honestly think they would try to track me down?"

"Honestly, I don't know. Till after the ruling, I'd like you somewhere no one can know about — " and in mid-flight, I think of Sevenoaks.

Will Christa go for it? Hymning its seclusion, its charm, I can't be all that far from Mara Herder, selling her on the Eagle's Nest; like Mara, if for more benificent reasons, I would like to keep Christa incommunicada, though a sudden failure of the telephone could be too much to believe.

She says it might be fun, having never seen more of England than a hotel in town and a taxi ride to Westminster Bridge to make parliament (and its staunch, upstanding clock) a backdrop for her posturing in billowy, impractical clothes.   Though Shakespeare is hardly Christa's cup of sack, she has pleasant recollections of my mother, vaguer ones of Dad. It will, at most, be three or four days.

The second time I came to Dusatia, I drove down from Berlin, and made a point of detouring to see the old church at Obdana (this was before it achieved its wider fame), so have a good idea of the general layout. We can and do approach the square by a series of narrow back-ways, and by good fortune arrive at almost the same time as a fresh batch of pilgrims to the shrine of Trudi, about two dozen in all, surging up from the bridge, cameras busy — one earnest old bloke is actually videotaping, giving rise to reflection on infinite layers of celebrity, having been filmed as a reason for filming. Most are no less than middle-aged, though there is a pair of young, oh, barmaids from Munich? of which the better-looking is going to be on quite a lot of the videotape, especially her very round bottom in taut jeans. The guide, a severe, sharp-nosed young woman in near uniform, a dark blazer, stands at the church door and for some higher purpose attempts to direct attention beyond the ghost of Trudi, pointing out felicities in the deep-relief carving, and speaking of the unique interior. Though a few mount the steps to stare through an opened doorlet within the door, no one is inclined to enter, and I suspect the last bladder stop was some time ago. There is a desultory eddying, and Christa and I join the fringes of the group.

She is still wearing the baggy cap and blue windcheater, but we're among cognoscenti now, and there is more than one lingering gaze; a stout grey woman in particular, lips parted, leaning forward, stays at the brink of certain, incredulous recognition.   The guide considers drawing attention to other treasures, the enamel-faced clock, for example, above the ancient saddlery, but recognises general sentiment, anticipated by general drift, is for a return to the coach.

As we move down towards the bridge, I see that while the normal contingent of almost functionless border guards has been reinforced by half a dozen vigilant *dzhăndarmi* in their black boots, they too are all genial smiles for the brief guests. There are, I believe, standing instructions from on high to be friendly, helpful and hospitable (in a word, *gemütlich*) to visitors from the Bundesrepublik, with which Miloczy desires improved relations. Not only as a source of revenue, but because it is in the German press that the harshest and most cogent criticisms of his works and aspirations have appeared.   I've been counting on this; if the provincial police are indeed on the lookout for us, it means they've been told at all costs to stop Christa Rasch and her companion, and at all costs do it unobtrusively; mutually contradictory orders to low-level officials generally result in paralysis.

I have found the tourist I'm looking for, younger than most, slung with a Polaroid. Nudging Christa to tell her this is it, I sidle up to him confidentially.

"Could I borrow your camera? I'll pay you for the film. I want to get a shot of Christa Rasch."

"Christa Rasch?" He puts a hand on his camera as if I might snatch it away, and at that moment Christa pulls off the cap, shaking out her hair, whirls away from the windcheater to suspend it on one finger, and turns at the bridge opening, a hip thrust out, the cover-picture smile blossoming. She is posing, but not for me; my Polaroider has gone, and is boring in on her; flashes are flashing.

While the border guards are all grins, their reinforcements are indecisive, as Christa swaggers onto the bridge to strike a new attitude, leaning against the handrail, head flung back, one knee up, a pose to assert this frock, this new scent, this stuff to do something to your hair will fill all your days with an ecstatic self-confidence. The flock follows and crowds, and not all are taking pictures; I can now state that a sixty-fivish, dumpy scalp-huntress can find a notebook and pencil and thrust them at a celebrity in approximately one ten-millionth the time it would take her to fumble out her money if you were waiting behind her at Safeway.

The *dzhăndarmi* are still in doubt, making hesitant steps to follow, and from the little wooden sentry-box office to one side I see the angry menace of a Rietz emerge, still with his taped-up forehead. He barks out urgent advice, but I, bearing our small luggage, am threading through the throng, swelled by other users of the bridge. Christa has graciously given an autograph, made a pretty show of wishing to disengage, then, in response to pleas, turned back after a few steps to pose again.

While the casual checkpoints are at either end, the border is at mid-river, indicated by a broad white stripe painted across the bridge. Going out ahead of Christa, I cross into Germany, and jog up to the guards, who are gazing with puzzled interest at the approaching crowd scene.

"It's Christa Rasch." My expression both proprietary and anxious, perhaps a personal manager, out of his depth. "We need some protection."

Whether an equally celebrated but less provocative name might have led instead to a debate about their proper duties, to reproach for my not having given the police advance notice, is impossible to say. Certainly the one woman among the guards, small and sinewy, little older than Christa, is no less quickly and probably more disinterestedly concerned than the bigger, blonder men, who gather themselves, putting on their masks of impassive competence. I trot out ahead of them, and re-enter Dusatia, where a steadily retreating Christa is conducting a kind of running rearguard interview with the tourists, yes, she expects to do more films, no, she's never met any of the transcendentally celebrated Elizabeths, what is the name of this alleged grandson whom her signature would so delight?

She is mere steps from Germany, where the border guards are prepared to sweep her up, their faces set on pleasant but firm. Snaking into the crowd, closing in on her, I see a trio of *dzhăndarmi* trying to maintain that same expression, and then there is a memorable, defining moment; their leader, a sergeant, turns round to catch the eye of Rietz, at the fringe of the crowd, and to indicate with a cock of his head the old buffer with the video recorder, getting it all.

Rietz, quietly frantic, gestures, never mind, go on, but the brief tableau has been enough for Christa to reach and cross the white line, to be passed through the waiting row of five German guards, who then stem the tide of their compatriots, good-naturedly chiding them for not allowing Fräulein Rasch some room.

For less than half a second, though distantly, Rietz's gaze meets mine, and I see that he loathes me with a deathless hatred — and that I've misread him up to now. With his history of exceptional service for *Schnur* under the Muscovites, followed by his assistance to Vock in outwitting the Red Army, I've assumed he's basically a highly competent mercenary with the capacity to change sides as often as necessary to preserve his second-level leadership position. Not so. It's weirdly conceivable that for him the secret-police work was an expression of twisted patriotism, or that he first found dedication as Vock's signals expert, or again that both were inspired by the loopy logic and highflown, passionate ignorance of Miloczy's rhetoric; wherever it comes from, the face he shows me is not that of a frustrated crook, but a thwarted fanatic, one whose adversaries can only be misguided fools or, like me, knowing agents of error. I'm glad of the broad white line that separates us, and incredulous that of my own free will I'll soon be returning to share a country with such venomous feelings.

We have underestimated him, underestimated them, Pavel and I. Oh, certainly, we've talked about crack troops and tanks, and given Rietz's technical capability perhaps more than its due, and have not been lighthearted about the rather fantastic idea of a coup, but because we find Miloczy's notions fatuous we make the very common intellectual error of behaving as if everyone, in the end, must dismiss him as a bad and anachronistic joke. To be kept in mind: they would do what they had attempted with Wirath and his beloved daughter not because they are unprincipled rogues, but because they have a cause that sanctions anything. They are on the side of right, and we the evil or dismissible obstructions; they are as sincere about this as I am about — and I'm obliged to concede that there's nothing about which I have that kind of justifying belief, very little that most people nowadays believe in to that extreme, enough to cheat for, threaten for, betray friendship for. Except money, of course.

Pavel says. "Hi buddy. You okay?"

"I'm in Germany. Christa Rasch is with me." We're at Schönefeld Airport, to be exact, near Berlin, after quite a good late lunch with a celebratory bottle of Clos de Vougeot.

"That's great news. I hear tell her father has been anxious about her."

"She's phoning him now." Patiently warned not to tell him where she'll be for Christmas.

"You sure?" He's cautiously taking into account the chance of other ears.

"Oh yes. It's all over; I'll tell you all about it when I see you. I should be in Korava a little later."

"With Christa?" Clearly not advised.

"She's making other arrangements."

"Fine."

"We have a lot of things to discuss."

"Yeah." Pavel is puzzled; with Christa's safety provided for he would speak openly of breaking the story, if he didn't know me so well.

"Oh, hey — You remember that mole we were talking about? I got him here, right in my back yard." Arni. He must be staying with Pavel for safety.

"I was wondering if he had been trapped."

"Yeah, well, they're not as dumb as they look."

I speak with my father, his career having made him especially susceptible to the hush-hush syndrome; if I were to murmur, "Actually, I can't say any more just now," damping my voice to the proper F.O., burn-before-reading, end-of-the-western-world-as-we-have-known-it tone, it wouldn't matter if we were discussing fish and chips, he'd respond, I'm sure, "Understood, 'nuff said."

Before I can begin, he says, "Your Albertson chap just rang, about an hour ago."

"Oh?"

Dad hears the subtext (*Oh, God!*). "Nothing, really. Thought he'd find you here, wanted to wish you Happy Christmas. Said he was just off to Norwich himself."

"Oh." Albertson has a place, a converted malting or something, in Norfolk. A very political wife, about three children, he's not such a bad bloke, really.

I felicitate Dad on his K, and he says, "Ah, well," quotes Hamlet (not quite appositely) on funeral baked meats, but allows my mother is "no end bucked," though I can tell he's wallowing in glory. Then I ask if they'd mind putting up Christa Rasch for a few days.

"Christa Wiradza that was?"

Exactly." I adopt the voice. "There's been some hanky-panky about the election, and we just want to be sure she's out of harm's way. I can't go into detail."

"I understand. Of course, she's a lovely girl, we'd love to have her. Your mother will enjoy having her here."

(I smile; my mother's slender shoulders are having to bear quite a weight of transferred delight.) "Only, it'll have to be kept rather dark — " the voice again. "If word gets out, you'll have paparazzi on the doorstep, and the whole point is lost."

"'Nuff said. Is there anything I can do?" He means, along the corridors of power, quiet words in the right ear.

"I'll let you know if there is." But it's my mother who decides that Don Forbes, often pompous brother to the new-blooming Stephanie, can pick Christa up at the airport, adding with some concern and uncharacteristic directness, "You're not going to *marry* Christa, are you? Not that she isn't — " What we can't deny Christa is too self-evident to itemise.

Grotesque from either end, but mothers of only sons notoriously believe no woman could refuse their treasures. "Not unless I might have another for working-days; her grace is too costly to wear every day."

A chuckle of approving recognition, then, "That little

group near Maidstone is doing *Much Ado* in February. They've asked me to direct them, but I don't know."

I do; protesting that she's an academic, that her style is too old-fashioned, that it takes too much time away from her book, she'll put on jeans and a moth-ravaged cardy, drill the bejabers out of them, moan in anguish at verbal slips, let her hair straggle, smoke one whole cigarette (probably during or after dress-rehearsal), give herself over to despair, and enjoy every minute of it.

There's only ten minutes between Christa's flight and mine; she is to have the rare experience of flying coach class. Even so, with the car rental to get us here, the extravagant lunch, I'm becoming uneasy; none of this can be charged off to the agency unless I end up with Christa as our story, and my decision to postpone revelation makes no sense to her, hot for retribution.

"They know what they did — " she means, specifically, the Herders. "And they know we know what they did. You're just giving them time to make up a good story, alibis and stuff."

"I'm giving time for there to be an effective government in Korava again. You think Dalerant is capable of handling the Loyalists?" It must be because I've gone over this in my mind so often that I now have the sensation of a debate renewed. "Five days from now, Gorat should be back in power — I'm assuming your father won't find for the Loyalist position."

"You think he would, after this?"

"I believe he would, yes, if it had merit." Wirath, the incorruptible, would recuse himself if he believed the threat against his daughter had affected his objectivity. "I don't think he's going to. In the meantime — " time is growing short, her flight has been announced — "You can't say anything to your manager, or your friends, anybody who's going to start chattering to the press." Her circle is like a primitive society with a single all-purpose staple, publicity; they cultivate it, live on it, wear it, build with it, use it in trade...

She looks at me, big-eyed. "I thought you liked me."

"Do you like me?"

Conceptually novel, but she recovers. "Sometimes."

"If I wrote a film for you, would you act in it for nothing?"
"What?"

"It's not that I don't enjoy trekking all over Dusatia, pointing guns at people, destroying cars, dodging avalanches. It's just that no one pays me for rescue work, and I have to live."

"You did, didn't you," eyes glowing. "You came and rescued me. That's fabulous." She kisses me, but still fails to make the connection, though this is stating the case in terms she should understand: she is my story, I've earned it. Why do I feel so shabby? She, equally, has made love with me.

"You can thank me by not talking about it for the next few days."

"Is that what you're saying, you want an exclusive? Well, but if they come and ask me, did you do this, did this happen, I can't lie, can I."

"In Sevenoaks, no one is going to ask you anything but would you please pass the stuffing."

She has given me no assurance; for Pavel's sake as much as mine, I do extract her promise that when she returns to Dusatia, after her father's ruling in the Yellow Ballot business, she'll do up to an hour with me at RTPD, before giving any other interview. Not binding, of course, and I know that if her manager decides her story is worth six figures to a syndicate, or one of the American news-magazine shows, I'm left with nothing better than my own account. But I've been as hard-nosed as I care to be, and if she'll just stay off the phone while we're saving Dusatia, I'll butter my bread with the consciousness of virtue. If Albertson gives me the boot, I can always get a job with a publisher.

"Someday when we're about eighty — " she moves to where the tips of her toes are touching mine. "We'll run into each other in Naples or someplace, and have a blast reminiscing about all this. The great escape."

"We'll be seeing each other in a few days." She agrees to that, too, but I know what she has just done: clearly she wants to convey that we are not an item. Fallen in love with on about an hourly basis, she's managing it rather kindly; I can scarcely reply that while I probably wouldn't decline another turn in the hay, I have no desire to be her long-term appendage. Our farewell kiss is soft and tender, regrets very generalised.

Formalities in Korava have never been gruelling, but this time I'm spared even the cursory comparison of passport photo and self, accosted in the tunnel leading from the plane by a couple of plain-clothes but blatant coppers, the marginally better-dressed of which asks if I'm not "Kehranz" (near enough). A door is unlocked, and I'm led courteously through dim back ways to a tiny room where a grave official stamps my passport, then to a larger lounge with one-way glass in its windows, where Pavel greets me.

"Whatja expect?" — he's answering my expression. "You're hot cargo, buddy. You and the Buckeroos — this town ain't big enough for the three of you."

Buckeroos? Pavel has strayed out of his normal genre — and then I recognise his tormented linguistic ingenuity; the word is, of course, a corruption of *vaquero*, cowboy, not bad for "Herder" treated as an English word.

It seems I am staying with Pavel and Katja; my clothes and other belongings from the Schweitzerhof have migrated there, Pavel, as with my short cut past more public exposure at the airport, indulging in a rare flexing of muscle. But the car which stays behind us, its two occupants, are private security arrangements, and Pavel warns me my movements are going to be circumscribed for the next few days, in part due to limitations of available manpower.

"Once we start to sing, the heat is off; you go on the record and there's no percentage in trying to take you out. Did you talk to Wirath?"

Pavel has. He managed to see him at his home; a careful journalist, he wanted confirmation of the link between Christa's kidnapping and the Yellow Ballot issue. Yes, it was Rietz himself who had delivered the ultimatum to Wirath; Pavel heard nothing from Wirath to suggest the strain he had undergone, but for a

momentary lapse, a crack in the voice speaking of his relief when
Christa phoned to say she was safe, news hardly an hour old when
Pavel arrived. Then, something like Christa with me, Pavel was
perplexed to find Wirath counselling, nearly ordering delay in
making the crime public, till after he had published his verdict in
the Yellow Ballot question.

Logically, I agree with Pavel, while the order of
occurrence counts, the sequence in which events are revealed
should make no real difference; though it isn't known till after, it
will still be true and evident that Wirath had been threatened by
the Loyalists, or at least by some of their supporters, before
reaching his decision.

Yet, as Wirath recognises, in reality the difference is
critical. No matter when the charge comes Miloczy will call it,
and some believe him, part of the eternal media conspiracy to
defame the Loyalists, but that climate of charge and counter-
charge would make it virtually impossible for Wirath to give a
ruling in the Yellow Ballot affair without appearing to choose
sides. By Pavel's account, Wirath, standing aside from personal
feelings, seems to regard the kidnapping attempt as an organic
chemist might some outside bacteria trying to confuse research
results, a potential source of confusion to be neutralised and
excluded.

That I, though not on precisely the same grounds, have
reached the same position was what made Pavel think I must have
discussed it with the judge, who did instruct his daughter.

"He says he told Christa to keep her yap shut if she wants
to keep her nose clean."

Wirath, of course, said nothing remotely like that; Edward
G. Robinson probably said it to some weaselly little punk in a
movie sixty years ago. But thinking back to my debate with
Christa at the airport, it's clear now that the feeling of rehash came
not from me but from her; she had already disputed this — no,
wanted to dispute this — with her father, and her meek acceptance
of Sevenoaks was acquiescence in his views more than mine.

"Okay, fine with me — " Pavel, shrugging, drops into a
congenial but highly misleading role, that of the simple newsman,
deferring to subtleties too complex for his wits. "But we better
find a way of staying alive that long. When we get 'em, we gotta

get 'em good, no slip-ups." Holding the wheel underhand, he gives me a searching look. "How did you — no, don't tell me. Katja wants to hear every word, no sense telling it twice."

I make myself at home in a comfortable back room decorated, I don't have to ask by whom, with racy Hogarth and Rowlandson reproductions. Arni has been adopted as a larger equal by the two boys, whose room he is sharing; Katja is resigned if not reconciled to having Vaclav greet all newcomers with a throaty "*Haah*!" striking an attitude with lethal hands at the ready. She is remarkable cheerful, not detectably perturbed by the security arrangements, a car parked not-quite outside with one vigilant watcher, his colleague drifting impassively about the house, ready to answer the door or investigate any unexplained noise.

Arni's further adventures are soon told. On his return to the Eagle's Nest, having delivered news of the car-crash, he was asked or instructed by Mara to meet Rietz at the Dvygarmicsz station — this must have been before Rietz's actual arrival there — taking Lisuk with him. Aware his supposed secret mission wouldn't survive a face-to-face encounter with Rietz, deducing Lisuk couldn't know the way, Arni instead had taken the Fridova road from Zrndja. Reaching a suitably deserted spot, he stopped the car, and used Lisuk's own gun to make him get out. He then drove back tamely to Korava, made his report to Pavel, and was taken in for his own safety, as I now am.

My story, lightly edited, is recounted after dinner, after the boys are bathed and bedded (though Arni is allowed to stay up late); I tell, for example, about the avalanche, but not Christa's tigrish defence of her virtue — there's no need to mention any of her exasperating ways. When I get to the night (only last night, though it seems far longer) in the shelter, Pavel's pupils noticeably dilate.

"You slept together?" We're in Dusatian, which accounts for the relatively colourless terminology.

"There wasn't much choice."

"You got to — " and here Katja pointedly decides we should have coffee, and goes into the kitchen.

"It was cold up there." Heroically resisting, I can't quite avoid a grin.

"Oh yeah, I tell the world — " in English, which doesn't trouble wide-eyed Arni. "Not for long, huh? That must have been something, that's a world class piece, my friend, those are some fabulous legs to have wrapped around you. What, she goes in for a little rough stuff, huh? "

He is indicating the scrapes on my cheek, but not irrationally, I'm reminded of Angèle, and tell Pavel about Herder's present to her. He has been making occasional jottings in a little notebook, and here he turns to a previous page to add this point.

"We can get that away from her without turning her in. Christ, she's an idiot, she needs a keeper. Your buddies Lisuk and Jenadju, they're both involved in penny-ante crime; the Korava police are going to pick them up when they come home; they got enough unsolved heists to hold them on suspicion a few days. That's as a favour to me, but as soon as the kidnapping case is out in the open they can be charged; they could turn into a great pair of canaries when they look at fifteen years in the big house."

Wirath even declined to discuss with Pavel the possible extent of the plot to kidnap his daughter, how far the National Loyalist party itself was implicated. Pavel is more hopeful than I that there will be direct links back to Vock and even Miloczy; both Herders and Erhardt Rietz seem to me the limit of sustainable charges, and I have no doubt the official party will without a blink throw them to the sharks, misguided enthusiasts who embarked on a course at utter variance with Miloczy's message of national renewal and respect for the law — at the extreme, might even show them to be undercover workers for Gorat, the entire plot an attempt to besmirch the sacred Loyalist banner. As for Pavel's draconian sentences, I am more than dubious; with a vigorous defence — and Herder can certainly afford that — it's going to be hard to prove any kidnapping ever took place; under cross-examination Christa will have to admit she went to Eagle's Nest of her own choice, and that she was never under any kind of constraint. The threat to Wirath is real, and his reputation will make him an unimpeachable witness, but to get a conviction the prosecution might be wise to limit the charges to some sort of conspiracy to commit a felony, which doesn't sound like fifteen years to me.

Katja, bearing three coffees and a cup of warm milk, has returned. "What you are saying, then, is that it is you, not the law, that must see justice done. You and Pavel, but Pavel can only follow; he can't make charges, only report them."

He nods resignedly. "You wanna say General Vock eats human flesh, then I can say, according to a report today on BBC, or wherever, General Vock is cannibal, the General denies the charge and claims the piles of human bones behind his house ain't nobody's business but his. You open up the can, I'll put worms on my menu."

"I want to consult with Niemek." More than ever.

"The old man? We ought to be able to arrange that. You can corner him at the President's Ball on S. Stepan." Very like Pavel not to ask how this followed from his half-challenge.

"Boxing Day," Katja says with pride, in English.

The event is a tradition, if hardly an ancient one, begun in imitation of Vienna's New Year's Ball. Dusatia's German connection historically was with Brandenburg, which replaced Poland as Dusatia's overlord early in the 18th Century; contrary to the cynical but pacifying principle which had ended the Thirty Years War, Dusatia was for a century a Catholic land with a Protestant prince; perhaps Slavs didn't count. Then, at the beginning of 1807, following Prussia's crushing defeat at Jena, Dusatia had asserted its independence, following the United States and France in declaring a republic.

It hardly lasted a season; as soon as the roads were passable, Polish cavalry came in to overthrow that government, supported by Bonaparte, who had assigned Dusatia to the Duchy of Warsaw (although in 1812, preparing for the Russian Campaign, he changed his mind and gave it back to Prussia), but the hundred-day republic became something of a legend, much as Niemek's brave, brief, liberal dawning did a century-and-a-half later.

In 1815, with Napoleon tidied away, the Congress of Vienna, redrawing the map of Europe, in a whimsical swap with Prussia for some Baltic territory made Dusatia part of the Austro-Hungarian Empire. This brought an oddly divided period; while nationalist fervour (mild pamphlets, madder pistols) fomented among artisans, artists and the intelligentsia, the merchant classes and of course the bureaucratic tribe, both led by the Dusatian clergy, fell in love with Vienna. Lanner and the elder Josef Strauss, followed by his all-conquering son, conducted waltzes in Korava in the 1840s and 50s, and Koravan society's taste for operetta, sentimental amorous intrigue and *Schlag* survived the country's reversion to north German rule after Austria's defeat in the Prussian war, and subsequent inclusion in the German Empire declared at Versailles in 1871. To a degree, a ghostly nostalgia for the Habsburg half-century, like a trace of *Schmalz* flavoured with Imperial Tokay, lingers still.

In that imitative time, Korava wished to have its own New Year's Ball, but Vienna wouldn't permit it; the Winter Republic had been declared on January 1, 1807, and the date was observed as an anniversary by open and secret nationalists, all those most worrisome to Metternich's spies. It was feared such a ball might become the occasion for public demonstrations embarrassing to Imperial rule. Instead, the day after Christmas was chosen, and in various forms, with an interregnum in the years when Nazi domination became Nazi occupation, the event, since 1919 called the President's Ball, has gone on ever since. Even during the most iron-fisted days of the Muscovite era (like an especially plushy production of *Sleeping Beauty* by the Bolshoi in Stalin's time, or Brezhnev's, there would have been a wry charm in seeing the commissars and *apparatchiki* aping the graces of a *fin de siècle* aristocracy).

"Me, at the President's Ball?" It is held at an adjunct of the Presidential palace, once the Winter Riding School, and as Pavel reminds me, discreet talks are as much a tradition as the dance itself, though business deals, political alliances, real estate transactions, ambassadorial chinwags, have largely replaced the flirtations, assignations and alleged consummations for which the numerous *salles privées* were formerly famed and maybe designed.

"You're invited. Foreign press."

"I have nothing to wear." (*My God! Perrault.*)

"Let me have the suit that fits you best for a couple of hours tomorrow," (*said the fairy godmother*). Katja knows the woman who, from a large and varied stock, hires out dozens of dress suits for the occasion.

"If I can find a pumpkin — "

"I'll turn it into a Bentley, but only till midnight." Katja and I share the same smile; it is very nice to be like that with someone; attuned.

"But now," she says, "Who's going to carry Arni off to bed?" After only a sip of his hot milk, the giant is slumbering.

VIII

Christmas Eve is a sour and muddled day, an alternation and sometimes a mixture of rain and snow icing the bare trees and filling the streets with a treacherous freezing slush; Katja at home, determined for the boys' sake to preserve a festive normality. At the studios, where I go with Pavel, there is again heightened security, but that has been true ever since Rietz's demonstrators first appeared. Pavel comes and goes, speaks on the phone a great deal, dispatches people with messages, while I do an enormous amount of writing, much of which is bound to be scrapped, since I compose alternative versions of news stories to fit various contingencies. We assume, Pavel and I, that Wirath, even if he invalidates the Yellow Ballot, will stop well short of vacating the entire election, but I have a megalomaniac fantasy in a Hemingway vein of ripe masochism, of broadcasting a virulent denunciation of Miloczy and Vock and all their works, as their storm-troopers close in on the studio intent on stilling all dissent; *Long Live Free Dusatia*! he cried, as the machine-guns opened up. As well to be prepared.

In a less melodramatic instance of that same Baden-Powell spirit, I write but don't yet transmit an immensely long E-mail for Albertson, avoiding substance, but priming him for the possibility of a very big story, the probable need for some hefty cash disbursements.

I have broken our journey to the studios, and maintained our probably overdone security, using a phone-box at the central post office to ring Kent, and find that Christa arrived safe, though a little miffed, having been unable to persuade Don Forbes to make a detour and stop at Harrods. My mother, who explained unnecessarily that it would have been folly to tackle the traffic, late afternoon so near Christmas, herself sounded faintly off-centre, but assured me all was well, Christa making herself at home. No irony detectable, but for me a peculiar stab of remorse, in the recognition of irreconcilable mismatch between Christa and a Sevenoaks Christmas, hibiscus in a herb-garden.

Now, at the station, I ring Sarajevo, and again fail to reach Mireille, perhaps for the last time; she is said to be holidaying in Dubrovnik, and her room-sharer, plain Lise from Lyon, who dislikes me, takes care to add, "*Avec son Américain.*" Another casualty of the Yellow Ballot crisis.

From one of his phone-calls, Pavel comes in grinning to tell me that Rietz's train-journey to the north and the plaster on his forehead have a single explanation supplied by Pavel's friend with the police; driving too fast (as he usually does) he struck a patch of ice in Grdacz Square; deprived of that friction between tyre and surface which alone makes motion controllable he achieved an involuntary stop by slamming into the rear of a furniture-van. Rietz had by far the worst of the encounter. I smile too, although it's possible that without that accident, Christa and I would have remained dead to our adversaries, and had an eventless journey back to Korava. On the other hand, Rietz, driving, might have arrived at the Eagle's Nest at much the same time as Arni and I, and that would have been disaster.

All Pavel's dealings are with the "blue" police, Korava's ordinary force, and without losing his cheerful face he tells me a Captain Iakadju with the *dzhăndarmi*, who wears National Loyalist colours on his lapel, and is thought to be close to Rietz, has been trying to find out what his blue colleagues are up to. Not surreptitiously, quite the contrary, he speaks loudly about "lack of cooperation," and complains of a breakdown in liaison, with dark hints of taking his grievance to higher authority.

"Some hopes, huh? Where's he gonna go? The minister is a lame goose till Wirath gives, and he's Gorat's man anyway. My guy at the ministry is civil service, they'll tell Iakajdu to file a written complaint in triple — what do you call it?"

"Triplicate." I don't correct his other lapse in idiom; one crippled fowl is as good as another, and why, in any case, is lameness so important to a bird that spends far more of its time on wing or water than at the waddle?

"They are running scared, my friend."

Well, but we knew that, or knew it should be so; Herder and Rietz must be wondering how soon they'll be facing charges, and can't be hoping for much from the Yellow Ballot decision. I wonder if Pavel is less blithe than he seems over this evidence of an internal struggle already begun; I am still filled with a hopeless dismay by the mere idea of policemen taking sides in a political struggle.

It's not quite that simple, as Pavel is aware; there is a question of critical mass; given political stability the opinions of individual officials don't much matter, whereas at a time like this their views and their potential actions only exacerbate the unstable condition, which all too easily can become the worm feeding on its own tail; what Dusatia needs, what all these fragile new-born countries need, is the kind of boring reliability that encourages foreign capital to invest (and domestically-generated wealth to stay out of Swiss banks). Yet political calm that reassures investors can only be maintained in conditions of economic stability, the necessary condition for healthy government, and so endlessly on. The trick is to create or simulate *enough* confidence that real reasons for confidence begin to take root.

Given access to the RTPD database, I do some neglected biographical research, particularly General Vock, who, I find, was quite an ordinary young officer, his career picking up momentum after his marriage to the daughter (now deceased) of the head Soviet military "advisor" — effectively boss over the Dusatian Chief of Staff. Tactical nuclear weapons training in the Crimea, armoured warfare in Thuringia with an ancient veteran of epic battles on the Steppes (I don't say on which side), command of an élite tank brigade, a jump in rank from colonel to major-general when, in response to some fresh American deployment of weaponry, the unit was expanded into a full division, equipped with new-model Soviet tanks — into, in fact, Javelin. Though the Russian wife died in a plane-crash in 1981, and was succeeded by a much-younger Korava girl in 1983, there's no real indication of when Vock's conversion came, from the perfect satellite to the Dusatian patriot who outwitted and embarrassed the Red Army; only weeks before his famous exploit he was publicly hymning the "indissoluable ties of friendship and mutual respect" between

Korava and Moscow — it is evident that his mastery of and reliance on the sonorous but null cliché long predates his entry into overt politics, or his empty interview with me.

Late, Pavel comes in with a print-out from the wire service.

"Hey, Boris Kalashnikov bought the farm. He was only 54 — "

"*General* Kalashnikov?" The name rings instant bells.

"Cancer of the pancreas — I guess he spent too much time at Chernobyl; they put him in charge of security there, in case anybody wanted to heist two-headed calves. That's what he was, the odd-job man. He headed the Kremlin team that negotiated the Red Army withdrawal from Strbjena, did a nice clean job, he was a civilised guy."

"He negotiated with Vock?"

"Uh-uh. Not after Vock had caught the Red Army with its drawers down — twice."

Most of this story I know quite well, but do not interrupt; small countries with little home-grown history to define them must be indulged in recitations of their folk-lore.

"Strbjena was supposed to be like, Moscow's Dusatian Gibraltar, but Vock had been reading their radio traffic, and knew had they had pulled out combat troops to send to Lithuania, which they thought was about to explode. Which it did, so when Vock jumped that Red infantry assault battalion, he knew there was nothing but cooks, clerks and truck-drivers manning Strbjena.

"So he shows up there with eighty tanks, all his choppers, there's a ten-minute fire-fight, one hero Russky M.P. killed, end of battle, four hundred more Red Army personnel disarmed. Now, Gorat has done business with Ivan before, I guess he figures they're ready to cut their losses, they got trouble in the Baltic, trouble down in Chechnya, trouble right there in Moscow, the only thing to make them dig in their heels is if it looks like humiliation. So he tells Vock, pipe down, and he names a special envoy, from outside the government — you'll never guess who."

"Juan-Micel Herder."

"You didn't guess, somebody told you."

"I found out today, doing research."

"*Gaspodi*, I never realised, that's where Herder and Vock must have first started getting palsy-walsy; Herder was supposed to be totally independent, just looking for a reasonable solution; when he *persuaded* Vock to release the last of his prisoners, hostages really, staff-level officers, as a kiss-and-make-nice gesture, it must have been a deal between the two of them. Anyway, it did the job; Kalashnikov okayed a complete pull-out, Herder okayed a Soviet transition team, who came in and packed up most of the Soviet hardware, they had a flag down, flag up party, and the Ivans handed over Strbjena."

"To Vock. And Javelin Division has held it ever since."

"Sure, to Vock. Whadda ya want? He was our national hero. You think anybody was gonna tell your Nelson he couldn't screw Dame Hambone after he won Trafalgar?"

"Lady Hamilton. Nelson died at Trafalgar."

"Bad move, ain't life a bitch? You onto something?"

"Perhaps." About three years ago, I couldn't be sure without checking my records, that same Russian general, Kalashnikov, in Ukraine for some negotiations to do with dismantling medium-range missile sites, speaking at a news conference on the disarmament process (the fleshy face of a cheerful farmer disguising a keen but brooding intellect) had remarked that "to his knowledge" there were functional Soviet nuclear weapons that had passed out of Red Army control. Most assumed he was talking about cases like the missile bases in Belarus, Ukraine and Slovenia, and Black Sea naval units now under the Ukrainian flag; but those were questions he'd already dealt with, and I'd been interested enough to try for a private interview with Kalashnikov.

"No dice."

"What he said must have upset someone; he was reassigned to Moscow; I lost track of him. I did a story on his news-conference, but hardly anyone wanted to use it, those who did buried it."

"Yeah. Nobody wants to hear about nukes, ding-dong, the wicked old witch is dead."

It is true; the unlooked-for disintegration of the Soviet Union, apparent end of Assured Mutual Annihilation, produced an unreal euphoria which has not yet dispersed — which is not allowed to disperse, resentment greeting any reminder of the realities, the thousands of armed and targeted missiles still in place, the instability of political control over their destiny, the battalions of bomb-building, bomb-designing technicians cut loose with no comparably remunerative reserve occupation. There are countries awash in oil, hard currency and endemic political irrationality who want nothing to complete their happiness except the weapons of terror, and countries energy-hungry, with desperate balance-of-payments deficits and nothing anyone wants to buy, except their unused weapons, or the components or the technology for making them; none of this can expect any sustained attention either in print or on the air.

"Kalashnikov said something else, about negotiations being subjected to inordinate pressure from both sides — at the time, most of us assumed he meant the Ukrainian discussions, and that was why Moscow brought him home. If I'd known he was the Russian man at Strbjena, I would have been even more interested than I was. I'll have to get a transcript."

"There's a chance it's in our database. Can you come any closer on the date?"

"I can get it off the web; it's bound to be in the files in Kiev." If necessary, I can probably get a tape; I am on good terms with Ukrainian State Television. "In the context, he can only have been talking about *tactical* weapons — otherwise, why particularly Red *Army* control?"

Pavel is disbelieving. "You're telling me that when they pulled out of Strbjena they left tactical nukes for Vock to play with?"

"Nuclear cannon, perhaps?"

"Couldn't happen. Where's the percentage for the Ivans? Somebody would have let the cat out of bag by now — "

"Only Javelin personnel have been there, besides Herder."

"American military intelligence, C.I.A., I hear they got every nuclear device in the world pinpointed down to about two metres."

"Up to the moment the Warsaw Pact started coming apart, American military intelligence and the C.I.A. were saying the Soviet system was good for another hundred years. They estimated the allied forces might suffer twenty thousand casualties taking Kuwait back from the Iraquis, but had the Chinese air force and half the army ready to join the students' democracy movement. A chap working for them, top security clearance, paid cash for a million-dollar house, his wife was spending fifty thousand a month, all on a sixty-thousand dollar annual income, this went on for years, and it took a Russian defector to tell them he was selling secrets. I wouldn't bet they know where every ocean in the world is."

I think about Vock, when I interviewed him, his undefined expansionist grandiosities, about Miloczy, his inspirer, who never seems more than five minutes away from proclaiming a crusade. "What we may have here is the world's only minority party that's also an independent nuclear power."

Every so often one becomes thoroughly convinced of a wild improbability, and then it's hard not to be annoyed when others fail to see the plain arithmetic. Pavel, though, is right to be sceptical; as he says, what was in it for the Russians?

All right, but suppose Vock knew where some bodies were buried — or better, Herder, the former C.I.A. man; he might have inside information on Red Army officers. For that muddled time, I couldn't guess whether exposure as a neo-Stalinist or a radical Westerniser would be fatal to a Soviet officer, but of course if somebody — Kalashnikov himself? — had actually been passing military information to the West, where his political sympathies lay would not be the issue — and Kalashnikov, as a colonel, had been military attaché in Washington for six years. That required no research at all to determine; it was in the wire service report of his death.

So Herder (let's say) blackmailed Kalashnikov into overlooking (let's say) a battery of nuclear cannon when taking inventory, and Kalashnikov reluctantly went along, but it gnawed at his conscience, and four or five years later he drops a great big hint into the middle of his news conference, which nobody is sharp enough to pick up.

"Something else to put on the table — " Pavel is laconic, not wishing to quarrel with me — "when you have your pow-wow with Niemek."

That, I find, is already prepared. Pavel, for the late news, has been assembling what he calls a "make nice" Christmas Eve piece, how the great and famous of Dusatia are to be spending their day; Dalerant being highminded and Catholic and prime-ministerial, Gorat at home with comfy Deresza, two sons, daughter, brand-new grandson, Vock with the languorous second wife saying hello to General Firkus and his old comrades of the Javelin Division, the President, beginning to look frail, in his modest, middle-class enclave in a mere corner of the palace, Mme. Niemek speaking with unimpeachable sincerity about the need to extend a hand to those for whom these are hard times. Not Wirath, which would be out of key, but for a serious moment there is a reference to the impending decision, with a held shot of the High Court building, before cutting to the archbishop presiding over early service (midnight mass will be on live). This would all normally be straightforward staff work, but Pavel took on the Niemek segment himself, largely to convey my wish for a private talk.

"The old guy says he'll be *enchanté* to see you again."

"If I don't get anywhere with Niemek, I'm going to do the story on my own."

"What story? You got nothing, guesses."

"Then you can go on the air and call me irresponsible. No matter how thin it is, they'll have to have a look." For the only time in my career, I plan to, in essence, fake a story, attribute my own guesses to a tip from anonymous sources. Pavel and I have been worrying ourselves over tanks in the streets of Korava, but if Vock has access to functioning nuclear weapons —

Still not accepting it, Pavel can't resist playing with the implications. "Jeez, he could hole up there in Strbjena, and who's gonna try flushing him out?"

It's worse than that. If he started to make threats, there's no doubt Nato or the United Nations, or both, would intervene, but it's hard to see what they could do once the weapons were in place, a couple of cannon concealed within range of Korava. If they began firing, they might be detected and destroyed, but when they start firing is too late; the chance of one round is enough to hold a whole country hostage. It may be difficult to imagine how a self-proclaimed ardent patriot, even when cornered, could make use of such a threat against his own country, but not necessarily more inexplicable than what his friends had already attempted with

Wirath; I had seen that crazy righteousness in Rietz's loathing eyes, Miloczy's audience in a frenzy of accord — oh, yes, I can believe it.

I am ridiculously sentimental about Christmas, and childishly resent having it turn into an irrelevancy, a day to be waited out, but with all my apprehensions continuing to churn, nothing can be done to put the Dingley Dell spirit back at centre-stage. No one else seems fidgety or abstracted; Pavel has turned the news department over to his most junior people; he's cheerfully certain there are bound to be patches of dead air, stories illustrated with the wrong footage, mispronunciations and missed cues, any of which would upset him if he witnessed them; the television is not turned on. TV news broadcasts on Christmas Day, he says, is like buttons on the cuff of a suit, nobody has any use for them, but they have to be there.

Katja demands instructions as to the pudding, taking it out in its small basin and asking if it will be enough for the six of us, seven if Vasz has some (at two, Thom isn't to be asked). "Seven?" I query, but assure her it is customarily served in very small slices; she has, besides, a rich indigenous holiday sweet, a kind of cake layered with cherries. There is between us today an indefinable constraint, which I try to ascribe to my own unhappy preoccupation, but remain with the conviction it is Katja who has removed herself, is it from the intimacy of last night's playfulness? What passes between us at any time is infinitely subtle, and the state which exists between any two human beings at any time infinitely resistant to analysis; we know who is a friend, who only an acquaintance, sense disparities of need or trust, adjust without knowing we're doing it to shifts in the receptivity or accord of even a very new or very old familiar. But there is no calibrated scale, not so much as a vocabulary, for bringing these matters into conscious consideration; perplexed by a sudden change in degree of closeness, all we can do is identify perplexity, although to do so may help first to fix and then to widen a gap which till then may be imagined, or caused by a toothache, a hangnail, an unexpectedly large phone-bill. Best is to be patient, and decidedly to avoid entry into that escalating spiral of estrangement which begins with a question such as, "Why are you being like this today?" passes through denial to counter-charge, and ends with wounds, and offended dignity in brittle voices.

While Pavel and I are cooking a lot of scrambled eggs, Katja's father arrives, cheerful, with presents for the boys and a very firm pat for his daughter's bejeaned bottom when they hug. There is a boisterous exchange of affectionate insults with Pavel, and for me a handshake with a deep bow, as he identifies me as "the famous English Duszacji." He has steel-grey hair, dark, ironic eyes and a hawk nose, happily not bequeathed to his daughter, though handsome enough on his long, strong face. He is so well-dressed as to verge on the dapper — he reminds me, in fact, of a gallicised North African diplomat, including the courtliness with me, but he is in fact a professor, teaching chemistry at the university. Except for the hair he could pass himself off as a weatherbeaten forty-five, ten years less than his actual age. I like him at once, and certainly no less when he produces and opens a magnum of Roederer, which we drink from tumblers with the scrambled eggs, Katja continuing to assemble an epic stuffing for the goose, engaging her father in a lively debate as to the relative merits of sour prunes and sour cherries as an ingredient. Arni, who is solemnly attentive to everything, has a small sip of the champagne, and returns philosophically to Pepsi-Cola. For which he must be saluted; at his age I already liked the taste (and even more, the fugitive texture) of champagne very much, but if I hadn't would have pretended to, so as not to fail as a person of taste and discernment.

Besides, when there's still five hours to go before dinner, a magnum isn't so much among four — not long after noon, five, when Marjenka arrives, mid-twenties, attractive, not quite pretty, chestnut hair, firm mouth, a tailored look, thick ankles. She is a statistical analyst in what for Dusatia is a foetal industry, polling and market research, and Pavel hails her with a loud heartiness and hair-trigger display of hospitality, pouring her champagne, adjourning us to the lounge so that she can be seated, making sure everyone is clear who she is and what she does — a performance which convinces me he doesn't much like her.

Apparently she's Katja's, fellow-member of a crafts society; very slowly and hesitatingly I begin to suspect this must be the brilliant, accomplished, beautiful friend I was offered as a bribe for being here, before circumstances made it inevitable. My still somewhat incredulous assumption is strengthened when Katja, emerging from the kitchen, has a sharp, assessing look to see how Marjenka and I are getting on; the answer, if I could give one, is politely, without the remotest chance of anything more.

Not that there's much objectively to find fault with in Marjenka; she laughs at jokes in the uncertain, sidelong manner of those lacking a sense of humour, and has a habit that could easily become tiresome of very humbly offering extremely tentative views, and having ready for anyone who takes the bait a crushing avalanche of incontrovertible evidence. These aren't fatal flaws, but it was Katja who praised her brilliance, Katja who hymned her beauty — I mean, if Schubert told you he had a friend who wrote good tunes, or Yeats that he knew a poet who could break your heart, you would expect something pretty special.

Actually, though far too young and not seriously to be considered, storied Ljuba attracts me more. Arni (who earlier, set by Katja to chopping up components of her stuffing, did so very deliberately, and with the absorbed precision of a neuro-surgeon) is absent for dinner, in the general unexplained relaxation of security permitted to drive off to see his family; it is a long, leisured dinner, and he returns in time for pudding, bringing Ljuba, small and trim in a tapestried top over close-fitting ankle-length grey underwear. When smaller Vasz greets her with his martial arts attitude and growl, she too goes *en garde*, launches a spectacular series of pirouettes and head-grazing kicks, to end by dumping him on his back and tickling him; pert, birdlike face, not really pretty except for her general vitality and youth, she then charms Pavel by hailing him with, "At last!" in a tone that echoes his legendary standing with Arni. Yet Katja likes her at a glance, and when Katja's father exacts his toll on her small, very firm, squarish bottom (intuitively omitted when meeting Marjenka), Ljuba responds in cheerfully robust kind, obviously to his entire satisfaction.

Katja asks me if there isn't something about "setting fire" to the pudding, and when we're together in the kitchen ends any possible doubt about the Marjenka case by asking, isn't she lovely?

"Lovely." Trying not to sound ironic, but disappointed with Katja, understanding now the origin of her distance today. She converted me to a project.

I'm in one of those times, I think everyone must experience them, when everything mysteriously, if not always happily, meshes with the theme of current preoccupation — likely, this phenomenon is due more to the organic nature of a human brain imposing its template on what is processed than to a sudden objective perception of mystical unities, but it's always strangely persuasive while happening.

Rietz, Vock, the Herders, the Loyalists, have fixed my thoughts on the fated immorality of corporate identities, their cynical expediency. Whenever people band together to share what they believe is some high and noble or useful purpose, the organisation that results may have a certain amount of dedication, very often idealism. Yet almost always, in striving to realise the common goal, the group is willing to trade virtue for effectiveness, and the individual allotment of scruples tends to neither the sum nor the average, but to nullity, as they pool their various justified exceptions to uprightness, moving towards a shared alternative universe where the cause may forgive any action.

It is hardly a closely-guarded secret that there still persists, among numbers of the world's married women, a little-formalised, mainly unspoken, largely unacknowledged international conspiracy to eliminate bachelorhood. Not a violent plot, it is aimed only at the condition, and is in its own view entirely benificent, though its means can be ruthless and utterly unprincipled, with lies and misrepresentations taken in stride *pour le bon motif*. Its participants, except in twos or threes, rarely consult, but what it has in common with more structured movements is the adoption of that collective mind where individual traits are sacrificed to indiscriminate principles. I'm afraid I've used a lot of words to analyze a lightning perception; subscribing to a corporate virtue, Katja has allowed the abstraction, bachelor, to efface the reality, friend.

Being on the same side with Katja, being with her in our own private conspiracy, is too important to me to pretend I'm not hurt, but perhaps I'm merely getting maudlin over a Christmas that declines to open and blossom, and Katja is not to blame for that killing frost. Forcing a bright patter, I warm a small amount of a Dusatian speciality, ferocious vodka with slight orange flavour and colour, and unheard-of proof; poured over the pudding it ignites at the touch of a match into a highly satisfactory garnish of flame, so that when I carry it in there is a burst of applause, and Arni, giving his woofing laugh, says, "Like that Cicada."

He gets a quick frown from Pavel, but Ljuba must already have heard the story, and the others smile politely at what they suppose the resurrection of a worn joke about the famous recall.

Finding that Ljuba is a runner, Katja's father, half avuncular but wholly flirtatious, plies her with an unlikely subject for a chat-up, the chemistry of anaerobic respiration, which he expounds with evidently spellbinding command. The performance perhaps inspires Marjenka; she launches into a detailed exposition of the *weighting* process for polls and surveys and the ever-more-refined technique of finding representative samples; still cheerleading, Katja interjects that her friend's work on behalf of an American soap-maker so impressed them that they want her to design surveys for several neighbouring countries.

While alert enough to remain polite, my attention is only marginal; I'm pondering the case of Katja's father. While the elapse of eight years, and the early death itself, may be responsible for some idealising, it can't be doubted that he loved Katja's mother, and that the marriage was a happy one; was she *complaisante* in the old-fashioned way, or happily oblivious to his philandering, or is it only since widowhood that he's become a player? Sentimentality aside, it's those who were happy who are most likely to marry again (among the widowed, that is; the miserably married who divorce often have a successor on hand), but his profession must put many a Ljuba in Katja's father's way, and I can sympathise with a reluctance to choose one, where it means saying farewell to all the rest, actual and as-yet unmet. Deplored by the international league which has tried to throw me and Marjenka together, we hesitators have at least the merit of taking marriage seriously; why subscribe to a vow so solemnly sonorous as *forsaking all others* until you mean to mean it?

Ebbing. Mingled with the remembered sadness of old Christmases where I wanted the magic not to end is my impatience for this one to be over and present reality to resume. Though Pavel has circumspectly omitted to ask just what I plan to say to Niemek, I want to rehearse with him, get his comments.

A restive Arni with no verbal armoury for duelling with Dad paws at Ljuba like a conditionally friendly bear. I don't know how (when neither is in intensive training) they manage their carnal congress; Arni, whose family is rural, in Korava shares one room with a male friend and a gas-ring, while Ljuba's parents are ruefully described as old-fashioned. Knowing that trait often demands a degree of willed blindness, where overnight absences may pass unremarked, I privately offer to swap beds and share the boys' room for tonight, but Arni glumly says Ljuba has to be back this evening; we achieve compromise by everyone not noting the absence of the young pair during Katja's promised showing of Alastair Sim's *Scrooge*, a virtuoso display on which it is hard to focus, my thoughts spiralling on like this sentence, unable to let go of questions to be answered only with events, except when Katja's father or Marjenka (to whom he has shifted his attentions) ask for clarification of some point, and I have to compose extempore entries for a Dickensian-Dusatian phrase book. It is, after all, in the family; my mother had to find equivalents for puzzles like *Each thing meets in mere oppugnancy*.

Film done, and coffee, the will to disperse comes uppermost. Pavel produces his car-keys but makes no move to use them; Marjenka arriving was dropped off by friends, and I gather the plan was for me in turn to violate security by driving her home. Katja's father, however, asks her where she lives and swears it is hardly out of his way, an inaccuracy given no respect by his daughter when they and the younger pair have left. She has noted and assessed without visible comment the courteous, formal nature of my parting with Marjenka, *sina die.*

"More snow," Pavel predicts.

From time to time I attend a function where a dinner-jacket is, if not required, strongly recommended, always complain for the sake of form, and always end by privately enjoying the sense it imparts of belonging to a particular fellowship — one which, properly considered, takes in not only elegant diners, the inner circle of a wedding, a few elect rows at a prize-giving or a gala performance at the opera, but also waiters and assorted masters of ceremonies, including those who bellow the next event from the middle of a boxing ring. Nevertheless, I've almost made my peace with what Mireille's new companion would call a tux — but *tails*! Though it should have, it never occurred to me that the preferred rig for the President's Ball would be a full set of tails, the absurdly long-waisted trousers, snowy waistcoat, tie to complete the predictable discomfort of a chin-lifting, neck-sawing shirt — now I am to belong to the company of conductors (musical, not bus), stage magicians and (lacking only a number on my back) competitive ballroom dancers.

At the shoes, Italian, patent-leather and halfway to being slender ankle-boots, I draw the line; a range of three pairs, labelled at or near my size, has been provided, but though one, a half-size larger than my norm, claims in the place where the heel would rest, to being *larga*, all three have a pencil-point taper such as no human foot ever possessed, certainly not my functional clumpers. Besides, despite elasticised inserts, the shoes are rigid enough to serve as coffins for small fish, and require, except no one could endure the agony, a fortnight of dedicated tramping to break them in. My own well-worn all-purpose black, buffed to a high shine, are going to have to serve.

Another waiting day, with some time at the studios; not till mid-afternoon does Pavel allow himself to become anxious over the fact that Arni has neither returned nor been heard from, at first surmising that he and Ljuba have found congenial surroundings. At three, after ringing Katja and finding there's still no word, he talks to Ljuba at home, and hangs up with a grimmer face; she has seen nothing of Arni since he dropped her off last night.

"Shit," Pavel says, after leaving Ljuba with airy reassurances. "We got sloppy. Christmas, what's that to those punks?"

I tighten my mouth and say nothing, having thought the same from the first.

"Let's see. He all of a sudden got a bright idea to run out and see his folks. Could be, that's some nothing place back east, Eridza way, but they're not on the phone. Naah, he would've called. Unless he figured I would blow a gasket — he could have laid odds on that — " while speculating, Pavel is tapping out a number.

It is that of the garage where Arni works, and there, too, he hasn't been seen. Actually, when he became my driver he was given a week off, supposedly to attend a muscle-building jamboree in Cracow, and now Pavel has to pretend a lapse of memory to explain his phone-call. Using one finger to disconnect, he fingers another number, and is talking to his friend with the police, and for the first time calling Arni *missing*.

He briefly describes him, listens, and says, "Well, you can look for the damned car. It's a late-model dark red four-door Toyota. I don't know, ninety-five, ninety-six, rental plates. No, I've got the number on the rental agreement at home, I can — " but I am already using the other phone to ring Katja.

"In the bin on my desk," Pavel tells her, and shortly is able to give the plate number to his friend.

"I understand," he says in answer to some disclaimer, "but this may be tied in with all the other stuff." He listens, and exclaims, "Shit," in response to some new information.

"Lisuk is missing, too," he tells me after ending his conversation with a renewed exhortation to "do all you can."

"How, missing?"

"They had to spring him and Jenadju — a fancy mouthpiece showed up and said, charge them or release them. Herder, you can bet, but he doesn't have to tell who's paying him. Lisuk lives in a — domestic hotel? — "

"Residential hotel?"

"Right, it's a real crap dump out by the brewery, about half the people who live there are small-time crooks, grifters and drifters. The cops had him staked out there, they wanna get his goat, they're pissed off about having to let him go. But they lost him, he didn't come home last night, and he still ain't showed up."

"It is Christmas," I offer. "Even petty criminals may have parents to see," (-*rents to see*, my mind idiotically supplies).

Pavel nods, but is not consoled. "I took Lisuk's heater away from Arni — he's not a guy you wanna see packing a loaded gun, but, shit! I'm an idiot, letting him go wandering around on his own — Christmas! Listen, my friend, you're not going one step without somebody's watching you, till we got these hoods behind bars."

Till then. The danger any of us are in, if it exists, comes mainly from letting our adversaries believe they can still somehow cover up the kidnapping; Pavel and I give urgent consideration to putting the story on the evening news and giving it to the agency, regardless of what Wirath desires, or Niemek might counsel. If the Loyalists have Arni — and while it's hard to see how his path and Lisuk's could have crossed, or how any of Rietz's people could have picked him up, an innocent absence is even more inexplicable — the story out in the open might convince them his capture is meaningless.

"Or that they might as well rub him out." Pavel is the one with the honesty to say it. Arni, you see, is a very important witness; it was to him Rietz boasted about the plan, and his evidence would confirm Wirath's. And mine, of course, where it would intersect with Christa's own account.

"No," Pavel says. "You got it right, buddy; we gotta get Niemek involved, throw everything at them all at once, arrest the Herders, pick up Rietz, get enough firepower out there to take care of his militia. That don't mean we're not gonna do all we can to find the kid."

He rings his man (I've always assumed, man) from the

Interior Ministry, finding him at home, and has a lengthy, grave discussion. "We're calling the Toyota stolen, maybe used in an armed robbery," he tells me. "Might be a hostage situation — that way, the cops take it seriously, but think before they shoot. What?" — he misreads my dubious mouth as an accusation. "What more can we do?"

Nothing, it seems, except pray or worry or both, according to temperament.

IX

We step from a dreary Koravan evening, snow dropping wetly in huge super-flakes, shed our coats, and I'm in a provincial production of *Der Rosenkavalier*, not knowing my part. To greet guests and examine credentials there is a major-domo in knee-breeches with a staff of office but no powdered wig, supported by two young toughs who look acutely uncomfortable in their flunkey costume with white silk stockings (I glimpse more security-men in normal dark suits, lurking in the background). Pavel, a familiar face, is not required to produce his invitation, Katja, quietly *ravissante* in dark-green taffeta, receives a bow, and so do I after Pavel identifies me doubly as his guest and a foreign correspondent ("distinguished" a makeweight). The major-domo, whose brocade tail-coat is overlong in the sleeve, consults a roster, and tells us the number of our table; gestured past, we descend half a dozen steps into the large, high hall, brilliantly lighted by chandeliers above, sconces set high on the fluted pilasters of the bracketing colonnade.

The wide floor is gleaming parquet. On its stone banks are rows of small square tables with upright white-painted iron chairs, many already occupied, though in the middle there is a good deal of social traffic, the cream of Dusatian business and bureaucratic, international diplomatic, society, few known to me, though both Pavel and Katja do much nodding and smiling, and one crescent clumping includes Jiri Podarny, young (well, near my age) titular head of Cicada, pink-eared and, in his tailored tails, a few abdomen inches the other side of svelte.

Many of the guests already have drinks, some passed out by an inadequate number of servers in traditional Dusatian dress, young men rather Tyrolean in short green rompers with broad braces, over long ribbed stockings, women with very close-fitting bodices and shortish skirts flared by a froth of petticoat, charming. More drinkers serve themselves at the long tables near the head of the hall, which, provided with an incongruous canvas awning, puts me in mind of the tea tent at a club cricket match.

An orchestra of near thirty, more than half strings (descending, 4,4,3,3,2, plus harp) is just about in place, tiered in a kind of shallow cavern amid flowers brought in from who knows what far southern climes, daffodils and hyacinths, which, with their leafage, comprise the national colours, framed by a pair of curved, wavy, rococo stone stairs. An oboe gives the A, and there comes that droning, harmonium sound of tuning, unbearable anticipatory joy for all music-lovers; a small, shaggy, long-necked conductor rather like an elderly cockatoo insinuates himself unobtrusively but cannot escape a patter of applause; he turns for a bow, or rather, a fierce nod, wheels back, gestures. Drum-roll, and the national anthem is launched.

Above and behind the orchestra, where the two stairs turn towards each other, there is a balcony, really more like a balustraded terrace to one of those pleasant villa-restaurants that look out on the Gulf of Genoa, anywhere between Savona and La Spezia. As the anthem comes to an end, President and Madame Niemek appear above. Prolonged ovation, but even while joining it I am filled with dismay. He looks old — as he is, but almost 80 is not ancient; he looks old and ill, his smile a fragile thing. When, eventually, the acclaim dies down, he speaks a few just-audible words of welcome and holiday, and the effort is mirrored in Mme Niemek's solicitous face. It is she who, over a fresh burst of applause, speaks the traditional, "*Let us dance!*" and then both step back to be seated among the favoured entourage. This, I'm heartless enough to remind myself, is the man we're looking to for strong, decisive action. Historically, his courage can't be questioned, but there comes a time when that fails, or is directed entirely into a personal struggle against encroaching weakness of the body and perhaps the mind as well. I glance over at Pavel, and he presses his lips together, shaking his head slightly.

The orchestra begins musing on then throbbing its opening curtsey to tradition, the most famous waltz in the world, followed in quick succession by a polka and a galop, all by the younger generation of Strausses. For this set-piece there has been salting of the mine; while some in the initial swirl are ordinary guests bravely doing their best, a high proportion are slender, accomplished young women in timeless, fluttering white and pastel gowns, their slender young partners too skilled and too well-tailored to be anything but professional; Pavel informs me these couples are from the opera ballet; after the echt Viennese prelude they vanish from the scene. Hereafter, too, most music the orchestra plays will originate within living if not always still dancing memory, when the waltz had become less flamboyant, more meditative, its melancholy worn openly on its simpler sleeve.

This first pause would normally be the time when the President and his lady descend to distribute personal greetings; in past years (I'm told) they have always danced the first slow waltz together to rapturous acclaim. Now, both have quietly vanished, though their chosen retinue comes down the stairs; Premier Dalerant at his most unctuous, the Gorats, he in mere dinner-jacket, Deresza not comfortable in a fussy grey gown with beads which does not downplay her dumpy tendency. Behind them, the Vocks, the General not in uniform, but converting his black mess-jacket into a coat of many colours with all his campaign and service ribbons, his wife moving cautiously on the stairs, one nyloned leg emerging from a clinging golden floor-length column, she probably claiming the evening's cleavage award. Next, Vock's former boss, General, no, now Marshall Svarin, Army Chief of Staff, very much Niemek's man, 68, tall, buzzard-faced, unsmiling in dress uniform. And there is a clutch of ministers, lame geese hoping Wirath's forthcoming decision will mend them.

At our tiny table somewhere near midpoint of the southern side, I am assailed by unreality; the occasion, my costume, Pavel in his equally resplendent, rather more aggressively geometric set of tails looking like the conspiratorial cousin, Black Michael. Across and little farther up — that is, in the direction of the orchestra — the Herders are seated; I can't be sure, but it's possible Mara nods to me. With them is a woman I don't recognise, and again Jiri Podarny, who is, remember, Christa's *fiancé en titre*. In all the hours I spent with Christa his name was never mentioned; while that may well side with general informed opinion that she has no intention of marrying him, it says nothing worse, and I don't believe he was party to the plot against her. He's not a conspirator or confidant I'd want with me, but while he may lack brains, he isn't devoid of a certain callow decency. But it does raise the question, what was to be the future of Podarny's personal and intimate financial connection with Herder when the kidnapping came to light?

As the orchestra begins to stir back into life, Pavel, saying he'll try to discover what gives with Niemek, orders me meanwhile to dance with Katja. She can have had few opportunities in the years since Pavel's wounding, and is on her feet at once, but I am doubly apprehensive, troubled by the thought of having Katja in my arms, as by her credentials, a dancer once good enough to win a year with the famous ballet in Petersburg, still Leningrad then.

At my best, usually after enough wine to loosen my father's dignity, without impairing my mother's physical assurance, I can be a reliable partner; I don't do tribal confrontation, or infrequent-contact convulsions, but can find my way through three or four standard ballroom codes without undue stumbling. Katja is light in my arms and graceful; eyes filled with enjoyment she is also touchingly pretty, and we waltz — something with the rather wearied and self-conscious sentimentality of the thirties, Coward, probably.

For a long time we're silent; I two or three times reject inane jokes that come to overcorrect the too-earnest things I want to say.

Catching her mood from the music, Katja sighs, "A Christmas I shall remember." Unexpectedly, she laughs. "I'm glad you didn't like Marjenka."

Confusion; what first? that it's not exactly true I didn't *like* her, that I thought she'd been brought in by Katja precisely for me to like? The music pauses on the dominant, and is halted by commotion.

At the head of the four steps down from the door the brocade major-domo is challenging someone's right to be here; in an edgy feminine range, the words, "I am *press*!" achieve optimal audibility in the silence as the music dies out, and a patter of applause fails to ignite.

With another late-arriving couple halted in the doorway, the disputed guest sidesteps the gate-keeper, who grabs at her arm.

She is Angèle, though that perception has to pass rapidly through three or more phases; it looks like, it can't be, it is; surely not. *She is wearing a frock.* The short, dark hair has been fluffed attractively out into something near stylish, and the layery gown, tulle over jacquard silk, though a half-metre short of floor-length, is unexceptionable, youthful, light blue with tiny puffs of pseudo-sleeve, not outrageously low in front, though it exposes throat and shoulders, unadorned.

The pair of less ceremonial chuckers-out are converging, but Angèle, whatever the unimaginable reason for her appearance here, has two instant, influential defenders; Juan-Micel Herder rises from his seat and moves to intervene, but is second by several lengths to Pavel, limping swiftly up the steps, to speak with conviction to the major-domo, who soon capitulates, standing aside with a self-deprecating flourish.

Watched coolly by Herder, Pavel comes back to the table with Angèle beside but slightly preceding him: if not my thumbs, but those of, say, large-handed Arni, were to be put together at the front of her waist, his forefingers could touch at the back; her neck and shoulders are very fine, what can be seen of silken legs, slender with keel-edged calves and lathe-turned ankles, elegant as a fashion-artist's pencil sketch; the feet, in irreproachable blue court shoes, are tiny, and in their moderate heels she comes short of Pavel's cravat. On our converging path, we greet; Angèle gives me a cool hand to press, while she and Katja nod at each other; there is no cordiality, but an inexplicable familiarity in their mutual dismissal.

Pavel, not meeting his wife's eye, pulls out our fourth chair, but Angèle never takes it; setting down a small silk bag, a match for her dress, she turns in my direction. She has brought a taut, suppressed excitement with her, yet her smile is placidly amused.

"Dance with me?" I assign Angèle a question-mark that may not be there, yet it's certainly not a command, while Katja's hand, still inside my elbow, tightens in a faint, possessive, negating tug.

For all that, and the momentary flash of savage envy from Pavel's hot eyes, I can't refuse; possibly the simplest explanation for Angèle's unexpected presence is also the best; the overwound young woman wants for a change to dance.

At the annunciatory flourish from the orchestra, however, if there were any way out compatible with good manners, I'd seize it. I've mentioned that *Evita* came late to Korava; when it did there resulted a craze for Argentine tangos, and a downtown restaurant with dance-floor which changed its name from *Polka* to *Tango* is still doing sell-out business. The rhythm is seductive, the dance well-done a model of sensuous elegance and sublimated passion, and I have ample less public ways of making a fool of myself.

It's a tune I know but can't name, something with *ojos* (and probably *mi corazón*) in it, and I mutter inaudibly to myself *keep walking*, instructions once hissed at me when first I had to muddle through this dance.

My anxiety is misplaced; I'm in excellent hands; Angèle, like one of her namesakes in a rococo canvas depicting the posthumous transfiguration of some stolid worthy, wafts me effortlessly to the heights. Technically, her contribution is all response, since there's no visible or even tactile suggestion she is leading; my initiative is in fact that of the planchette or an inverted glass at a home séance, answering to consciously imperceptible pressures as if I have a mind of my own; we merge into figures undreamt, and she is all yielding, the epitome of domination by surrender. That her truculent advocacy of a lunatic cause could conceal such grace, both natural and accomplished, is like an ultimate condemnation of opinions *per se*. Dancing, she possesses something conspicuously lacking in her opinionated life, a distancing humour. The tango (as an institution, I mean) is, let's confess, always wobbling on the brink of ludicrous self-parody, and Angèle, without a smile, stylistically acknowledges that possibility, rebuking it with the (dare one say Chaplinesque?) perception that a spoof can double back on itself to evoke the emotions it guys.

I shan't say the other pairs cease dancing and form a ring to observe us, like Fred and Ginger, but Angèle dressed up, Angèle dancing, Angèle mute, is noteworthy in itself, and more than one couple is simply marking time so as to enjoy the spectacle; my suspicion is that the conductor has signalled a spur-of-the-moment *da capo*; few simultaneous achievements go on this long, and when it does end I'll want to roll over on my back and pant.

Yes, it would be absurd to deny eroticism to a paired activity where the partners' hips, though sometimes beyond a yard apart, move in sinuous mirror simultaneity or significant contrary motion, yet this is nothing like foreplay, or the mating rituals, purposefully elaborate, of certain birds; sexuality has been completely subsumed in its analogy, the dance its own completion. Not to say...

It ends, Angèle twirling back to rest her head in the hollow of my shoulder; too abruptly we stop being each other and are discrete. All but a musing first-chair trio of the orchestra is resting; there is applause, of which a considerable proportion is for us — for Angèle, if the clappers have any eye. Among them, sleepy Mme Vock in her fluid gold scabbard is wondering whether she might pick up some tips for similarly managing her leaden-footed husband.

Angèle doesn't give any general acknowledgement, but resuming arm's length makes me a formal little curtsey, head nodding down; she is wearing a small silver coronal with what look like sapphires. She thanks me.

"No, thank you — " with bow and smile. "I had no idea I danced that well."

She pauses on this, and for a nasty moment I anticipate extension into a strained political metaphor, the vast untapped spring of human possibility to be set free by the abolition of government (I'm prepared to point out that the dictatorial rhythms of dance are anything but anarchic). No; her holiday mood survives; she laughs, repeat, laughs: is this an occurrence within the living memory of anyone present? "It was fun. We must never dance together again."

There are, instantly, five or more available interpretations of this gnomic utterance; I'm reminded, for one, of an anecdote about Lenin listening raptly to a gramophone record of Beethoven, then recalling himself to annihilating fury over the impermissible solace it proffered in a wickedly capitalistic world, and for another, more melancholy but less repellent, that Angèle recognises a magic not to be recaptured.

A look back to the distant small table, but we're far nearer the long boards where refreshments are, and she moves in that direction. Still on her best conventional behaviour, she does not plunge into the mild throng there, but waits demurely for me to ask what she'd like. She chooses the alleged champagne cup, and I secure for myself a tall glass of the bland chardonnay now being bottled in Dusatia, at the expense, sadly, of hectarage formerly devoted to riesling and sylvaner.

Returning, I note that she is a sort of exhibit; there are those who approach but lose their nerve when about four feet distant, others, no doubt prominent in some social circle, who station themselves rearward, and watch as if she might be about to do something anarchic and memorable. Apparently unaware, she tastes her drink, makes a face and passes it to me for a try. Bubbly from Azerbaijan, most likely, mixed with some sort of syrupy near-fruit drink.

"Champa-Cola," she says, but turns down my offer to change it for something more drinkable.

She is also declining my wordless suggestion, a matter of sway and half-step, that we return to our table, and I discover that despite apparent absorption I have never stopped being perplexed over Katja's strange last remark.

"Katja doesn't want to see me. Pavel's angry, with me, too. He used to love to dance."

A dizzying shudder in this, considering how Pavel got the wound that ended his dancing. Knowing I ought to confront her about the gun she was given for her birthday, I've doubted I'd have the heart to, but now take her small wrist to lead her through the line of tables, passing stonily quite near the interested Herders (she fails to see Juan-Micel, with a high-chinned, could it be? defiance), and under the colonnade, where the outer reaches are divided into numerous large alcoves or small, high-ceilinged rooms, a great window occupying most of the outer wall. These are not the *salles privées*, which are reached by mounting either of the twin wedding-cake stairs, but only a scattering of sippers and chatters are here, and it is private enough for my purpose.

"Do you have that gun with you?"

The change from our till-now mutually teasing tone makes her blink. "Gun?"

"The one Juan-Micel gave you."

"Who says he gave me a gun?"

"Christa Rasch."

"Christa Rasch — " and Angèle can be seen to gather herself, to banish the gown and the silk stockings, the jewelled coiffure, all the holiday ameliorations — "is completely typical of the useless adornments exhibited to distract the people from their condition of slavery. I have nothing against her personally; it's not her fault."

Am I angry? I know I might be, and am not; what catches at me is a bitter sorrow over this incurable disease that disfigures and cripples Angèle, who could be so radiant.

"Your good friends the Herders — " I can go on only by making myself gruff and forbidding — "They have nothing personal against Christa, either." And rashly, I'm sure Pavel would say, I tell Angèle all about the kidnapping and its purpose, and come to the brink of what I suspect was to be her part in the extended plot.

She says, "If Christa *is* his daughter — " nothing new; on form Wirath's participation is problematic, his bride's infidelity quite likely, but, as I tell Angèle, utterly irrelevant when Wirath certainly brought the child up as his own, and continues to give her all his affection.

"Juan-Micel is not stupid, and he is not a Loyalist. He would be an anarchist, if he didn't like money so much."

"If he were someone else." (this is a mistake; I'm debating with her)

"Why not? if the world were not structured by power."

"You're not going to improve that with a gun."

"If you think I'm so evil, why did you stop that policeman from arresting me? That's why I wanted to dance with you."

Lightly enough, we call people mad, loony, loopy, dotty, out to lunch (chiefly U.S.) every day; it's such a common assessment that the current vogue word for insane, cuckoo, bananas, bonkers, round the bend, not playing with a full deck (U.S.), soon wears out its novelty and has to be replaced; there are incomparably more colloquial synonyms for batty, crackers, gaga, off one's head, nut, onion, out of one's mind, gourd (U.S.), up a tree, than any other adjective in the language (*intoxicated* its only possible rival, falls well short). Maybe in anyone's makeup there's enough that is goofy, nutty, barmy, kooky, wacky, non compos, to sustain the charge, but in general it's not a serious clinical diagnosis, rather a lazy-minded way of dismissing the bewildering question of human variance, taking shelter within a tight circle of agreed (and sub-literary rather than empirical) convention.

Yet when Pavel calls Angèle crazy, it isn't jocular hyperbole, or his exasperation with an isolated instance of irrationality, not even the impatience of a man in confessedly absurd love; with Angèle two and two really can make three or five, and to guess how her mind will work requires a miraculously matching lunacy. There's no instruction manual for talking to the quiet, pretty person you seriously believe could be goaded into murdering the Chief Justice.

There is nothing left but an ultimatum, give up the gun or face arrest, and certain imprisonment. But before I can frame it, Pavel arrives, to chide me for vanishing, when I'm expected "upstairs."

"Where upstairs?"

"You'll know the room; there's a guard on the door — " he says this without taking his eyes from Angèle. It is completely impossible; far beyond the oddity of discussion with Angèle, the cross-currents here are too much for me to make sense of. Pavel has agreed with me about disarming her, and I hope he'll deliver the same ultimatum, but guns are not a subject I can bring myself to mention between these two. There's also the thought of Katja, and before fleeing I say with a vague wave, "Angèle left her handbag at our table."

"Thanks for the dance," she says, as determined not to look at Pavel as he is to cause her to.

One of two security-men outside opens the door for me. Wall-fixtures high up throw all their light against wall and ceiling, giving a muted, shadowless, underwater effect. The room is carpeted, windowless, with a dark sideboard, a couple of spindly chairs with high, curving backs, and a wide, low ottoman, on which is seated Mme Niemek, much as some odalisque or naughty young wife must have awaited *milord* in that long, voluptuous

European autumn before the Archduke went to Sarajevo; she is, however, soberly dressed as befits her years. She rises, smiling, presses my hand between both of hers, and gestures for me to sit beside her.

The President is resting; nothing grave, he has a chill, and asked her to meet me; she will, of course, report our conversation to him, since she understands from Pavel Orbicz that this is not simply a courtesy-call. On the whole, I'm relieved; Niemek's fragile appearance would have obliged me to tread softly.

Her grey eyes are very astute. Age, the long hiatus from public life, and perhaps her own conscious choice have turned the latter Mme Niemek into a benign national grandmother, bestowing sympathy and benedictions in exchange for numberless bouquets presented by adorable and well-scrubbed little girls, but we should not forget her beginnings. More than fifty years ago, she had (I've seen pictures) a pert, bright-eyed, fresh-cheeked prettiness, employed ruthlessly to introduce a powerful bomb into the bar of the old Schweitzerhof, then used as a German officers' club, and there are bloodcurdling (or at least throat-cutting) legends of her even more direct participation in the grim business of the Resistance.

At double the age, in the 1962 debacle, she was, as portrayed in interrogation notes only recently brought out of secrecy in Russia, more defiant than her husband, and would (or said she would) have armed women and children with Molotov cocktails for use against the invading Soviet tanks, but that Niemek saw further bloodshed as futile. On the other hand, according to home-grown anecdote (this I had from my father), when one of their firebrand associates wanted to embarrass the U.S. into intervention, by making public all the empty hints and near-promises of help with which the State Department had encouraged the insurrection, it was she who dissuaded him, whether for fear of leaving Dusatia entirely friendless, or out of an aversion to seeing Korava become the opening battlefield of the Third World War can't now be said; the point is she was never Niemek's mere consort, but a formidable force in her own right.

She begins by asking for news of my mother, and when I mention her directing *Much Ado*, somewhat surprisingly, knows the play.

"Beätriz and Benadich — that was Niemek and me when first we met, except not so nice — you know little Angèle? Me at sixteen, exactly. In many ways, exactly."

I doubted that adverb. "Madame, I think it might be many girls at sixteen, and you, besides, had the Nazis to hate. The trouble is, it's still Angèle at twenty-six."

A nod. "You young ones, very rightly, are sick of hearing the old fossils tell about that war. But the world got a disease then from which it has never recovered. Not that we learned how to hate, I think that has been an easy accomplishment for anyone, always. But to be proud of hating and pleased with the terrible things we did out of hatred. As you say, there were the Nazis, but that pleasure became like an addiction for the world, and when there were no more Nazis, there were too many who could still be proud of their hardness. We won against the Nazis by becoming like them, even your British *gentlemen* — " she uses the English word. "And after — I know, this is your world, you don't believe it could ever have been much different."

Does she think I've come, thus emptyhanded, for an interview? I have no idea why she's decided to speak for history, but can scarcely hope for a better opening.

"The National Loyalists — " the connection brings a grim smile, but she holds up a warning hand.

"Like the President, I have to keep out of party politics."

"What I want the President to know, though it involves a party, is by no stretching of the term, legitimate politics." Mme Niemek's silence is encouraging, and I tell her everything known and conjectured, beginning with my conviction Javelin, hence Vock, has access to nuclear weapons. She is listening attentively, but with all judgement withheld, and at this point she turns, and from the dark mahogany sideboard takes a small leather notebook and a pencil or pen.

"Kalashnikov, yes — I remember the man, we had him to dinner; he gave us a Fabergé egg." She makes a note, while I hand over from my inside pocket a Dusatian translation from the relevant portion of the Kiev speech, having obtained the exact text from the electronic files of Ukrainian State Television.

She unnecessarily smoothes it on her lap, and reads with the help of a tiny, highly decorative *pince-nez.*

"I see that someone, somewhere, according to Kalashnikov, may be in possession of Soviet nuclear arms — or may have been, three years ago. But from there to Strbjena — "

I am prepared for this; it was in my rehearsal with Pavel, though I now disregard his advice to tone down the answer I gave, and give: "To me, it is extraordinary enough that no one outside of Javelin division can be sure the nuclear weapons aren't there, not the premier, nor the former premier, nor the defence minister, nor Marshall Svarin — no one, that is, except General Vock, whose formal divorce from Javelin seems not to disallow continued cohabitation. I would be delighted to be wrong about this, but shouldn't someone have a look before calling me a scaremonger?"

"No, no, you have a reputation as a careful and responsible journalist." (*wormwood, wormwood*)   "You recognise that premature publication of your suspicions, whether or not they prove to have any substance, would be a great embarrassment for any government, at a time when international confidence is absolutely vital to the future of Dusatia."

(Adversarial, inevitably, but I'm pleased to have come so far) "Madame Niemek, if it was my intention to embarrass the government, I would hardly have sought this meeting."

"Then you don't intend to publish this story?" — the swift swoop of lightning chess; I can visualise her hand banging down the plunger on the clock. Could she, if circumstances came, succeed her husband as president?   I'm not sure of the constitutional process; Niemek was first installed virtually by acclamation, and was unopposed for re-election. Candidates, I know, are nominated in parliament, and I believe are supposed to be former premiers and others of high rank (both Gorat and Dalerant might want the job for their twilight years), but an exception, surely, might be made in Mme Niemek's case, if she were to become a widow.

She is waiting. "There is another matter which is related, though obliquely." And I launch into the history of Christa's kidnapping, on firmer ground here, since my own experiences can't be disputed, and for confirmation of the purpose I can invite her to ask Wirath.

"Juan-Micel Herder — " her face declining to show surprise. "He is an influential man, an important player in the economy."

"I am aware of that."

"That's not to say I trust him. Or have ever liked him — he always reminds me of a high-class pimp, and that frozen bitch — well. Are the police involved in this?"

"So far, only informally, Madame, through personal contacts of Pavel Orbicz."

"Why? There has been a crime, or an attempt at one. Why hasn't Justice Wirath brought charges? You say his daughter is safe?"

I explain what I understand to be Wirath's reasoning, and link it to my own. "If my surmise about nuclear weapons is correct — or if no more is true than that General Vock retains de facto command of Javelin — it would be dangerous to proceed against the Loyalists piecemeal before certain steps are taken — "

Anger. "What are we, a country of brigands and warlords? If what you tell me is true — and I have no reason to doubt your word, hard as it is to believe the Herders could act so stupidly — there might be criminal charges against them, and this Rietz, and a few underlings. We cannot arrest an entire party, and I don't believe Mr Miloczy is going to start a civil war over the indictment of Juan-Micel Herder. Do you, seriously?"

"If I didn't, by now I would have had the kidnapping story on front pages from here to New York. I think that if, as seems likely, the decision goes against them in the Yellow Ballot question, the Loyalists may be desperate enough for anything." Herder doubly desperate, faced with the loss of position and prestige, even if he escapes imprisonment. As, probably, chief source of financing, his influence with Miloczy's party might well be crucial.

I am done. Mme Niemek sits silent a long minute, then turns a page in her notebook. "The President must be informed. You are staying in Korava?"

I give her Pavel's phone-number, but am dissatisfied. "You understand these things can't be kept out of the press much longer."

She glares, and her shift of posture is like the bristling of a cat's fur. "Are you making a threat?"

"Madame Niemek, I am a working journalist; I had no professional duty to seek this meeting — on the contrary, the delay in publication could easily cost me my livelihood."

Though her eyes don't leave me, her expression softens to merely grave. "Of course. We — the President will be grateful. We must decide what is to be be done. But do you blame me — " the intimate manner returns, and still disarms me, though I'm aware the effect is calculated. "In our position, we would like to settle everything behind closed doors, then summon the press to tell them how very clever we have been. Unfortunately, you can't trust us so far. Oh — " a coy look that must recall younger, flirtatious days. "My opinion of the Herders — "

"Nothing said here is for publication."

"The President will want to talk to you tomorrow, I think. You are available? You can give us twenty-four hours?"

"I am not the only newsman."

A nod. "When you speak with Elena, give her my love. Does she still remember Barry?"

A British intelligence officer with a taste for poetry. "Her first love."

"So she thought. She was only a schoolgirl. Fourteen? Barry and I were going to be married, after the war, and live at Ox Ford."

"She never told me that."

"She has never known. I would have been like your mother, a proper English wife, but he was captured. Niemek got me back — *on the bounce*, do you say?"

"*On the rebound*." Like my mother, she says, but it's not hard to trace a time-track where, without this woman beside him, Niemek does not begin the 1962 liberalisation, there is no Soviet suppression, hence my father never comes to Korava; in that odd sense if Barry hadn't died, I would never have been.

"We lived, everything, two hundred kilometres an hour, a month was like five years, then, never knowing who would be alive next week. I'm glad she brought you up to be a good Dusatian."

I'm standing now, and bow. "So am I."

But have no idea why my eyes should blur with tears, as I return to the ball, taking the left-hand stair so that I can stop for another glass of wine. The dance-floor is thronged, orchestra playing Andrew Lloyd Webber, but *Cats*, not *Evita* (actually, it's still well short of midnight). Moving behind the colonnade, I am face to face with Herder.

"The very man I wanted to see." The exact opposite of my feelings. As if meant for that, he puts a glass filled with white wine into my hand, and darts back to his table to get another. It is a cool chardonnay, infinitely superior to my last, at a guess Puligny-Montrachet.

"You have nothing to fear from me."

Am I that easily read? I was remembering Pavel telling me Korava was too small to hold me and the Buckaroos, and now it seems we are to share one alcove, the same one where I was with Angèle, the many squares of the great window now more than half obscured with piled and spattered snow. As best I can tell in the slant of distant lights, it is still coming down thick.

"Mara, I'm sorry to say, is quite upset with you, stealing away our favourite guest."

Not Angèle, Christa. Is this what he's up to, laying the foundation for a preposterous claim the kidnapping was all in my mind? "I knew she must be unhappy, when she sent Erhardt Rietz all the way to Obdana to invite us back."

Not a blink. "Christa is well? Is she in Korava now?"

"No."

"I kind of think she doesn't share our profound interest in the future of Dusatia — a true internationalist, hm? Or should we say, she belongs to the world. Like Coca-Cola — or Moët et Chandon would be more Christa."

Does he actually think he's bloody hilarious, or is there purpose in the asinine performance? I think this is where I'm supposed to suck in my cheeks and match suavity for suavity, but I'm horribly miscast, and trample all over the convention. "If

Miloczy's babble is your idea of Dusatia's future, I don't share it, either."

"Babble is the future of the world, isn't it? Or — you don't actually believe in democracy? — Oh, you're not going to quote your Winston Churchill to me, are you? What Churchill meant by democracy was the common people's right to choose who from the ruling classes would be their masters — Marlboroughs, Roosevelts; three-quarters of their hostility to Adolf Hitler was nothing but snobbery, the officer caste and the upstart lance-corporal.   But democracy is of its nature institutionalised hypocrisy, a false religion posing as a science.   What you intellectuals really dislike about Miloczy is the complete absence of humbug; there's no pretence."

"Or sense."

A keen look. "You have never interviewed Miloczy, have you?"

"I've tried. He was always out somewhere, raising the rabble."

"Try again, you should talk with him, you really should. Oh, he knows what they want when he speaks in public, but you'll get an entirely different impression in a quiet one-on-one situation, he's quite a visionary, with some remarkably sound ideas. Gunther Üwe almost caught the real Miloczy, his interview had seven or eight minutes that were really worthwhile, but then he had to go creative and intercut it with Hitler at Nürnberg, and totally irrelevant concentration-camp stuff — the Germans lap that up, naturally, and you must admit they have a case; the *Endlösung*, by all means, was a terrible crime, but far from a unique one — the Americans *resettling* their Indians, or pacifying the Philippines, Kemel and the Armenians, Stalin and the kulaks, the Chinese cultural revolution, Pol Pot in Cambodia, Iraq and the Kurds, the Serbs in Bosnia, that business in Rwanda, Indonesia in Timor —"

"We should stop making a fuss about mass murder, it's an everyday occurrence."

"No, no, not at all. Can you find me one statement by Miloczy that advocates, that so much as condones, violence against anyone?"

"There were the ethnic riots when he was first elected."

"Which he publicly deplored. The Hindu-Moslem massacres when India was first partitioned — would you blame those on Gandhi? He was the one, after all, who did most to get the British out of India."

"I hadn't heard that Miloczy was a champion of passive resistance."

"That's not what I said. When Miloczy speaks, because he's a spellbinder, because he knows the importance of involving his audience and leading their response, he's constantly compared to Adolf Hitler — there have been other great orators, Lord knows why it should always be Hitler."

"Perhaps, for example, because Miloczy talks about the purity of the race and the destiny of his people, chooses red, white and black for his party colours, and dresses his provincial police to look like the S.S."

Not a ruffle. "In any event, you forget that leaving aside the unfortunate Jewish obsession, the message of Hitler was hope; he took a defeated, bankrupt, despairing country and gave it new pride and national purpose."

"And after he'd marched them to even worse disaster, Konrad Adenauer did the same and more, without putting them all in uniform, or threatening powerless neighbours, or opening a single death camp." This is really quite idiotic. There is some point to preserving social conventions when you find yourself in a nonsensical debate with, for example, your employer, the father of your fiancée, a relation from whom you might expect an inheritance, a head of state, but I don't know what bone-deep taboo keeps me from telling Herder I'm beyond my limit for non-sequiturs, and walking away. He holds, of course, all the sartorial cards; whatever his dialectic shortcomings, his tailoring is beyond reproach, and my own resplendence looks like what it is, off-the-peg, next to his Savile Row complacency. But it's not quite true that I want nothing from him.

"If Miloczy has anything in common with any of the historic national leaders," he resumes, not acknowledging my riposte. "It is a refusal to pay lip-service to the sacred democratic ideal — paradoxically, an elitist notion, with an aesthetic rather than an intellectual basis. Those who, having the ability to rephrase the common clichés of their time, imagine that they think for themselves, come to believe that illusory ability a *sine qua non* of happiness, and are not deterred by the self-evident fact that by far the majority at any time have no desire to share their self-congratulatory fantasy. Most people, Kearns, though they are indoctrinated, in the west, to some undefined treasure called `freedom,' don't want to choose for themselves — that's why they all listen to the same shoddy music, eat the same awful food, buy the same gym-shoes and go to the same mindless hit mega-movies; they want to have their thinking done for them. The articulate exceptions, of which I judge you to be one, because you hate to be told what to do, imagine it must be an intolerable burden for everyone else, but you have no evidence for that assumption — that's why I call democracy a religion. And hypocritical because those who rise to the top know this in their hearts, make use of it: how clever you are, they say, how wonderfully independent-minded to let me tell you what you want!"

"You're saying democracy is nothing but a coercive form of dictatorship, under another name."

"Largely. A prescriptive oligarchy, let us say."

"Then why not let it be? Why should Miloczy attack democracy, and advocate what you say, de facto, already is?"

"Because — understand, I can't speak for Premier Miloczy, but I imagine his objections are the same as mine. Because it is untidy; the need to preserve the illusion of choice can sometimes have unpredicted and damaging effects, and delay the implementation of necessary measures — the chronic inability of the world's richest nation to guarantee security for its aged and infirm is a case in point; Bismarck could tell you, a strong leader, free from the necessity of coddling an electorate, could solve the question with two strokes of the pen — but the need for some apparent distinction between tweedledum and tweedledee turns the question of funding into an eternal, unresolved political squabble: a single oligarchy, yes, but paralysed by its need to blandish the voter with conflicting lies. Not that the people's belief in something for nothing, today, tomorrow and forever, has anything to do with freedom, quite the reverse. Under a well-run authoritarianism, once *vox populi, vox dei* is on the scrapheap where it belongs, there will actually be more freedom, for that relative minority which knows how to use it. The rest can still have their bread and circuses."

The aged and infirm! their welfare has hardly been a priority for Miloczy, much less for Juan-Micel Herder. I very nearly laugh out loud, but at a recollection. Up in the frigid shelter, when Christa revealed Mara Herder's eerie admiration for Magda Goebbels, I half-rejected the consequent analogy, on the grounds that her husband had never seemed anything like the twisted theoretician of the National Loyalists, the necessary crook philosopher. Well, here he is, in full bloom.

Not that everything he says is without merit, but reasoning always distorts when tugged at by conclusions already reached, instead of allowed to grow from within by its own logic; when one considers the ancient and hallowed centres of learning where Herder has put in time, he becomes a devastating illustration of the impotency of education to alter minds already hostage to a burning conviction; all his studies at Oxford and Stanford, Sorbonne and the rest merely provided that fire with fuel. As with those shabby, dotty philosopher-kings you see shambling along Great Russell Street, or with their dynastic father, Marx, scuttling to earth in Hampstead, their strident female counterparts preparing to detonate yet another historical condemnation of the male sex; they read prodigiously, and call it study, but it is not, because study would retain the possibility of minds being changed; had Marx really studied history he might have concluded that capital, beginning with the first peck of wheat beyond its grower's immediate needs, though unchecked can produce great evils, is the necessary catalyst in our progress from dingy, drudging survival to comparatively leisured comfort. They aren't looking for learning, those who prove that the English are the Twelve Lost Tribes, or that Erse is the basal language of all mankind, or that all male dealings with women are the equivalent of forcible rape, but for inevitable confirmation of a predetermined answer, and could as certainly (though with less prestige) find it in a Tarot pack, the I Ching, or the entrails of a slaughtered kid.

"I have truly been disappointed — you are, if I may say so, on a different intellectual plane to the majority of journalists, which is why it's disappointing to see you handling the National Loyalist movement so conventionally. More wine?"

My patience, though extensive, has its limits. "I have met two people who have spent far more time with you than I have, who both at first denied you could be an adherent of the Loyalists — "

"In my position — "

"It's not unreasonable to conclude there must be something disreputable about a party where membership can't be openly acknowledged. And when it comes to threatening a gentle man with harm to the only person he loves in order to further your dubious cause, I'm afraid my feelings are completely conventional; contempt."

"Oh, dear. Well, I suppose I expect too much."

I hand him my empty glass. "There's a boy named Arni Abczik, he was with me when I visited the Eagle's Nest. Now he's missing."

"I know nothing about it." He appears authentically perplexed.

"Your friend Rietz may. You should tell him, he's in trouble now, but if Arni doesn't come safe home — "

"Oh, if we're going to talk about people in trouble — " an empty glass in either hand doesn't make it easy for Herder to be menacing. "You should realise you're on thin ice yourself; your mother's *entrée* doesn't guarantee you unlimited immunity, you should know."

"Give it up, cut your losses. You can't help yourself by harming me, or anyone else. There are some headlines Miloczy isn't going to thank you for."

He wants to say more, but I turn away before the tremble of my anger becomes uncontrollable. It's a consolation to know Herder is also furious.

Back at the table I learn that in my absence there has been an announcement; because of the weather the ball will break up early. Pavel suggests I might dance the forthcoming final waltz with Katja, but she, very subdued, shakes her head. "We should start for the car. It's going to be a mess when everyone leaves." Sensible enough, but still I feel rebuked.

Outside, conditions are awful; the temperature has fallen and the snowflakes are smaller now, but there are blindingly more of them, often on a gusting wind driven almost horizontally, with excruciating effect. Pavel has said he would fetch the BMW while we waited under the portico, but cars already are wallowing and howling in the drive, spinning churned snow into black ice, and we go together like a harried knot of stragglers from the Grande Armée, wondering whatever became of *l'Empéreur*.

"What became of Angèle?" What I really want to know is whether Pavel tackled her about that gun. "Did she dance again?"

"Not that I saw. I'm going to go see her tomorrow, she's gonna gimme her heater."

From the back seat I can practically see the tension between Pavel and Katja, like a shimmering force-field in a starzapper movie. I say with maximum inconsequentially, "Who would ever have guessed she could dance like that?"

Katja, darkly patient: "Certainly she can dance. We were in dance-class together. She was the best, better than me, but they would never send her to Lenin — to Petersburg. Even at fifteen she was considered politically unreliable." Their cool familiarity explained, but as Katja relapses into pensive silence, I know with absolute certainty what's in her mind, equally that she's never allowed herself to consider it before; this is an evening for alternative time tracks. If Angèle, instead of Katja, had gone to work with Kirov, is it possible she would have been completely different, happy, even? if she had gone on to a career?

"She has demons. No one can help it." I'm leaning forward, and Katja, grateful for my attempt at absolution, reaches across herself to put a hand over my fingers grasping the back of the seat. Phantom reconciliation for the unacknowledged ghost of a quarrel; we're back again where we were, a longitude and latitude I still can't plot.

But Pavel duelling with the snow; he disliked my dancing with Angèle, no doubt loathed that Angèle made us dance so well, and very much resents anyone else explaining his Angèle.

"What that bugsy little broad needs — " and I wince, knowing what's coming — "Is a guy to fuck the devils out of her."

"I understand that remedy is in bad repute nowadays." Pavel is more intelligent than this: even in other ages of the world when its arrogance might have gone without comment, it would have been an extraordinarily stupid thing to say about a woman he's just told his wife he'll be seeing privately tomorrow; Katja can't be altogether unconscious of his inexplicable passion.

He scarcely hears me, swivelling round with a big grin. "What about it, Kearns? You had your chance there, she must've been hot to trot after it turned out you were Rudolph friggin' Valentino. Whatsa matter, still got a yen for the delectable Miss Rasch?"

"The road," Katja suggests. For the completely vigilant, it is only marginally visible, and Pavel faces front with a giant shrug, both hands gripping the wheel. Oh, yes, he is very angry with me; no one who knows his habitual generosity, his good-humoured competence on the job, would ever guess at this potential for destructive anger.

"When we do the story," I say. "You're going to have to interview Christa."

"For Dusatian TV, sure."

"No, in English, for everywhere."

"Huh? Me muscle in on your big moment?"

"I can do the story itself, but I can't grill Christa. It would be absurd: 'Then what happened?' 'Well, then you came and told me I was a prisoner, but at first I didn't believe you.' 'So how did I convince you?' — it's Abbot and Costello."

"Will your guy go for it? Albertson?" Pavel sounds about as genuinely casual as my father deprecating his K.

"He's not going to have much control. For that part of the story, there aren't very many sources." I'll have to get him to tone down the gangsterese, but I'm not going to write his questions.

"I can interview you both together — "

"Oh — " I am reluctant, but have to admit the journalistic logic of it.

"Hey, I'm gonna be on the British Broadcasting Corporation — " grandiloquently rolling all the r's.

X

    Morning comes with a mockingly gentle snow, tiny points like the stars of a distant galaxy, sedately tumbling down, adding imperceptibly to the accumulation. It has snowed, as Vaclav observes in a piercing voice of wonder, all night, and it has also blown, carving the arcs of a weird sculpture in the unfamiliar garden, the redesigned street; drifts are shoulder-high, head-high; instructive to view this white world in imagination through the eyes of Thom, who, one step beyond the back door where a narrow swathe of apron has been scoured almost clear, has no vista, only the towering walls of snow, impenetrable Himalayas.

    The BMW is trapped, and will be for some time, perhaps days to come; snow ploughs are certainly at work on the main thoroughfares, but while snow continues to fall there'll be nothing to spare for lesser roads, and clearing, when it is attempted, will be complicated by the large number of cars abandoned where immobilised, either wedged in drifts or having emptied their tanks spinning snow into ice.

    Pavel makes phone calls, reports tersely that the airport is closed, the railways mostly so, the provincial police forces at full stretch rescuing travellers stranded along major roads, not even the motorways entirely passable. News from outlying parts is sketchy, but many telephone and power lines are down. From the studios he learns that while few of the day's personnel have been able to get there, this is offset, on the operational side, by the inability of the night crew to go home.

    Assuming, correctly, that I'll join him, he supposes that once we reach a main road we'll find a taxi, or at worst a bus. After big mugs of coffee fortified with a dollop of *sliwowicza* we set out, accompanied by a security-man, like me in borrowed galoshes. He is recently married, the younger of the two who remained with Vaclav and Thom while we were at the ball; apparently as a result, to Pavel's expressed disbelief, he is now sentimentally eager to begin a family of his own.

Conditions are easy for no one, but brutal for Pavel's injury; he refuses to complain, more than once asking with a set smile for a brief pause, eyes defying me to ask about the pain. Because of drifting it is hard to estimate the actual amount of fall, and we're still discussing the point, narrowing the plausible range to somewhere between 30 and 50 cm, when we attain the studios an hour and a half later, Pavel's predictions of available transport having proved wildly optimistic. On major thoroughfares, some cautious traffic is nosing along, but the ploughs have been so far inadequate to clear more than narrow lanes. It is always easy to overlook that the operators of emergency vehicles themselves have to find a way to get to work, and we have seen only one bus, going in the wrong direction.

We arrive at the same time as a grinning Firenc on skis, and he settles our debate by telling us the National Weather Station at the useless airport had measured 32 cm by seven a.m., say 38 by now, which would give Pavel the jackpot if we'd had a sweep.

Seized by a Dunkirk, Battle of Britain, D-Day spirit, we have a marvellous few hours — well, I do, and Pavel, frowning, employing many curses, muttering darkly, is also enjoying himself. As Director of News by far the highest-ranking personage on the premises, he is in effective control of Dusatian State Television, though the Programme Director, trapped in the southwestern suburbs, is in touch by phone with many recommendations, few of them feasible in our understaffed state — I say "our" because, short of voices, Pavel presses me into unseen service reading, as they come in, short lists of what is and long lists of what isn't open. With one channel, normally a succession of magazine, panel and chat shows, for which none of the hosts or guests are in evidence, he wipes out the entire roster and runs films, which he can interrupt about every half-hour with crisis news; lamenting he doesn't have *Nanook of the North*, *Scott of the Antarctic*, or *Siberian Railway*, an equally icy Soviet epic, any of which might be taken for live current reports, he puts on *Lawrence of Arabia*. The other channel is to stay on with news and crisis reports.

That settled, the superfluous floor-director for several of the usual programmes, brash and barely twenty, is told he is now replacement for the missing driver of Remote Unit One, which is to get out there and shoot.

"Shoot what?" The cameraman, too, has never worked outside before.

"Snow," Pavel succinctly instructs. He ostentatiously consults his wristwatch. "Your first segment is on live in twelve minutes."

Enter a furry woman with hair of brass and at present a voice to match, demanding why, only minutes before air time, after she has ordained miracles to be here, her stage is unlighted, her cameras unmanned. She is named (or so she has always alleged) Karla Karola, and does daily a numbingly tedious revelations programme, in which young wives or near-wives complain about their husbands' or fiancés' philandering, mothers-in-law about their sons' demon spouses, frequently varied with girls who have had visions of the Virgin, or those of either sex with their near-death experiences, or reminiscences of former lives as Romanovs, renaissance popes, pharaohs, about any of which the reincarnate swear an astonishing and absolute ignorance "before I started getting these memories," though subsequent study has been sufficient to confirm the detailed accuracy of their recollections.

Placating Pavel gently explains near-death reality to Karla, and then, inspired, suggests she go as voice with the remote crew. Coyly, she resists, protesting inexperience, for fully eight seconds, and capitulates when Pavel assures her she'll be great, and that "everyone knows her."

"Phone," Firenc tells me as he passes, making the gesture, rolled hand next to his ear. "Line A." Back with his first love, like any meteorologist he is proprietorily exultant over weather at one of its extremes, flaunting lists of the dates and amounts of former heavy snows, and of December, post-war and all-time records now in jeopardy.

"Mark Kearns?" An alto, indeterminate as to sex. "This is the Presidential Palace. Stay on the line, please, the President wants to talk to you." The momentarily muted phone comes live again.

"Mr Kearns? How are you this morning?" Niemek's voice, certainly, and he sounds far stronger than last night.

"Mr President, I have to warn you that this phone may not be secure."

A sharp, impatient noise, like a suppressed sneeze. "We'll take our chances, shall we?" Contempt proper for one who once put Stalin right, but I note as we go on that he is not too proud to show caution.

"Sir."

"I'm sorry I could not keep our appointment last night, but my wife has given me a very full report, and I have made further enquiries this morning; Justice Wirath and I had a very interesting meeting." On Wirath's part, getting there must have been equally fascinating.

"Your story concerning Justice Wirath is a very grave matter, Mr Kearns, and I think you'll agree that those who actually took part must suffer the full consequences of the law. But we must always guard against guilt by association, do you agree?"

What he wants could hardly be clearer. "Mr President, I intend to report only what can be certainly known; the story is sufficiently shocking without adding any lurid conjecture."

"Excellent. I think you and Justice Wirath concur as to the proper timing."

"I believe so, sir. It is not entirely in my control, but I'll continue to do what I can."

"Not in your control?"

"There are other principal figures whose silence can't be compelled, sir, or guaranteed. However, the time is quite near now." Less than twenty-four hours, unless the weather causes Wirath to postpone.

"The other question — " Niemek is willing to let it go at that — "Arising from the death of General Kalashnikov — it's really an unpleasant little group of questions, isn't it. If this were a news conference, and you had asked me, what was being done, et cetera, I would reply that the matter is in hand, and that decisive steps are being taken. You, I suppose, would call that evasive."

"I'm aware, Mr President, that there can be compelling reasons for evasion."

"Compelling indeed. You know, Mr Kearns — may I call you Mark? I am a little less of an ancient monument if I can think of you as Elena's boy. When the American president was murdered — that would be before you were born, would it?"

"Three years before." The Washington where I came unwilling into the light must have been a bitterer place for the last survivors of what they'd been fatuous enough to call Camelot (in reference, moreover, to a coy, Disneyfied, Broadway travesty of that noble theme), most moved out to make room for Texans, the brother only two years away from his own rendezvous with a gunman; Johnson and his Great Society were sinking into the greedy mud of the Mekong Delta, and hitherto docile white youth was turning on and taking dissent to the streets.

"I mention it, because I believe that was a time when good men were obliged in effect to conspire with the bad to hide the real truth, because the facts about the murder would have been more destructive than the act itself. People cannot live where justice is seen to be a whim of the rulers, and the defenders of their freedom are assassins. There is no special merit in justice which can tear a country apart, don't you agree?"

"In principle, Mr President — " a large gulp of air, for courage — "I don't know that I do agree. It is not clear what benefit the people are supposed to derive from a false belief in the virtue of their institutions."

"They still must be governed, and by their own consent, not by force."

"But wouldn't they be right to reject government which believed no evil mattered, so long as it could be kept secret?" This is a realler, less one-sided continuation of last night's discussion with Herder, and it's disturbing how neatly Niemek's sincere concern dovetails with Juan-Micel's cynicism; democracy does indeed decline into conspiratorial oligarchy where its leaders decide how much truth the common people can be trusted with.

"Right? Well, in principle, Mark, I'm with you." The faint mockery here is, I think, self-mockery; Niemek recalling his own idealistic past. "In practice, one finds next year is always going to be the time for complete frankness, which at present would be too dangerous. But in this actual instance... "

"In this actual instance, I would see no object in raising fears, once satisfied the threat no longer exists. If it ever has."

"Exactly, if it ever has. But if it does, you understand it is a very delicate business, like a mine with a trembler-fuse — one cannot *breathe*, much less speak."

"For my own satisfaction, Mr President, with no thought of publication — "

"Oh, yes, I'll let you know. When the weather is better, you must come to dinner — we'll have Wirath, perhaps, if we can get him out of his books."

"Speaking of the weather, Mr President — " it wasn't till hours later that I flushed with shame at having given no reply to his invitation, "is there action at the national level, to deal with this crisis?" It is, I might note, still snowing.

"Ah. In point of fact, we were just discussing — one moment." Without covering or muting the phone, Niemek engages in a brief, low-voiced talk with at least two others, ending with, " — no reason not to — Ah, Mark, you are working with RTPD? We intended to call them in any event, but you may as well know; Premier Dalerant will declare a general emergency at noon, and immediately following, there is to be a press-conference at the Defence Ministry. It would be excellent if RTPD has its cameras there."

"I'm sure that's possible, sir." I'm not. Choice of the Defence Ministry doesn't necessarily presage emphasis on the army's role; it may have been chosen for its accessibility, just off Grdacz Square.

We part with mutual compliments, and I go to find Pavel, who is in Control Room One, on the radio telephone, telling the remote unit they'll be on the air in one minute.

Karla, harried, tells him it isn't possible. She'd been on her way to Central Hospital to see how they were coping, but there was this bus that had skidded three-quarters of a circle before ending wedged broadside across the road, well, blocking two roads.

"Passengers?"

"Half a dozen, maybe."

"Hurt?"

"Might be some bruises. They're terribly shaken up. The driver is practically in tears with the police."

"That's your segment. Driver, passengers, police — " though she can't see him, Pavel is ticking off his fingers. "Anybody who saw the whole thing.   In...twenty-five seconds...*mark*!"

"Oh — " and Karla makes reference to a bodily function in terms she would certainly reprimand (and blip) a guest for on her own programme. We can overhear her exhorting the crew to get their balls moving, and then she's on the monitor, dulcet and smiling compassionately, arm round a shrivelled bus-driver.

Pavel rolls his eyes, and rolls them again when I tell him about the presidential press-conference.

"I can't send Karla, she'll ask Niemek whether he's wearing his long-johns — " although she's making a rather neat job of the foundered bus. He summons Firenc, and tells him he'll be his own driver for the second mobile unit; assigning a cameraman leaves only one for the studio, a lean and leathery veteran who's been up all night. Before leaving Firenc cheerily informs us that another massive depression, having wandered in off the Baltic, is following precisely the track of the one still with us, and may bring us a further 20 cm ("or more") of snow.

In a breathing-space with coffee, I recount my conversation with Niemek.

"You sure he's not just fluffing you off?"

"He sounded serious."

"Yeah. They're all good at that."

On the monitor a captain of police is urging all except those with essential occupations to stay at home, pointing out that disabled cars in the streets are an obstacle to the hard-pressed police, fire and ambulance services.

Just before noon, Albertson reaches me with the message, *Call me. Urgent.* That's as may be; we are about to show and view the Niemek event on both channels (leaving Col. Lawrence on the Sun's Anvil).

It is poorly attended, a few newspapers and Firenc for us, with a handful of representatives (some I recognise from last night) from the nearby cluster of embassies, American, German, Russian, some Slavonic neighbours. Probably they're bored.

First we have Premier Dalerant, and he has at last found an effective image-building device; always as conservative in his dress as restrained in his manner, he is now in rather baggy unpressed work-trousers and a lumberjack shirt, as if ready to grab a shovel and personally exhume Korava. Despite which and a self-deprecating preludial grin as flash-cameras capture the sartorial moment, he becomes gravely formal, and on his own authority declares a General National Emergency, an act which confers extraordinary powers on the president, though parliament must meet to ratify or reverse the declaration within forty-eight hours. The peculiar current political situation is reflected in this concern for constitutional punctilio.

Niemek comes next to the rostrum, to thank Dalerant, and to remind us that his titular authority as commander of the armed forces becomes effective control only with such a declaration (it is in fact a question of providing the money for any contemplated action). While most of Dusatia, he tells us, is hard hit, it is the western half of the country, from the Korava region to the Czech border, where conditions are worst, with some two dozen or more villages and hamlets completely isolated, without telephone service and, in many cases, electricity; the lack of medical services and food is certain to become acute without swift action, such as only the army is equipped for.

He then turns the proceedings over to Marshall Svarin, tall, balding, wearied man, with a thrust of bony nose over the nether lip and mournful jaw of a Velázquez Habsburg, who lowers over the rostrum like a gaunt revivalist preacher with some especially nasty news about brimstone — but an apparent gloom is Svarin's norm, and he is actually quite a pleasant man in private. The problems, he says, of rescue, communications and supply for the west require maximum co-ordinated effort. To this purpose, a structural change long contemplated for purely administrative purposes, is to be immediately effective: the Fourth Division, the Second (Mountain) Division, Combat Brigades XI (Parachute) and

XII, together with Second Engineer Battalion, and a number of other transport and medical units, are now to be under a unified command, as Army Corps West.

While Javelin Division, based in Viczonjy, is already deployed to conduct road-clearing and rescue efforts in the east, some twenty of its helicopters and pilots are temporarily reassigned to the west. Also from Javelin, its commander, Major-General Firkus, is advanced to Lieutenant-General, and is to command Army Corps West. Born and brought up, as he was, in the Czech borderlands, he knows the country. His proven ability makes him the ideal man to direct these emergency efforts, and beyond that, to instill cohesion and effectiveness in the western command.

And behold, there is Firkus, standing to be recognised, in battle-dress, attempting a look of determined purpose; he must have been helicoptered in, and may be a little dazed by this.

Pavel and I exchange looks of a perplexity which vanishes with Marshall Svarin's little footnote: "Brigadier Cebju, of my personal staff, is to become interim commander of Javelin Division."

At the studios, a persistent trickle of personnel has been arriving with tales of adventure, of more-than-human determination that got them here, and some have stopped work (more have never started) to watch the presidential event. A writer, one of the gopher-girls and a couple of technicians are bewildered to witness unrestrained enthusiasm over what seems to them some fairly arid administrative detail; can anything that happens to Cebju be the reason for whoops of joy?

As a frequent spokesman and colourless appendage to the Chief of Staff, Cebju is a familiar figure, self-effacing list-maker, compiler of feasibility studies, cost-efficiency authority, Svarin's drudge. It doesn't matter that Firkus now commands more troops, they're not Javelin troops, the officers not Vock's disciples; he'll be talking to division commanders, and divorced from the Javelin infrastructure of potential coup. Either Niemek, or Madame Niemek, or conceivably Svarin himself, deserves a place among the great opportunists of history; under cover, as it were, of the blizzard, Javelin is being taken off the political board. Cebju! if there were any threat of war, the appointment would be bizarre;

Firkus, despite the compliments, must know he's being kicked upstairs, and Vock, suspecting he's suspect, is going to see it additionally as a personal insult; the storied armour that took on the Red Army under a man who is more accountant than soldier.

Indeed, when there is a pause here for questions, the man from *Novjétny*, the right-wing tabloid, queries the wisdom of depriving Javelin of Firkus, and wonders further if there might be a place for General Vock in the present crisis.

Niemek waves off the Chief of Staff to give an answer; snow, at the moment, is a more pressing concern than the kind of operation for which an armoured division is particularly trained, and General Firkus is highly qualified for his new responsibilities. As for *former*-General Vock, while it would be inappropriate in the midst of the current political quarrel, to appoint him to any position of authority, he, Niemek, would be grateful for any counsel Vock might wish to offer, based on his wide experience and well-known commitment to the needs of his country.

Pavel, after hugging me, is jumping up and down (note for any translator: this absurdity is thoroughly established idiom, and means "making small, repeated jumps." He really jumped only *up*, while *down* was involuntary), chanting, "That old bastard! That old bastard!"

Niemek, that is, and the term is strong approval tinged with something beyond respect, containing implicit relief he's on the right side.

The remainder of the conference is a succession of officials asking for calm, and patience in paralyzed residential sections, exhorting not to drive, completely banning cars without tyre-chains from national ways, threatening forcible removal of cars blocking emergency routes, giving out numbers to call for various forms of distress. A bird-like woman from the Ministry of Power suggests that those deprived of electricity can store their perishable foods out in the snow, possibly oblivious to the fact that those same people have no means of hearing her. There are some dreary questions and plain or evasive answers, but for me the euphoria brought on by the blunting of Javelin persists into my talk with Albertson.

He demands elucidation of my obscure but expensive-sounding letter, with an aside about my having remained so long in Korava; there's some top-notch blizzard footage coming out of Warsaw and Prague. Here I'm able to promise him all the snow he could possibly desire, with the added attraction of impending political drama ("As this beleaguered country waits tensely for resolution of its leadership crisis..."); I have already begun putting together a montage of storm scenes.

I tell him then what has just come to mind, that unless there is an unexpected sudden improvement in conditions, I'm likely to be the only representative of the world press when Wirath announces his decision. Albertson is moderately gratified, but says Dusatia as a subject has rather gone off the boil, unless we're going to have riots or something. We have, I tell him, better than riots, and for the first time that it involves Wirath's celebrated daughter; even Albertson doesn't need reminding who she is.

With Niemek in firm control, I can see no real reason left for caution. I don't like the complete lack of any news about Rietz, who has dropped from sight, but he must know by now that his only hope is that Wirath, against all expectation, will decide the Yellow Ballot issue in favour of the Loyalists, and if that happens (Vock, as premier, intervening to block any prosecution, leading to a new constitutional crisis) what I say now, overheard or not, is of no importance.

There follows a lengthy and complicated discussion, sometimes exclamatory, sometimes a wrangle, especially when I reveal my fifty-fifty arrangement with Pavel and RTPD, which I can defend on the grounds that we'll be entirely dependent on Dusatian Television's technical resources, and (even more tellingly) that Pavel himself is part of the story. For a man in whose pockets I'm putting, oh, I don't know, a hundred thousand pounds, a quarter of a million, who can tell? Albertson is ungratefully grumpy when we finally reach, if not accord, truce.

After that, there's an odd talk with my parents, telling them when Albertson calls it's all right to admit Christa is there, and that I'll be making arrangements for her return to Korava as soon as the airport reopens.

My mother says, "Why must she return to Korava?"

"I imagine her father very much wants to see her." It is remarkable evidence of Wirath's iron will that he has made no apparent attempt to discover where Christa is, and has simply accepted Pavel's second-hand assurance that she is safe.

Cryptically, my mother says, "I suppose we can spare her. You'll bring her back when you come?"

I agree to, without finding words to ask why Christa has become so indispensable there.

As I finish that call, my glad mood is dissipated, and I descend with a thud into gloom, which I trace back to the debate over Pavel with Albertson. I told him it was an informant of Pavel's who had first brought us word of the kidnapping, and now I'm nagged at by Arni's disappearance, an unreasonable feeling of guilt, which I know Pavel shares.

No longer needed as an auxiliary RTPD announcer, I tape some pieces of my own, and when the mobile unit puts in, have Firenc drive me over to the High Court so as to be filmed getting snowed on while talking, a mandatory scene. If snow is still falling; gusty wind makes it hard to tell. It had definitely stopped for a time in early afternoon, when there was a gleam of feeble sunlight; the airport was open long enough for a couple of departures, before blowing snow again made the runways unusable.

On the way back I notice that a little semi-basement bakery is open and doing business, and since the only safe place to stop would be squarely in the single lane cleared for and kept trampled by traffic, have Firenc circle the block while I go in for some bread, which Katja has cited as our sole urgent need. It is very good, crackling, crusty bread, and the baker is worthy of it, a tiny man not much more than Angèle's height and weight, with the florid, confident face of a heavyweight.

He cheerfully defies anything the weather can do; he lives immediately behind his shop, has a couple of tonnes of flour stored, and his fuel, as with most of Korava, is unfailing natural gas, piped, as far as he's concerned, from Poland, though I know its origins lie three thousand and more frozen kilometres farther to the east, the bleak shores of the Obskaya Gulf. His name is

Fischer, his paternal line of Austrian origin, though he claims the family have been bakers in Dusatia for seven direct generations, first where the Magadu department store now stands, then at this spot since the 1920s.

As for blizzards, well, his grandfather (still living, expert custodian of the "mother" for yeast) went on baking through all the worst days of the Second World War, right through the liberation, undeterred by small-arms fire and a blazing tank outside. By that time, shortages had reduced him to selling half-loaves, and there was a famous loaf which ended by being shared unawares between the last German officer, pausing in his retreat, and, five minutes later, the first Red Army soldier to arrive.

Going outside with my loaves, I signal to Firenc to block traffic for a few minutes (there isn't much to block) so as to get the indomitable Fischer on tape. The crew moves in, but the combination of lights and camera, his having rehearsed with me, and Firenc's too-blandishing manner, turns the little baker into a large ham, with all the winking, chuckling folksiness of — well, of Gorat, campaigning. With that comparison in mind, I suppose the tape is good enough to put on the air, and Firenc, I'm a little disappointed to find, is delighted with it.

Back at the studios, I compose, ready for use, the link between tomorrow's coverage of the Wirath announcement and the now-it-can-be-told story of the kidnapping, though actually I'm hoping to prompt Wirath, when I put a question to him, to introduce the subject himself.

Pavel comes with a glum face. "They found the car."

"The Toyota." A large stone drops in my belly.

A nod. An alert provincial policeman attached to road-clearing operations eastward had spotted the orange number-plates when the car was partially uncovered, and found they matched a missing car circular. The car was empty, and had been left beside the Viczonjy road, thirty kilometres east of Korava. It had been left in *park*, engine off, but the handbrake was not on, and the keys were still in the ignition. The petrol tank was about half full, and the engine started when tried. Nothing unusual was found in the interior of the car, nor in what Pavel, forestalling my apprehensive question, calls the trunk.

It was not possible, of course, to make the normal search along and in the vicinity of the road, and Arni's disappearance is complete.

"There's no way it adds up," Pavel protests. "Okay, worst-case scenario, let's say Rietz or one of his hoods manages to hijack the car with Arni in it — "

"How?"

"After he dropped off Ljuba, he went back to his own place, to get something, or maybe he had to take a leak. Rietz, or Lisuk, maybe, had the place staked out, pulls a gun and makes Arni drive out to the sticks. Okay. They get someplace quiet, he tells Arni to stop, makes him get out of the car, and they go into the woods, and he takes Arni out. Then what?"

Reluctantly I offer, "Suppose there are two people — there could be more, but two at minimum — watching Arni's rooms, and they have a car. One gets in with Arni, as you say, and the other follows. They execute Arni, and drive off leaving the Toyota. Or — " I see a fresh objection coming, and am compelled to make plausible what I hope is not true — "the killing is done somewhere, they drive both cars away, and leave the Toyota miles from the scene, so as not to lead searchers to the body. Dead or alive, Arni could still be anywhere."

"He can't be dead. He's a good kid."

XI

Morning is brilliant, gusty, bitterly cold, still with stinging clouds of snow wind-driven, though the clouds have all departed. Not before adding fresh overnight layers to the accumulation: the airport is still shut down, the railways operating only as far as the suburbs, we are unreachable by road from Berlin, or Prague, or Warsaw. Unless Wirath, in an atypical acknowledgement of external conditions, postpones his announcement, Pavel I and seem certain to have the world stage virtually to ourselves.

But this is to underestimate the tenacity and ingenuity of our colleagues. We ride in the back of Mobile Unit One (now manned by regulars) to the High Court building, and while mounting those steps are first astonished and then showered with snow agitated by the descent of a large military helicopter into the cramped forecourt. It has Ukrainian Army markings, which explains the attendant presence of a pair of armed Dusatian helicopters hanging just overhead. As the massive, drooping rotor comes to a stop, a front-seat passenger warmly, even passionately embraces the female pilot, slides, legs first, through the door, and becomes Ludmilla Matsirova, smiling opulently, and waving to us, waving her credentials at the police who close in on her. She is followed by a small, wiry man with a small wireless camera; Russian TV is here, she having made use of somewhat irregular contacts to be ferried in from Lvov after a late-night flight from Kiev.

There is more. Once inside, in the foyer of the small auditorium, we find ourselves preceded by an improbable pairing, both known best by nicknames, Dufoireau, begging to be asked about his cleverness in getting here, and "Kitty O'Hara," Nippon TV, whose real name is Itiko Ohanura, the Irish alias bestowed by Trev Hassett, with whom she learnt fine points of her trade during a longish liaison. She is far too Japanese, tittering with a hand to her mouth, portraying agonizing embarrassment and abject humility as if doing Cìo-cìo-san in, let's say, an Albanian production of *Butterfly*, at times descending to the level of an overdone Yum-yum. This, while it might be almost passable in flowered kimono and oversized obi, becomes outlandish in Kitty's ordinary work-costume of twill shirt and French blue-jeans, and shouldn't deceive anyone; she speaks excellent English, good French and two kinds of Chinese, is polite, pretty, ferociously competitive, and tough. It's said the affair with Hassett ended after she cleaned out and embarrassed him in an all-night poker game in Bangkok, the other participants being the chief of police, the owner of an enormously successful child-brothel, and the biggest opium producer in all Asia (these are storied scenes I have no desire to experience first-hand).

Their epic (which I suspect owes more to her determination than the little grey cells of Dufoireau) began in Prague, where there were no planes. Learning that Korava might still be reachable overland from the southwest, they took the train to Brno, and fought their way through in a hired car, taking eleven hours for less than 200 km., more than half the time practically under the back wheels of a monstrous, crawling machine ejecting beside the road an endless thick ribbon of snow.

The Dusatian print news is here in force; all the newspapers, last evening and this morning, have had variants on the "Day of Decision" headline for their front pages, *Novjétny* a page three "conversation" with Vock (pictured defying the blizzard, fists thrust in the pockets of a manly pea-jacket) expressing confidence in his vindication, as well as undefined "reservations" about the wisdom of taking General Firkus away from Javelin, though this, of course "is not to imply any criticism of President Niemek or of Marshall Svarin." I once interviewed a local candidate in Ukraine who called his main opponent a depraved moron, hastening to add he meant nothing personal by that.

Though the weather has kept any potential demonstrators indoors, security is as extensive as I've ever seen; the judiciary possesses its own small force, now reinforced by the cordon of city police we've already passed through, and, for firepower, a contingent of brown *dzhăndarmi*, their deadly little machine-guns slung at their chests; I wonder not so idly how many would fall into Pavel's category, cops with a soft spot for those opposed to the egghead loony queers. But Pavel turns aside for a few quiet words with the commander of the normal guard.

"I wised him to keep eyes peeled for Angèle, not to let her in." Conditions prevented Pavel from going to see her yesterday, but he had her briefly on the phone, and reported she said she wasn't going anywhere while the weather was like this, but, "She gets some great idea, you can't trust her to behave, crazy bitch."

Yes, but since the evening of the ball, there has been another untold story lurking. From Angèle's remark about Pavel's former love for dancing, contrary to the impression always (I believe, deliberately) given, it's perfectly clear that they knew each other quite well *before* the shooting incident. If she knew his dancing habits, it's hardly likely she didn't have some idea of where he stood politically, and certainly did not shoot him as a symbol of collaboration with the oppressive Muscovites. Was there a triangle, Pavel and the two young dancers; was Angèle's student assault on RTPD the camouflage for a crime of passion? That would give a different but certainly not less credible reason for Pavel's refusal to testify against her. I'm never going to know.

Inside, in anticipation of reduced attendance, the first couple of rows of seats have been removed, and a lectern placed not on the low stage, but an even lower portable platform in front of it. But there is a large folding screen for back-projections set up on the stage. Also a row of half a dozen chairs, and these are progressively occupied, first by a wispy-haired, rather stooped young man with wire-rimmed glasses, who might well be a computer-programmer, then an almost elderly, sober woman I vaguely recognise as the incumbent in a virtually powerless but constitutionally stipulated appointive office, Commissioner or Certifier of Elections, something like that. Next, robed, come the four other High Court judges, two of whose names at minimum will have to be appended to any decision Wirath proclaims; conventional assessment is that their numbers contain one right-winger, one ultra-liberal, and two who simply follow Wirath's lead, a condition which turns the quartet into something like a rubber stamp.

Then, with no sounding brass or rumble of drums, comes Wirath, briskly, at the lower level, shadowed closely by a familiar figure, Rosza Smed, *née* Grdacza, great-granddaughter of the national novelist, excellent stand-up interpreter, poor translator (accurate, but with no ear; her Dusatian paperback versions of *Pride and Prejudice* and *Catcher in the Rye* are like the work of a single monochrome writer).

Wirath: an ordinary grey suit, looking rested and composed; I wonder if my unilateral relaxation of secrecy has resulted in his hearing again from Christa. All having risen at his entry, he waves us two-handed to be seated, saying, "Good morning. I shall try to be finished in time for the next blizzard — " a joke, unexpected from this source, which therefore, first for the Dusatian-speaking, then in translation for those who can follow English, gets a double laugh beyond its actual merits.

I'm seated on a rather irregular aisle, chairs being haphazardly aligned, and as we settle am jostled slightly by a latecomer, pushing by to be seated to my right front; with surprise I see the strawlike mop and dark glasses of Reuters' little Amy Highcote. As she sits I note that in place of the usual trousers she is wearing boots and a slit skirt, and wonder why I've not noticed before that Amy has more than passable legs, at least as promised by those sleek calves. Something else, and after a moment it comes to me; when she scrambled past I was not assailed by her characteristic, clinging, musty aroma of vegetable combustion; can it be that she has anticipated the New Year and resolved to give up cigarettes?

Ask her later, and probably hear of one more ingenious way of getting into snowbound Korava: now, Wirath is launched.

He is at his most professorial, giving an exact account of the complaint as it reached the High Court, and enumerating the various elements to be considered, first of which was the nature of the disputed ballot itself. In their specification, those who brought the suit maintained that its colour, being identified with one party, or rather group of parties, unfairly influenced voters to cast their ballots for that coalition. Before discussing the merits of that assertion, Wirath had thought it desirable to establish whether the colour of the disputed ballot did indeed violate the constitutional stipulation on that point, and, if so, whether it could properly be termed *yellow*.

All this must be said twice, and already there is some restiveness apparent, but I perceive Wirath, in his quiet, pedantic way, is rather enjoying himself, as anyone might have predicted who knew, from his writings, his love of making a point perfectly, indisputably clear. Now he introduces the earnest young man up on the stage proper. A German, Manfried Thomas, professor of optical physics, colour consultant for Agfa, he activates the slide-projector using a hand-held control, and begins a painstaking analysis. He speaks very nearly correct English, giving Rosza Smed a chance to go the other way, and occasionally to struggle with some stiff technicalities.

"The constitutional specification of white as the colour of legal ballots," he begins, "is of course not intended as a scientific or technical description." He then shows us on-screen a square of "absolute white," and retaining a bar of that stark shade for comparison, eight samples of paper designated as "white," obtained from German, Swiss and English as well as Dusatian suppliers.

"Clearly, we see there is considerable deviation from absolute white to be found in what is ordinarily designated and sold as `white' paper. Sample three, for example; this is a paper used for many of the undisputed ballots in the recent election. All these samples, let me say, are photographed against an opaque, matt-white surface under full-spectrum white halogen light." He would, I think, go on to describe the film, its characteristics and the exposures used, but senses a certain impatience in his audience, and moves ahead to the next point.

We are shown the paper of the so-called "yellow" ballot, which is then compared simultaneously to the undisputed though impure white and to eight samples supplied in answer to a request for "pale yellow" paper, all of which are a great deal more yellow; the eye irresistibly groups the ballot paper with the "off-whites." Finally, Thomas tells us samples of that ballot paper were sent to his international array of suppliers, asking them to define the colour. "This was on the letterhead of my own offices, making it impossible for any respondent to know in what matter the query was made."

Not quite idiomatic, but adequately clear.

"The French, *pale ivory* — " Thomas reads from a list of responses. "*Light cream, cream white,* and, from the British source, *warm white.* Two of the suppliers contacted, then, though with qualifications, used the word *white* to describe this paper, while none used the term *yellow*, or its equivalent in any language."

There is a pause. Is he finished? He is. "Some," he says, "may have questions, which we have agreed to have at the end of Mr Justice Wirath's presentation, but for the most part the answers can be found in this printed explanation — " he holds it up — "which is to be distributed for everyone, and describes the assumptions, methods and controls made use of in this investigation."

This brings a slight patter of applause, and Wirath expresses thanks for his thoroughness. It is by now quite clear which way the decision is going, but we are going to be given every step.

Wirath resumes. "This analysis takes us to the heart of the complaint, and allows us to save a great deal of time and argument in discussing intent and effect. If the ballot in question cannot fairly or reasonably be described as yellow, then the question of whether a yellow ballot might or might be intended to affect the outcome of an election becomes purely hypothetical. We find, then, that there was no 'yellow' ballot, and that part of the complaint is, therefore, without substance.

"However," he proclaims warningly, just as I (not alone), somewhat startled by how the long way round has turned into a short cut, am preparing to rejoice, marvelling at Wirath's stroke of genius in turning *Is this yellow?* — the angry rhetorical question expressed by Pavel — into an expert enquiry.

"There remains the question of whether these ballots, if not yellow then arguably non-white, are constitutionally valid. In the strictest interpretation, the answer must clearly be, no."

(A whispering ruffle of shock, growing in the second wave as the translation comes; for the first time there is genuine tension, and no one's attention is merely marginal.)

Wirath rests his forearms on the lectern, and the desire to make himself perfectly plain transmutes into a kind of benign didacticism. "A very long time ago, as a student, I became convinced that there is no such thing in law as an abstract question. Though we must strive, so far as is possible, to isolate eternal principles from specific instances, the laws of man are not the laws of physics, and to apply the words of a law without considering the intent behind its making is to create nonsense rather than order, undue burdens and restraints in place of justice."

(Long wait while Rosza, going carefully, catches up.)

"Now, it is crystal clear that the constitutional proviso as to the proper colour for our ballots was intended not to express a captious preference, but to prevent precisely the species of partisan influence as we have conclusively determined was not and could not have been present in this instance; if there was no yellow ballot there was no actual or intended influence, and we may go to another principle I learnt as a very young man; *de minimis non curat lex*; the law does not extend to trifles. Though technically perhaps not white, the difference of hue, as Doctor Thomas has so ably demonstrated, is just such a trifle, and it is the decision of the court — "

(Once more, Rosza, at this dramatic juncture, is permitted to bring her audience up to date.)

" — that the complaint falls far short of the standard necessary for a substantive challenge to the validity of the General Election of December 12th, and the temporary injunction granted in Korava State Court on December 17th is, therefore, set aside."

It is over. There comes, perhaps inappropriately, a substantial burst of applause, to which Wirath, putting his notes in order, sedulously avoids any reaction, while up on the stage, Madame Commissioner or whatever she is, taking the hand-held mike used by Professor Thomas, intones to no effect at all that no other objection having been heard, it is her duty to pronounce the election of December 12th as lawful and binding. The Loyalists have lost, and Gorat will be premier again.

I don't know why I ever assented to the general perception, through Pavel, of Wirath as a severe adherent to the exact letter of the law, when his books, so far as they are readable at all, are replete with dry advocacy of just the sort of common-sense humanism in interpreting law as he has here displayed. It is from attempting to browse those books that I've called him colourless, another misapprehension; the literary style is not always the man, and today Wirath is quiet one-man show.

Kitty O'Hara asks, "Would you say, now we have a decision, that this was, from the first, a frivolous objection?"

Wirath twinkles at her, and without waiting for the interpreter says in English, "What I would say is, I hope, always what I do say. The law has spoken, and the case is now in your hands, not mine."

The man from *Novjétny* stands ponderously, and is recognised. "Mr Justice, was this decision influenced by a desire, or shall we say a tendency, in the current political climate, to preserve the *status quo ante*?"

Very nasty in its implications, but Wirath points whimsically at the man, and asks, "Have you just come in?"

After the laugh: "I rather tediously outlined the elements of our deliberation, and I don't believe the `current political climate' was anywhere amongst them. However — " relenting a bit. "It is naturally axiomatic that the law must begin with the presumption that the *status quo ante* has met the test of constitutionality and is therefore to be preserved, and those who seek to challenge that *status quo* have the task of marshalling sufficient argument to prove that presumption incorrect. Here, the evidence woefully failed to sustain the challenge, is that an answer for you?"

It is more, but the partisan from *Novjétny* has provided me with a context, and I'm on my feet, quickly acknowledged. "Justice Wirath, would you like to comment on the unusual outside pressures to which you have been subjected during your consideration of this case?"

This brings a murmur, while Wirath stares, ponders, and breaks out in a smile. "Mr Kearns, isn't it? Mark Kearns?" Standing out from behind the lectern, he beckons with four hinged fingers. "Would you?"

With great reluctance, I move in his direction; this is not what I wanted, but it can't be stopped now.

At the edge of his low platform, he grasps a hand, bends to murmur in my ear, "I can never repay you," and right hand on my left shoulder, turns me to face my double dozen peers.

"Most of you must know Mr Kearns, who is of your number, and a welcome visitor in our country. Now I wish to tell you of the great debt I owe him." Lacking his former ease, he pauses, moistening his upper lip, and I perceive personal emotions are about to take him in one step from effortless command to stammering inarticulacy.

"When this matter of the so-called Yellow Ballot first came to me, my daughter — I'm sure you know my daughter, who is really quite celebrated in her own right — my daughter was here in Dusatia, although I fear, because of this urgent question I was unable to — was here in Dusatia. There was a man — "

He breaks off. There is a man. Coming at us is one uniformed as an officer of the *dzhăndarmi*, a captain, and I at first think he must be weirdly anxious about my proximity to Wirath. His hand is at his leather holster, unsnapping, drawing the pistol, and as he looks up I see it is Erhardt Rietz.

His eyes meet mine, absolute hatred, the pistol is cocked, and at the strangely hyperactive tempo of my perceptions I note that leftward little Amy Highcote is on her feet, fumbling at her shoulder bag.

Rietz intends to kill me, or kill Wirath, or both, only the order is unsure. I twist away, ducking, there is a tremendously loud bang, practically overlapping with the first of three quick cap-pistol, Christmas-cracker pops.

I have not (and this is going to have to be denied over and again) made the smallest attempt to "shield Wirath." I'm not the sort of person to whom such an act would occur; when a gun is going off in my vicinity my reactions are pure instinct, and my instincts pure self-preservation. I have a sensation that I've been shot but am still alive, and when I turn back (probably, "and open my eyes"), the Justice is almost overwhelmed by a sudden rugby-scrum of his own security-guards, Rietz is down and bleeding, nearly all the Fourth Estate is cowering behind and as far as possible beneath chairs, and a second horde of uniforms is converging on Amy Highcote, wresting a tiny pistol from her small hand.

Only it isn't Amy, never was, and I must have known that from her arrival. It is Angèle, in a flaxen wig and dark glasses, and she has saved Wirath's life, or my life, or both, only the order is disputable. My right side is burning, and it occurs to me I might as well sit down on the edge of the platform.

Someone has taken away my jacket and wastefully torn away my shirt; possibly the same vandal who is pressing a pad painfully against my side. Not ten feet away, motionless Rietz is being ministered to with oxygen mask and bottled elixir; he is not at his best, with a dark little hole in his head and a far messier wound in the throat; his always pallid complexion has a blue-green cast. Angèle is gone, Wirath has vanished, behind me the four judges, the Delphic Oracle and Professor Hues have all been spirited away, and I decide I must have been daydreaming here for some minutes.

Pavel's large features come near, and I ask, "Have we got it all on tape?"

"Oh, yeah."

I begin to be impatient with the white-coated young man and his dabbings at me. "What's the time? We've got an edit to do. We have to get Wirath on tape, otherwise — " I'm interrupted by arrival of an oxygen-mask, and my arm is being swabbed preparatory to my connection to unwanted fluids.

"You're going to the hospital, buddy."

"I'm bloody not — " prying away the mask, seldom more certain of anything. The wound is nothing, though I feel as if someone has kicked me very hard in the ribs, there clearly is no bullet in me; mostly I'm suffering from shock. "I'd like a cup of tea." Made by Katja, I don't say, cozy and strainer and scald the pot. For Pavel's sake, or the sake of hard-boiled tradition, I should have demanded three fingers of rye whisky.

But he looks unduly harried. "Are you still on live?"

"Don't worry about it — " but I note a shouldered camera is there when a wheeled stretcher is ratcheted down to receive what's left of Rietz, and follows its rushed exit.

"Where's Angèle?"

"They took her downtown. I'm, I oughta go there, they can't hold her now."

This (my brain is coming back up) seems to me quite probably untrue; they can hold her, and it's going to take some time to sort out the white and black hats in this morning's events.

"What did Rietz think he could accomplish? Even without Angèle, he would never have got out of here alive."

"The guy snapped. He sees old man Wirath about to start naming names, the whole Yellow Ballot gimmick is a bust, last straw, you — he went bughouse, buddy."

Well, but he hadn't come here, disguised as a copper, to applaud politely, and that was something else that needed looking into — his connections, I mean, to the *dzhăndarmi* that had let him borrow his uniform.

Rietz, I reflect, couldn't know he would only have one shot, but even so he could have killed me, or killed Wirath, but for a last-instant vacillation. His primary target must have been Wirath, but seeing me for the first time since humiliation on the bridge at Obdana he was muddled by rage, and couldn't decide between his enemies. Which, except for taking a notch out between my ribs, is pretty much where his bullet went.

The majority of the remaining press are now ranged strategically near, being kept back by police, and I realise not one of them has a clue how Wirath and Rietz and I are connected; they would like elucidation of his expressed gratitude to me, and especially of the reference to his daughter — all my own property as a journalist, but now I'm fair game, part of the story, too. Given time they are sure to elude or wear down the resistance of the police cordon.

Here, Kitty and to a lesser extent Ludmilla have an unfair edge, since our societal adherence to gender stereotypes permits them to approach under the guise of sympathetic concern for a felled colleague; Kitty could manage a look of feminine solicitude while picking the pope's pocket. When another medical person arrives, trundling a wheelchair, to say the second ambulance is standing by, the women are in its wake, and Ludmilla calls out, "Hey, Kearns — " pronouncing it with about five r's — "You gonna be okay, baby." (*am I so sentimental as to be touched by codswallop?*)

They are all round, Poirot, too, and the newspaper people, as I allow the medics to help me into the chair, even let them savage my arm with a great steel spike connected to glucose; sheltered behind the oxygen mask I am proof against any question, and Pavel, to whom I have muttered, "Stay with me," is tightlipped and impermeable, Bogart (or is it Cagney?) clamming up.

At the hospital, we'll be able to find out whether Rietz is alive or dead, then slip away and get to work editing film and recording commentary for what's going to make a marvellous story, even more so now.

"*Gaspodi*," Pavel says, struck by a thought, when we're in the back of a slow-moving ambulance. "If I had collected Angèle's little toy heater yesterday, you and the judge might be dead, my friend."

The American vice-president with the appropriately robotic manner might as well have called our miracle of integrated communications the triviality super-highway, or the garbage autobahn, or the misinformation motorway; the old rules still hold, and the value of technology remains no more than the value of what it has to communicate. Coming back to the studios Pavel is barely in time to prevent the radio news from opening with a story slightly rewritten from the wire service, which in turn acknowledges copying from the French agency; it therefore originates with that bungler Dufoireau; nonsense has flashed and splashed round the world and come back to be given credence here, where we showed what really happened, not two kilometres and two hours from the events misrepresented.

Poirot's version, in brief, is that Angèle, a well-known anarchist, has been arrested after wounding a journalist and fatally wounding a security-man who intervened in her apparent attempt to kill the Chief Justice; it does not fail to quote Angèle's old advocacy of "a few timely assassinations."

I flash the most urgent of red lights to my people, telling them on no account to copy and in fact explicitly to refute the story, following with a bare outline of the true facts; it then takes me ten minutes to write a fuller story, linked to the already-written account of the kidnapping, and to transmit the whole thing.

All this time Pavel is in a rage, though a productive one. The first channel is continuing live coverage, by now consisting of forlorn pictures of various people waiting in various places; our woman at the hospital waiting for news of Rietz, our man at police headquarters not being allowed to see Angèle or speak with the officer in charge of the case, the dazed lingerers at the High Court building, and Firenc, obviously shivering, outside the residence of Gorat, whose certain reinstallation as premier has become "the other story," but who, once buttonholed, might be good for a comment on the shootings.

Pavel orders these watches to continue, while he writes furiously at a computer, uses his stopwatch, bullies editors and the archivist to give him footage he requires. For a time we work together on selection and mix, and will refine it later for our joint presentation, but then I'm called to the phone.

It is Wirath, who tells me he rang the hospital for news of me, and was told I had "discharged myself," a singularly appropriate term.

He asks how I am, and I tell him, fine, though really I'm nothing, an out-of-body experience in an overlarge short-sleeved shirt (Pavel, who tends to sweat, keeps a supply at the studios); in my veins instead of blood an exotic mélange of distilled water, common salt, glucose, antibiotics, morphine, and finally, none of that having succeeded in killing me, a double brandy. I still seem to be alert — but use of the personal pronoun is misleading; there is alertness, there is function, there is a dreamy sense that pain is only veiled, not banished, but the containing *I* is absent.

After another tentative exchange or two, it's plain to me that Wirath feels responsible for my wounding, and after reassuring him it is nothing but a slight inconvenience, I shamelessly make use of his concern, getting him to assent to a visit from a camera crew, so that he can describe his first encounter with the gunman, Rietz.

"It was Rietz, then? It all happened so fast. Was he killed?"

"No. He hasn't regained consciousness, and is undergoing cranial surgery at this moment."

A hum of doubt. "Since I did not recognise him, it would be improper for me to speculate on the motive behind the attack."

"I don't see that, sir." (In full possession of my normal faculties, would I dare debate Chief Justice Wirath on such a point?) "If you had never seen the man before, and were reliably informed later he was, for example, Rietz's brother, there would be no impropriety, as the intended target, in your speculating as to his motives."

"But, eventually, you see, I may have the case to review."

"However, sir, there is no need for you to refer to this morning's events at all, if you could simply recount your former meeting with Erhardt Rietz, and what he proposed to you."

"And how I subsequently learnt my, ah, my daughter was safe — " there it is again, the change of voice. "In fact, the account I was about to give when we were interrupted. When would this be?"

"Almost immediately, sir." The forlorn survivor of the original High Court coverage will be glad to have something fresh to film, and can be at Wirath's threshold in five minutes.

"With pleasure. I have still had no real opportunity to express my gratitude for what you did."

"No need." Possibly, with me not displayed beside him like a prize marrow, he won't dwell on my role; I make a much better reporter standing on the boundary applauding the shots than out in the middle myself.

Since the man filming him will not know enough to put any questions, I suggest Wirath might want to make some notes of what he wishes to say, and we part in mutual esteem, with on my side some wonder that he asked nothing about the young woman who saved his life, the prime subject of Pavel's frenzy.

For what he has required in the way of technical support, he is ready in unimaginably little time, and spot on the stroke of three p.m. suspends the live remotes for what he calls a Special Edition News.

Though he still appears interviewing and ringmastering round-table events, Pavel seated behind the news-reader's desk is an image from the past, but for Dusatians, accustomed to the factual, dispassionate, even-handed style of reporting he did as much as anyone to establish, his vehemence is altogether new — as is twenty-three minutes devoted to a single subject.

He begins with a forty-second montage of the morning's events, the High Court Building, Wirath's entry, Professor Thomas and his slides, Wirath pronouncing his verdict, and then the chaotic finale (it is the first time I've seen myself shot, and it guiltily reminds me I must let my parents know it is far less catastrophic than it appears).

Back to Pavel, grim-faced. "This," he says, "Is what the world is being told — " and he outlines the Poirot version, though so far leaving out Angèle's name.

That done, he is unleashed. He runs the tape repeatedly, slows it down, freezes it, uses highlighting, arrowing and isolation to show plainly that Rietz was moving in on Wirath and me before Angèle ("the young woman") stirred, and that his pistol was ready before she went for hers. It is plain, Pavel emphasises, that Rietz had no other target but one or both of the two men, and the young woman no other object but to stop Rietz.

Turning then to the description of Rietz as a security officer, Pavel proclaims he was no such thing, that in his whole life his only official connection with the police was as a rapidly-promoted member of the SNJR, *Schnur*, the notorious Communist secret police; in some magical fashion the archives have retrieved a photograph of Rietz's service record. More recently, he has been well-known to the police and the press as an organiser of political demonstrations (footage of Rietz, again highlighted, conducting the siege of the RTPD studios) and of a street-militia prepared for civic violence on behalf of the National Loyalist Party.

These, Pavel goes on, now moving into dangerous territory, are activities which stem naturally from his long association with their parliamentary leader, General Vock, initially as chief communications officer for Javelin Division.

(This more than suggested implication of Vock is what causes Pavel to be on the carpet next day with the General Director, a tempestuous meeting capped by Pavel's threat of resignation. But by then the tide is running so strongly in his favour that the D.G., himself a political creature, has to climb down as ungraciously as possible, making clear he was criticising only certain aspects of the broadcast, Pavel's partisan tone, his failure to make clear that there is nothing to show Vock has been part of any illicit activities.)

From his redefinition of the victim, Pavel moves to Rietz's motives for wishing to kill Wirath (and me), and that launches the first reference to the kidnapping of Christa Rasch, for which, just in time, the supportive contribution from Wirath, on tape, is transmitted from the High Court Building.   Freed from the necessity of connecting him to the shooting, Wirath roundly names Rietz as the man who had come to see him, to threaten harm to his daughter (inset: much-used, enormously attractive still of Christa) unless he decided in favour of the National Loyalists. Together with his history and reputation, only Wirath's precise manner could make believable his assertion this visit did not play, and could never have played a part, either way, in his Yellow Ballot decision; if the Loyalist case had merit he would have decided for them despite the threat, but in fact would have been obliged to decide against them, even if (and here the detectable tremor in the voice) he had not received word that his daughter was out of danger.

With this (there is also a wholly irrelevant tribute, which will be omitted when we use this tape again) Pavel moves to a promise of the complete story of the attempted kidnapping and how Christa Rasch was freed, on another Special Edition of the evening news. Meanwhile, the young woman, Angèle, whose swift reaction almost certainly saved the life of the Chief Justice, is being held behind closed doors by the police; this fact is deliberately set against a live report from the hospital on the condition of the "would-be assassin."

There, the woman tells us, clinging to her mike and dodging various medical and security persons, Rietz is still in surgery; a harried, understandably waspish chief surgeon says, in effect, that a bullet in the head is nobody's idea of a joke, that while prognosis is premature he doesn't think much of Rietz's chances of a full recovery, and that he is not going to answer any further questions.

"Listen," Pavel, as they tell him he's off, compares his watch to the big clock. "You can get started on your own? I gotta get over to headquarters."

"It isn't going to help. They're not going to release her till there's been some sort of official hearing."

"Damn, this is the dame who saved your life, whadda you want? Shit, it's true, what my father always said about you frozen-ass English — "

Possibly, but this won't help, either, and Pavel with his intelligence intact would allow that one may be grateful, but still recognise that the presence of Angèle, disguised as a Reuters correspondent, needs some explaining. "What we ought to be doing is getting her a lawyer, and you should talk to your friend at the Interior Ministry. The most you and I can do for her is more of what you just did."

He mutters, "A national heroine, so she has to have a lawyer?" But he makes for his office, and once there, for the phone, not his overcoat.

He picks it up, then stops, and points a finger at me. "Sorry. I'm half crazy myself. My old man was full of crap."

"Everybody's father was. Mine thinks the Dusatian national obsession is prudence."

For all his calls, he is restricted to the same line, the one with an unpublished number, the others being jammed with incoming calls: Pavel's secretary keeps arriving to convey the particular importance of some caller, and is repeatedly told it will have to wait; the pile of blue (priority) message slips grows, as does her discreet exasperation. With the broadcast, my correction and amplification of the Poirot story, the cork is out of the bottle, and everyone is demanding film, information, Christa's current whereabouts; we're told the main switchboard downstairs is equally besieged.

A squad of police arrives, wanting tapes and formal statements, at the same moment as the lawyer Pavel has been in touch with rings back.

"She's already got a mouthpiece — " ending that conversation with a baffled face. "Vítor Kaepfky."

Complacent, silvering, Dusatia's best-known, and certainly most expensive practitioner, though hardly for criminal work. He came to wider fame when, for Jiri Podarny, he defeated the Gorat government in its attempt to delay restoration of family property, including what became the Cicada factory, and has since been invariably, suavely successful in a number of prominent commercial cases, the labyrinth of torts and contract law being a peculiarly appropriate venue for one belonging to what claims to be the Dusatian branch of Franz Kafka's family.

The question, as Pavel says, coolly deferring police business, is who hired him?   He has made an unheralded appearance at police headquarters, very briefly seen his client, applied for her release, and announced he will be prepared to put up bail in "any reasonable amount," if she is not set free by the hearing, first thing in the morning.

"Herder?" Pavel names one of the few who has the money needed to make such a blank-cheque commitment; I wasn't going to be the first to. But the gun was his, and someone helped Angèle with her disguise, supplied her, presumably, with credentials. Our conjecture, ages ago, was that she might be the one primed to kill Wirath, but Herder after talking to me at the ball, would have seen that nothing could keep the story of the kidnapping from being told. He might have decided his own chief danger, and Mara's, came from Rietz, the sole real connection between Christa's sequestration at the Eagle's Nest, and the threat delivered to her father — indeed, if Rietz dies, or survives in a speechless condition, convicting the Herders of anything may become impossible. Lisuk and Jenadju have dropped from sight, and the housekeeper at the Eagle's Nest, nice Mrs Bacewicz, obviously wasn't in on the plot; there are the makings here of a line of defence already inadvertently anticipated by Wirath, when I mentioned the treachery of the Herders; "I don't *know* that," he said, meaning he knew only what Rietz had told him. And the attack on Wirath and me can only assist in a portrayal of him as a deranged megalomaniac, making up the kidnapping to dovetail with Christa's innocent mountain holiday.

Has Herder enough control over Angèle to have persuaded her Rietz was the one who had to die? That would mean he knew Rietz intended to be at the Wirath conference; surely it's too much to postulate Herder as a sort of Edgar Wallace or Saxe Rohmer villain, able in some mesmeric way to influence Rietz to kill Wirath, Angèle to kill Rietz?   Although it is true that Herder himself would be no worse, quite likely better off, no matter how partially such a plan succeeded, no matter which among five possibilities was killed.

This is rather a far-fetched speculation to stem from the appearance of a high-priced lawyer. I share none of it with Pavel, but know his thoughts run at least some of the way parallel with mine, entailing his necessary minimal acknowledgement that Angèle's armed presence there, though fortunate for me, was not fortuitous, enough irreconcilables to cause him to let the subject lapse, and lose his brooding gloom in a new fury of work.

Our man in the street somewhere, reading a written statement from the office of General Vock. Deplores shooting, repudiates any recent connection with his former Chief Signals Officer (Rietz), though naturally disappointed, unreservedly accepts Wirath's decision ("Ain't that sweet — " Pavel).

Working without a pause (somebody brings sandwiches from the RTPD canteen, fully international in their desiccated dreariness), doing parallel versions in Dusatian and English, we take our joint production as far as we can without the presence of Christa. So that she can be smuggled to the studios with no competitive ambushes, tomorrow I'll fly back to England and fetch her. Word has come that Korava airport is open and operating, and, as I learn later, the delayed afternoon arrival from Berlin is to bring Hassett, Üwe, Scheiden and the rest, including the authentic Amy Highcote (still chain-smoking), a whole new battalion for the army of our besiegers.

More lurid events have driven the war against the snow into the margins, but RTPD has a team, complete with helicopter, out in the western regions, and there are pictures of relief coming to remote hamlets, an air-drop of crucial supplies, the airlift out of a medical emergency. Also a bulletin from the Ministry, mainly a puff piece about General Firkus taking vigorous command, heartwarming joint efforts with the Czechs, the Poles, and international agencies, the stoic indifference of ordinary soldiers to sleep, rest or sustenance so long as lives are endangered. As an aside, though as if related, there is the offhand news that the Defence Minister, together with Marshall Svarin, is on a tour of inspection, beginning with the Strbjena military base, where they were flown at about midday.

It hardly matters whether Gorat issued the instructions as soon as he heard the Yellow Ballot decision, or Niemek persuaded Dalerant to exercise his fleeting authority. Pavel, grinning, decides to tease me about my alleged softness in passing up a story like nuclear weapons at Strbjena. "Never mind if they don't find anything, they oughta pin a medal on you."

Though none was made, I feel it would be breaking a promise to Madame Niemek if I did write anything about Soviet nuclear cannon, but to save my historical conscience, as a long dependent clause in my main written story, I include the observation that together with yesterday's changes in command, this inspection signals a quiet, profound reorganisation of the military, one which appears to "promise more effective civilian control."

Albertson gets through to find out when I'll be sending pictures; America is greedy for footage. To be fair, he does make sure my wound is not a grave one, before asking anxiously whether we have all the gunplay on tape.

"Oh, Katja called," Pavel, reminded. "Call her back when you got time. She's not gonna believe you're okay without she hears your voice."

Leaving, quite late, we hope our internal access to RTPD's underground garage, where a car and driver are waiting, will allow us to defeat the siege, but the lift stops on the ground floor, and, so that we can be grilled, alert journalists pounce to prevent the doors from reclosing.

It's my first experience on this side of a feeding-frenzy, and it's far better being one of the sharks. We are, of course, a special case, and are treated with a volatile mixture of fellowship, blandishment and rancour — the last especially for me, since Pavel is generally liked for his efficiency and courtesy in making tapes and facilities available (and is still needed for more of the same), whereas I am merely a fellow-infantryman who happened to stumble into an undefended stronghold, and am now claiming credit for its single-handed capture.

The real Amy Highcote: "Kearns, what is your relationship with this Angèle?" Understandable she should be interested in the woman who posed as her, but all the rest of the old hands know the public Angèle, at least by reputation. Dufoireau, by the way, isn't among the throng; he may be nervous about showing his face after Pavel's broadcast annihilation.

"Relationship?"

"I understand you once prevented her being arrested."

"Yes, and I also interviewed her, before the election. RTPD did a profile on the evening news."

"Is that a *No Comment*?"

Trev Hassett: "I was told you have information about the current whereabouts of Christa Rasch."

"Now that's a *No Comment*."

(Chorus of outrage)

Kitty: "Why is it necessary to hide her away? Surely she isn't still in danger?"

Pavel, with a winning smile: "Like we see this morning, nobody's totally safe, huh?"

His attempt to distract and shame them with the reminder of my wounding is only momentarily successful. We escape at last.

XII

Late in January I come back to Korava, sodden in a steady, thawing drizzle. Out in the country there is widespread flooding, the yield of melting snow unable to run off in rivers and streams still blocked by ice. I am here for the trial of Angèle, to testify as a witness. An absurd one if I am restricted to what I actually saw, probably less of Angèle's actions than any person present that day, and the RTPD tapes are far more objective than any eye-witness could be, but the defence having listed me among possibles, the prosecution pre-empted them, which I suspect was exactly Vítor Kaepfky's strategy from the start.

That except for smiling, healing Katja, with the boys (Pavel is at an all-day planning conference), there is no one waiting to waylay at the airport is a promising sign my life is returning to its ordained obscurity, after twenty days or so spent mostly on the wrong side of the cameras and the wrong position in the stories, as part of the text. I say that not only in conventional disdain; after a sample, it's unimaginable to me that anyone could wish to spend months, years, most of a lifetime being recognised, mobbed, subjected to inquisition or the licensed touch of total strangers — and yet in candour I must admit there are some faint pangs of regret at sinking back into mainly welcome anonymity; he who says he doesn't want any special treatment is either a liar, or trying to establish a far-famed reputation as an ordinary bloke, to be pointed out and coddled for that. Christa can arrive unheralded at a vogue restaurant, fully booked well into next century, in the absolute assurance of getting a table, or flout with impunity the double yellow line to collect a parcel; celebrity is power, but in the end the cost is too high in lost privacy, and beyond that the risk of losing anything worth being private about.

That danger began for me, predictably, when I brought Christa here for the first exposing of the whole tale, logically unfolded, from genteel captivity at the ski lodge to the shoot-out in Korava. Only thirty-odd hours later, I returned to England for my father's do, and again Christa was with me. We had to run a gauntlet at Korava airport, but might have temporarily lost the press, except that we had two hours between planes and a change of airports in Berlin; Christa by some mysterious means like the silent signals of the wild that bring solitary leopards together to mate, informed her pals in the fashion world, and there was a sort of raucous celebratory safari with flawless young women mainly wasted on emphatic young men, right across Berlin; as I celebrated Christmas with Roederer from a tumbler, so New Year's Eve (though long before time for the Scots song) was a vintage Krug from styrofoam cups at Tempelhof.

Though all the women and a good part of the men were faces you would at least vaguely recognise (simpering at you in a new shade of lipstick, or doing weirdly androgynous things on a beach dominated by a colossal phial of costly fragrance), Christa and I were hot, hot *hot*, and our festivities. unfortunately, highly visible as well as extravagantly audible. The result was a new melée of reporters and cameras to greet us at Heathrow. Christa's manager, Art Redstone, Manhattanised Mancunian, was also there, and had to be insistently convinced I was in earnest about not turning my parents' place either into a command post and communications centre, or the site of a fresh siege. Though our hired Bentley was tailed from the airport, I had rung young Don Forbes to meet us as Gatwick; it was dark, and in the car-park there we achieved a quick switch — Christa and I did, that is — leaving baffled pursuers with the impression we must have left on a late flight for New York.

By then, I knew the origin of my mother's sudden possessiveness about Christa. On Boxing Day, about the time I was dancing with Angèle, four young members of the Maidstone theatre group had descended on my mother to intensify pressure on her to direct their *Much Ado*, and she suggested a run-through might be fun. She keeps a five-foot shelf stuffed with multiple copies of the Pelican Shakespeares, largely for such impromptu readings (Dad usually ends by taking on a whole bundle of *comprimari* parts, cutthroats, confidants, constables, curates, peripheral kings), and she has from time to time coaxed memorable performances out of improbable players — I recall a junior Thatcherite cabinet minister (junior in rank, not years) who was hair-raising as Cassius, striking a mother-lode of corrosive envy in *Upon what meat does this our Caesar feed, that he is grown so great?* a haunting resentment in such lines as *we petty men...peep about to find ourselves dishonourable graves.*

Well, this time, Christa, who had irked my mother with her too-evident boredom, was peremptorily informed she was to read Hero, which she did with increasing interest, in winning deference occasionally asking for clarification of the words, and at the end wondering modestly if she might be considered for the part.

My mother was amenable ("*Just about anyone, really, with a little coaching, can play Hero, but it does help the play if she's beautiful.*"), the other actors enthusiastic, even when they recognised it meant tailoring their rehearsal timetable to Christa's availability ("*They're only in it for love of the theatre, but, after all, Christa in the cast might bring a reviewer or two down from London.*").

As a measure of Christa's determination, in the end it's going to cost her several thousand pounds, not even counting the money she might be making elsewhere; more than once she has sped expensively from the ends of the earth to attend rehearsals. A union member, not permitted to appear unpaid (this can't be called a charity), she grieved Art Redstone by floating Hero Films, a phantom company committed to a notional backstage documentary about amateur production of a Shakespearian comedy, with her compensation to be twenty-five percent of its gross take. Although Guy has appeared in Maidstone, and moodily shot some hand-held, available-light footage, it is hardly compatible with his doggedly perverse world-view (that the nominal heroine is Hero may briefly have kindled his interest), and hugely unlikely there will ever be a finished film, much more any receipts to divide.

In this brief, packed span, Christa and I were, for a rather large slice of the public, the inevitable duo, beauty and the beast, Jeanette and Nelson, though in real life we saw much less of each other than might have been assumed, than obviously was desired by much of that public, who wanted romance.

Particularly true in America — yes, I let myself be persuaded into flying the Atlantic, initially to appear on a relatively respectable network magazine-programme, which stood us to first-class air travel, and Lucullan accommodation at the Plaza in New York.

Even so, I almost begged off when the trip began expanding into further appearances on other programmes in more cities, but Albertson and Art Redstone coalesced to rebuke me, pointing out that for this span of fleeting fame I owed it to dependent others to maximise potential profits. My publisher, too (all at once I have a publisher), urged it as an opportunity to create an improbable frenzy of anticipation for my forthcoming book, and a mock-up was created overnight to hold up for the cameras; it's mainly a collection of my weightier pieces, slightly revised and with some new connective matter. The American market in mind, the chosen title is *Out of One, Many*, an inversion of the (Latin) motto of the United States, marking the hardly fresh but still astonishing fact that the breakup of the Soviet Union, followed by Yugoslavia and Czechoslovakia, has given Europe a dozen new countries for us to worry and pontificate about. The sober tone, I'm afraid, is going to be a grievous disappointment to those who buy it expecting to find more adventure on the order of flaming Cicadas and mountain treks, the gunfight at High Court corral, the romance-novel flavour for which we had been adopted by television. Though it was a print journalist, headline-writer for a London tabloid, noticing the name of the village nearby the Eagle's Nest, who was first (but far from last) to call Christa *The Prisoner of Zrndja*. Hope springs anew.

Of hosts, the women were the more explicit in trying to find something more than shared experiences between Christa and me, most actually having the gall to ask, more or less, "You two must be denting a lot of mattresses together?" Well, that's what I took to be the subtext; in fact it would go with a back-and-forth gesture, more on the lines of, "Is there any... any, like, romance?"

It doesn't do to disappoint a voyeuristic public, so Christa, having a wondrous technique for ambiguous denial, usually took this question; she would tilt her head back, smile, slide her eyes sidelong over to me, reach for my hand, and say, "Mark and I have a very special friendship." The mixed noise this drew from an audience, blended of half-approving reproach for her reticence, the pure *aah* of triggered sentimentality, knowing chuckle, and, on top like the trumpet in Scriabin's tone poems, whoops or yelps of encouragement and vicarious arousal, will remain in my ears for the rest of my life.

If my list is complete, I appeared, in New York, Los Angeles and Chicago, on fourteen different programmes in five days — it could easily have been forty — eleven of them jointly with Christa; I have no idea how many she did without me. We shared flights twice, had lunch together twice, breakfast once, and that was almost the extent of our keeping company — not counting the several times the host for our next appearance took us for drinks or a meal so as to run over the kinds of question he or she intended, and sound us out for any mandatory or taboo topics. In Chicago, the (as it turned out) rather dim host of an afternoon hour sent a surrogate, an associate producer, to vet us, and we met, the three of us, in my hotel room. She, Debra, was young, attractive and formidably intelligent, but just when it seemed I was making promising progress with her, she deferred to that recurrent misapprehension, and with charming, exasperating tact withdrew to leave Christa alone with me.

The truth was, we were bored with each other, Christa chiefly by the taxing necessity of maintaining gratitude, I by the strain of being its object, and by the obvious fact that (notwithstanding her raid on Shakespeare) we had nothing whatever to talk about.

It was the other show in Chicago, what posed as a serious-minded discussion programme (for which I was Christaless), that ambushed me with an ancient Ukrainian, Vasylenko, who had spent more than two-thirds of his life in the U.S., having left Kharkov twenty years before I was born; he was retired from a teaching post at Northwestern University, and had (as I later was told) produced a Ukrainian nationalist newspaper, subsidised by the C.I.A., for almost forty years, until abrupt achievement of its forlorn-seeming goal made it redundant.

His one visit to his old home and the new country he evidently felt he'd invented was five or six years ago. Plainly offended not to be offered at least an important post in the cabinet, his new grievances fastened on the old enemy, and decided that the "so-called break-up" of the Soviet Union was fraudulent, fresh instance of immemorial Russian perfidy. He contradicted everything I had to say about developments anywhere from Prague to Minsk and Tailinn to Skopje (to none of which four, and not much in between, he had ever been), and since he looked like a Slavonic leprechaun, and habitually referred to the United States as "this wonderful country, my adopted home, the greatest country in the world," a discriminating audience demonstratively endorsed his outmoded fantasies over my recent and careful observations; I was evidently alone in detecting an undercurrent of impartial hatred for Jews and the Orthodox Church in Vasylenko, which must have been a marketable asset in the middle years of the war; his retreat from Ukraine at about the same time as the Germans may have had other than nationalistic motives. But the encounter was salutary reminder that deprived of Christa's radiance (she was making one of her lightning raids on Shakespeare in Maidstone but reappeared in L.A. next day, fresh and flawless) my popular appeal was distinctly limited.

Though coverage was scant now, I kept up with events in Dusatia, phoning Pavel where necessary; the Herders had been arrested, charged with an obscure nosegay of mainly attempted crimes, but let go when they put up a very large bail, increasing the furor over Angèle's unconditional imprisonment. Soon this became a question in parliament, but the unforgiving Gorat, with whom her "old goat" remark still rankled, answered blandly that the law must take its course, and that it would be improper for him to intervene. His legal advisors, he said, informed him that bail in such a case could not be granted to someone with Angèle's extensive record of violent acts.

I would have wanted to be there, if I had dared, for the rally Miloczy held so as to identify all the allegations against Rietz and the Herders as part of the conspiracy against the National Loyalist Party, actually descending on the capital and hiring the football stadium just across the river by Prjanu. Herculean labours cleared the venue (of snow, not horse-manure), which normally holds about thirty thousand, but could take at least forty for an event like this, where the pitch itself can be occupied. Miloczy blamed the low gate (twenty thousand according to his estimate, twelve at most to independent eyes) on the weather.

Notable among the hordes who stayed away was General Vock, and he, next day, forswore his affiliation to the Loyalists, announcing the formation of a new party, heavyhandedly named National Morality (tactfully, or tactically, he remained among the few leading political figures with nothing to say on the question of Angèle's imprisonment). About one-third of the parliamentary Loyalists defected with him, and Vock made overtures to Gorat, expressing a willingness to support the centrist coalition in "questions of national importance." Gorat was therefore rapidly able to pass his so-called Foreign Workers act, which, while making it somewhat harder to get into Dusatia, guarantees full protection of the law to those already admitted.

He seems likely also to succeed with new legislation curbing the powers of provincial premiers — a measure Miloczy complains, quite accurately, is aimed specifically at him — chiefly by denying funds for road-building, education and law-enforcement where provincial practice fails to conform to national policy. Since the revelations about the attempted kidnapping, and the Rietz attempt on Wirath's life (as it is almost universally seen), the polls conducted by Katja's Marjenka depict a precipitous drop in support for the Loyalists, even suggesting Miloczy may fail to be re-elected next year. These things are volatile, and everything may depend on Gorat's ability to stimulate the economy, but in the absence of catastrophe it may be that Miloczy, like Enoch Powell, will simply cease to be interesting.

As the Christa-and-Mark show traversed the continent, certain portions of the tale became guaranteed show-stoppers; burning the Cicada, of course, Christa's laughing account of how she posed and autographed her way into Germany, and for more thoughtful moments, my half-ironic theory that Rietz's failure to kill both Christa's father and me was traceable to vanity, the vanity that made him disguise himself as a captain of the *dzhăndarmi*; as an ordinary member of that force he would have been carrying a fully-automatic weapon on a lanyard at his chest, and could have squirted out thirty rounds before anyone could move; as an officer his far slower pistol was holstered at his hip, and it was the opening of that holster that alerted Angèle.

It is, ultimately, impossible to resist seduction by applause, and no matter how passionately a belief is held, it begins to take on shadings of the meretricious when, having once been accorded an ovation, it is repeated for a new but similar audience. Nevertheless, it was never principally for the power and pleasure of evoking response that I habitually linked this part of the tale to a description of Angèle's current plight, repeatedly denied bail, her relentless prosecution delayed only by the possibility that the comatose Rietz might die, so that the charge could be upped from attempted to achieved murder. Gorat, I explained, playing Pilate with his chaste refusal to intervene, was in fact pursuing a spiteful personal vendetta against Angèle, who had once, only too accurately, insulted him. Dusatia, I said, was rightly proud of its hard-won independence, but by no means immune to the influence of the kind of international outcry that was a-building on Angèle's behalf.

The first time, I wasn't sure of what Americans do in such cases, but the host, an ample woman, whose audience bayed and clapped on cue like trained seals, prompted, "You mean, all of us could help, by writing to our congressman, or to the President?"

I agreed; telegrams, E-mail, respectfully suggest America should use its influence in this case; everything helped.

My last day was a Sunday, and I was up early for one of the few programmes actually seen while it's happening, the network hour *Confront!* with a format I enjoy, once the mandatory recounting of familiar events has been endured, sitting at a table with other press people to discuss the political and economic future of Central and Eastern Europe.

It might have been worthwhile. Aware of the deficiencies of a survey made while travelling at high speed from hotel to hotel, restaurant to studio, studio to airport, I've resisted the sort of all-embracing assessments of America that come so often from those visitors who walk eight blocks on Fifth Avenue or attend a political convention, and fly home as authorities, but I can say that, together with the three weekly news-magazines, the network news departments form unquestionably the most powerful mechanism for the gathering of information that the world has ever known, which the compulsion to package, to titillate, to scale everything down to the shortest attention-span in a population of two hundred and fifty million, deprives of almost all its potential effect, as if the entire staff of the O.E.D. produced nothing but the column-fillers in the *Reader's Digest*.

One result is that there appears to be a great deal more certainty than there is knowledge; I'm thinking of the black woman in Los Angeles who told me it was time for Europeans to get out of wherever it was I'd been, and was sure the civil war in Zaire was caused by refugees from across the border in Bosnia, the absurdly angry post-adolescent in New York who assailed Christa as a bad "role model," because "most women nowadays aren't gonna wait for some man to come rescue them," or the rather nice, muddled chap in that same audience who objected to my expressing a distance in kilometres, on the grounds that the assault on English measure (as he definitely would not have called it) was part of the conspiracy to take away American livelihoods by having shirts made by twelve-year-olds in Taiwan and the Dominican Republic; hobby-horses, hobby-horses, rolling roughshod over any chance to learn.

But there are formidable Americans, too, who speak effortlessly in complete sentences and summon recondite facts and statistics at will; seldom entirely free from the national delusion that inventing a new and longer word to describe an ancient condition represents progress, they are quite a match for anything encountered on European television, and at times make those Sunday morning programmes an exception to the reign of vapidity; though I'm told the aggregate audiences at that time for all three networks are a mere decimal of the most popular sitcoms and soaps, they are said to be influential beyond their "numbers."

My anticipation of a stimulating discussion was disappointed by the inclusion of Burnwhit Farlen, the network's darling, last seen in full combat fig in what he called and kept calling "strife-torn" Korava. He pretended to remember me, and was as bad as old Vasylenko in Chicago, not as contradictory, perhaps, but equally determined to monopolise the scene with ill-informed opinion, based on his "recent tour of that area." What was called the moderator, though she did very little to moderate anything, would throw out a theme, and on cue came Whitburn, with his, "Well, when I was there," "Well, when I spoke with President Niemek," "Well, from what I saw in Warsaw," followed by a summation as expert as I could have given of conditions in general in Los Angeles. With only hours of my largely sleepless American sojourn remaining, I eventually mislaid my humour, and left behind a probably permanent reputation for waspishness by cautioning all against the distortions of "snapshot analysis."

Not to bestow the same legacy here, I need to say that another American national characteristic I encountered is a breathtaking generosity and hair-trigger friendliness; on the West Coast and again when I returned to New York I was welcomed by complete strangers like the prodigal son, not, I think, because I was the momentary celebrity, but because that's how they are; it was, by the way, an unfailing well-spring of naive delight to mention my American birth. Not to doubt I was as quickly forgotten; in a country of such mobility, rootlessness, where a *career-related* move from coast to coast or windswept lakeside to sweating Gulf is routine, it's only natural to have bosom friends, like cities, that are interchangeable, and still it's very pleasant to be greeted with all the signs of heartfelt joy.

Now, Katja's first words to me are that I'm expected for dinner at the Presidential Palace, invitation delivered by telephone this morning. They knew I would be here because at JFK Airport in New York last night (about four in the morning here) a CNN crew had spotted and grilled me, and Pavel used the piece on the noon news, as part of the run-up to Angèle's trial.

"Informal," Katja adds.

Which I take not to mean jeans and a polo shirt, and wear a dark suit as does Niemek, though the other main guest, Wirath, appears in a dinner-jacket of antique cut, shiny about the lower sleeves; his bow is palpably a clip-on. The Niemeks' private dining-room is small, unpretentiously furnished, the meal an unassuming match for its surroundings.

I am deluged in gratitude; Wirath resumes, though less publicly, the panegyric interrupted last month by Erhardt Rietz, and a little later Niemek draws me aside to tell me in absolute confidence that a battery of four nuclear cannon with fourteen projectiles was indeed uncovered at Strbjena, for which, again, I am to be thanked. They were stored, wrapped, in an otherwise disused communications bunker, and had received no expert maintenance, so that no one could say how functional they still were: the Soviets possessed a conventional H.E. shell that was compatible, and used for test firings, but had not left any stock at Strbjena.

"I doubt, sir, that anyone would wish to gamble on their state of repair, once they were trained on Korava."

"As you say."

A United Nations team, more or less smuggled in, is seeing to dismantling and disposal.

Questioned by Marshall Svarin, General Vock predictably denied any knowledge of the lethal cache; his failure to support the Miloczy rally, followed by his break with the Loyalists, and offer of co-operation with the ruling coalition, came in the wake of that interview.

Contrary to my expectations, Wirath does make reference to the trial about to open, but only to begin a discussion of law in general, and of differing procedures; he asks whether I have been in an English court.

The first rough sketch for the original Constitution of 1919, he tells me, at Versailles, was contributed to by a young American lawyer, a protégé of Woodrow Wilson's, and an enthusiast for his own country's constitution, and Anglo-Saxon legal precepts in general.

As, I learn, is Wirath, though he admits the impossibility of grafting common law onto a Continental tradition, which in Dusatia quietly digested and transformed most of the alien features in the constitution; any hybridisation, he tells me, is now visible only in certain procedural matters.

Procedure, the rules of evidence, are where he most sees need for reform, but he is not an admirer of developments in

America, where the virtuoso defence attorney, commanding astronomical fees, has enormously increased pressure on the prosecution to present a more-than-watertight case, where necessary by improving and even fabricating evidence, intimidating witnesses with threatened indictments. "Prosecutors are all-too-often elected officials, there, and the political pressure on them causes them to seek convictions rather than justice."

He smiles. "We know all about political pressure here in Dusatia; the communist period left the scales weighted in favour of the prosecution, and many of the young lawyers of that time who privately advocated reform are now our prosecutors and judges, resisting any change that might make their jobs harder."

He speaks approvingly, also, of some aspects of Scandinavian legal practice, where they avoid the English tendency to over-reliance on the necessary integrity of the right sort of people. I am very tired; sixty apparent and fifty-one actual hours ago I was in Los Angeles, and I have traversed continents and oceans, swallowing time-zones, rushing to meet the rising sun; lathering myself in compliment I have begun to see this circle of eminence as my ordained place, but now, though remaining polite, am grabbed by a sudden, guilty, embracing disgust, for the ostentatious modesty of this occasion, for outdated folk-ikons with their well-earned complacency, not so much resting as mouldering on their laurels.

Angèle is no national hero on the order of either Niemek or of Wirath, consciously and coolly choosing a moral but dangerous course, but an unstable young woman who was almost perversely in the right place. Yet she was there, and is now a prisoner awaiting trial, while Wirath is alive to generalise about justice; I am fairly sure that his merest hint in the right place would have changed the judge's mind about granting bail.

And Niemek, with his serene wife who says she used to be just like Angèle; there has been some speculation in the newspapers that a presidential pardon might be extended if Angèle is convicted, but why must he wait for a conviction? Unlike Gorat, he has an unlimited credit balance of goodwill to draw on — although I judge it would in any event be a popular decision.

None of this can be brought up here; Wirath I'm absolutely certain would tell me he can't possibly comment on a case *sub judice*, while the Niemeks would be offended at my stinking up a convivial little gathering more or less in my honour. In my present barely-controlled mood of infantile, over-tired irritability, anything I say might end by making things worse. But I do know Angèle has to be acquitted.

She may be, as the editorially hostile *Novjétny* says, a danger to society; if so society has to watch out for itself; we have to free her because if we don't we're terrible people. And because it may be, very likely is, the last chance of freeing her from her demons.

The Criminal Courts are, as is often sardonically noted, very near parliament, a big, square stone building, shallow steps in front, eight of them, across almost the entire width, today effectively reduced by a double line of police to an aisle mounting to the central doors. Something near one hundred spectators are gathered, mostly simply to stare, though there are some placards, all in support of Angèle or opposition to her captors. On the pavement, a little apart, a youthful contingent, seven or eight of Angèle's anarchists, are holding up their *FREEDOM* banner, and maintaining a less than spirited chant of "Free Angèle!" They show symptoms of weariness, and I have no difficulty believing, as Pavel says, that they have maintained a presence, though in planned rotation, through the night.

Inside, as if belatedly to guard against the reason for this trial, there are metal detectors and, for the press, a painstaking scrutiny of credentials; the vigilant police assigned to the court are wearing photographic identity-tags.

The largest courtroom has been chosen, to accommodate the press and perhaps eighty additional spectators on long pews; notwithstanding the vexations of being subjected to interrogations, scans and over-intimate pattings, every available space is filled, and is to be so throughout the trial.

As Wirath forewarned me, there is no presumption of innocence, and the judge often becomes a second prosecutor, cross-examining witnesses, openly drawing attention to inconsistencies or expressing scepticism about alibis. Since the judge's charge to the jury comes after the closing speech for the defence, and frequently is a meticulous reconstruction of the initial prosecution case, it is somewhat surprising that the conviction rate, high as it is, isn't in the neighbourhood of one hundred percent.

The jury is ten, and a verdict, either way, may be reached by a "substantial majority" — in effect, two-thirds. But since jurors can, and in difficult cases, often do, abstain, and a new trial is required only if half or more fail to reach a verdict, it is possible to achieve a conviction with (work it out) as few as four `guilty' ballots. Nor is the fact that a majority failed to vote for conviction an allowable part of any appeal, which can only be lodged on strictly-defined principles, an allegation of judicial error being virtually never sustained. Wirath believes this is one of the places where reform is overdue.

"By way of compensation," he said, "Though it might be dangerous to assume this will always be so, there's no doubt that our police and prosecutors have shown great responsibility in seldom bringing to trial a case where the evidence would not be compelling in any court in the world."

As, in strict law, is true here; it cannot rationally be disputed that Angèle was in illegal possession of a firearm, that she illegally concealed it on her person, or that she discharged it at Rietz with intent to cause his death or serious injury; nor that as a result of her actions Rietz is injured beyond reasonable hope of recovery.

An abridged list; there are in all nine titles in the indictment, some of which, such as "endangering public safety" could be, but seldom are, tacked on to any major charge involving firearms; somebody, as Pavel snarls on hearing the entire menu, some premier, is sure out to get Angèle.

For which the chosen prosecution team is confirmation; chief prosecutor is Horvach, tall, lean, barely thirty but with a killer reputation, assisted by Hannah Sjuc, very experienced, law-learned, tenacious, with, I am told, a disarmingly courteous manner.

"What about the judge?"

"Polenaczny. He's Gorat's stooge. He was a lawyer, raised big bucks for the Social Democrats, he ran for parliament himself but was skunked by an independent. So Gorat makes him a judge."

"The premier doesn't appoint judges, does he?" A strange process for a country whose constitution prescribes a strict separation of powers.

"Tell me about it, and a cabinet minister can't get a parking ticket fixed, sure. Gorat wanted to make Polenaczny solicitor-general, but he's too hot politically, next thing, he's a judge. Horvach, Sjuc and Polenaczny, this is gonna be *A Night at the Opera*, with Polenaczny as Groucho."

Of their early performance I have to rely on Pavel's partisan reports; as a witness listed by the prosecution, I am not permitted to be in court for the opening moves, which consist of an excessively detailed recounting of the events, together with the first showing of the crucial twenty minutes of the RTPD tapes — the only complete showing, as it is to be, though several short portions will be seen again, as well as Pavel's early edit, complete with highlightings and isolations.

After that first day, Pavel, still maintaining the whole case should be summarily dismissed, is impatient with Kaepfky, who, after stating straight off that the defence is not to be based on any dispute of the incidents as shown, has hardly had a question, except for one policeman, who seemed to be trying to resurrect the Dufoireau version, with Wirath as Angèle's intended target, but admitted on cross-examination he had seen nothing before the shooting started and Rietz went down.

"What would you want Kaepfky to ask?"

The Cagney-Bogart snarl. "He's turning it into a parade. You gotta shake them up some, send some kind of message to the jury."

"But if he niggles over details of what happened, it only weakens the effect of his main defence, that Angèle acted to prevent an assassination."

"Yeah, but frigging Polenaczny ain't buying that. Twice already he told the jury they can only decide it on the law, it don't matter what they think of Rietz."

"He can say it."

"Shit, the mouthpiece I got for her doesn't get manicures, but he's been in criminal cases before. Who hired this monkey? How do we know he ain't selling her down the river?"

"Angèle is satisfied." She could choose another lawyer; there is now available to her a publicly-subscribed defence fund of at least three hundred thousand crowns, mostly coming from many small contributions (though I know Pavel made a substantial one, and I gave one-half of all my fees in America).

"Yeah, but she's nuts."

The prosecution really would have done better to have let the defence call me, since in Dusatian law I could then have been questioned only about what I saw, opinions disallowed. As is, when it comes to his turn, Kaepfky will be able to introduce no topics not touched in direct examination, which, but for a mistake by the prosecutor, could have been confined to an eye-witness account distinctly inferior to what could be seen on the tape. The stand is a little circular dais, four steps up, like a dismounted pulpit, just right of centre in front of the high bench — stage right, the judge's right. I am surprisingly at ease there, though Kaepfky, with whom I had a half-minute encounter, has given no instructions or suggestions.

In pigeon-steps, we go through the story, and come to the critical few seconds.

"You knew Mr Rietz by sight?" I am being questioned by Horvach, keen-jawed and aquiline, though his nickname is Shark.

"By sight, and by reputation, yes."

(*Worth a try, but no bite.*) "Never mind reputation. You recognised Mr Rietz."

"I knew he was not a police officer, and had no legitimate reason for being there."

(*The mistake, with something like a sneer.*) "How could you *know* that?"

"I was personally aware of Mr Rietz's involvement in the abduction of Christa Rasch, and had been reliably informed — "

"I wish to withdraw the question in the form proposed."

Judge Polenaczny, a man in his fifties with a round face in a state of eternal surprise, doesn't know what to make of this. He asks, "Is that your answer, Mr Kearns?"

"Sir, I had been reliably informed that Mr Rietz was the man who visited Chief Justice Wirath — "

"The question," the prosecutor objects, "Concerned Mr Kearns' personal knowledge of Mr Rietz, not what he might have been told."

Kaepfky: "The witness should be permitted to finish his answer."

But I am not, not now, nor even soon; the prosecutor sits down, and Kaepfky has no questions, reserving his right to cross-examine during the case for the defence. Perfectly permissible, but considered dangerous, since the jury might well forget my original testimony. But now I can take a seat beside Pavel in court. From habit, I make notes, although I have no assignment to report the trial; outside Dusatia, coverage is patchy, though the verdict is sure to make at least inside-page headlines everywhere. Looking about, I scan the jury, and recognise its short foreman (the Dusation term is "speaker") as Fischer, the anecdotal seventh-generation baker of bread, sitting upright, alert as a meerkat.

The finale for the prosecution case is the defendant. In Dusatian law she has to submit to questioning, and there is no inherent safeguard against self-incrimination.

She has been very attentive during my testimony, and I assume throughout. When she comes to the witness stand, she is demure and tiny in a quiet button-up dress of linen, warm beige in hue, lips and eyelids barely brushed with discreet colour. It has never before occurred to me that denial of bail deprives a defendant of the chance to rehearse properly with her attorney, but Kaepfky must have done all the coaching he could to keep her calm, keep stridency out of her voice.

And it goes quite tranquilly, Angèle giving quiet, minimal answers, in harmony with Kaepfky's strategy, to Hannah Sjuc's bland tour of the events. Hannah is of a shape hard to describe, wide rather than broad or stout, iron-grey hair and a bee-stung lower lip. Discord arrives when the prosecution moves on to what it sedulously avoids calling Angèle's reputation, and Sjuc tries to get in Angèle's "former problems with the law."

Kaepfky is at once on his feet. Though there isn't anyone in the court, including the jury, who doesn't know about the shooting of Pavel, it is inadmissible as evidence. So the judge is obliged to rule, purely educationally explaining to the jury that they are to consider only the facts in this case, not any past events, "not even if, in your minds, they appear to suggest a pattern of behaviour." Outrageous, but Kaepfky has no remedy.

There is further dispute when Sjuc seeks to question Angèle about her writings, but this time Polenaczny rules for the prosecution, so long as they confine themselves to statements which "may have relevance to the present case." No help, and not an Angèle-watcher present who doesn't know what's coming.

Hannah Sjuc nods to the bench. "`A few judicious assassinations'," she reads, "`May be necessary if our freedoms are to be saved.' Did you write that?"

"In 1993."

"Sir?" appealing to the judge.

"You must answer the question; did you write this statement?"

"Yes, in 1993."

Sjuc again. "And subsequently, were you asked about this statement in the course of a radio interview over the RTPD?"

"In 1993, yes."

"Whenever it was, did you then say, `Yes, I stand by that...sometimes assassination is the only way to bring about needed change.'?"

"My colleague — " Kaepfky, not looking up from the transcript he is following — "Has inadvertently left out a phrase."

"I am giving the essence."

"The court can determine the essence, if it is given the words, all the words."

The judge hesitates, and Sjuc, with the air of one humouring an unreasonable nit-picker, reads the entire passage: "`Yes, I stand by that. It is always better if great goals can be achieved by peaceful means, but sometimes assassination is the only way to bring about change.' Did you say that?"

There is some more niggling over Angèle's recall of her exact words, but eventually she admits to having said something closely similar. And to once more affirming that position in a subsequent television appearance — which she should remember, since it was the real start of the furor which led to her being dropped by her newspaper.

" — at the time — " she tries to expand, but Hannah Sjuc breaks in to say there are no further questions, and abruptly sits down.

"How would you define *assassination*?" Kaepfky begins conversationally.

"The murder — " Angèle thinks it through. "Of some powerful or prominent person, for political purposes."

"In the hopes of some political gain."

"Yes, or of creating a situation which might be politically exploited."

"The remark about assassinations, made some years ago, which we have heard quoted here more than once — does that still reflect your views?"

"No. It is an immature statement, the statement of an immature person."

"Would you regard Mr Rietz as a powerful or a prominent person, in the political sense?"

"No."

"Did you know Mr Rietz prior to the incidents of December 28th?"

"Slightly. I had met him, and knew of him as an organiser of political demonstrations. I have seen him leading demonstrations in the streets."

"Did you dislike him?"

"I didn't much like him. He was unimportant to me."

"You wouldn't say you disliked him enough to attempt to kill him?"

"No, of course not."

"Why did you shoot Mr Rietz?"

"It was obvious to me he was about to kill Mr Kearns, or the Chief Justice, and probably both. He had already wounded Mr Kearns."

"Your action, then, was entirely unpremeditated."

"He had to be stopped."

"Thank you."

Kaepfky sits down; very deft, as much in its omissions as what was brought out, but Angèle is not yet dismissed.

"A moment, please — " Horvach, who is then engaged in a furious *sotto voce* discussion with the older assistant, Sjuc. Obvious what it is; one of them, probably the elder, wants to go into the question of why Angèle was there armed, but that leads immediately into all that was earlier skirted for tactical reasons: the defence doesn't want it because it brings in premeditation and upsets their picture of an impulsive and public-spirited act; the prosecution wants premeditation, but not Juan-Micel Herder and the kidnapping, which would place Rietz firmly among the villains.

Eventually, with Polenaczny growing impatient, Hannah persuades the chief prosecutor that it has to be risked. Horvach rises.

"Was it with the purpose of, as you put it, stopping Rietz, that you were there that morning?"

"No." Angèle might have expanded, but for the first time I notice a signal from her attorney, a quick clenching of a fist slightly raised above the polished breastwork behind which he sits.

"Did you have any advance information of what Rietz might attempt?"

"No. If I had — "

"*No* is sufficient. What was your reason for attending the Chief Justice's news conference?"

"I am a working journalist."

"Ah, yes — " a gratuitous bit of superciliousness, with meaning only for those who know the dingy publications in which Angèle's latter work has appeared. "And do you always carry a gun on your assignments?"

"No." Fist signal again.

"But you decided to on this occasion."

"It was in my shoulder-bag."

"Is that where you normally kept it?"

"Sometimes." Angèle is labouring now.

"But you knew it was there on this occasion?"

"I suppose so, yes."

"You suppose so? You could hardly have reacted as swiftly as you say you did, unless you knew your gun was readily available."

Angèle opens her mouth, and Kaepfky intervenes. "That is not a question. The prosecutor is testifying."

Polenaczny, appearing to agree, nevertheless doesn't let this point drop, putting a highly editorial question of his own. "What I think the prosecutor is asking is, and you must answer this carefully — " eye on the jury — "since it does go to the whole question of premeditation: did you know from the first that you had your gun with you that day?"

"Yes, sir."

"You did not, as it were, slip your hand into the bag and suddenly realise the gun was there?"

"No, I knew it was there."

The trouble with judge as auxiliary prosecutor is that it's impossible to object to his little bits of re-emphasis on the grounds that the question has already been answered. This patch of re-examination has been far more damaging to Angèle than the original questioning, and Kaepfky has to decide whether to attempt putting a better face on what is the weak point in his defence, or to leave ill enough alone.

After fully fifteen seconds of meditative silence, Horvach having sat down with a deferential and no doubt grateful bow to the judge, Kaepfky rises again.

"When my colleague asked you if you had any prior knowledge of Rietz's intent, you answered *No*, and began to say *if I had* — . If you had?"

"If I had been given any advance information about an attempt on the life of the Chief Justice, or anyone else, I should, of course, have notified the authorities."

"Thank you." Kaepfky sits down satisfied, but this new notion of Angèle as a pillar of law and order has sounded a tinny note in my ear.

Hannah Sjuc, the old hand, is on it at once. I understand the rule is the prosecution can come back for more so long as the preceding questions introduce new material, but the judge is obviously ready to stretch more than a point in their favour.

"You said you are a journalist," the woman asks. "Isn't it true that your journalism is written from an anarchist standpoint?"

Up pops Kaepfky with a strong objection as to relevancy.

Challenged, the questioner is very nearly smug. "The defendant, in her reply to counsel, used the expression `the authorities.' It might be instructive to the court to discover what *authorities* she recognises."

"The question is permitted."

The clerk reads: "Isn't-it-true-that-your-journalism-is-written-from-an-anarchist-standpoint."

"Philosophical anarchist, yes."

"And isn't it true — " Sjuc ruffles with her left hand a sheaf of pages. "We can, at need, submit a number of your published articles as evidence, but for the sake of brevity, isn't it true that the rejection of all authority is at the heart of your *philosophy*?"

"All authority — " Angèle, absorbed, positively rushes to the slaughter. "As it is now constituted, yes. We envisage a different kind of authority, founded in mutual respect, and in a shared concern for all the peoples of the earth, not in force and the threat of force, which is the basis of most present authority."

"Such as, the police, for example?"

"The entire structure of current government, of which the police are a part, depends on the immoral actual or potential use of brute force."

"And would that be your description of the *authorities* you say you would have *notified*, if you had known of Rietz's intentions?"

Trapped, and Angèle looks it. "There are times — " she is floundering. "When the institutions we have must be used, to prevent a greater evil."

"But it is better — more moral, in your view — to rely, where possible, on your own personal resources?" (*Damn, this woman isn't stupid*)

"Oh, always, yes, where we can."

"Including the use of deadly force?"

"If that's the only way to — to prevent something worse happening."

"Thank you for clarifying that point." She sits down. Kaepfky, solely with the object of leaving a more positive impression, stands up and asks a few more questions, trying to shade some of Angèle's defiant answers, to make a distinction between a theoretical assertion and behaviour in the real world. He has collaborated well with Angèle in presenting, throughout the trial, an earnest, attractive, calmly contained middle-class young woman, and is, I think, belatedly discovering that he has for client a perilous fanatic, who, if it means twenty-five years in prison, cannot make the concession he wants the jury to hear.

An oddity, here and throughout, is that while Angèle's wig and forged credentials are mentioned several times, there's never any attempt to find out how she acquired them. The probable solution for me is a tremendous irony; they must have been supplied by Rietz, the former secret police agent, at the time when Herder was priming Angèle (as I firmly believe) to assassinate Wirath.

There would have been a plan to prevent the real Amy Highcote from attending — they couldn't have anticipated the blizzard — though quite possibly she would have decided, as so often, to cover the event on television, from the smoke-fogged comfort of her hotel room.

The night of the President's Ball, Angèle's friendliness, Angèle's dance with me was, and was perhaps intended to be, a signal for Herder that he'd lost her, and that was when Rietz himself took on the job of killing Wirath, but his failure to prevent Angèle using her disguise is a near-fatal omission that can never be properly explained. Yet while there would have been a possible logic in the original plan (if that's what it was) of having a celebrated revolutionary attack a national symbol of law and justice, that Rietz could ever think anything was to be gained from his very public killing of Wirath is sufficient evidence of growing irrationality. By the way, his borrowed uniform was not explained, either. Myself, I would have interrogated Captain Iakadju, Miloczy's cheerleader with the Korava *dzhandarmi*.

It has been a long session, and when Kaepfky winds down, we break for lunch. The morning — and especially early afternoon — have been, as Pavel and I despondently conclude, unmitigated disaster.

"Why the hell is Kaepfky pussyfooting? He's been all round the Rietz thing, I tell you Herder's paying this guy to keep his name out of it."

Possible, but I don't believe it; the connection to Christa's kidnapping had been on the point of coming out in my interrupted evidence, but with Angèle Kaepfky had still been trying, impossibly, to keep the jury's minds from the obviously planning that went into her presence there that morning.

"He has to let it go now, and go after Rietz." It's not clear whether Kaepfky has consciously recognised that his strategy boils down to trusting that the jury will refuse to convict on the evidence, which depends on their perceiving the shooting of Rietz as a public benefit. Or rather, he must know it, but all his training and experience compel him to keep trying to find a victory based on law.

"He better go after him. If he doesn't, I'll do it for him." Pavel could be recalled, though his brief appearance early on was only to authenticate and explain the "editorial" version of the tape.

XIII

"Mr Kearns, when you were questioned by the prosecution about your knowledge of Mr Rietz you indicated you possessed other information."

"Yes, that it was Mr Rietz who approached Chief Justice Wirath to threaten him, tell him the safety of his daughter depended on a decision favourable to the National Loyalist side in the so-called Yellow Ballot issue." What the hearsay rule might be in Dusatian law I don't know, but Horvach is on his feet, and I quickly add, "I'm certain Justice Wirath would confirm this." It has, in fact, been a part of newspaper stories for every continent but an unpeopled one.

Prosecutor, with what he thinks is shrivelling sarcasm: "Do you propose to call the Chief Justice as a witness?" But why not, if he is one?

Kaepfky is complacent. "No, but, if I may sir? — " to the judge. "Justice Wirath has volunteered a sworn deposition, which I now propose to enter in evidence." An efficient clerk has produced three copies, one of which Kaepfky passes up to the judge, the other going to the prosecutor, who studies it unhappily.

"This will be read into the record when we are finished with the present witness," Kaepfky advises. "But I may say that the account of the Chief Justice does indeed confirm that Mr Rietz threatened him, just as this witness has stated." Precisely true; when the deposition is read Wirath, typically, has made a careful distinction between personally recognising the gunman as the same person (which he did not), and subsequent identification by name and description. The practical difference is small, and the prosecution will not attempt to do anything with it.

Meanwhile: "The kidnapping having failed in its objective — " in theory, as a question to me — "Rietz's motive for an attack on both you and the Chief Justice becomes clear."

"Yes." Leave needed legal reforms to Wirath; this, technically, is cross-examination, but I've noted throughout, even in direct examination, an extravagant tolerance for leading by counsel. More follows.

"Is it your belief that he hoped to silence the two men who could connect him to the kidnapping attempt?"

"Partially." Kaepfky would prefer my unconditional assent, but the point, surely, is to make sure the jury recognise Rietz as the villain, and that can't be strengthened by an untenable motive. "It would, of course, be irrational to try to save oneself from a charge of kidnapping by committing two very public murders."

"Then Rietz's behaviour was, you believe, irrational?"

Here, Horvach at last wakes up, and objects to my being invited to speculate on *the victim's* state of mind, and this leads to an extended, low-voiced wrangle just beneath the judicial bench, the entire essence being contained in a single somewhat more audible exchange:

Kaepfky: "Well, we can't question Rietz about his motive."

Horvach: "We are not here to try Erhardt Rietz."

Formally true, and a point made more than once by Polinaczny, but in reality we are. That's exactly what we're doing.

Kaepfky's manner seems deferential, but he didn't take on the Gorat government (and win) without some reserves of steel; instructed to abandon the enquiry into Rietz's mental processes, he puts his next question under the judge's hard scrutiny, and steers the finest of lines.

"Without trying to define what those motives might be, are you satisfied that Rietz had adequate motive for attempting to kill either you yourself, or the Chief Justice, or both?"

"Certainly."

"To what do you ascribe his failure to do so?"

"To the swift and decisive actions of the defendant, as depicted on the tape."

"Of my client."

"Of Angèle, yes — " surprised we both got away with the double re-emphasis.

But when Kaepfky presses his luck, beginning, "I take it then you are profoundly thankful — " Horvach pops up with a near-howl of protest, and my gratitude is ruled irrelevant.

As, later, is Pavel's attempt to steer his reasons for preparing the "editorial" tape into his opinion of the entire proceedings against Angèle. Afterwards, he is angry with Kaepfky for not trying harder, but I suspect the attorney is, on the whole, relieved. As was, Pavel was grazing the edge of personal feelings about Angèle, in danger of permitting the prosecution, after all, to open up the whole business of her wounding of him. A story which speaks highly of Pavel's fine, forgiving nature, but is far worse than no help to Angèle.

The second overnight pause is at the threshold of closing arguments, and Katja is confident there can be no guilty verdict. Her friend Marjenka (of the Christmas gathering) has published a just-completed poll, showing that almost two-thirds of all Dusatians (or all who have an opinion; there were large numbers of Don't Knows) believe Angèle should never have been tried, and only a slightly lesser majority that Gorat (never mind the constitution) should have intervened to halt the proceedings. There is also strong support for a presidential pardon in the event of conviction.

"This," she says, "is language Gorat understands. Dalerant supports his refusal to intervene on principle, but some of the Catholic Renewal deputies don't, and none of the Liberal Front; about a dozen Social Democrat members are ready to revolt — " all this inside parliamentary information comes from Marjenka's younger brother, who works for an S.D.D. member.

"Yeah," Pavel says grimly. "But Gorat may have started something he can't stop."

He's right of course. If Horvach and the judge between them succeed in browbeating the jury, Angèle's conviction might accomplish what Rietz and the Herders, Miloczy and the former, unrepentant Vock could not, breaking of the centrist coalition, and the fall of Gorat.

Third and surely final day. A quiet beginning, though the tension is high; everyone expects a verdict today. Or rather, that it will be in the hands of the jury; Trev Hassett has got up a little sweep among the press on how long they'll deliberate, and the experienced are putting their money on four, six, ten hours, even overnight.

Kaepfky makes a last point, recalling the chief arresting officer to make absolutely explicit that Angèle made no resistance to being disarmed or attempt to evade arrest, and that when he took the gun from her she remarked, in a conversational tone, "If you were on your job, I wouldn't have needed that."

Conversational, perhaps, but vintage Angèle tactlessness; she was lucky to have found an honest sergeant; a less scrupulous and more vindictive man might have made up something more damning.

After another of their animated whisperings, Horvach and Sjuc decide to let it alone, whereupon the defence case is closed.

Taken together, the two summations and closing arguments are a demonstration of how exact truth, by omission, can be made to lie. Horvach deals with the immediate facts simply but selectively: the defendant, in possession of an illegal firearm, illegally concealed about her person, disguised herself to gain admission to the news conference, and shot Erhardt Rietz, resulting in near-fatal wounds from which he was unlikely to recover; no reasonable person could doubt that was her object from the start. That prior intent, then, was not affected by the fact that Rietz himself was apparently engaged on a murderous attack at the time of his shooting; "if this were the act of a vigilante, it could not be condoned, but might be regarded with some leniency; this was not vigilantism, but a premeditated attempt at murder."

He leaves Angèle's history to Hannah Sjuc, who, by all means, brings up the "assassinations" statement once again, but also contrives, without mentioning specifics, to remind everyone of "not only a philosophical advocacy, but a demonstrated capacity for reckless acts of violence — " Pavel's wounding. There has been, she observes, a concentrated effort to portray this vicious young woman as a victim of over-zealous law enforcement, but unless she is convicted, it is law itself, and justice, and public safety which are the victims.

Today, then, is either the beginning of that nightmare era envisaged by the defendant, when murder is a legitimate tool of revolutionary social change, or else its end; the decision is in the hands of the jury.

Commercial and contract law don't lend themselves to the stirring of passions, and Kaepfky has no oratorical resources for competing with Sjuc and Horvach; wisely, he aims his appeal at common sense. A man with a long history of sordid and provocative where not demonstrably illegal acts had somehow acquired the uniform of a police officer, with no other intent but to commit murder. It was scarcely material whether he had one or two victims in mind; there was strong evidence, including his presence in that particular place on that specific occasion, to suggest his primary target was the internationally renowned Chief Justice, Wirath, but there is no question he also had motives for an attack on Mr Kearns, a distinguished visiting journalist, and little doubt that he would have succeeded in accomplishing one or both objects, but for the swift intervention of the defendant. Rather than honouring Angèle as the rescuer, the Dusatian state has made the shameful error of putting her on trial, and forcing her to endure this long ordeal. It is clear that the government's actions can in no way be said to reflect the will of the people, of whom the overwhelming majority regard this young woman as the heroine of that frightening episode, a view which he has no doubt the jury will wish to endorse, by acquitting Angèle on all charges.

Pavel, beside me, mutters, "That's great." Astonishingly, it is not ironic; for the only time during the trial he approves of Kaepfky. I would have expected him to want something more hyperbolic and hortatory — in a word, more Hollywood — but as he says (later), juries don't necessarily go for that golden-tongue crap.

The temperature of the rhetoric falls almost to freezing point for Polinaczny's contribution, managed with much shuffling of notes and insistent emphasis on the need to separate fact from opinion, and mortify the latter. With the judge, this also involves dividing fact from fact, since he omits any identification or characterisation of Rietz and barely mentions that I was shot, declaring that the jury has only to decide whether the defendant fired the shots which caused a near-fatal wounding, whether this was a deliberate act, whether she was illegally in possession of the gun, and so forth, a definition for each item of the indictment.

It is, he insists for the last of many times, a question of law. A jury is entitled to differ on the interpretation of events, but not to make law; if they believe these acts occurred — and not even the defence has attempted to dispute the plain facts — they have no choice but to convict.

The jury, six men and four women, and rather more middle-class and middle-age than a true cross-section of Korava would be, is stolid and attentive; there is no hint of how, individually or collectively, they are going to deal with what is as close to a directed verdict as Polinaczny dare come, with (he no doubt feels) the eyes of the world upon him — besides me, half a dozen familiar faces from foreign newspapers and agencies are in the court. Not Dufoireau, whose original, wildly inaccurate story on the shooting was the final flourish in an idiotic career; the French agency is now personified by an elegant and exceedingly supercilious young man from Châlons-sur-Marne, who on the first day complained that the *Guide to Eating Out in Korava* is available in German, Polish and English but not French translation. When he deigns to, he speaks fair English.

The jury is out, by my careful timing, eighteen minutes. Trev Hassett comes over to chat, but is put off, as anyone might be, by Pavel's grim taciturnity, and is relieved to be able to say, "Christ, already?" and make his escape as we are called to order.

The foreman, Fischer, the anecdotal seventh-generation baker, stands to respond to the clerk's questions. They have reached a verdict. They have reached verdicts for all the charges on the indictment (an average rate, I note, not deducting travel time, of two minutes deliberation per charge).

"One," the clerk prompts. "Attempted murder, with premeditation."

"Not guilty."

A stir, and the judge admonishes us.

"Two. The deliberate causing of grievous bodily harm."

"Not guilty."

Polinaczny says, "*Not* guilty?" He's right, this is a key point, virtually a simple question of fact. Kaepfky turns to his client with a faint smile.

"Yes, sir," Fischer says, small, but living up to the family tradition, unintimidated.

"You have considered the evidence?"

"Yes, sir."

"And this is your verdict?"

"Not guilty, sir."

In the face of the judge's undisguised displeasure, he is to say it seven more times; the jury refuses even to convict Angèle of possessing, carrying or concealing an illegal firearm. By this time Polinaczny is struggling with a court at the point of jubilation, while the defendant with a truly angelic smile embraces her attorney, and a number of the press people sidle and skulk away to file reports. Pavel is among them, no doubt to alert his waiting cameras, and make sure Firenc has all possible exits covered.

As he may, Polinaczny demands to know what the vote was in each instance. Fischer accepts a fresh page of notes, clears his throat, and says doggedly, "A majority of the jury also wish me to say this prosecution should never have been done, and that the defendant is a public benefactor."

O, shrewd loafmaker; had he tried to put that at the end he would have been cut short; now it is the final catalyst, and applause, even cheering, erupts everywhere, a furious judge snarling for order, threatening to eject us all.

Relative quiet achieved, he is still angry, and admonishes Fischer: "You are not entitled to give an opinion beyond the verdict itself."

"Yes, sir." He looks out on the world unrepentantly. His several-greats grandfather ignored the uprising of 1849, his grandfather kneaded on while Panzers and T-34's duelled in the streets.

Thwarted, Polinaczny asks again for the jury vote for each charge. Like the verdict itself, it is identical throughout, nine not guilty, no guilty, one abstaining.

We all can guess the abstention, the deputy-foreman ("alternative speaker") next to Fischer, a well-dressed, tight-lipped woman near forty, who never looks at him, but stares out on the court with a chin as stubborn as his — or not quite, perhaps, else she would have voted for conviction, however hopelessly. But even with her dissenting note, the acquittal is too resounding for Polinaczny to upset.

As surely as Angèle once ended her career in journalism with a single phrase, Polinaczny now commits judicial suicide. There were, in any event, to be adverse comments in the press about his conduct of the case, but his speech now means a storm, questions in parliament, and an embattled Gorat throwing his protégé to the wolves by *recommending* the judicial enquiry which is to end by defrocking Polinaczny.

He says, "This is, beyond a doubt, the most wrongheaded jury verdict I have had to deal with in my years on the bench, absolutely contrary both to the evidence, and to my instructions. It is impossible that any sane person can doubt this defendant's guilt on all of the charges, or endorse the wisdom of setting free such a defiant and unrepentant danger to our society. If it were in my power to overrule, I would do so, not only with a clear conscience, but with the utmost enthusiasm. As the law is, however, I have no choice. I cannot overstate the displeasure with which I am obliged to state that having been declared Not Guilty on all charges, the defendant must be set free. I trust that her future activities are to be kept under close and continual scrutiny by the police."

This last part, after the word *free*, has to be recovered from the official court report; here it is lost in pandemonium; cheers and shouts of encouragement for Angèle, whistles and angry shouts for the judge. Who mimes dismissal, and quickly vanishes. As do the prosecutors, although I note that Horvach leans over with a quick congratulatory handshake for the triumphant Kaepfky; for the legal profession the disposal of a young woman's remaining lifetime is, in the end, a sporting question; we do but jest, revile in jest, no offence i'the world.

Outside, the annual late-January thaw is over and winter is closing in again. Supporters, reporters and the simply curious, waiting for a glimpse of Angèle have a raw wind to endure; red-nosed, bright-cheeked, hunched, few if any give in, though the wait stretches out to half an hour, to forty minutes.

At last a sentinel by the double-doors at the head of the eight broad steps calls, "Here she is," and here she is, or so we must assume; hemmed by a tight phalanx of four well-dressed but formidable security-guards, she is scarcely visible. More of Vítor Kaepfky can be seen, and it is he who answers or parries the questions; he is pleased with the verdict, naturally his client is pleased with the verdict, no, she may have a statement later, no, he wasn't surprised, he has always had faith in the common sense of juries.

Someone's gigantic pull has caused there to be a large clear space by the kerb where the steps come down, and into this harbour now sweeps a vast dove-grey Lincoln, very oblong, a chauffeured limousine with dark one-way windows in the rear. A car all Korava knows as the "Super-Cicada," in jocular reference to the profits which enabled its owner not to drive his own success; Jiri Podarny.

As the tight cortège descends, a blazered chauffeur swings open the rear door, and a blazered, bland-faced Jiri emerges. Completely ignoring the questions now choosing him for target, he grasps the hand of Vítor Kaepfky, then hugs him warmly, both men with canary-ingesting smiles.

Kaepfky steps back; Podarny takes the small hands of Angèle, stoops for her to murmur in his ear, and they embrace with a long kiss, before vanishing into cushioned dim, Podarny with a final appreciative cupping of Kaepfky's elbow.

Pavel, at my side, mutters in savage irony touched with hysteria, "Somebody buzz Christa Rasch. The engagement's off."

On the pavement, jostled by the dispersing reporters and merely curious, the tiny band of Angèle's faithful, FREEDOM banner drooping, hold their ground in stupefaction. They received no gesture from their saint.

Driving, he is in the same restless, volatile mood as the night of the blizzard, coming home from the President's Ball.

"Podarny, we should have figured; he's through with Herder, you know? Well, had to be, how can he stay palsy with the jerk who tried to kidnap his fiancée? Some engagement, huh? She's off in America banging — " a quick look for me — "Who knows, maybe the president. And this little bitch — how she look at herself in the mirror, she's supposed to be totally against big dough. Got any ideas for the Defence Fund, I guess she won't be needing it?"

"Keep it in the bank to help with the legal fees of anyone who can't afford a good lawyer?"

"Like a, what do you say, fundation?"

"Foundation — " though actually I like Pavel's Joycean coinage.

"Great, we can call it the Angèle Foundation, make the goddam' tramp immortal."

"Did you know her before? Before she shot you, I mean." Worth a try. Waiting for a traffic signal, we are right outside *Hybicza* with its discreet front windows and lurid posters, another dance-restaurant, like *Tango* (ex *Polka*) just round the corner, but with a very different reputation; couples patronise *Tango*, but *Hybicza*'s clientele is unattached men, and the establishment provides a wide range of dance-partners to choose from, with two floors of tiny private rooms, or cubicles, above.

"What? Oh, sure. Loudmouth little pain in the ass, from the word go, but I met Katja via Angèle. What are you doing tonight?"

"Packing. That should keep me busy for, oh, seven minutes."

We move forward again. "Katja's got tickets for Schubert tonight, you wanna take her? We already got a sitter for the boys."

It's part of a chamber cycle, quartets and quintets. "You're not going?"

"My quarterly report is overdue; I was behind, and now with this trial I'm way behind. I better go back to the studios and work on it."

"I thought you usually brought it home."

"Yah." An immense pause. "Okay, my friend, you wanna know, I'm gonna go get me the best blow job in town, only this Katja doesn't need to know about, right?"

"I have no reason to tell her."

"Yeah? well, you might have, except your mind don't work that way. They got girls there — " a backward tilt of the head to indicate *Hybicza*, now far behind — "for money, you can hurt them. One I know is really into that, only she charges the same price."

I ask nothing.

At the studio where we are for an hour, there are two pieces of news. The first is for Pavel, a phone-call from a friend with the police, whom he thanks after a brief conversation.

Because of the thaw, he relays to me, in the near vicinity of where the Toyota driven by Arni was abandoned, a male body has been found. Dead a month, they estimate, though decomposition has been slight, buried as it was in snow.

"Uh-uh," Pavel responds quickly to my expression. "Not Arni. They just got a positive I-D. It's Lisuk. They think he was strangled, but he's got bruises, too."

Nearby, the police found a revolver, one shot fired, but slushy conditions were hardly conducive to further investigation.

"Lisuk was the one — " I try to think it through — "Arni dumped in the middle of nowhere, from that same car, the evening we helped Christa escape. He may have wanted to return the compliment."

"Plus shooting him? What, did he miss?"

"I think Arni could be hit more than once, and still have the strength to throttle Lisuk." Easily; I could picture those large hands picking Lisuk up by his neck, like a big-jowled tom-cat with a scrawny mouse. "But if Arni survived to kill Lisuk, where is he? Why did he abandon the car?"

It is to remain a mystery, though I don't believe Arni's body is still to be found, deeper into the woods on whose fringe Lisuk was lying. My idea is that in his muddled way he believes he's wanted for that killing, and has slipped across the border into Poland (he spoke passable Polish); he may be repairing cars in Cracow or Warsaw, still wondering when it's going to be safe for him to come home.

The second bulletin, from Central Hospital, is for the world; about an hour after Angèle's acquittal, Rietz was pronounced dead. It would be theoretically possible for her to be re-arrested and charged with murder; I promptly and generously offer Pavel five-to-one odds against it, and he suggests five hundred to one might be nearer. Gorat's ill-will for Angèle must surely stop short of political suicide.

As it does; as we're leaving Firenc comes in to tell us the Prosecutor's office has quickly advertised the absence of any plans for a fresh indictment.

"Maybe she'll marry Podarny," Firenc says, all innocence.

Pavel grins. "One thing Dusatia needs, a rich-bitch revolutionary, just like civilised countries."

The ensemble is visiting from Prague, adding a local second cellist for the wonderful quintet, and to my joy they conclude with G-Major Quartet, another miracle, not as famous as it ought to be. I have never been able to watch Katja enjoying music, as she genuinely does. For many ballet people, Adam, Delibes, Prokofiev or plundered Bach and Beethoven, there's not much distinction to be made, it all becomes so much useful rhythmic noise, cut to measure. But Katja is of the elect, serenely attentive while it lasts, stimulated after.

After, like young students, we stop for coffee and talk. Though not quite like students; coming in I hold open the door for two real ones, he with a bulky bound score tucked under his arm — and I recognise my own signs of aging; I have (for some time now) come to a place where it's possible to wonder what on earth deliciously attractive young women are doing in the company of boringly immature boys.

A soon as Katja and I are seated, this particular astonishingly pretty distraction, brushing off her escort's dissuasive hand, approaches shyly.

"Excuse me — " in careful English. "Are you not Mister Mark Kearns?   We believe what you have done is so praiseworthy."

I dip my chin dismissively (*Praiseworthy*! what do they use for a text, *Phoebe Becomes a Prefect?*).

"It is most wrong that you are, were shot, but I hope you will know not every Dusatian are bad persons — "

"I am Dusatian myself — " In English; it would seem a rebuke otherwise, when she's labouring so gamely. "My mother is Dusatian."

"Oh. Now I think you will always be famous in Dusatia — " and she proffers her concert programme for me to "write name on."

Odd, but I ask her name (Irena) and inscribe a salutation; she retires in obsequies of gratitude.

Katja is wry. "What a shame! If you were going to stay, you could give her private English lessons.' But mention of my departure makes her serious, and she adds, "And me, too. Korava is much more exciting when you're here."

"I come here when exciting things are happening."

"No, not exciting like that. I thought you came to see me."

"Pavel thinks I'm in love with you — " lightly, though I'm thinking, *this is never going to come back; this is the only time Katja and I, pleasantly pie-eyed on Schubert, are going to bow our heads to each other over coffee.*

"Pavel says that? Well, you see, if someone's in love with me, he can be in love with Angèle."

(This equation doesn't balance; many men could be and probably are in love with Katja, just because she's Katja.) "Poor Pavel," she sounds sincere. "How can he ever sleep with her now?"

"Did he, before — did you steal Pavel away from Angèle?"

A startled laugh. "Not exactly — oh, if I tell you, you're never going to want to see me again, you're going to hate me."

I assure her, accurately, that there's nothing she could tell me that could make that true.

"You've got it backwards. It was Pavel who stole me away from Angèle. Or so she believed. Yes. Oh, it was just a phase I went through — for Angèle, too, I think, but it meant more to her. We were very young — it began just when my mother died, if that has anything to do with it."

"You were probably lonely." Proper orientation of the triangle at last explains why it was Pavel who was attacked. To judge by Rietz, Angèle's marksmanship has improved; Pavel was wounded in the upper leg, and the nature of his offence suggests she had in mind another, nearby target (Hannah Sjuc's characterisation, if partial, isn't so far from the truth). And he refused to press charges so as not to expose Katja's private life; everything dovetails, but the origin of his latter extravagant passion for Angèle has to lie down among the dark, insoluable mysteries.

"For me, it was just something we did together, friends, I didn't dream a woman could be really in love like that with a woman. I had never slept with a man, till Pavel. He's still the only man I ever went to bed with — isn't that ridiculous! Just like the middle ages, or Jane Austen."

"It isn't ridiculous if that's what you wanted. Sleeping with a lot of men you don't want, because this is now, that would be ridiculous."

She gives me a long, quite deliberately sexual stare, but resumes where she left her account. "Once I had slept with Pavel, the other was all over. I was so naive, I thought I could just say that to Angèle and she would understand. She went insane." A dour little laugh. "I almost told her what Pavel suggested, when I told him about me and Angèle. That would have made it worse."

"A threesome." Not among my conscious fantasies, but asking supplies a slight, undeniable tingle. Perhaps, in any context, I am roused by the thought of Katja, stripped and bedded. "Did you want that?"

"Oh, no. It was revolting — I was in love with Pavel. I was very young, and I thought, if that was what he wanted — It's better now, now he works late; his wife is his wife and his whore is his whore."

"What about you?" With all her revelations, we've been using many words, like other people, but now we're back knowing what we mean.

"Revenge, you mean? That's all it could be. I don't want to have just sex, pay for it and forget it. That's important for some men, for Pavel; he can do things he can't do with his wife, the mother of his sons — he thinks he can't; you know, really filthy things that wives don't do."

Though her flushed irony virtually proclaims Katja's aptitude for all and any erotic variants, I recall Pavel's hot eyes when he spoke about hurting a woman, and think he may have it right after all, as near right as it can be, given these elements.

"With me, if I wanted someone else — you know American films, TV shows as well? the children are with their mother, and the father comes to take them for the weekend, and she has a lover and he has a new girlfriend, et cetera. In the films, the children are very clever, and it all ends up *okay*, but even the *okay* is horrible, and in real life it must be much worse, a nightmare. Pavel is a nice man, he makes love very well, we hardly ever quarrel. Do you know anyone more generous than Pavel?"

"No one who comes close." But this counting of blessings, rejection of unthinkable alternatives, sounds like the state of play in a long internal debate, the reasoning of someone who can no longer resort to the unanswerable *I love him.*

"When shall you be back in Dusatia?"

I have been dreading this. I don't know. When not in crisis, Korava is a backwater. If my life was unchanged, it might be years, but as another side-effect of sudden prominence, I am only a signature away from becoming editor-in-chief and what they call "anchor" (a large stone on a rope?) for a syndicated news-magazine show dealing in depth not with celebrity piffle, but with serious world events and issues. We plan versions in half-a-dozen languages — it is, in fact, much the idea proposed by Svoboda in Prague, except that this one is properly financed and has access to world distribution; sight unseen the English version is already sold in a number of cable and broadcast markets, and my salary is generous. Albertson, who has been very civilised, warns me it could all go down the drain in a year or so, but even if that's true, I'll have time to put together a couple more books. Actual production is to be in Brussels, but I'll be able to live in London.

"In London," Katja says, rapt with her romantic anglophilia. I don't tell her how dead is the literary London she dreams of, Johnson's London, Dickens' London, Conan Doyle's London, all gone, except for a few blessed backwaters, replaced by characterless Cosmopolis.

A parallel for the notional Englishman I, under false pretences, represent for Katja, who was, if he ever existed, a transient phenomenon. That poetry-reciting Barry once loved by both the young Mme Niemek and my adolescent mother may have been among the last, and the species was definitively extinct with the death of Winston Churchill, a little less than four centuries after that of Phillip Sidney, who might be the first. And he was immediate precursor to Shakespeare, who gave them all a tongue, down to the last lion — because the real undimming empire was not the fleet, or bits of Africa and Asia coloured red on a map, but the imperium of language, fresh and confident and rich enough to make heaven-storming aspiration stand in place of, sometimes *become*, reality; Thomas Jefferson was of that breed as well as Drake and Nelson and Burton, almost T.E. Lawrence, and absolutely Coleridge and Elgar and H.G. Wells, till, like their country, they grew tired and despondent, at best scholarly, at worst, rancorous.

Now, because America is still confident and consequential, we disdain Americans and copy them in everything; knowing absolutely nothing about baseball we speak of striking out, batting a thousand, getting to first base; we mock and then soberly adopt the polysyllabic pomposities of American academic, bureaucratic, sociological and business talk; loving the smell of power that clings to them, transplant and utterly misapply political terms such as lame duck and favourite son, like boys aping the incidental mannerisms of a favourite footballer; perhaps if we sound enough like Americans, we can still matter in the world, too. But we no more resemble Katja's fabled Brits than Onassis did Achilles.

For the show, I have demanded and been assured complete editorial control; I intend still to do interviews, but unless they're heads of state (and sometimes even then) my victims will come to me.

"Might you not be bored, sitting still, after — this?"

Not really; if I am, I can always send myself, not limited to my past linguistic bailiwick, to witness civil war in Sri Lanka, poverty in Peru, a coup in the Congo. But mostly I'll be seeing others off without regrets on what has been my life of hotels, breakfasts of bread, coffee flecked with milk-skin, early flights and late flights, dismal airports and hit-and-run sex. Only now do I recognise how much I have longed for a fixed domicile with a library and CD's, a few decent bottles of Bordeaux; a cat, certainly.

"A wife," Katja prompts. Moving my head in possible agreement, I shake loose another unexplained mystery.

"When we danced. Why did you say you were glad I didn't like your friend?"

"Oh — " She smiles with an onset of shyness. Of *shyness*?

"Wasn't I supposed to like her?"

"You should be married. If you were married — " it's simple, "I should have to stop thinking about you. But thinking about you is my best secret."

Our cab and the BMW pull up at the house in near succession, and Pavel, tieless, a little bleared, but (he insists) fully sober, leaves again shortly to take home the boys' minder, a ruddy, elderly lady, grandmother to one of the gopher-maids at the station.

Among the English prints, I accomplish my slight packing, struggling against an insidious melancholy. Emerging, I search for Katja, and find her looking like an Arthur Rackham princess, high-collared, close-fitting, brocaded dressing-gown, hair coiling free, in the kitchen making tea.

Tonight's music is running in my head, and I'm thinking how, with that very small company of godlike composers, the greatest moments are often achieved with the simplest effects, a half-step modulation, sudden absence of a syncopation, a couple of passing-notes; mysteriously, because the same procedures are banal in lesser hands. It is the simplicity of achieved wisdom that moves us, and this connects, not solemnly, to the disproportionate pleasure there is in watching Katja, the absorbed precision of her moves.

Really boiling water poured, pot lidded and cozied, she looks up and smiles at my catlike vigil.

"What do you think, Mark? Do people really fall in love, or do we only want to hold on to the one who lets us love ourselves?"

I put up a hand as if to fend off such portentous questions, and she (I'm glad to say) laughs.

"No, but isn't it difficult to know?"

"Impossible. If that's all anyone ever does, then that's what falling in love is." But at best, it's a sometime truth; long ago the late stages of being in love with Germaine filled me with contempt for myself. Oh, shut up, this isn't a time for syllogism.

"But it ought to be something happy." In the coffeeshop, when she was explaining how useless it was for her to think of paying Pavel back, she was telling me why we would never go to bed together. About some things, I'm moronically slow.

She squints at me earnestly, and speaks English. "Dear Mark, would you do a thing for me — a favour?"

"Of course."

"Kiss me now. We shall kiss goodbye when you really leave, but now I would like for you to kiss me — " a shy struggle. "As you would kiss me if we had made love all night."

Overwhelmed, one recognises the impossibility; I don't have a detached monitor to note and remember those morning kisses; the spontaneous can't be consciously reconstructed. So I do what must be wanted, certainly what I have always wanted, and for the only time kiss Katja with no prudent reservations. As if we might make love all night.

Right away, my ill-informed web of nerves, feckless endocrine system, believe it might be true; circulation, respiration, tactile perception all move to action stations. There is nothing in existence softer than Katja's lips, nothing in imagination as desirable as Katja. We fail to stop at one kiss, and she is equally responsible for what, beyond kissing, there is, caresses, the striving encounter of clad bodies.

We hear the car-door thud. As if arranging her on a shelf, I grasp Katja's shoulders and put distance between us. She is trembling, but I am gasping like the death-throes of a salmon.

She sets three cups on their saucers, and goes to the refrigerator for milk.

It is a late-morning flight, and Pavel, who is to drive me to the airport, puts in an early appearance at the studios, and returns when, eye on the clock, I am on the point of phoning for a taxi. He is wearing the smug face of Pavel with some news.

"Hey, buddy, maybe you should stay, I got a great place for you, ritzy fully-modernised eighteenth-century villa in la-dee-dah suburbs, luxury furnished, Christ knows how many bedrooms, state-of-the-art communications centre, concert grand pie-anno, immediate occupancy."

"The Herders have scarpered." The only available answer.

"Scarpered?"

"Taken it on the lam." I'll have to send Pavel a selection of the classic Ealing comedies, so he can add some dated British underworld slang.

"Jumped bail, yah. Last night sometime — boy, somebody got paid off. They crossed the frontier into Slovakia around one a.m., the Merc and a good-sized van, so I guess they took the Monet and the ikons."

There is much more, a Chippendale cabinet and Louis XV escritoire, a Sèvres coffee-service, a Sung screen, a Canaletto, first editions, some of all which must have been left behind.

"Why now? — " I think it through, Pavel amusedly encouraging me: "Angèle's acquittal must have given them the idea that the political climate was against them. But then, with Rietz dead, the chances of a conviction were just about nil, unless — "

"Yeah, yeah... "

"Rietz left behind some written evidence. Either that, or the other hood from the Eagle's Nest surfaced. The bald one, Jenadju."

"Hey, we gonna make a reporter out of you yet. How about both? Before the hospital finished yanking tubes out of Rietz, the cops pulled a raid on his place, out at the rifle range, you know. They heisted all kinds of records, who he paid to do what, a ton of guns and ammunition, and Jenadju is hiding out there, the poor bastard must have frozen his ass, all there is is a pot-belly stove, he was down to burning cartridge-boxes."

"And the Herders were tipped off, naturally."

"Shit, they probably heard about it before the commissioner did."

A costly decamping, though less expensive than at first blink; their bail, an unprecedented one, was two million crowns the pair, but of that they were required to put up only half, and so forfeited about seventy-seven thousand pounds sterling, tip money for Juan-Micel. If I may carry their saga a little beyond the bounds of my story, they are eventually to reappear in Singapore, whose notoriously draconian penal code is suffused with a spirit of mercy for those who bring a half-billion (U.S.) dollars of new venture capital into the economy; attempts at extradition are to be suspended helpless in a sticky web of procedural technicalities, and the Swiss, German and American ambassadors become their frequent dinner guests. They steadfastly decline to be interviewed for inclusion in my very successful series *The Money Barons*, and Christa Rasch is to deny a report she stayed with them on a promotional swoop through the Orient.

Everyone goes to the airport, Vaclav and Thom bundled like Amundsen; the wind is unforgiving under a virginal innocence of sky. At the gate, Pavel hugs me, and wishes me well in my new career.

"We gonna see you some more?"

"I can come for a holiday."

"Any time. Hey, maybe we could all go someplace, Greece maybe, Venice."

"Sounds good to me." This is never going to happen.

Pavel, unnecessarily, is seeking a defining word. "I think we smashed up the Nazis, you more than me. We oughta name a street after you, a building, maybe.

"You know what I mean — " answering my grimace.

I do, and we clasp hands solemnly once more. "But it was fun."

"I'll tell the world."

Thom, whose normal forward progress is a continuous, lurching flirtation with falling on his nose, twenty feet away comes up short, face to face with a grave little girl of similar size but greater age, or greater sophistication; from a distance of five inches they stare transfixed at each other, he amazed, she intrigued by his amazement. The mother, young, Polish, tries to impose an irrelevant, alien convention, informing her daughter that this is a little boy, urging her to say hello. Pavel, towing Vaclav who is walking backwards and looking open-mouthed at the ceiling, goes to collect his second son.

Katja and I fold together, and the counterpoint, in our decorous kiss, of impractical mutual hunger, is very subtle. I murmur, "Pavel had it right. For always."

She breathes, "Oh, God," and I suppose tears are permissible at a parting of friends. Mawkish to acknowledge, dishonest to deny the wrench of agonised affection for her blurred beauty.

Then I do get on that plane, and regret it, soon, and so far as I can see, for the rest of my life. Not that I believe, as Korava, as Dusatia dwindles below, is curtained off by cloud, there was even an illusion of choice.

XIII

"Mr Kearns, when you were questioned by the prosecution about your knowledge of Mr Rietz you indicated you possessed other information."

"Yes, that it was Mr Rietz who approached Chief Justice Wirath to threaten him, tell him the safety of his daughter depended on a decision favourable to the National Loyalist side in the so-called Yellow Ballot issue." What the hearsay rule might be in Dusatian law I don't know, but Horvach is on his feet, and I quickly add, "I'm certain Justice Wirath would confirm this." It has, in fact, been a part of newspaper stories for every continent but an unpeopled one.

Prosecutor, with what he thinks is shrivelling sarcasm: "Do you propose to call the Chief Justice as a witness?" But why not, if he is one?

Kaepfky is complacent. "No, but, if I may sir? — " to the judge. "Justice Wirath has volunteered a sworn deposition, which I now propose to enter in evidence." An efficient clerk has produced three copies, one of which Kaepfky passes up to the judge, the other going to the prosecutor, who studies it unhappily.

"This will be read into the record when we are finished with the present witness," Kaepfky advises. "But I may say that the account of the Chief Justice does indeed confirm that Mr Rietz threatened him, just as this witness has stated." Precisely true; when the deposition is read Wirath, typically, has made a careful distinction between personally recognising the gunman as the same person (which he did not), and subsequent identification by name and description. The practical difference is small, and the prosecution will not attempt to do anything with it.

Meanwhile: "The kidnapping having failed in its objective — " in theory, as a question to me — "Rietz's motive for an attack on both you and the Chief Justice becomes clear."

"Yes."   Leave needed legal reforms to Wirath; this, technically, is cross-examination, but I've noted throughout, even in direct examination, an extravagant tolerance for leading by counsel. More follows.

"Is it your belief that he hoped to silence the two men who could connect him to the kidnapping attempt?"

"Partially."   Kaepfky would prefer my unconditional assent, but the point, surely, is to make sure the jury recognise Rietz as the villain, and that can't be strengthened by an untenable motive. "It would, of course, be irrational to try to save oneself from a charge of kidnapping by committing two very public murders."

"Then Rietz's behaviour was, you believe, irrational?"

Here, Horvach at last wakes up, and objects to my being invited to speculate on *the victim'*s state of mind, and this leads to an extended, low-voiced wrangle just beneath the judicial bench, the entire essence being contained in a single somewhat more audible exchange:

Kaepfky: "Well, we can't question Rietz about his motive."

Horvach: "We are not here to try Erhardt Rietz."

Formally true, and a point made more than once by Polinaczny, but in reality we are. That's exactly what we're doing.

Kaepfky's manner seems deferential, but he didn't take on the Gorat government (and win) without some reserves of steel; instructed to abandon the enquiry into Rietz's mental processes, he puts his next question under the judge's hard scrutiny, and steers the finest of lines.

"Without trying to define what those motives might be, are you satisfied that Rietz had adequate motive for attempting to kill either you yourself, or the Chief Justice, or both?"

"Certainly."

"To what do you ascribe his failure to do so?"

"To the swift and decisive actions of the defendant, as depicted on the tape."

"Of my client."

"Of Angèle, yes — " surprised we both got away with the double re-emphasis.

But when Kaepfky presses his luck, beginning, "I take it then you are profoundly thankful — " Horvach pops up with a near-howl of protest, and my gratitude is ruled irrelevant.

As, later, is Pavel's attempt to steer his reasons for preparing the "editorial" tape into his opinion of the entire proceedings against Angèle. Afterwards, he is angry with Kaepfky for not trying harder, but I suspect the attorney is, on the whole, relieved. As was, Pavel was grazing the edge of personal feelings about Angèle, in danger of permitting the prosecution, after all, to open up the whole business of her wounding of him. A story which speaks highly of Pavel's fine, forgiving nature, but is far worse than no help to Angèle.

The second overnight pause is at the threshold of closing arguments, and Katja is confident there can be no guilty verdict. Her friend Marjenka (of the Christmas gathering) has published a just-completed poll, showing that almost two-thirds of all Dusatians (or all who have an opinion; there were large numbers of Don't Knows) believe Angèle should never have been tried, and only a slightly lesser majority that Gorat (never mind the constitution) should have intervened to halt the proceedings. There is also strong support for a presidential pardon in the event of conviction.

"This," she says, "is language Gorat understands. Dalerant supports his refusal to intervene on principle, but some of the Catholic Renewal deputies don't, and none of the Liberal Front; about a dozen Social Democrat members are ready to revolt — " all this inside parliamentary information comes from Marjenka's younger brother, who works for an S.D.D. member.

"Yeah," Pavel says grimly. "But Gorat may have started something he can't stop."

He's right of course. If Horvach and the judge between them succeed in browbeating the jury, Angèle's conviction might accomplish what Rietz and the Herders, Miloczy and the former, unrepentant Vock could not, breaking of the centrist coalition, and the fall of Gorat.

Third and surely final day. A quiet beginning, though the tension is high; everyone expects a verdict today. Or rather, that it will be in the hands of the jury; Trev Hassett has got up a little sweep among the press on how long they'll deliberate, and the experienced are putting their money on four, six, ten hours, even overnight.

Kaepfky makes a last point, recalling the chief arresting officer to make absolutely explicit that Angèle made no resistance to being disarmed or attempt to evade arrest, and that when he took the gun from her she remarked, in a conversational tone, "If you were on your job, I wouldn't have needed that."

Conversational, perhaps, but vintage Angèle tactlessness; she was lucky to have found an honest sergeant; a less scrupulous and more vindictive man might have made up something more damning.

After another of their animated whisperings, Horvach and Sjuc decide to let it alone, whereupon the defence case is closed.

Taken together, the two summations and closing arguments are a demonstration of how exact truth, by omission, can be made to lie. Horvach deals with the immediate facts simply but selectively: the defendant, in possession of an illegal firearm, illegally concealed about her person, disguised herself to gain admission to the news conference, and shot Erhardt Rietz, resulting in near-fatal wounds from which he was unlikely to recover; no reasonable person could doubt that was her object from the start. That prior intent, then, was not affected by the fact that Rietz himself was apparently engaged on a murderous attack at the time of his shooting; "if this were the act of a vigilante, it could not be condoned, but might be regarded with some leniency; this was not vigilantism, but a premeditated attempt at murder."

He leaves Angèle's history to Hannah Sjuc, who, by all means, brings up the "assassinations" statement once again, but also contrives, without mentioning specifics, to remind everyone of "not only a philosophical advocacy, but a demonstrated capacity for reckless acts of violence — " Pavel's wounding. There has been, she observes, a concentrated effort to portray this vicious young woman as a victim of over-zealous law enforcement, but unless she is convicted, it is law itself, and justice, and public safety which are the victims.

Today, then, is either the beginning of that nightmare era envisaged by the defendant, when murder is a legitimate tool of revolutionary social change, or else its end; the decision is in the hands of the jury.

Commercial and contract law don't lend themselves to the stirring of passions, and Kaepfky has no oratorical resources for competing with Sjuc and Horvach; wisely, he aims his appeal at common sense. A man with a long history of sordid and provocative where not demonstrably illegal acts had somehow acquired the uniform of a police officer, with no other intent but to commit murder. It was scarcely material whether he had one or two victims in mind; there was strong evidence, including his presence in that particular place on that specific occasion, to suggest his primary target was the internationally renowned Chief Justice, Wirath, but there is no question he also had motives for an attack on Mr Kearns, a distinguished visiting journalist, and little doubt that he would have succeeded in accomplishing one or both objects, but for the swift intervention of the defendant. Rather than honouring Angèle as the rescuer, the Dusatian state has made the shameful error of putting her on trial, and forcing her to endure this long ordeal. It is clear that the government's actions can in no way be said to reflect the will of the people, of whom the overwhelming majority regard this young woman as the heroine of that frightening episode, a view which he has no doubt the jury will wish to endorse, by acquitting Angèle on all charges.

Pavel, beside me, mutters, "That's great." Astonishingly, it is not ironic; for the only time during the trial he approves of Kaepfky. I would have expected him to want something more hyperbolic and hortatory — in a word, more Hollywood — but as he says (later), juries don't necessarily go for that golden-tongue crap.

The temperature of the rhetoric falls almost to freezing point for Polinaczny's contribution, managed with much shuffling of notes and insistent emphasis on the need to separate fact from opinion, and mortify the latter. With the judge, this also involves dividing fact from fact, since he omits any identification or characterisation of Rietz and barely mentions that I was shot, declaring that the jury has only to decide whether the defendant fired the shots which caused a near-fatal wounding, whether this was a deliberate act, whether she was illegally in possession of the gun, and so forth, a definition for each item of the indictment.

It is, he insists for the last of many times, a question of law. A jury is entitled to differ on the interpretation of events, but not to make law; if they believe these acts occurred — and not even the defence has attempted to dispute the plain facts — they have no choice but to convict.

The jury, six men and four women, and rather more middle-class and middle-age than a true cross-section of Korava would be, is stolid and attentive; there is no hint of how, individually or collectively, they are going to deal with what is as close to a directed verdict as Polinaczny dare come, with (he no doubt feels) the eyes of the world upon him — besides me, half a dozen familiar faces from foreign newspapers and agencies are in the court. Not Dufoireau, whose original, wildly inaccurate story on the shooting was the final flourish in an idiotic career; the French agency is now personified by an elegant and exceedingly supercilious young man from Châlons-sur-Marne, who on the first day complained that the *Guide to Eating Out in Korava* is available in German, Polish and English but not French translation. When he deigns to, he speaks fair English.

The jury is out, by my careful timing, eighteen minutes. Trev Hassett comes over to chat, but is put off, as anyone might be, by Pavel's grim taciturnity, and is relieved to be able to say, "Christ, already?" and make his escape as we are called to order.

The foreman, Fischer, the anecdotal seventh-generation baker, stands to respond to the clerk's questions. They have reached a verdict. They have reached verdicts for all the charges on the indictment (an average rate, I note, not deducting travel time, of two minutes deliberation per charge).

"One," the clerk prompts. "Attempted murder, with premeditation."

"Not guilty."

A stir, and the judge admonishes us.

"Two. The deliberate causing of grievous bodily harm."

"Not guilty."

Polinaczny says, "*Not* guilty?" He's right, this is a key point, virtually a simple question of fact. Kaepfky turns to his client with a faint smile.

"Yes, sir," Fischer says, small, but living up to the family tradition, unintimidated.

"You have considered the evidence?"

"Yes, sir."

"And this is your verdict?"

"Not guilty, sir."

In the face of the judge's undisguised displeasure, he is to say it seven more times; the jury refuses even to convict Angèle of possessing, carrying or concealing an illegal firearm. By this time Polinaczny is struggling with a court at the point of jubilation, while the defendant with a truly angelic smile embraces her attorney, and a number of the press people sidle and skulk away to file reports. Pavel is among them, no doubt to alert his waiting cameras, and make sure Firenc has all possible exits covered.

As he may, Polinaczny demands to know what the vote was in each instance. Fischer accepts a fresh page of notes, clears his throat, and says doggedly, "A majority of the jury also wish me to say this prosecution should never have been done, and that the defendant is a public benefactor."

O, shrewd loafmaker; had he tried to put that at the end he would have been cut short; now it is the final catalyst, and applause, even cheering, erupts everywhere, a furious judge snarling for order, threatening to eject us all.

Relative quiet achieved, he is still angry, and admonishes Fischer: "You are not entitled to give an opinion beyond the verdict itself."

"Yes, sir." He looks out on the world unrepentantly. His several-greats grandfather ignored the uprising of 1849, his grandfather kneaded on while Panzers and T-34's duelled in the streets.

Thwarted, Polinaczny asks again for the jury vote for each charge. Like the verdict itself, it is identical throughout, nine not guilty, no guilty, one abstaining.

We all can guess the abstention, the deputy-foreman ("alternative speaker") next to Fischer, a well-dressed, tight-lipped woman near forty, who never looks at him, but stares out on the court with a chin as stubborn as his — or not quite, perhaps, else she would have voted for conviction, however hopelessly. But even with her dissenting note, the acquittal is too resounding for Polinaczny to upset.

As surely as Angèle once ended her career in journalism with a single phrase, Polinaczny now commits judicial suicide. There were, in any event, to be adverse comments in the press about his conduct of the case, but his speech now means a storm, questions in parliament, and an embattled Gorat throwing his protégé to the wolves by *recommending* the judicial enquiry which is to end by defrocking Polinaczny.

He says, "This is, beyond a doubt, the most wrongheaded jury verdict I have had to deal with in my years on the bench, absolutely contrary both to the evidence, and to my instructions. It is impossible that any sane person can doubt this defendant's guilt on all of the charges, or endorse the wisdom of setting free such a defiant and unrepentant danger to our society. If it were in my power to overrule, I would do so, not only with a clear conscience, but with the utmost enthusiasm. As the law is, however, I have no choice. I cannot overstate the displeasure with which I am obliged to state that having been declared Not Guilty on all charges, the defendant must be set free. I trust that her future activities are to be kept under close and continual scrutiny by the police."

This last part, after the word *free*, has to be recovered from the official court report; here it is lost in pandemonium; cheers and shouts of encouragement for Angèle, whistles and angry shouts for the judge. Who mimes dismissal, and quickly vanishes. As do the prosecutors, although I note that Horvach leans over with a quick congratulatory handshake for the triumphant Kaepfky; for the legal profession the disposal of a young woman's remaining lifetime is, in the end, a sporting question; we do but jest, revile in jest, no offence i'the world.

Outside, the annual late-January thaw is over and winter is closing in again. Supporters, reporters and the simply curious, waiting for a glimpse of Angèle have a raw wind to endure; red-nosed, bright-cheeked, hunched, few if any give in, though the wait stretches out to half an hour, to forty minutes.

At last a sentinel by the double-doors at the head of the eight broad steps calls, "Here she is," and here she is, or so we must assume; hemmed by a tight phalanx of four well-dressed but formidable security-guards, she is scarcely visible. More of Vítor Kaepfky can be seen, and it is he who answers or parries the questions; he is pleased with the verdict, naturally his client is pleased with the verdict, no, she may have a statement later, no, he wasn't surprised, he has always had faith in the common sense of juries.

Someone's gigantic pull has caused there to be a large clear space by the kerb where the steps come down, and into this harbour now sweeps a vast dove-grey Lincoln, very oblong, a chauffeured limousine with dark one-way windows in the rear. A car all Korava knows as the "Super-Cicada," in jocular reference to the profits which enabled its owner not to drive his own success; Jiri Podarny.

As the tight cortège descends, a blazered chauffeur swings open the rear door, and a blazered, bland-faced Jiri emerges. Completely ignoring the questions now choosing him for target, he grasps the hand of Vítor Kaepfky, then hugs him warmly, both men with canary-ingesting smiles.

Kaepfky steps back; Podarny takes the small hands of Angèle, stoops for her to murmur in his ear, and they embrace with a long kiss, before vanishing into cushioned dim, Podarny with a final appreciative cupping of Kaepfky's elbow.

Pavel, at my side, mutters in savage irony touched with hysteria, "Somebody buzz Christa Rasch. The engagement's off."

On the pavement, jostled by the dispersing reporters and merely curious, the tiny band of Angèle's faithful, FREEDOM banner drooping, hold their ground in stupefaction. They received no gesture from their saint.

Driving, he is in the same restless, volatile mood as the night of the blizzard, coming home from the President's Ball.

"Podarny, we should have figured; he's through with Herder, you know? Well, had to be, how can he stay palsy with the jerk who tried to kidnap his fiancée? Some engagement, huh? She's off in America banging — " a quick look for me — "Who knows, maybe the president. And this little bitch — how she look at herself in the mirror, she's supposed to be totally against big dough. Got any ideas for the Defence Fund. I guess she won't be needing it?"

"Keep it in the bank to help with the legal fees of anyone who can't afford a good lawyer?"

"Like a, what do you say, fundation?"

"Foundation — " though actually I like Pavel's Joycean coinage.

"Great, we can call it the Angèle Foundation, make the goddam' tramp immortal."

"Did you know her before? Before she shot you, I mean." Worth a try. Waiting for a traffic signal, we are right outside *Hybicza* with its discreet front windows and lurid posters, another dance-restaurant, like *Tango* (ex *Polka*) just round the corner, but with a very different reputation; couples patronise *Tango*, but *Hybicza*'s clientele is unattached men, and the establishment provides a wide range of dance-partners to choose from, with two floors of tiny private rooms, or cubicles, above.

"What? Oh, sure. Loudmouth little pain in the ass, from the word go, but I met Katja via Angèle. What are you doing tonight?"

"Packing. That should keep me busy for, oh, seven minutes."

We move forward again. "Katja's got tickets for Schubert tonight, you wanna take her? We already got a sitter for the boys."

It's part of a chamber cycle, quartets and quintets. "You're not going?"

"My quarterly report is overdue; I was behind, and now with this trial I'm way behind. I better go back to the studios and work on it."

"I thought you usually brought it home."

"Yah." An immense pause. "Okay, my friend, you wanna know, I'm gonna go get me the best blow job in town, only this Katja doesn't need to know about, right?"

"I have no reason to tell her."

"Yeah? well, you might have, except your mind don't work that way. They got girls there — " a backward tilt of the head to indicate *Hybicza*, now far behind — "for money, you can hurt them. One I know is really into that, only she charges the same price."

I ask nothing.

At the studio where we are for an hour, there are two pieces of news. The first is for Pavel, a phone-call from a friend with the police, whom he thanks after a brief conversation.

Because of the thaw, he relays to me, in the near vicinity of where the Toyota driven by Arni was abandoned, a male body has been found. Dead a month, they estimate, though decomposition has been slight, buried as it was in snow.

"Uh-uh," Pavel responds quickly to my expression. "Not Arni. They just got a positive I-D. It's Lisuk. They think he was strangled, but he's got bruises, too."

Nearby, the police found a revolver, one shot fired, but slushy conditions were hardly conducive to further investigation.

"Lisuk was the one — " I try to think it through — "Arni dumped in the middle of nowhere, from that same car, the evening we helped Christa escape. He may have wanted to return the compliment."

"Plus shooting him? What, did he miss?"

"I think Arni could be hit more than once, and still have the strength to throttle Lisuk." Easily; I could picture those large hands picking Lisuk up by his neck, like a big-jowled tom-cat with a scrawny mouse. "But if Arni survived to kill Lisuk, where is he? Why did he abandon the car?"

It is to remain a mystery, though I don't believe Arni's body is still to be found, deeper into the woods on whose fringe Lisuk was lying. My idea is that in his muddled way he believes he's wanted for that killing, and has slipped across the border into Poland (he spoke passable Polish); he may be repairing cars in

Cracow or Warsaw, still wondering when it's going to be safe for him to come home.

The second bulletin, from Central Hospital, is for the world; about an hour after Angèle's acquittal, Rietz was pronounced dead. It would be theoretically possible for her to be re-arrested and charged with murder; I promptly and generously offer Pavel five-to-one odds against it, and he suggests five hundred to one might be nearer. Gorat's ill-will for Angèle must surely stop short of political suicide.

As it does; as we're leaving Firenc comes in to tell us the Prosecutor's office has quickly advertised the absence of any plans for a fresh indictment.

"Maybe she'll marry Podarny," Firenc says, all innocence.

Pavel grins. "One thing Dusatia needs, a rich-bitch revolutionary, just like civilised countries."

The ensemble is visiting from Prague, adding a local second cellist for the wonderful quintet, and to my joy they conclude with G-Major Quartet, another miracle, not as famous as it ought to be. I have never been able to watch Katja enjoying music, as she genuinely does. For many ballet people, Adam, Delibes, Prokofiev or plundered Bach and Beethoven, there's not much distinction to be made, it all becomes so much useful rhythmic noise, cut to measure. But Katja is of the elect, serenely attentive while it lasts, stimulated after.

After, like young students, we stop for coffee and talk. Though not quite like students; coming in I hold open the door for two real ones, he with a bulky bound score tucked under his arm — and I recognise my own signs of aging; I have (for some time now) come to a place where it's possible to wonder what on earth deliciously attractive young women are doing in the company of boringly immature boys.

A soon as Katja and I are seated, this particular astonishingly pretty distraction, brushing off her escort's dissuasive hand, approaches shyly.

"Excuse me — " in careful English. "Are you not Mister Mark Kearns?   We believe what you have done is so praiseworthy."

I dip my chin dismissively (*Praiseworthy*! what do they use for a text, *Phoebe Becomes a Prefect*?).

"It is most wrong that you are, were shot, but I hope you will know not every Dusatian are bad persons — "

"I am Dusatian myself — " In English; it would seem a rebuke otherwise, when she's labouring so gamely. "My mother is Dusatian."

"Oh. Now I think you will always be famous in Dusatia — " and she proffers her concert programme for me to "write name on."

Odd, but I ask her name (Irena) and inscribe a salutation; she retires in obsequies of gratitude.

Katja is wry. "What a shame! If you were going to stay, you could give her private English lessons." But mention of my departure makes her serious, and she adds, "And me, too. Korava is much more exciting when you're here."

"I come here when exciting things are happening."

"No, not exciting like that. I thought you came to see me."

"Pavel thinks I'm in love with you — " lightly, though I'm thinking, *this is never going to come back; this is the only time Katja and I, pleasantly pie-eyed on Schubert, are going to bow our heads to each other over coffee.*

"Pavel says that? Well, you see, if someone's in love with me, he can be in love with Angèle."

(This equation doesn't balance; many men could be and probably are in love with Katja, just because she's Katja.) "Poor Pavel," she sounds sincere. "How can he ever sleep with her now?"

"Did he, before — did you steal Pavel away from Angèle?"

A startled laugh. "Not exactly — oh, if I tell you, you're never going to want to see me again, you're going to hate me."

I assure her, accurately, that there's nothing she could tell me that could make that true.

"You've got it backwards. It was Pavel who stole me away from Angèle. Or so she believed. Yes. Oh, it was just a phase I went through — for Angèle, too, I think, but it meant more to her. We were very young — it began just when my mother died, if that has anything to do with it."

"You were probably lonely." Proper orientation of the triangle at last explains why it was Pavel who was attacked. To judge by Rietz, Angèle's marksmanship has improved; Pavel was wounded in the upper leg, and the nature of his offence suggests she had in mind another, nearby target (Hannah Sjuc's characterisation, if partial, isn't so far from the truth). And he refused to press charges so as not to expose Katja's private life; everything dovetails, but the origin of his latter extravagant passion for Angèle has to lie down among the dark, insoluable mysteries.

"For me, it was just something we did together, friends, I didn't dream a woman could be really in love like that with a woman. I had never slept with a man, till Pavel. He's still the only man I ever went to bed with — isn't that ridiculous! Just like the middle ages, or Jane Austen."

"It isn't ridiculous if that's what you wanted. Sleeping with a lot of men you don't want, because this is now, that would be ridiculous."

She gives me a long, quite deliberately sexual stare, but resumes where she left her account. "Once I had slept with Pavel, the other was all over. I was so naive, I thought I could just say that to Angèle and she would understand. She went insane." A dour little laugh. "I almost told her what Pavel suggested, when I told him about me and Angèle. That would have made it worse."

"A threesome." Not among my conscious fantasies, but asking supplies a slight, undeniable tingle. Perhaps, in any context, I am roused by the thought of Katja, stripped and bedded. "Did you want that?"

"Oh, no. It was revolting — I was in love with Pavel. I was very young, and I thought, if that was what he wanted — It's better now, now he works late; his wife is his wife and his whore is his whore."

"What about you?" With all her revelations, we've been using many words, like other people, but now we're back knowing what we mean.

"Revenge, you mean? That's all it could be. I don't want to have just sex, pay for it and forget it. That's important for some men, for Pavel; he can do things he can't do with his wife, the mother of his sons — he thinks he can't; you know, really filthy things that wives don't do."

Though her flushed irony virtually proclaims Katja's aptitude for all and any erotic variants, I recall Pavel's hot eyes when he spoke about hurting a woman, and think he may have it right after all, as near right as it can be, given these elements.

"With me, if I wanted someone else — you know American films, TV shows as well? the children are with their mother, and the father comes to take them for the weekend, and she has a lover and he has a new girlfriend, et cetera. In the films, the children are very clever, and it all ends up *okay*, but even the *okay* is horrible, and in real life it must be much worse, a nightmare. Pavel is a nice man, he makes love very well, we hardly ever quarrel. Do you know anyone more generous than Pavel?"

"No one who comes close." But this counting of blessings, rejection of unthinkable alternatives, sounds like the state of play in a long internal debate, the reasoning of someone who can no longer resort to the unanswerable *I love him*.

"When shall you be back in Dusatia?"

I have been dreading this. I don't know. When not in crisis, Korava is a backwater. If my life was unchanged, it might be years, but as another side-effect of sudden prominence, I am only a signature away from becoming editor-in-chief and what they call "anchor" (a large stone on a rope?) for a syndicated news-magazine show dealing in depth not with celebrity piffle, but with serious world events and issues. We plan versions in half-a-dozen languages — it is, in fact, much the idea proposed by Svoboda in Prague, except that this one is properly financed and has access to world distribution; sight unseen the English version is already sold in a number of cable and broadcast markets, and my salary is generous. Albertson, who has been very civilised, warns me it could all go down the drain in a year or so, but even if that's true, I'll have time to put together a couple more books. Actual production is to be in Brussels, but I'll be able to live in London.

"In London," Katja says, rapt with her romantic anglophilia. I don't tell her how dead is the literary London she dreams of, Johnson's London, Dickens' London, Conan Doyle's London, all gone, except for a few blessed backwaters, replaced by characterless Cosmopolis.

A parallel for the notional Englishman I, under false pretences, represent for Katja, who was, if he ever existed, a transient phenomenon. That poetry-reciting Barry once loved by both the young Mme Niemek and my adolescent mother may have been among the last, and the species was definitively extinct with the death of Winston Churchill, a little less than four centuries after that of Phillip Sidney, who might be the first. And he was immediate precursor to Shakespeare, who gave them all a tongue, down to the last lion — because the real undimming empire was not the fleet, or bits of Africa and Asia coloured red on a map, but the imperium of language, fresh and confident and rich enough to make heaven-storming aspiration stand in place of, sometimes *become*, reality; Thomas Jefferson was of that breed as well as Drake and Nelson and Burton, almost T.E. Lawrence, and absolutely Coleridge and Elgar and H.G. Wells, till, like their country, they grew tired and despondent, at best scholarly, at worst, rancorous.

Now, because America is still confident and consequential, we disdain Americans and copy them in everything; knowing absolutely nothing about baseball we speak of striking out, batting a thousand, getting to first base; we mock and then soberly adopt the polysyllabic pomposities of American academic, bureaucratic, sociological and business talk; loving the smell of power that clings to them, transplant and utterly misapply political terms such as lame duck and favourite son, like boys aping the incidental mannerisms of a favourite footballer; perhaps if we sound enough like Americans, we can still matter in the world, too. But we no more resemble Katja's fabled Brits than Onassis did Achilles.

For the show, I have demanded and been assured complete editorial control; I intend still to do interviews, but unless they're heads of state (and sometimes even then) my victims will come to me.

"Might you not be bored, sitting still, after — this?"

Not really; if I am, I can always send myself, not limited to my past linguistic bailiwick, to witness civil war in Sri Lanka, poverty in Peru, a coup in the Congo. But mostly I'll be seeing others off without regrets on what has been my life of hotels, breakfasts of bread, coffee flecked with milk-skin, early flights and late flights, dismal airports and hit-and-run sex. Only now do I recognise how much I have longed for a fixed domicile with a library and CD's, a few decent bottles of Bordeaux; a cat, certainly.

"A wife," Katja prompts. Moving my head in possible agreement, I shake loose another unexplained mystery.

"When we danced. Why did you say you were glad I didn't like your friend?"

"Oh — " She smiles with an onset of shyness. Of *shyness*?

"Wasn't I supposed to like her?"

"You should be married. If you were married — " it's simple, "I should have to stop thinking about you. But thinking about you is my best secret."

Our cab and the BMW pull up at the house in near succession, and Pavel, tieless, a little bleared, but (he insists) fully sober, leaves again shortly to take home the boys' minder, a ruddy, elderly lady, grandmother to one of the gopher-maids at the station.

Among the English prints, I accomplish my slight packing, struggling against an insidious melancholy. Emerging, I search for Katja, and find her looking like an Arthur Rackham princess, high-collared, close-fitting, brocaded dressing-gown, hair coiling free, in the kitchen making tea.

Tonight's music is running in my head, and I'm thinking how, with that very small company of godlike composers, the greatest moments are often achieved with the simplest effects, a half-step modulation, sudden absence of a syncopation, a couple of passing-notes; mysteriously, because the same procedures are banal in lesser hands. It is the simplicity of achieved wisdom that moves us, and this connects, not solemnly, to the disproportionate pleasure there is in watching Katja, the absorbed precision of her moves.

Really boiling water poured, pot lidded and cozied, she looks up and smiles at my catlike vigil.

"What do you think, Mark? Do people really fall in love, or do we only want to hold on to the one who lets us love ourselves?"

I put up a hand as if to fend off such portentous questions, and she (I'm glad to say) laughs.

"No, but isn't it difficult to know?"

"Impossible. If that's all anyone ever does, then that's what falling in love is." But at best, it's a sometime truth; long ago the late stages of being in love with Germaine filled me with contempt for myself. Oh, shut up, this isn't a time for syllogism.

"But it ought to be something happy." In the coffeeshop, when she was explaining how useless it was for her to think of paying Pavel back, she was telling me why we would never go to bed together. About some things, I'm moronically slow.

She squints at me earnestly, and speaks English. "Dear Mark, would you do a thing for me — a favour?"

"Of course."

"Kiss me now. We shall kiss goodbye when you really leave, but now I would like for you to kiss me — " a shy struggle. "As you would kiss me if we had made love all night."

Overwhelmed, one recognises the impossibility; I don't have a detached monitor to note and remember those morning kisses; the spontaneous can't be consciously reconstructed. So I do what must be wanted, certainly what I have always wanted, and for the only time kiss Katja with no prudent reservations. As if we might make love all night.

Right away, my ill-informed web of nerves, feckless endocrine system, believe it might be true; circulation, respiration, tactile perception all move to action stations. There is nothing in existence softer than Katja's lips, nothing in imagination as desirable as Katja. We fail to stop at one kiss, and she is equally responsible for what, beyond kissing, there is, caresses, the striving encounter of clad bodies.

We hear the car-door thud. As if arranging her on a shelf, I grasp Katja's shoulders and put distance between us. She is trembling, but I am gasping like the death-throes of a salmon.

She sets three cups on their saucers, and goes to the refrigerator for milk.

It is a late-morning flight, and Pavel, who is to drive me to the airport, puts in an early appearance at the studios, and returns when, eye on the clock, I am on the point of phoning for a taxi. He is wearing the smug face of Pavel with some news.

"Hey, buddy, maybe you should stay, I got a great place for you, ritzy fully-modernised eighteenth-century villa in la-dee-dah suburbs, luxury furnished, Christ knows how many bedrooms, state-of-the-art communications centre, concert grand pie-anno, immediate occupancy."

"The Herders have scarpered." The only available answer.

"Scarpered?"

"Taken it on the lam." I'll have to send Pavel a selection of the classic Ealing comedies, so he can add some dated British underworld slang.

"Jumped bail, yah. Last night sometime — boy, somebody got paid off. They crossed the frontier into Slovakia around one a.m., the Merc and a good-sized van, so I guess they took the Monet and the ikons."

There is much more, a Chippendale cabinet and Louis XV escritoire, a Sèvres coffee-service, a Sung screen, a Canaletto, first editions, some of all which must have been left behind.

"Why now? — " I think it through, Pavel amusedly encouraging me: "Angèle's acquittal must have given them the idea that the political climate was against them. But then, with

Rietz dead, the chances of a conviction were just about nil, unless
— "

"Yeah, yeah... "

"Rietz left behind some written evidence. Either that, or
the other hood from the Eagle's Nest surfaced. The bald one,
Jenadju."

"Hey, we gonna make a reporter out of you yet. How
about both? Before the hospital finished yanking tubes out of
Rietz, the cops pulled a raid on his place, out at the rifle range, you
know. They heisted all kinds of records, who he paid to do what,
a ton of guns and ammunition, and Jenadju is hiding out there, the
poor bastard must have frozen his ass, all there is is a pot-belly
stove, he was down to burning cartridge-boxes."

"And the Herders were tipped off, naturally."

"Shit, they probably heard about it before the
commissioner did."

A costly decamping, though less expensive than at first
blink; their bail, an unprecedented one, was two million crowns
the pair, but of that they were required to put up only half, and so
forfeited about seventy-seven thousand pounds sterling, tip money
for Juan-Micel. If I may carry their saga a little beyond the bounds
of my story, they are eventually to reappear in Singapore, whose
notoriously draconian penal code is suffused with a spirit of mercy
for those who bring a half-billion (U.S.) dollars of new venture
capital into the economy; attempts at extradition are to be
suspended helpless in a sticky web of procedural technicalities,
and the Swiss, German and American ambassadors become their
frequent dinner guests. They steadfastly decline to be interviewed
for inclusion in my very successful series *The Money Barons*, and
Christa Rasch is to deny a report she stayed with them on a
promotional swoop through the Orient.

Everyone goes to the airport, Vaclav and Thom bundled
like Amundsen; the wind is unforgiving under a virginal innocence
of sky. At the gate, Pavel hugs me, and wishes me well in my new
career.

"We gonna see you some more?"

"I can come for a holiday."

"Any time. Hey, maybe we could all go someplace, Greece maybe, Venice."

"Sounds good to me." This is never going to happen.

Pavel, unnecessarily, is seeking a defining word. "I think we smashed up the Nazis, you more than me. We oughta name a street after you, a building, maybe.

"You know what I mean — " answering my grimace.

I do, and we clasp hands solemnly once more. "But it was fun."

"I'll tell the world."

Thom, whose normal forward progress is a continuous, lurching flirtation with falling on his nose, twenty feet away comes up short, face to face with a grave little girl of similar size but greater age, or greater sophistication; from a distance of five inches they stare transfixed at each other, he amazed, she intrigued by his amazement. The mother, young, Polish, tries to impose an irrelevant, alien convention, informing her daughter that this is a little boy, urging her to say hello. Pavel, towing Vaclav who is walking backwards and looking open-mouthed at the ceiling, goes to collect his second son.

Katja and I fold together, and the counterpoint, in our decorous kiss, of impractical mutual hunger, is very subtle. I murmur, "Pavel had it right. For always."

She breathes, "Oh, God," and I suppose tears are permissible at a parting of friends. Mawkish to acknowledge, dishonest to deny the wrench of agonised affection for her blurred beauty.

Then I do get on that plane, and regret it, soon, and so far as I can see, for the rest of my life. Not that I believe, as Korava, as Dusatia dwindles below, is curtained off by cloud, there was even an illusion of choice.